THE MAYOR OF SUCCESSIVE MIRACLES

Hamlin Tallent

EDITED BY

Dell Putnam

CHAPTER ONE

The USS Eisenhower floated serenely in the early morning dark of Naples Bay, the sun's daily struggle over Vesuvius having just begun. As the tentative rays topped the mountain, they breathed light onto the foothills below and upon the waters beyond and, of course, brought the hope of a great, new day.

The brightening sun turned Ike from black to gray and opened the panorama of Southern Italy to the men on her deck. Those men found their eyes wandering to the pastel squares and cubes that mixed with the red-tiled creaminess of old concrete homes. Of course, the eyes invariably strayed to Vesuvius, and her timid smoke, just now visible in the growing light, gave little hint of her violent past.

The Ike was foremost among the ships, a grand and gray lady and a most fitting visitor to this bay, for these waters had hosted warships since the time of sails. She twisted gently on her anchor, obedient to the breeze against her side, and the squeak of the chain was her only protest. Despite the early hour, Ike's liberty party was already going ashore. A coterie of hardship-bound sailors bent upon enjoying the sights and food and pleasures of the port. They were, for the most part, young men, a mix of pasts and backgrounds. A combination of colors, too, but unified by their service. Their youthful shouts, their brazen and unashamed boyishness, masked the seriousness of their business. They had spent the past six months together and were a honed, fighting force of unprecedented power. But, they were also old hands as tourists and visitors. Their liberty jars back on the ship were full of all manner of coins and bills, money that would soon be of no value to them and destined for some cause the chaplain had yet to announce.

But despite the joy of leaving the ship, the crew did not buzz with the energy of previous liberty outings. They were nearing the completion of their six-month voyage, and in some ways, Naples stood in the way of home. It was a fact that a sailor always wanted liberty, but there was one thing and only one thing that would have him lose interest in a port of call: the lure of home. For most on Ike, Naples was an unwanted nightcap after a big party, a postscript to a story already known.

For the previous half-year, the sailors of Ike had carried their nation's flag, and its interests, with pride and resolve and had visited England, France, Monaco, Palma de Mallorca, and Israel. It was time to get home.

As the sun rose and looked down at the ship, one party of revelers stood out from the rest, and that is because they were boarding the admiral's barge. The barge was a beautiful, twin-screw craft with a roomy, comfortable cabin, and a service staff designed to host the guests of America. Her black hull and gleaming brass had cut a wake from the Spanish coast to the French Rivera and across the waters to Italy and Israel. Many a visitor had disembarked her with fawning gratitude for Uncle Sam.

But on this last port call of the cruise, the barge was loaded with the commander of the air wing, referred to as the CAG, and his deputy as well as the nine squadron commanding officers. They were recipients of the admiral's treat, gratitude for such a significant deployment. Stewards had filled the lockers in the galley with shrimp, roast beef, cookies, wine, and beer. The admiral greeted them aboard with handshake and smile, and his two-star blue flag fluttered in the breeze.

One commander, however, was absent from the gay group on the barge. He was Jack Grant. Jack was absent because he was waiting in flight deck control for the admiral and their helicopter ride to the beach. What Jack did not yet know was that there would be no admiral and no helicopter. Jack's JOs, junior officers, fed up with his selfishness and shenanigans, had purloined letterhead from the admiral's office and had penned the following:

Skipper, tomorrow the barge will be taking the CAG, DCAG and squadron commanders on an outing to celebrate our successful deployment. However, I would like you to accompany me as the airwing representative to a meeting with the president of the Naples Navy League, the Mayor of Naples and others. CAG suggested you as the best representative, and I agree. Our helo leaves at 0800 so meet me in flight deck control. I may be a few minutes late as I will see the barge off.

Warmly,

Titan

Jack's JOs knew he would take the bait since his ego blinded him to much of life's realities.

When Jack first read the letter, he feared that the CAG had split him from the group of his fellow skippers for some punishment. However, that didn't make sense.

No! No, he was selected to join the admiral because the admiral chose him!

Jack Grant was a physically appealing man, tall and slender, with dark brown hair and gray eyes. Some thought him to be the archetypical image of the dashing fighter pilot--- flashing white teeth, charismatic, and, of course, a magnet for the ladies. He knew he was attractive to the opposite sex and poorly hid the fact. Jack thought he could have his way with any woman he wanted. Of course, that included wives and girlfriends of his squadron mates when he could get away with it. Integrity, or the lack of, did not hamper Jack, so his desire to manipulate those around him was limitless. With unmatched skill, he applied false sincerity, the appearance of compassion and understanding, and ass-kissing. He was exceptionally skillful in the handling of his bosses as he remembered the precise mix of compliments, humor, self- deprecation, and military starch to overcome even those who didn't quite believe him. He leveraged the fact that as many officers became more senior, they grew more vulnerable to charm, wanting and needing to think that they were, in fact, a cut above the rest.

While Jack did not hesitate to take advantage of his juniors to get what he wanted, his most significant advancements came in beguiling those senior to him, and it was entirely believable to him that the admiral had chosen him above all others to accompany him to the beach. So, it was a selfish and self-righteous Jack Grant that waited for his helo and the admiral, in the small room adjacent to the flight deck. He heard the 1MC ship's speaker announcement for all squadron commanders to lay to the fantail and he knew that meant the barge was ready for boarding. He smiled when he heard it because it said the others were going to leave the admiral to him! Jack busied himself with an ancient copy of The Stars and Stripes, irritated by the fact the crossword puzzle was already filled but soothed by the thought of his privilege. However, upon glancing at his wristwatch and seeing 0815, he frowned and went to find the aircraft handling officer. He found the man down in the wardroom, wolfing a stack of pancakes. Jack pulled a chair across the gleaming, waxed floor, and sat down.

"Handler, when is the admiral's helo arriving? The schedule says 0800."

The handler frowned and licked a drop of syrup from his lip. "There isn't any helo on the flight schedule."

"What?" Jack frowned. "What about this?" He whipped out his copy of the ship's flight schedule and placed it on the table. It had appeared under his door last night.

"See, right here." Jack pointed to the helo line on the schedule.

The handler wiped his hands on a napkin as he looked at the paper.

"See, right there. It shows a 0800 launch to the beach. You can see the two-star annotation for the admiral as a passenger."

"I see that," said the handler, as he placed his clipboard in front of Jack. "I don't know what you have, but THIS," he pointed at his board, "THIS is the flight schedule for today. You can see there is no helo line on it."

Jack looked at the clipboard and frowned again. The helo line was clear.

What the hell was going on?

He looked up at the handler, "I don't get it?"

7

The handler smiled back at him. "I'd say somebody played a trick on you. Where did you get this?" He pointed at Jack's schedule.

"Somebody slid it under the door last night."

The handler smiled again. "And that someone is who pranked you. As I said, there is no helo on today's schedule. The admiral is off on the barge with all the skippers and the CAG. Well, except for you."

Jack felt his face grow hot. He glanced at the handler and saw a smirk on his face and the look in his eye that said, "I know that you know that I know you have been screwed." Jack swallowed and stood.

"Okay, thanks." He turned and stomped out of the wardroom and down the passageways to his stateroom. He flung open the door, entered the darkened room, and slumped into a chair. He knew it was his JOs that had pranked him! He knew it! What frustrated him was his inability to manipulate THEM.

As the liberty parties left the ship and as Jack fumed--- critical things were beginning to bubble on Ike. In CVIC, the ship's intelligence spaces, Special Category SPECAT messages began to scream across the circuits. Ike watchstanders, confused at first, alerted their bosses. Much of the leadership was off duty, so the first petals of the chaos flower opened to young eyes. Soon, pentagon telephones, connected by satellites, found those on watch and the truth became known.

Saddam had invaded Kuwait!

Lieutenant Commander Doody Mullins, the air wing duty officer, was eating a breakfast of bacon, with more bacon, when a breathless, swan-necked ensign from CVIC found him and relayed the news about the attack. Doody was unsure what to do, so he followed the ensign. The place was abuzz with activity, and in the center of the room, surrounded by the chaos, stood the senior intelligence officer and the admiral's duty officer. They were engaged in the timeless navy officer game of trying to pin ownership of a brewing mess on the other. The cardinal rule of those moments was that when given a steaming turd, you must pass it to someone. Upon seeing Doody, they saw a turd holder.

"Is one of the skippers onboard?" The admiral's duty officer needled his brows at Doody. "The Chief of Staff needs us to start planning."

"Yes, sir. I saw Commander Grant in the wardroom earlier. He was talking to the handler. Planning for what?"

"Could you please ask him to come down here? We need some help."

Doody looked at one, then the other, and seeing the gravity of the situation in their eyes, gulped. "Sure, I'll call him."

Jack was still stewing in his room when the phone rang. "Skipper, can you come down to CVIC?"

"Who is this?"

"Sir, this is Doody Mullins, the air wing duty officer. We have a situation."

"Well, what kind of situation?"

"Not sure, sir. They won't tell me. Top Secret or something."

"Are you fucking with me?" Jack had had enough of JO pranks.

"No, no sir," Doody stammered. "No, sir."

Jack frowned and took a deep breath. He knew Doody. He had manipulated him often to curry favor with his boss, the CAG. Jack knew Doody wasn't going to kid around with him. "Okay, I will be right down."

As soon as Jack entered CVIC, he knew it was no joke. The place was going nuts! It was pandemonium!

Doody escorted him into a top-secret space where he found the ship's intelligence officer and the airwing intelligence officer scanning charts. They flipped them back and forth, then flipped them again, obviously hoping that somehow they would gain an understanding of what they saw.

"What's going on?" Jack frowned at the ship's intelligence officer.

"Sir, it looks like Iraq has invaded Kuwait. We can't contact the barge on the satellite phone. The Chief of Staff says we need to start thinking about air plans and you are the senior air wing officer on board."

"What? What kind of plans? What are you talking about?" Jack sucked in a sharp breath. He was going to get screwed.

Wasn't Saddam our pal against Iran and where the heck was Iraq and Kuwait anyway?

Ike had steamed around on her summer Mediterranean cruise like a tour boat and had enjoyed the largesse of the Soviet implosion. Her contingency war plans centered on messing around with Libya's Kaddafi. No one onboard had considered anything to do with Iraq; they didn't even have the right charts!

Jack quickly read the messages and began to panic.

What the heck was he supposed to do? Where was everybody? He sat and slumped over a desk and put his head in his hands.

"Sir. Sir."

Jack looked up and, seeing it was just Doody, slumped his head again.

"Sir, we could begin to develop some significant metrics about time, distance, fuel and command and control requirements from various launch points in the Red Sea and Eastern Mediterranean."

"What?" Jack sat back and shook his head. "What are you talking about?"

"Sir, the most likely launch points for us, should, you know, the powers task us, are from the Eastern Med or the Red Sea. Problem with the Med is we would have to fly over Lebanon and Syria, or Israel and Jordan and both those options have challenges."

"What?" Jack looked at the chart Doody placed on the desk.

"The Lebanon and Syria option is not good because the Syrians hate us. The Israel and Jordan option is not

11

good because if Israel lets us fly over their space, then the whole thing gets tainted with the Jew, Arab thing. I bet that they send us into the Red Sea. That is if we go anywhere."

Jack looked at the chart and brightened. Doody made sense and, even better, it was something he could do while they tried to make contact with the barge. At least it would look like he was taking the initiative. Jack knew CAG liked guys that took the initiative.

"Get on it, Doody," he said. "Get everybody working on it."

"Yes, sir," beamed Doody. He ran back into the planning spaces, yelling to the other officers as he went.

Jack stood and reached for the phone. He rang central communications and directed the officer on watch to try to contact the barge every two minutes until he made contact. Then, "come and get me."

Ninety minutes later, the ship contacted the barge, and Jack, ensuring Doody was elsewhere, briefed the admiral on what he had initiated. The admiral agreed and effusively thanked Jack for taking action. Moments after the barge returned to Ike the admiral's staff prepared a SPECAT message to Sixth Fleet, listing the suggested launch points and critical metrics.

Ike's leadership began recall procedures to get the shore party back on board, and the massive warship prepared to get underway. By the time Kuwait City fell to Saddam, she was steaming at full speed towards the Suez Canal and the Red Sea. While she churned through the blue waters of the Mediterranean, onboard planners frantically poured over the charts and computed times, distances, and fuel requirements to potential targets from Red Sea launch points. Maintenance personnel tweaked radars and weapon's systems, ordnance men built bombs and guidance flowed from national command authorities to Ike's embarked battle group staff.

From the Pentagon to Ike's command center, concern grew with each hour. The fear was that Saddam, encouraged by his lightening takedown of Kuwait, would proceed south toward Dhahran, Saudi Arabia, and its precious oil fields. His tanks would be able to move quickly down the freeway into the heart of production, and once in place, he would be very, very difficult to dislodge. The disruption to the flow of oil would be catastrophic!

In CVIC, CAG took Jack's initial numbers and quickly developed a plan. The air wing would launch six-plane strike groups around the clock to interdict Saddam. The idea was to have enough firepower to stop the tanks on the highway or at least drive them off the road and slow them down. The groups needed to be potent enough to cause destruction but small enough to be refueled efficiently with the limited assets in theater. Four of the aircraft would be bomb droppers: A-6 Intruders and F/A-18 Hornets loaded with Mk-20 Rockeye cluster bombs and Mk-83 1,000- pound general purpose bombs equipped with laser guidance kits.

The other two were F-14 Tomcats loaded with AIM-9 Sidewinders, AIM-7 Sparrows, the enormous AIM-54 Phoenix, and the M61 20mm Gatling gun. The Iraq air threat to the group was unknown, but with 400 enemy aircraft within striking distance, the fighter mission was a necessity.

Ike sped across the Mediterranean, flying as she went. The aircrew had to be on the top of their game when tasked to defend their allies.

The danger did not come just from the Iraqi military but also the enormous logistical challenges. The sheer distances involved in the battlespace and the lack of resources plagued planners. On the seventh of August, Ike entered the Suez Canal, and while the massive ship slipped past the sand and its Egyptian dwellers, her crew made final preparations for combat.

**

Lieutenant John "Jocko" Barnes frowned as he read the report chit. It was a standard, US Navy charge sheet, given for an infraction. He and Senior Chief Petty Officer Franklin were standing on the flight deck, as flight operations had not started yet. He looked at the senior chief and shook his head. "The Ike's command master chief wrote up Perkins? Wants him to go to Captain's Mast?"

"Yes, sir," said the senior chief. "Caught him wearing an earring at ship's landing, in Haifa."

"But why the recommendation for mast? And I read here that you highly recommend the same?" Jocko frowned again. Jocko was the Aviation Weapons Division officer in Fighter Squadron 142's maintenance department, and Senior Chief Franklin was his top enlisted man. AVWEPS was the largest division in the squadron.

"Well, sir, he WAS wearing an earring." The senior chief's tone was not defiant, but it was insistent.

"I see that," said Jocko. "But, senior chief, wearing an earring is a violation of uniform regulations. It's like

14

having your shirt unbuttoned, or not having your dungarees stenciled. Why mast?

Perkins has never had any problem, has he?"

"No, sir, he has a clean record."

"He's a good worker?" "Well, yes, sir. Yes, he is."

"Then why would we take him to mast?"

"Sir, we don't need any hippies wearing earrings. Besides, it is the command master chief that wrote him up. He is the senior enlisted man on the ship."

"I respect the command master chief," said Jocko. "I respect all of you. It was chief's that raised me from a pup," Jocko laughed and clapped his senior chief on the shoulder.

"Yes, sir." Senior Chief Franklin chuckled.

"But, I don't think we can select what violations we don't like and hammer people for it. Hell, I don't like earrings either. Do you see what I mean?"

"Yes, sir, I suppose so." Franklin nodded and pursed his lips.

"If Perkins had been unshaven, would he be facing mast?"

"Well, no, sir."

"What would he be facing?"

"Me, getting into his shit," laughed Franklin.

"I tell you what, let's throw this away, and you get in Perkins's shit. I will find the command master chief and explain. I do owe him that."

"No, sir, I think I will go find the master chief. I should explain it, chief to chief."

"Even better," said Jocko. "Thank you, senior chief." Jocko clapped the man on the shoulder again and turned toward the island. He started toward the hatch when it opened and Lieutenant Commander, "Polyp" Boil stepped out.

"Just the man I was looking for."

"What's up Polyp?"

"Jocko, I've been directed to make some aircrew changes for the Iraqi ops. I am crewing you with the skipper."

"What? I'm crewed with Tagger. What changed?"

"What changed was the skipper wants some experience with him when he goes over Indian Country. He wants you."

"But, Polyp…"

"No buts," said Polyp. "Look, Jocko, you're one of the best RIOs we have. You run that back seat like a magician. I need you to step into this without squawking."

"I'm not squawking," said Jocko. I am whining. It's my right as a junior officer." He knew there was no reason to argue. Might as well prepare for the challenge of flying with the worst fighter pilot in the universe.

16

"Glad to see an upstanding JO like you taking this like a man," laughed Polyp. "Whining and all."

Jocko watched him go, then headed toward Wardroom One. He stepped down into the catwalk, ducked through a hatch and entered the ship on the 03 level passageway. He headed forward toward the smells of fried stuff and floor wax.

"Christ," I'm-fucked." Jocko sighed, dropped his tray on the table, and slumped into a chair.

"Yes, we know," Tubby looked up from his salad. "But is this new or just the old stuff you are always fucked about?"

Jocko narrowed his eyes and looked at Tubby's salad. "What are you doing eating salad?"

"The XO said I had to lose weight, or I would lose my flight pay."

"Let me see that." Jocko leaned over and stuck a fork into the salad. Sure enough, Tubby had hidden a one-eyed Jack beneath the lettuce. "Aha! Just what I thought!"

"What the heck. I'm starving." Tubby scowled.

Jocko laughed and leaned back in his chair. He took a drink of bug juice.

"So, as I asked, is this new or old; you're fucked?"

Jocko rolled his eyes and groaned. "It's new; I' m-fucked stuff."

"Is it something that is going to get us up, too?" Spooge Carter frowned and lay his slider down.

Jocko looked up and grinned despite his misery. Spooge was always worried about getting rounded up in group executions.

"Yeah," piped Flea Jonas, "what is the frag pattern of your fuckedness?"

Jocko sighed again and glanced around the room. The four men were sitting in Wardroom One. Jocko and his pals always ate there even when not in flight suits. They said they did so because they didn't want to associate with the shoe snobs down in Wardroom Two. The truth was they didn't dislike their surface warfare brothers; they just liked giving crap to them. "Shoe" was a derogatory term that aviators used for surface warfare officers, SWOs. Naval aviators based the name on the fact that they wore brown shoes with the khaki uniform while the SWOs wore black shoes. Naval aviation had adopted brown as a shoe color in an attempt to offset the dust from the primitive airfields of its birth and, truth be known, the aviators probably just wanted to be different too! In any regard, hoe was a term used for their non- flying colleagues. Wardroom Two and its black-shoed inhabitants were down on the main deck, and it was more formal and carried the culinary culture of the US Navy. Stewards set its tables with linen and silver.

"Don't worry, this is just me being fucked," said Jocko.

"How so?" Tubby took a gigantic bite of his "hidden" one-eyed Jack and Jocko quickly looked away. A one-eyed Jack is a slider or hamburger, with two patties of meat, cheese, bacon, and an egg. Since Tubby always had the egg cooked over-easy, it would squirt and run into a horrific, yellow-streaked mess as he worked it. The idea that he could hide such a thing under lettuce was a mystery. The gouge was never to make eye contact with Tubby when he ate, or you would undoubtedly vomit.

"I am flying with the skipper for the Red Sea ops."

"I thought you were with Tagger?" Flea looked at Jocko, and Jocko saw the suspicion in his eyes. Flea flew with the skipper.

"Skipper changed it all a minute ago," said Jocko. "Says he created the plan and he should lead it. He wrote himself into Tagger's place for the first event."

"He didn't create the plan," said Tubby. "He gave CAG some time, distance, numbers, and the A-6 skipper created the plan."

"Man, I was looking forward to this," said Jocko. "I mean, a chance to get into something real. Not this training bullshit, but real. And to fly with a guy like Tagger made it perfect."

"But I'm crewed with the skipper," whined Flea. "What happens to me now?"

"Don't get your panties in a bunch," said Jocko. "You are a first tour ensign, a fucking new guy. The skipper wants me to fly with him to keep him out of trouble. He wants an old hand for this. It's business, not personal."

"So what do I do?"

"Well, it looks like Tagger's back seat is open now. I think you should go and get crewed with Tagger," said Jocko.

Flea frowned again, then jumped to his feet.

"Where are you going?" Tubby squirted egg and bits of hamburger.

"Got to go talk to Ops about crewing with Tagger." Flea grinned at Jocko. "Now that he needs a RIO. Tagger and I will get the MIGs while YOU will be arcing around looking for the tanker." He scurried for the door.

"No shit," said Spooge. "If there are any MIGs out there, Tagger will get 'em."

"Well, Jocko, think of the good news," said Tubby. "You will most likely get to be famous! By flying with the skipper, you may well be the first prisoner of war since Viet Nam. Quick, write to John McCain and see if he will send you the Hanoi Hilton tap code."

"Fuck you, Tubby! This is not funny." Jocko picked up a fry and grimaced as the cold starch caught in his throat.

"Hey, don't worry, son," said Tubby." This stuff will probably launch at night. You know the skipper never flies at night. Jack Grant sucks at night landings."

Jocko sneaked a quick peek at his friend. The vomit burger was on his plate, and his face was reasonably free of egg and grease. He made a wary eye contact, "The first event is launching in the morning. No chance to have to land at night."

"Well, that explains that," said Spooge.

"Oh well," said Jocko. "I will make the most of it. How bad can it be?"

"Are you shitting me?" Tubby laughed. "Jack Grant is the worst fighter pilot in the navy. The COD drivers could gun him."

"I'll never forgive him for 207," said Spooge. He looked down at his plate and stabbed a French fry.

"I remember that," said Tubby. "He said the fuel system was all screwed up, right?"

"Right," said Spooge. "And my guys in power plants had to work the entire Haifa in-port period because of it."

"I don't remember it, what happened?" Jocko splatted some ketchup on his fries and looked at Spooge.

"You know how if you leave the fuel dumps on in the Tomcat, it will drain down to 4,000 pounds." Spooge picked up a pickle and bit into it.

"Yeah, right," said Jocko.

"So, the skipper is coming in on his normal pinky, and he is heavy, so he hits the dumps and tells his RIO, Radar O'Reilly, to remind him to turn them off at 7200 pounds. Well, Radar was a new guy and forgot, so they dump down to the automatic cut off."

"I remember this part," said Tubby. "I was in the control center down in CATTC when it happened. We were in the middle of the Med, and the divert fields were closed, and they call the ball with 4,000 pounds of gas instead of 7,000."

"Anybody that knows the Tomcat knows they had fucked up as soon as they heard the ball call," said Spooge. "But, the skipper downed the airplane when he landed. Said that he had turned the dump switch off at 7200, but it kept dumping."

"Jesus," said Jocko.

"No shit," spat Spooge. "And so my guys had to work the entire port period to fix the thing. There was nothing to fucking FIX! I finally told the chief to sign it off by saying he found a bad thermistor. Thermistors are always useful for that kind of shit. Whatever a thermistor is."

"I'll also never forgive him for Haifa," said Tubby. "The skipper hooked up with some chick and took her to the rack in the squadron hotel suite. Locked everybody out and banged her for half a day. Everybody had to wait outside the door until he got his rocks off."

"Oh great," said Spooge as he stood. "Now, I hate him even more. He looked at his watch. "Got to go brief, see you guys later."

Jocko watched him go, then stood and walked to the "auto-dog" machine. Auto-dog is what naval aviators call soft-serve ice cream. Jocko knew it had something to do with the way a dog takes a dump. He pulled the lever, and the brown ice cream flowed in his bowl. He looked over his shoulder. The room was empty except for the two of them.

22

"Tubby, you're the rumor monger and master of all trivial knowledge around here, how the hell did the skipper ever screen for command anyway?"

"Oh, that's a good story," said Tubby. "Bring me some dog."

Jocko dutifully filled another bowl and carried them to the table.

"So, how did he screen for command? Tell me the story." Jocko handed Tubby a bowl.

"Did you ever hear of Red Bannister?" Tubby spooned a blob of dog in his mouth.

"Wasn't he the guy that jumped out in Sigonella or something?"

"Yep, that's him. Red was the skipper of 143 during a med cruise, and so he launches as the alert five one night."

"Why would they launch the alert in the Med?"

"Who the fuck knows. They just did. So old Red flies around doesn't find anything and comes back to land. He bolters a couple of times, and the ship launches a tanker to give him gas. The tanker turns out sour, so they send him to Sigonella to get fuel." Tubby leaned back in his chair, a glisten of fresh dog on the front of his flight suit. "Remember, he had boltered, right? So he had his hook down when he missed the wires, right?"

"Yeah, right."

"So, he forgets to put his hook up. He lands at Sig, and his hook sends this shower of sparks into the air and the Italians in the tower scream "FUOCO, FUOCO!"

"Fire in Italian," said Jocko.

"Exactly," said Tubby. "But old Red thinks they are saying 'Fuck you, Fuck you' so what the hell, he keys the mic and says, 'FUCK YOU. FUCK YOU.'"

Jocko nearly fell off his chair, laughing.

"Red's airplane sparks down the runway amid all the FUCK YOUs and FUOCOs, and he never realizes his hook is down.

However, his RIO knows Italian, sees the sparks in the mirrors and ejects!"

"NO! You've got to be shitting me."

"Nope. He ejects, and Red and his RIO fly up in the air, get good chutes, and land back on the runway. Nobody gets hurt, but their Tomcat runs all over the place for a while before it hits a tree and explodes."

"So, how does this lead to our skipper screening for command?"

"Aha," said Tubby. "The skipper is a department head in Red's squadron at the time. He is the admin department head, but he is behind two guys that are Red's pals--- Squeezer McGinnis and Bunny Smith. They have ops and maintenance, and our Jack Grant is so far back in the pecking order he will never get a chance. But," Tubby held up a finger. "But, the post-accident blood work shows

old Red has a blood alcohol count of 1.6. He was
DRUNK!"

"What?"

"No shit, CAG initiates an investigation and a
couple of the squadron JOs spill the beans that Red,
Squeezer, and Bunny were drinking in the skippers'
stateroom the night of the crash."

"Really? The JOs ratted them out?"

"Hey, Red was a total prick and ran the squadron
like his kingdom. He had the morals of a fucking coyote
and didn't give a crap about anyone but himself. He would
force RIOs to plan cross countries to fly to places like
Pensacola or even out to San Diego with him, and then
after take-off, he would cancel the flight plan and fly over
to Norfolk."

"That's twenty miles away from Oceana. Why
would he do that?"

"Because he would spend the weekend with some
girl he met at the officers' club. His wife thought he was
away on business, and he would be shagging some chick
down on the beach."

"What about the RIO that went with him?"

"The RIO had to hide for the weekend. That was the
problem. Everyone felt sorry for Red's wife. She was a
sweetheart, and thought Red was the greatest thing in the
world. So, the RIOs, everybody in the squadron, had to
participate in Red's fucking crap even if they didn't want
to."

"I can see why they ratted him out." Jocko took a sip of water and leaned back in his chair. The dog was a little too sweet this time.

"Yeah, and Squeezer and Bunny were chips off that block. They were just as bad, so it was pretty easy for the JOs to approach the investigators. Old Bunny even tried to cop a plea, and he is the one that told them Red had heard the alert called away over the 1MC and had decided, "He was the guy to fly it!"

"That kind of thinking gets a trailer burned down every Thanksgiving," said Jocko.

The two men laughed, and Tubby continued. "So the next day Red, Squeezer, and Bunny are sent off on the COD, and the XO of 143 takes over as skipper. Jack is the senior of the two remaining department heads, and the new skipper makes him ops. Jack gets the number one ticket and screens for command."

"Wow! Just fucking wow!"

"Wow is right. For a while, the JOs gave Jack the nickname Phoenix, as in rising from the ashes."

"Why didn't it stick?"

"The JOs realized it was too disrespectful to the Phoenix missile."

Jocko laughed again and spooned the last dog from his bowl. "He just goes by his initials now, JG. You would think with Jack's ego, he would insist on being called Superman or something."

"Or how about, "Lucky," said Tubby. "Lucky " is the perfect call sign for a guy like him. The guy has nothing but good luck."

"The guy has incredible luck," agreed Jocko. "Think how hard it is to screen for command, and he came out of nowhere to do it. Then, he gets slotted into the Ghostriders between one of the best skippers in history and best XOs in history. Hell, anybody would look good in that position."

"Yeah, you're so right," said Tubby. "And the luck of being left back so he could develop the initial plans for our Red Sea ops. Just think of that! He was the only skipper on the ship, and even if all he did was crunch some numbers, he was the guy talking to the Pentagon, he was the man talking to Sixth Fleet, talking to the admiral on the bat phone. He comes off, looking like a hero."

"And we did that." Jocko shook his head and leaned toward Tubby. "We did that, you and I! We thought we were dicking him with the fake helo ride, and he comes out smelling like a rose."

"Yep, the guy is truly blessed. Well, except as a pilot."

"Christ," moaned Jocko. "Why did you have to remind me? I am fucked."

"His nickname should be Elisha," said Tubby.

"What are you talking about?"

"Elisha, you know, in First and Second Kings."

"Again, what in the fuck are you talking about?"

"Kings, the Bible, that book you might have seen in a hotel room?"

"What does that have to do with Jack Grant?"

"Elisha listed the miracles of God in Kings. Eight in Kings 1, and sixteen in Kings 2."

Jocko shook his head and stared at Tubby. "Why is it you know everything that everyone else in the world has forgotten or doesn't give a shit about?"

Tubby grinned. "So, in Kings, there is the belief that God, and, in fact, religion itself, must have successive miracles to stave off the devil and hell. And certain people must have the ability to perform successive miracles."

"I don't think the skipper performs miracles; I just think he is somehow the recipient of them."

"Hence, the call sign, Elisha. The miracles he lists can all be about himself!" Tubby laughed again.

"Tubby, how do you know all of this? Do you sit around and dream it up?"

"No, I just know what the Bible says." Tubby grinned. "Remember, I was a Religious Studies major in college."

"Oh, yes, of course," laughed Jocko. "How could I forget that? By the way, how did a religious studies guy get into the navy?"

"I couldn't get a job."

Jocko grinned and rocked back in his chair. "But according to you, certain people must perform successive miracles to save religion, not benefit themselves. So, the skipper doesn't fit. He is the recipient of miracles. If he tripped and fell face-first into a pile of cow shit, he would get up with two diamonds in his nose."

"I haven't worked the theory out completely," laughed Tubby. "Maybe the skipper's energy is from a place in heaven that produces miracles. He got misplaced with someone good."

"Okay, I think I understand." Jocko laughed and rocked his chair forward. "In heaven, there is a town called Successive Miracles and babies that come from there are magic. And somehow Jack's divine essence got mixed up with Mother Teresa's."

"Not magic, more like divine, but you are close enough." Tubby laughed.

"Well," said Jocko, "If there is a place in heaven called Successive Miracles, where idiots with massive luck come from, then Jack Grant is the Mayor of Successive Miracles."

CHAPTER TWO

While Jocko and Tubby were sitting in the wardroom, the subject of their conversation, Jack Grant, struggled over the speech he was going to give at that evening's all officers' meeting, or AOM. While AOM's were not unusual--- the squadron had them for training every day--- this one was going to be different. He had called this special AOM to discuss war! Jack knew the JO prank that led to his opportunity as the initial war planner was divine intervention. The Ike was the only war machine in the theater for the time being. She was America's, she was the WORLD'S, first response to Saddam! And Jack Grant had been the man alone in the ring when the page was blank! He was the one who wrote the first line! He was the one who authored the first response to a brutal dictator.

Jack had never felt so important. The entire staff in CVIC had turned to him and had supported him. He had discussed options with the colonel in the Pentagon, and he had spoken for a moment with VADM Jolly, the Sixth Fleet commander! Saddam's invasion had set the stage for Jack Grant, and he knew it was for a reason. Tonight's AOM would be his chance to describe the situation and to share his philosophy. It would also be a time for the handful of young JOs that had precipitated the prank to stew in their juices.

Tonight, Jack Grant was going to turn the corner and join the "greatest of all skippers" list. He was going to be a skipper that everyone talked about. He was going to say something short but riveting. Something that everyone would remember.

The surprise would help him tonight. He never discussed feelings or emotions when he addressed his officers, or to anyone else for that matter. He had his XO do all of that kind of thing. But tonight was his time to invoke the inner thoughts; his time to usher in the quiet, introspection. It was Jack Grant's time to introduce the contemplation of conflict as the man who had planned it.

He was also going to tell his men that he, the planner, was going to lead the first event into the unknown. That would surprise everyone because they knew Tagger was scheduled to lead the first package. But Jack had already instructed his ops officer to put him on that event. He deserved to lead it! Jack knew Tagger had been selected by CAG, but Tagger was his XO, and Jack was the skipper, and that was that. Jack knew he was not CAG's favorite, and it bothered him that he couldn't get CAG on his side. For some reason, CAG did not dig his chili. However, if things went well, he could change that perception. Jack wasn't keen to fly in combat, but he didn't think Saddam would go south. He had quickly studied the history of Saddam and the region and was convinced this was all bluster.

There would be no Iraqi invasion of Saudi Arabia. It would all be over in a couple of weeks. But that did not diminish the opportunity now. A hero could be a man prepared to die for a great cause; it didn't have to be a man who died for one. No, this would be an exercise and an opportunity, and he intended to make the most of it. He had even penned a suggested line on his fitness report:

Jack Grant developed this battle group's plan to turn back Saddam's aggression and to lead the first combat operations against Saddam's forces.

He knew the CAG would spruce it up a lot and make it sound better. He planned on handing it to him after the flight.

Jack leaned back in the gray, metal chair and dropped his pen on the fold-out desk that was standard issue in a navy officer's stateroom. Since Jack was a commanding officer, he had a room to himself. It was a 20 x 20 space, all in gray of course, with a stand- up metal locker to complement the bureau of drawers that folded out for the desk. He also had a head, toilet in navy parlance, he shared with another skipper. He immensely enjoyed the fact he no longer had to flip-flop down the passageway, towel clutched around his waist like some douche, with his bag of toiletries dangling from his hand.

Space was the perk of seniority on ships where berthing ranged from sixty man compartments to a suite of quarters for the captain and onboard admiral. Junior officers lived in three or four-man rooms, mid-grades in two-man rooms and commanders and seniors in singles. Jack enjoyed his perk.

He picked up his pen and flipped it in his fingers, trying to come up with something memorable. He struggled because he didn't have a talent in relating to people and so he didn't know what to say. It had been that way all of his life. An image of George C. Scott and the Patton speech flashed in his mind. He smiled and straightened the pen to write, then frowned and shook his head. It was too long, and the ready room was too small and close for that kind of thing. It wouldn't work.

"I need something more personal," Jack whispered to the room as he rocked in his chair. "I need something about death. I need something about the danger." He sighed and looked up at his bookshelf. Jack liked to read and routinely checked books from the ship's library. He glanced at the titles, then grinned as he stood. He pulled a worn copy of *The Dirty Dozen* from the shelf and blew dust from its cover.

Lee Marvin, as Major Reisman, was looking right at him.

Jack quickly burned through the pages, licking his fingers once, then twice, there it was; Lee Marvin's speech to the Dirty Dozen. Jack loved that scene in the movie where they were all sitting at a long table after having tricked their way to success. Major Riesman had molded a group of convicts into a lethal machine, and the dinner was the culmination. Jack especially liked the way the group responded to the major when he stood and delivered the speech. The way they replaced their sullenness and mistrust with respect and open camaraderie. Jack grinned when he remembered Telly Savalas' smile as he took a drink of wine. The smile said the major had won his hard ass over! Jack began to read Reisman's words. Soon, they would be Jack Grant's words:

We still have one operation to go. If you guys foul up on this one none of us will ever play the violin again. Cause up until now it's all been a game. But as of tomorrow night, it's going to be the real thing. And if you want to know how real, I'll tell you. It's my guess that a lot of you guys won't be coming back. But there's no sense in squawking about that, right? Cause the army never did love you anyway. And besides, you all volunteered, right? That's more than I did.

Jack grinned as he reread it. He would have to tweak it a bit, but all in all, it was, perfect!

33

***

"Standby!"

Jack stood outside the ready room and smiled as he heard the duty officer's voice. He listened to the sounds of flight boots scuffing against the polished tile. He inhaled a quick breath and walked into the room.

"Attention on deck!" The duty officer yelled.

Jack kept his face stern as he strode to the front. He felt the heat of the bodies and caught the smell of the lair of naval aviators--- Sweaty flight suits, cigarettes, day-old coffee, and floor wax. He lived for these "being the king" moments. As a junior officer, he had been awed by navy protocol and, particularly, the treatment of commanding officers. Now, as the skipper himself, he drunk it in. His favorite was this grand entrance when his people came to attention to honor him and then waited for his release from their ramrod positions.

"Seats," he declared!

The men quickly settled into their heavy, steel, ready room chairs. Jack slowly and purposely strode to the center. The Ghostrider ready room was an ample space for ship standards, located athwartships on the 03 level. It was rectangular with a false, low-ceilinged overhead and the chairs all faced forward along a center aisle. A duty officer's desk was at the front of the room and a coffee mess and mailbox cubby hole at the rear. The walls were painted a bright yellow with black and white trim. The black-tiled deck triumphed from vigorous buffing and gleamed in the overhead lights. A yellow death's head, red blood dripping from its sword, was inlaid in the center front

34

of the room and Jack took care not to step on it. Doing so was a sign of disrespect and a one-dollar fine!

Jack took a deep breath as he looked out into the audience. "Men, this has been a great cruise. We answered our country's call for the past six months, and we answered it with professional excellence." Jack liked the term "professional excellence," and he used it a lot. He even had it printed under his signature block. Or, at least he used to. The JOs kept changing it to pornographic excellence, so he had to stop using it. That said, he still thought of professional excellence as his personal byline.

"As you know, "professional excellence" is a hallmark of Jack Grant-led organizations, and this one has been no different."

Jack paused and smiled at the assembled crowd. Thirty faces looked back at him and, as always, he wondered what they were thinking.

"It was professional excellence that led me to create the first combat plan for this battle group, and it is professional excellence that drives me to lead the battle group into the unknown." Jack slowly walked to the other side of the death's head, careful to avoid the fine. "As you might not know, I am leading the first event tomorrow because that is what real leaders do, they lead."

Jack glanced at Tagger and saw his eyes slit with a frown. Tagger would just have to get over it.

"But we need to think about what is in front of us." Jack paused for dramatic effect. "You know, I have been doing a lot of thinking since we pulled out of Naples." He walked over to the large, white briefing board on the forward wall. An assortment of plastic aircraft models hung there by hooks. The aircrew used them during briefings and following a flight to demonstrate maneuvers. He selected a Tomcat model and turned to the room. He looked at the model and rolled it in his hands for some more dramatic effect. A cough from the back of the room was the only sound.

I have them!

"I have been thinking about what is important," he continued. "Thinking about what is in front of us and what the nation, the world, expects out of us. I have some personal words I want to say to you. Words that I wrote as they came out of my heart." Jack reached into his trouser pocket and pulled out a paper square. He unfolded it as he looked around the room; pleased with the somber mood. It was precisely what he wanted.

Time to kick in some Lee Marvin. He began to read.

"However, we have one more operation to go, and we can't foul it up. If we do, we will never play the violin again." Jack paused and looked at Tagger. His XO was frowning, and as he looked at the other officers, he could see the confusion in their eyes too. Must keep on reading. The violin bit had been too much.

"Because up until now it's been a game. But as of tomorrow, it's going to be the real thing." He paused again. They were all looking at him, concern in their eyes, just what he wanted.

"And if you want to know how real, I will tell you. It's my guess that some of us won't be coming back." Jack looked at the room and took a steady, loud breath. It was the purposeful breath of a great moment. The thirty sets of knotted brows and set lips in the room were focused entirely on him.

"But there's no sense in squawking about that, right? I mean the navy never did love you anyway? And besides, you all volunteered anyway, right?"

Jack smiled, folded the paper, and put it in his pocket. He put his hands akimbo, and scanned the room, expecting to see heads nod and perhaps, even some clapping. He smiled wider and looked at the back rows where the JOs dwelled. Surely they would support his drama. He looked at Jocko, then moved his eyes. He looked at the rest of the crowd.

What the Fuck?

There was no nodding. There were just frowns of confusion. JOs in the back looked sideways at one another, then looked back at him. Jack shot a glance at the lieutenant commanders; those fuckers owed him! More confusion.

"Right?" He swallowed, a ragged chuckle caught in his throat. "Questions, then?" Jack licked his lips. He felt his face grow red.

"Ghostriders, are we ready to get 'em?" He pumped his hand.

He smiled and held his hand higher. They all looked at each other, then back at him.

What the fuck? What the fuck?

Jack stared at the people he didn't know for a second longer, then turned to his Ops officer. "Okay, then, Ops, what about tomorrow's schedule?"

Jack quickly stepped forward to his ready room chair and sat down.

Jesus Christ, what happened?

He felt his face glow, and an uncomfortable tightness gripped his chest. He forced himself to breathe calmly. He had bombed. He swallowed and looked forward, feeling Tagger's eyes on the side of his face. Jack quickly glanced at him and hated himself for doing so. Tagger smiled weakly and gave him a thumb's up.

Jack knew he did that because he had to.

Jack forced himself to look at the Ops officer, but he wanted to run out of the room. He forced himself to listen, but he wanted to crawl away.

What the fuck?

The rest of the AOM was a hash of the next days' schedules and a threat briefing from the intelligence officer, but Jack barely heard it. He had failed in his big moment.

How could I have been so far off the mark? What made the speech work for Lee Marvin but not for me? What the fuck?

When the AOM ended, Jack ran to his room to hide.

Jocko watched the skipper scurry out of the ready room, then strolled to the back of the room to his mailbox. He found a motorcycle magazine from *American Iron*, so he started to read an article about the Evolution Engine versus the Knuckle Head. But something about the skipper's speech seemed familiar. He walked over to the duty desk and dialed his stateroom number.

"Bridge club." It was Tubby's voice.

"WHO IS THIS? MISTER, WHO TAUGHT YOU TO ANSWER THE PHONE LIKE THAT?" Jocko roared into the receiver.

"Uhh. Uhh."

Jocko grinned when he heard Tubby's stammer.

"Uhh, sorry, sir."

Jocko hesitated a second. He could hear Tubby telling everyone to be quiet.

"Uhh, sir, this is Lieutenant Wainwright. Can I help you?"

"WHAT? WHO IS THIS?"

"Sorry, sir, this is Lieutenant Wainwright, Can I help you?"

"Hahaha, you tool. This is Jocko; I'm just messing with you man."

Jocko grinned into the receiver. He could hear Tubby's brain cells puking on themselves.

"Jocko! You turd. You miserable turd!"

Jocko laughed again. "Hey, who taught you to talk like that, mister?"

"Screw you, Jocko!"

"Hey, do you still have a tape of *The Dirty Dozen*?"

"I have a copy of every Lee Marvin movie, but fuck if you can see it."

"Hey, I'll bring some dog. Que it up, I'll be down in a minute."

"Okay, but screw you!"

Jocko hung up the phone and walked the dark passageways to Wardroom One. He got four cups of dog and headed to the room he shared with Tubby, Spud, and Mooch. It was a four-man called the bridge club for some reason nobody remembered. Nobody played that game anymore. Anyway, it was a much better arrangement than the six-pack, and, for heaven's sake, the pit of pits, the octagon.

Jocko kicked the open door wide and walked in. He handed the dog to his mates and sat down.

"Boy, was the skipper ever weird tonight." He unlaced his boots.

"Was he ever," grunted Tubby.

Jocko shook his head. "Do you think he was drunk or something?"

"No, he wasn't drunk, he was just fucked up," laughed Mooch.

"Ops normal," said Spud." But, it was so unusual to hear him say stuff like that. You know, something other than just rattling off policy."

"Yeah, the skipper reminds me another Grant, you know, the actor, Cary Grant."

"How's that," asked Mooch?

"He is a chick's type of guy but has no real guy guts. You know?"

"Yeah, you're right." Jocko frowned and pursed his lips. "But, I think I heard his pitch before."

"What do you mean?" Tubby paused over his dog.

"I mean, I have heard the violin thing before. In a movie." He motioned to Tubby. "Play that tape we talked about."

Tubby inserted the tape and sat down. Jocko fast-forwarded it, and images of Lee Marvin, Charles Bronson, Telly Savalas, John Cassavetes, and others flickered across the screen.

"Here we go." Jocko hit the play button, and the screen filled with the dirty dozen sitting at a long table. Lee Marvin stood and began to talk.

We still have one operation to go. If you guys foul up on this one none of us will ever play the violin again. Cause up until now it's all been a game. But as of tomorrow night, it's going to be the real thing. And if you want to know how real, I'll tell you. It's my guess that a lot of you guys won't be coming back. But there's no sense in squawking about that, right? Cause the army never did love you anyway. And besides, you all volunteered, right? That's more than I did.

"You've got to be shitting me!" Jocko shook his head and leaned back against the wall. "So much for the words that came out of his heart."

41

"Yeah, the guy has no morals. He is a douche-bag."

"And I get to fly with him over Indian country."
Jocko banged his head against the wall.

Tubby ejected the tape and returned it to the locker. "Don't trust him, buddy. That's all I got to say."

CHAPTER THREE

Ike entered the Red Sea on the eighth of August, and by the ninth, she was abreast Medina on the Red Sea coast of Saudi Arabia. She was prepared to launch her first interdiction team, and she turned into the wind.

Jack snapped on his oxygen mask and gave a thumbs up to the yellow-shirt. He kept firm pressure on the brakes as the man returned the signal and directed the brown-shirted plane captains to unchain the Tomcat. Jack glanced to the left and right to ensure he had room to taxi forward.

"Why do they always have to squeeze us in so fucking tight?" He glanced in his rearview mirrors at Jocko and set the intercom to "hot mic."

"You're clear on the sides, skipper." Jocko's voice was crisp and sure.

The yellow-shirt held his hands over his head with the clenched fists signal for brakes on! He slowly moved them apart and then back together, a message to the pilot to move. Jack released pressure on the brakes and wiggled the throttles. The big fighter groaned out of the spot and rolled forward. Jack tapped the brakes and rechecked the clearance.

"We clear? We clear?"

"We're clear, skipper. We're clear."

Jack strained to look around the jet. He hesitated, and the yellow-shirt impatiently motioned him to keep rolling forward. He knew they all called him "creepy-crawly" because he was so hesitant. Jack added a little power and shot a glance up at the tower. He wondered if the CAG was watching the launch and if he had found Jack bumped Tagger for the flight. Tagger was one of the best strike leads in the air wing, a former TOPGUN instructor, and a great ball flyer. These were all things that Jack wished he was, and it frustrated him that he was not. He glanced again to see if CAG was in the tower.

But, the hell with it! He figured it was his squadron and his flight schedule. Hell, he signed the flight schedule every day, and he should be able to decide who flew on what event.

Jack's yellow shirt pointed toward the center of the ship where another director motioned him to keep moving. Jack hesitated again.

"You okay, 201?" The air boss's voice crackled in Jack's headset.

"You bet, boss," replied Jack.

"Well keep it moving then, we have a launch to make."

"Yes, sir, boss," said Jack.

"Wings are clear, skipper." The hot mic allowed Jocko to speak freely to Jack without having to hit the transmit button. Jack liked to fly in hot mic and would remain there for the entire flight.

They moved slowly to the catapult and on a signal, Jack shoved the lever forward and the Tomcat's wings slowly swung into the takeoff position. He followed the yellow shirt's directions, lowered his flaps and dropped the launch bar which allows the cat crew the ability to "connect" the airplane to the catapult. Jack and Jocko held their hands up as the ordnance men pulled the flags off the Sidewinder, Sparrow, and Phoenix missiles, and armed the gun. A minute later, Jack saluted the cat officer; and in two seconds, he and Jocko accelerated to 160 miles per hour and leaped into the sky.

As Jack and Jocko climbed away from the ship, Captain Hulk Townsend, deputy CAG for the airwing, worked his way through the passageways of the 03 level for his meeting with CAG. He frowned as he thought of their task. It was to rank the skippers for their fitness reports. In his opinion, the CAG was partial to his A-6 community. He stepped over a knee-knocker, bent down to avoid a head-knocker and rapped his fist on the door to his boss's office.

"Morning CAG," he said, as he entered the room. Captain Frank Wright, Commander of Air Wing Seven, grinned when he saw his deputy and motioned to a chair. "Sit down, Hulk; we don't have much time. I need to get to the flag spaces once our strike package checks in with Dragon, the air force AWACS. As you know, the situation is chaotic at best. General Horner is setting up a JFACC, but there is no formal air tasking order yet. Central Command approved our interdiction plan and is providing the command and control and tankers, but we are pretty much on our own."

"Yes, sir." Hulk took a chair facing his boss. "I checked with CIC. The package won't get to Dragon for at least 90 minutes."

"Got it," said Frank as he looked at his watch. "Okay then let's see how far we can get." He looked at the papers in his hand and sighed. He hated this part of his job.

45

The purpose of the meeting was to rank the nine squadron commanders in the wing. It was a critical process since only the skipper ranked number one or two would get a following command such as an airwing, aircraft carrier, or significant shore installation. Such rankings occurred each April and after the CAG's tour. Since Frank was leaving in less than a month, the meeting had to take place.

"CAG, first of all, any chance you might be extended? You know, due to this Iraq thing?"

"Nah. I think this will develop slowly, unless of course, Saddam pulls a dumb shit and heads further south."

"Any chance of that?"

"Who knows?" Frank handed a sheaf of paper across his desk to his deputy. "You will see from this spreadsheet that I have taken some critical factors, critical in my mind that will indicate the strength of our commanding officers. I want us to use this data, but I also want your opinions on who is who in the zoo. Hulk, you are here because you are the second most experienced aviator in the air wing and because you will inherit this kingdom when I leave."

"Yes, sir."

"So, what's your take on this line-up?" Frank leaned back and watched Hulk with interest. The spreadsheet he had provided listed the names of the squadron commanders against the categories of retention rates, discipline rates, advancement rates, boarding rates, sortie completion rates, ordnance delivered, flight time, and safety incidents.

Hulk cleared his throat and looked up. "Well, from this it looks like Guido Beckindale from the Blasters is number one."

Frank nodded and looked at his deputy closely. He relied on Hulk's judgment for many things, and he was a smart and good man. But Frank thought it was right to prioritize specific warfighting capabilities vice giving them all equal value. For instance, he tripled the value of ordnance delivered and doubled squadron flight time. True, this presented a massive advantage to the A-6 squadron and the two F-18 squadrons because of their bombing mission. It further singled out the A-6s because of the number of missions they flew. The Blasters were the only A-6 squadron in the wing, and they flew all the tanking missions plus their tactical missions. Frank realized that his model made it difficult for a unit that didn't drop a lot of bombs to compete. He also knew he was probably a little parochial in favor of his community. Frank knew that Hulk favored weighing all of the categories equally and this allowed him to argue for his Tomcat pals. He had explained all of this when they did the rankings the previous April. Frank felt he was on solid ground. After all, the primary mission of an aircraft carrier was to deliver ordnance on the nation's enemies, and therefore; the primary ordnance deliverer should be ranked number one.

Hulk looked up from the spreadsheet and frowned. "CAG, I know the reasoning on this, but shouldn't we also take a look at the man we are recommending? The whole package? After all, who we pick will go on to be the next CAG, carrier skipper and so on."

"And be in the running for flag," Frank interrupted.

"Absolutely, sir."

"Okay, so who do you have?" Frank picked up his letter opener and began flipping it in his fingers.

"I have Jack Grant as number one."

Frank took a deep breath and looked at the ceiling. The letter opener danced. "You mean because of the CVIC planning?"

"That has something to do with it, sure."

"Geez, Hulk, he had a couple of hours and guidance from me, and he produced some good numbers. But that doesn't make him the number one guy." He narrowed his eyes and looked at Hulk. "He IS a Tomcat bubba…like you."

"Sir, that has nothing to do with it.!" Hulk straightened in his chair. "It's just that his squadron is near the front of many of the numbers for one thing. He has his maintenance shop humming; his ops guys are always on point, and the Ghostriders never miss a sortie. His people programs are first rate. He is just a very polished guy. "

Frank continued to twiddle with his letter opener. "I agree with everything you said about that squadron. They are phenomenal. But I am not so sure I cherish the polish like you do. Do you think he is better than Guido? Do you think he would make a better CAG, for instance?"

"I do. Guido is fantastic, don't get me wrong. I rank him right behind Jack. But Guido doesn't have the élan that Jack has. Guido is a great bomber and tactician, but he doesn't have the sophistication Jack has."

"In what way?"

"Well, Guido can land an Intruder on the three-wire in the middle of a hurricane and drop a bomb inside a needle's eye, and Guido did take Jack's numbers and did come up with our interdiction plan. But Jack worked with a chaotic situation and pulled together a group of young officers to develop the numbers around our lack of strategic tanking and command and control. Guido provided the strike plan and ordnance plan to Jack's numbers."

"Excuse me, but the strike and ordnance plans are pretty important to an interdiction mission." Frank grinned over tight lips. "I know what Jack did, or at least what the team did. There's some talk that Doody and the guys in CVIC did all the real work, and Jack just took credit."

"Sir, Jack spoke to his numbers with a deep understanding of what they meant. I don't think anybody developed them but him."

"Well, maybe," said Frank. He twiddled with the letter opener.

"Yes, sir. Bottom line, sir, is Jack is the complete commander in the wing, and I think that makes him the best candidate to go forward."

Frank grimaced and took a deep breath. "Jack is smooth, for sure." He swung his chair around and frowned at Hulk. "But, sometimes I think he is a little too smooth. He is too much David Niven and not enough John Wayne for me. He is also a bull- shitter."

Frank looked at Hulk and took a deep breath. His deputy's eyes fell to the floor. "And it doesn't make any difference how polished he is if he can't relate to people."

"Sir, I think he relates to people just fine."

"Hulk, he relates to you because he kisses your ass."

"Sir!"

"Relax, DCAG," Frank grinned to ease the tension. "He kisses everybody's ass. Everybody that is senior to him that is."

"Sir."

"But have you seen him around his guys? I go to all of his functions when they need CAG's presence, and there is a distance between him and his guys."

"But CAG, he is the skipper. There has to be a distance."

"Yes, I know what you are saying," nodded Frank. "But this is more than rank and position. It's like they don't like him at all."

"I don't know what you mean."

"I visit the ready rooms frequently and stick my head in to say hello. You know that. But every time I dropped by the Ghostrider ready room, Jack was sitting in his chair. Nobody else but the duty officer was in the room. And that is in the middle of the day! That isn't normal."

"Yes, sir. But…"

"I can see why you like Jack because what you like is the Ghostriders. They are indeed a class outfit. However, much of that was put in place by Jack's predecessor and maintained today by his XO. The problem with guys like Jack is that they aren't believable and they aren't good leaders. Jack isn't a good leader. You've seen him in the skippers' meetings. He is a snake oil salesman. As I said, the XO runs that outfit, and Jack goes along."

"But CAG, how can the squadron be so good with that kind of guy at the top?"

Frank laughed. "Heck, DCAG, we would like to think we are the reasons for greatness," He leaned back in his chair. "And, sometimes we are, I suppose. But I think personal greatness often happens because the supporting cast is so great. I believe that is the case with the Ghostriders. You heard the rumor about why he wasn't on the barge in the first place, didn't you? That his JOs had conspired against him? That isn't normal. Even for naval aviation."

Frank heard Hulk sigh and watched as his deputy looked at the floor.

"Hulk, Jack looks the part, usually acts the part, and he is just fantastic at the receptions we have. He is especially effective with our foreign guests who visit the ship. I have received several personal comments about him during this cruise. He is a superficial guy that can flitter through a crowd and delight almost everyone. But, he isn't knowledgeable when it comes to the business. He doesn't know anything about the strike mission and doesn't seem interested in it. He wants to be a fighter guy. I don't think his aircrew, or the squadron, want to follow him. Jack doesn't have a good reputation around the boat either. He only flies at night to stay current, and he always takes the pinky recovery. I don't think he could get it aboard if it were dark."

"But sir, at some point, all of that becomes irrelevant. For instance, the day after your change of command, your skill as an actual pilot doesn't mean anything. You will have all of your value based on your experiences and how you handle yourself."

"I get what you are saying," said Frank. "But that experience and skill with a crowd, especially a powerful crowd, has to have a strong foundation. Jack has to have some solid concept of tactical leadership." Frank took another deep breath and looked at his deputy. "Jack isn't ready to lead an airwing or ship. I don't see him as a CAG or carrier skipper. I don't see it."

"I understand, said Hulk. "But I want to say I think we need to pick someone who has the polish and experience to provide value beyond the ship. That's all."

Frank took a sharp breath and looked hard at his deputy. "When we fight the next war, are these polished types you seem so fond of going to do the actual planning and are they going to fly THEIR plan? Guido planned the interdiction missions, and he briefed them to the Admiral. And, he is going to fly his plan into combat. I didn't even put Jack on the line up to fly on these missions because I don't think he would execute very well."

"Sir, is that because he is just a Tomcat guy and not a bomb dropper?"

Frank narrowed his eyes. "Hell no! I put Tagger down to lead the first event. He's a Tomcat guy. Look, Hulk, I want someone who will fly in against the SAMs and the AAA and hit the target. I want someone who will find the courage and engage all those MIGs out there. I don't want some guy that knows the best wine to go with Norwegian cod."

"Well, CAG…"

"Imagine a scenario where we go with your suggestion. Let's make Jack number one, and he selects for CAG, and his air wing has SWO as the flag. You know, another pentagon trained thinker that doesn't understand or embrace tactics and doesn't know shit about air combat. Now, you have a guy developing a plan to go downtown in some raghead hellhole, briefing strike warfare, something he never has personally done, to a shoe admiral who knows even less than he does. What fucking sense does that make?"

"Does that mean I'm not qualified? I fly the Tomcat."

Frank regretted his comment. "Of course not, Hulk. But you are not a typical Tomcat guy. You and Tagger both gained a lot of strike experience with your tours up at Fallon and your tour as a CAG Ops officer. You dropped a lot of bombs back then. You are a far cry from Jack Grant. Look, DCAG, it makes no sense for a guy with Jack's experience to be in the running to be a CAG. It makes no sense. We have enough casual guys hanging around as it is. We need guys that can get into the dirt and stab the fuck out of people. Bomb the shit out of them. Engage in air combat with them and gun their brains out. Make them wish they had never fucked with us."

"CAG, I..."

"Listen, Hulk. You are a good man, a great man, in my opinion. And you will be a great CAG when I leave. But whatever you do, you never leapfrog over the real mission of this carrier and think that somehow we are the breeding ground for all things wonderful back in the pentagon. The only reason we are here lies down there in the armory. Oh, we can do the other stuff. We can, and we should deliver water and rice to starving ass-kicked folks.

We can, and we should have our parties and invite people on board, serve big shrimp and Budweiser, and kiss their asses for being in the French Navy League. We can, and we should have our Marines perform the sunset, silent drill in dress uniforms while they coo and ahh. We can, and we should do all that stuff. But the only reason we are here, the only reason we are here is to bomb the ever-living fuck out of those that threaten us. If you don't substantially contribute to that, then you won't ever be a CAG in my book. We understand each other?"

"Yes, sir." Hulk looked down at his boots then back at Frank. "Yes, sir, we do."

"Look, Hulk, I appreciate your insights, I do. But, I am going with Guido as number one and probably Lassie Collier over in the Wildcats as number two. We can talk about the rest later."

"Yes, sir." Hulk stood to go. "I'm going to drop by CIC then go to my brief. I am flying on event four."

"I'll be down in a minute," said Frank.

***

Jack rendezvoused overhead Ike with his wing Tomcat crewed by Lieutenant "Headly" LaMarr and his RIO, Lieutenant Commander "Chain" Sawyer. As the other strike team members launched, they joined in loose formation. Once all were on board, Jocko transmitted to the ship, "Dakota 201, package complete and outbound." Jack led the formation to the planned aerial refueling point northwest of Riyadh while Jocko established communications with Dragon, the USAF AWACS command, and control plane, as well as the KC-10 tanker. All six birds topped off their fuel tanks. Jack took his group north of the refueling point and set up an orbit with the six aircraft flying in sections of two each, separated by 1000 feet of altitude. This allowed the group to keep sight while relaxing the requirement of division formation flying. As he flew, Jack surveyed the landscape below. The sheer nothingness of it was breathtaking. Jack smiled as he thought of his position.

I am so glad I bumped Tagger and took this flight! It will look good on paper, and there was no risk. Saddam isn't going to do anything provocative.

Jack was content in his orbit when the AWACS controller, call sign Dragon, jolted him from his reverie.

"Dakota 201 from Dragon, bandits,' bullseye zero one zero for sixty miles!"

What? Jack snapped into focus as he heard Jocko's quick reply.

"Roger Dragon, Dakota."

What the hell?

"Skipper, come to a heading of zero one five." Jocko's voice was crisp and confident.

"Are you sure? Is it a vector or just information"?

"It's a vector. Skipper, come to zero one five."

"What's, was going on? Are there MIGs out there?"

"Skipper, come to a heading of zero one five." Jocko's voice was stern.

"Roger," said Jack. He couldn't believe what was happening. He looked in the mirror at Jocko, but all he could see was the top of the RIO's helmet. Jocko was working the systems. Jack was glad he had Jocko in the back seat. He swung his Tomcat to the left and shoved the throttles forward. He glanced over his shoulder to see that Headley followed him and keyed his second radio.

"Stay put Guido."

Guido, flying his A-6 Intruder, was the attack lead. The plan was to leave the attack planes and their heavy bomb loads at the orbit point if the fighters got vectored — no need to get them involved in a dogfight.

"Roger." Guido's radio crackled in the headset then went silent.

"Dragon, Dakota, say status." Jocko prompted the AWACS.

"Dakota, Dragon, two groups of suspected horses vectoring south towards you. Ten-mile trail. Lead group now bullseye zero one zero for fifty-five. Hail Mary. Hail Mary."

"Dragon, Dakota copies horses, and Hail Mary," replied Jocko. "Skipper, ensure Master Arm is on. Select Phoenix."

"Roger," said Jack. He lifted the Master Arm switch to the "on" position and toggled the weapons to Phoenix.

"Horses and Hail Mary," echoed Chain in the wing plane. He wanted the flight leader to know he heard the controller. Horse was code for MIG 23, the supersonic swing-wing Soviet jet that Saddam liked to use. Hail Mary was code for visual identification required to fire. There was much confusion in the battle area, and despite the capabilities of the AWACS, the code meant that U.S. fighters had to visually confirm what they were shooting at before weapons' release. There was too much risk that Saudi planes were in the area, and USAF F-15s were also streaming into the theater. This requirement put a tremendous burden on the Tomcats, but it could not be avoided.

"Dakota has a contact bearing zero one five at forty-five, Angels twenty-four." Jocko barked the contact.

The mic keyed, and Dragon responded. "Roger, Dakota, that's your lead bandit. Watch for the trailers. Hail Mary."

Roger," said Jocko. Moments later, he continued, "Dakota has a single zero one five for forty-three miles, Angels twenty-four, airspeed 680!"

"That is your bogey," replied Dragon.

"Holy shit." Jack gulped into the mic. "That guy is moving!"

"We are closing at over 1200 miles per hour," said Jocko.

"Dakota Two is targeting the trailers." Chain's voice sang over the radio. "A flight of two bearing zero one seven at fifty miles, Angels ten." Chain's comments told Jack and Jocko that he had the trailers low at ten thousand feet and seven miles in trail of the lead. He also said he was targeting which meant he would keep his radar on the trailers, allowing Jack and Jocko to track the lead bandits.

"Lead is on my nose at forty miles, level," said Jocko.

Jack's pulse pounded. *Maybe they should turn around! What if they couldn't identify the MIGS until too late? What if the MIGS fired first!*

He sucked oxygen and glanced left. Headley was still in position.

"Skipper, I'm taking a lock on the lead bogey to slave the TCS to the radar. Maybe we can get an ID on these guys."

"Good idea," blurted Jack.

Seconds later, Jocko shouted into the intercom. "Got him! I got him! Look at your display."

Jack looked down at his Horizontal Information Display to see why Jocko was so excited. The bright image of a MIG 23 popped into view.

"C-confirm horse," he sputtered over the radio.

"There are two of them," said Jocko. "Welded wing."

Jack looked at the image again, and, sure enough, there were two MIG 23's. They were so close the radar had only detected a single target.

"Confirm, TWO horses in the lead group!" Shouted Jack.

"Roger, two horses," said Dragon. "Green Lantern." Green lantern was code for cleared to fire.

"In range for the Phoenix, skipper."

Jack hesitated. The MIGs were still over thirty miles away.

"Shoot now, and they will never see the missile coming," insisted Jocko.

Jack hesitated. He knew the numbers, he just wasn't sure and didn't want to screw it up. He looked at the image. They sure looked like MIGs.

"Take the shot, skipper!"

Jack hesitated. *What if he was wrong? A MIG 23 looks like a Mirage F1 at certain angles. What if he wasn't supposed to shoot?*

"Take the shot, skipper!"

What if it's not MIGs? The TCS could be wrong. Fuck!

Whoosh!

Jack felt the thump of the 1,000-pound Phoenix missile leave the Tomcat and saw it streak in front of his nose. He watched it accelerate vertically and out of sight.

"Fox three!" Shouted Jocko.

"What happened?"

"I launched it, skipper. If we waited any longer, they would have seen its smoke trail. It will be doing Mach five by now and will hit them from directly above. They won't see it coming."

"What? What?" Jack was confused.

What just happened? Jocko launched the Phoenix?

The Phoenix was the only weapon that the RIO could launch, and Jocko had done it.

Jack gulped. Once a missile launches, the game is on. There was no turning back now.

Holy crap!

"Trailers on my nose for thirty," said Chain.

"Skipper, we need to stay up here until we see what the Phoenix does. The missile goes active at fifteen seconds from impact. We are almost there!" Jocko shouted.

Jack looked left and saw Headley's Tomcat below him. "Okay," he said. He thought about turning away. Not too late to stop this. They could be making a colossal mistake. What if they weren't MIGS?

"She's active!" shouted Jocko.

Jack shook his head, took a deep breath, and pushed the nose over.

"Stay up here!" Jocko yelled. "We need to support a second shot if we have to."

"On my nose for twenty-two," said Chain.

"I'm locking our lead target for a follow-on Sparrow," said Jocko.

What the fuck? What the fuck? Jack wanted to turn the jet around and run away.

What was happening?

Jack glanced at Headley he was so low he could hardly see him. He looked back up and suddenly a massive fireball exploded right in front of his eyes! Angry coils of orange and black billowed, and the wreckage of two aircraft wheeled out!

Their Phoenix had hit both MIGs!

"Splash two horses!" Jack screamed before he realized he was talking on the intercom. He keyed the UHF and shrieked," Splash two horses!"

"Looking for the trailers," said Jocko.

Jack shoved his nose down and looked at his wingman. He saw a missile come off of Headley's Tomcat.

"Fox one!" shouted Headley.

Jack saw the Sparrow whipsaw forward, then accelerate into an arc to the left. He lost sight of it.

Shit, it missed!

Then he saw a fireball!

"Splash one horse!" screamed Headley.

"I have the second guy locked," said Jocko. "Skipper, come hard left and put him on the nose."

Jack jerked the stick to the left and flew over Headley, "Crossing over."

"Mile and a half," said Jocko. "He's turning into us. Shoot him, skipper!"

"Fox one," said Jack as he pulled the trigger.

Nothing happened, so he pulled the trigger again. The MIG was turning hard into them.

"Select Sparrow!" screamed Jocko.

Jack looked at his weapons display. He still had Phoenix selected.

"Fuck!" He screamed over the ICS. He selected Sparrow and pulled hard on the stick. He squeezed the trigger, and the missile leaped off the rails. It instantly headed for the ground.

"You shot too late!" roared Jocko. "We're in min range now; the radar broke lock! Select Sidewinder!"

Jack lost sight of the MIG as it whizzed under his wing. He pulled harder and caught sight as it headed down. He rolled in behind it.

"SHOOT!" screamed Jocko.

"I can't get a tone! I can't get a tone!"

"You still have Sparrow selected. Go to Sidewinder!" Vapor poured off the MIGs wings as it turned hard into the Tomcat. Jack planted the stick in his lap and stomped the left rudder. He slammed the throttles to idle as the MIG closed. Christ, he was right on it! Jack jammed the weapon's selector switch down with his right thumb.

"I can't get a tone! I can't get a tone!"

"You're not in Sidewinder you're in Guns! You're in Guns!" screamed Jocko. "Just pull the trigger!"

Jack was confused.

What the fuck? What the fuck?

"Skipper, just pull the trigger!" screamed Jocko.

Jack pulled the trigger, and the Tomcat's M61 Gatling Gun belched hundreds of rounds of depleted uranium, peppering the MIG.

What the fuck?

The MIG filled his windscreen, and Jack jerked the stick to the right and pushed forward to avoid a collision. The MIG hurtled by.

Jack saw flames licking the wing roots. It sailed past them, then exploded!

Holy shit, he had gunned him! He had gunned a MIG!

"Splash one horse!" he shouted.

Jack screamed over the ICS and gave a thumbs up in the mirror. Jocko screamed with him!

THREE MIGS! WOW!

Jack and Jocko were still screaming and laughing in their headsets as Headley and Chain joined on the right side. They had their oxygen masks dangling from their helmets, huge grins plastered on their faces. Jocko and Chain exchanged hand signals for status and fuel while Headley joined for a visual inspection of his flight lead's jet. When he finished, he gave Jack a thumbs up.

"Wingman is good to go," said Jocko. "Vector is one 183 for seventy to the rest of the package."

"Roger," said Jack. Man, he was glad he had Jocko with him!

He pointed the nose south and began the climb to rendezvous altitude.

"Dakota, Dragon."

"Go Dragon," said Jocko.

"We, uh, heard most of that, but can you say status?" "Affirmative. We splashed four horses and have available ordnance for vectors. Attack group remains up for full tasking, but we need Texaco."

"Roger, that," replied the Dragon controller. "Vector 160 for forty-five to Texaco."

Jack led the six-pack back to the tanker and all aircraft topped off. They swung back north to the orbit point when they heard the relieving six-pack check-in with Dragon. The party was over, time to go back to the ship.

As Jack led the six-pack back to the carrier, he felt his euphoria drain into concern over how he would sound on the tape. He tried to remember what he and Jocko had said over the ICS and what was just in his head. He tried to recall the events, and he remembered his hesitation to shoot the Phoenix.

But how would it sound?

He felt he had been behind the entire engagement, struggling to catch up with the action. He had been out of sync. It was like he had been in shock the whole time. The dumb-shit switch errors would be especially hard to explain. Jocko had to repeatedly remind him he was in the wrong setting for the weapon needed. Jack sighed. There was no doubt. The tape would indicate he was a clown that was saved by his RIO.

Christ!

The matter of fact of killing the MIGs was huge. But, when people played the tape, well, that would be a different story. And, for sure, the tape would be played. Over, and over and over. He had blown his big chance to impress CAG, CAG, and everybody on the fricking planet! Fuck, the Pope would think he was a wimp!

If only I had just not been such a dumb shit! What am I going to do?

Jack could see the guys in the ready room, listening to the tape.

He shook his head as the image of his humiliation played in his mind.

"Hey, play that back again. Stop right there. Play that again. Do you hear that? Holy fuck, the skipper is total dumb shit."

Christ, they would play it on television, maybe even play it around the world. After all, it was becoming an international effort to dislodge Saddam.

Christ, what am I going to do?

He wished it was in the old days in the Phantom. He didn't have any fucking tape in the Phantom.

And then, a plan began to emerge. A way out began to form. Jack grinned in his mask as he thought about it.

"Jocko, how do you feel about going back again?"

Jack waited for Jocko's response. He would surely be confused.

"Uhh, sure skipper."

"Great. Put me up with the E-2. On the back radio." Jack waited for Jocko to switch frequencies.

"You're up on frequency with him, skipper."

Jack keyed the UHF mic, "Black Eagle, Ghostrider, over." He waited a second and repeated, "Black Eagle, Ghostrider, over."

"Ghostrider, Black Eagle, go." Jack could hear the faint hum of the airplane's big propellers in the background.

"Black Eagle, call the ship and get my XO on the line."

Jack waited a couple of seconds, then impatiently keyed the mic again. "Black Eagle, you copy?"

"Black Eagle copies. Wait, out."

"What's up, skipper?" Jocko sounded confused.

Jack looked in his mirrors and saw his RIO craning his head around the ejection seat. He had his visor up, and Jack could see the concern in his eyes.

"Jocko, there is something about actually being in combat versus just training for it. You know, the shock

66

factor. You handled that today like a pro. You epitomized professional excellence." Jack grinned at the use of his byline. "Those MIGs came at us supersonic, in a trail, with a high low split. You and Chain both caught it, but Jocko it was you who led the intercept. Now, we can brief all this to the guys that follow us, but what if they change their tactic? We need somebody with a clear head who has seen this stuff out here, so I am going to have the XO get the ship prepared to hot switch you into the outgoing launch."

Jack looked in the mirrors and watched Jocko's eyes over his oxygen mask.

"We need your leadership out here Jocko. You good with that?"

He watched Jocko look out the side of the airplane for a second then look into the mirror. "Sure, skipper. Sure. I can do it."

Moments later, Tagger keyed the mic, and Jack told him the plan. Tagger said he would pass the request on to the ship and have maintenance and the aircrews briefed.

Jack led the group back to the ship, and the Intruders, Hornets, and Tomcats proceeded to their holding altitudes. There was no radio traffic as the ship was operating in "zip lip" conditions. As the last launching aircraft rolled down the cat, the airborne Hornets hit the break, turning sharply over the carrier's island structure.

The Tomcats, Intruders and remaining aircraft followed in sequence.

Jack flew the ball to touch down and after the plane came to a stop, raised his hook, and cleared the landing area. He followed the director's signals, and after the remaining missiles were de-armed, and he was chained down, he shut the engines down. He watched Jocko exit the jet first and climbed down the ladder where a brown-shirted maintenance man held a flight book for the new airplane Jocko was to man. Jack stepped down the boarding ladder and watched Jocko flip open the book. The pages almost blew away! The deck was a cauldron of aircraft in various stages of being shut down, refueled, and in the case of the Ghostriders, re-armed. The noise was deafening!

Jack saw a green-shirted technician hand Jocko the TCS tape from their plane. The technician had retrieved it from the nose wheel well. It was customary for the RIO to take it to the de-briefing of the event. Jack watched Jocko put the tape in his helmet bag and continue to read his airplane status book.

"I'll take the tape," said Jack. He leaned into Jocko, yelling over the noise. "I'll take the tape to CVIC and de-brief for us. Good hunting out there!"

Jocko looked up briefly and frowned. He reached into his helmet bag and handed the tape to Jack. "See you when I get back, skipper." He gave the book back to the plane captain and headed for his new mount.

Jack walked down the flight deck and around the island, exiting on the 03 level. He went to his stateroom, unlocked the door, and ducked into the darkness. He stood there for a moment inhaling slowly, getting himself together. He turned on the light and removed his helmet.

What the fuck am I doing? Jesus, Jesus, Jesus, what the fuck am I doing?

Jack opened his desktop and saw his unused TCS tapes.

Aircrew erased the recordings for re-use, and Jack always had a couple in case he wanted to preserve some event.

The point of no return. Well, here goes.

Jack put the tape Jocko had handed him into a drawer and picked up a blank tape. He exited the room, locked the door, and proceeded to his ready room.

CHAPTER FOUR

Jack hurried down the passageway, high stepping the knee-knockers and ducking through hatchways. The going was tough as officers and sailors boiled all over the ship. He threw open to door to his ready room.

"SKIPPER!"

A crowd of Ghostriders mobbed Jack! The officers and Sailors swarmed him, roaring excitement and pride!

They had gotten MIGs! The ultimate goal of all fighter squadrons everywhere! Four MIGS, two with a Phoenix, the first-ever Phoenix kills!

Jack grinned and shook hands. He hugged, grabbed shoulders, and high-fived until his hands burned. Jack felt a momentary twinge of guilt that Jocko was missing the celebration but quickly shrugged it off. He had to get Jocko out of the way so he could destroy the tape.

Jack was overwhelmed with back slaps and hugs!

Headley and Chain walked in, and the crowd mobbed them too!

Suddenly, someone shouted, "Attention on deck!"

Jack and the others snapped to attention and turned toward the shout. CAG strode toward him with his hand outstretched and a huge grin on his face.

"I was pissed when I found you bumped Tagger. But, what the hell," he smiled. "Looks like it worked out!"

He vigorously shook Jack's hand, then turned to the joyous room, "Looks like the Ghostriders rule!"

The ready room roared anew, and they swarmed Jack, Headley, Chain, and CAG. The crowd grew larger as more squadron members squeezed through the door. Red-shirts, white- shirts, green-shirts, brown-shirts, shirts of all colors mingled with the green flight suits and khaki uniforms of the aircrew and chief petty officers.

Jack beamed. He had never felt so good.

I am a fucking stud!

"Skipper! Skipper!" Jack looked toward the duty officer. He held a phone, "It's the admiral's aide. He says the admiral wants to talk with you. He also wants to know if CAG is there."

"I think we need to go talk to the big guy," said CAG. He clapped Jack on the shoulder.

"Yes, sir," said Jack. "Let's go!"

"Sir, what about the flight debrief in CVIC?" The duty officer shouted again. "They called twice."

"Chain, you and Headley go on and debrief. Tell them I'll be right down after I talk with the admiral." Jack turned to the door.

"Skipper, what about the tape? The TCS tape, do you have it or is it still in the plane?" The duty officer walked around his desk. "I can have that sent up there."

"No, I have it right here," said Jack. He reached into his helmet bag and brought out the tape. "No idea if it recorded or anything, but here it is."

"Let's go, sir." He nodded to CAG, and they walked out the door.

Jack led the way, and he and CAG wound their way down the passageway to the flag spaces. A dark blue partition marked the boundary of the area, and the standard green deck tile turned to a highly waxed blue. Everything was bright, clean, and shipshape. Jack opened the door into the flag wardroom, and he and CAG were mobbed again by the admiral's staff. The Chief of Staff, Captain Hollis Wayfield, gripped Jack's hand and hugged him.

"You bring us all glory," he said with glistening eyes.

The noise and joyous celebration overcame Jack. The skipper of the ship, Captain James "Hog" McNamara, grabbed him in a bear hug and pumped his hand until he thought his shoulder would separate.

The door to the flag cabin popped open, and Rear Admiral Stan "Titan" Turner, the carrier group commander, beamed. He walked forward and grabbed Jack's hand. "Fantastic, skipper, just fantastic! Come into the cabin." The admiral pulled Jack's arm and turned toward the hatch that led to his private room. "Come on, CAG, Hollis you too."

Jack was in heaven! He felt comfortable with the admiral. He knew the two-star liked him, and as a fellow fighter pilot, would revel in the fact the F-14 community had scored the MIGS. He followed the admiral through the door, and soon he and the CAG and Chief of Staff sat around a small, felt-topped table.

"I heard you got two with a buffalo and GUNNED the third." The admiral slapped the table. Jack thought he saw tears in the man's eyes.

"Is it true?" asked Hollis.

"Yep," grinned, Jack. "And my wingman got the other!"

"That's great training and leadership," said the admiral. He leaned over and slapped Jack's shoulder "This is great for the Tomcat." He looked around the small room. "This is great for the fighter community. Man, to get two kills in one shot with a missile, then gun a third! And have your wingman mop it all up is just fantastic!"

"Sir."

The admiral looked at his door. It was ajar, and his Intel officer, Commander Stevie Cooper, had his head halfway inside.

"Come in, Stevie, come in."

Stevie slid through the opening. "Sir just wanted to give the first report. There are some indications that Saddam was moving south until the MIG encounter. It appears all of that movement has now stopped."

"What?" The admiral stood, and the other officers stood too. "Say that again."

"Sir, there are some preliminary indications. Nothing firm just yet, but some indications that Saddam was moving across the Kuwaiti border, but after the MIGs were shot down that movement stopped." Stevie nervously licked his lips, then turned and left the room.

"Did you hear that? Jack, you and the Ghostriders averted an invasion!" He grinned and slapped Jack on the back. "With a buffalo and a couple of bullets!"

"By the way, what did it feel like to shoot that thing anyway?" Hollis grinned. "Nobody has ever shot a Phoenix in combat."

"Yeah," said the admiral. "What did it feel like to pull the trigger and have that behemoth leap off the rails? That thing weighs, what, a thousand pounds?"

"Yes, sir," said Jack. "It makes a thud when it leaves, and you can hear the whoosh when it takes off!" He was feeling better and better. The tape thing would work out.

"What did it feel like, what went through your mind when you pulled the trigger?" The admiral's eyes sparkled.

Jack hesitated, he thought of Jocko's launch of the missile. "Well, Sir, I don't know. I just pulled the trigger when the timer went down. I wanted to launch it far enough away so they wouldn't see it but close enough so it would get into a no escape zone."

"No escape zone," said the admiral. "I freaking love that! No escape zone."

Jack imagined a photo of Duke Cunningham, holding a MIG 21 model. Now, it was Jack Grant, who was a war hero!

74

"Sir, if you would like I could give you the ejector pin the Phoenix leaves behind in the launcher. You know, as a souvenir."

"Jack, I couldn't accept that. It should be something you keep forever." The admiral dropped his hands and stepped back.

"Sir, I want you to have it."

"Jack, I appreciate that. Thank you."

"Sir, could Hollis call my ready room and have it brought up here?"

"Sure, Jack, Hollis, call 142's ready room and have somebody run the ejector pin from the skipper's aircraft to my cabin." The admiral turned to Jack. "Thank you, son. Thank you. So tell me, what happened after you pulled the trigger and the Phoenix left the rails."

"The whole airplane shook when that beast lit off," said Jack, and everyone in the room laughed.

Jack never felt so alive.

"It went straight up. I followed the smoke trail for a second, but it went out of sight. Besides, we were still in an engagement, and my wingman had two bandits on his radar. "

Jack leaned back in his chair to drink in the moment. "I looked down at my wingman but knew I needed to stay high in case we had to go for the lead MIGS again. Then, I saw the fireball with two MIGS whirling out of it. It was a thing of beauty! I headed down to support my wingman."

"Fantastic! Just fabulous airborne leadership, Jack." The admiral shook his head and smiled.

"About then, my wingman took a shot at the lead MIG in the trailer group and smoked him. I dove over him, got a lock on the other guy, and closed. The MIG driver must have seen my Tomcat because he reefed into me. I mean the vapes were pouring off his wings! I knew I was too close for a Sparrow shot, so I switched to Sidewinder. But, in a second he was inside Sidewinder range, so I switched to guns. I filled the windscreen with the bastard and fired. He blew up!"

The small group in the cabin erupted with cheers and a fresh round of back-slapping and high-fiving.

Jack was not just in heaven; he was in the middle of paradise.

"You know I used to fly Crusaders, right?" The admiral interrupted Jack's thoughts.

"Yes, sir," said Jack. "I know you flew the F-8 and I know you got a MIG kill in Viet Nam."

The admiral grinned and nodded. "Yep, got a MIG-17 over Kep airfield. Got him with a Sidewinder." He looked away for a moment. "I liked flying the Tomcat, but man I LOVED the Crusader. Now that was a jet. Simple, fast, deadly." He continued to look away for a second, then smiled at Jack. "Of course, you have the help of a second guy, right?"

"He's not that much help," blurted Jack. He instantly regretted his remark.

"Jack, Jack." CAG put his hand on Jack's shoulder and smiled. "Jack, please tell me you have this on tape. Please tell me." He shook Jack's shoulder.

"Oh, man, that would be fantastic," said Hollis. "Imagine the playback on the news!"

"CAG, can we get an S-3 ready to take that tape ashore? What do you think? Get it to Qatar then over to Fifth Fleet?"

"Absolutely," said CAG. "Consider it done!"

"So, you did tape it right?" CAG looked at Jack.

"Absolutely," said Jack. I gave the tape to the duty officer. Should be viewing it in CVIC now."

"Hollis, go tell Stevie to preview that tape." The admiral stood. "NO, hell, I want to see it myself." The other officers jumped to their feet. "Okay guys, I got to report to the boss at Fifth Fleet."

"Sir, someone from 142 is outside, says something about an ejector pin?" The admiral's yeoman stood at the door.

"Send him in," said Hollis.

The door opened, and Tubby walked in. "Here is the ejector pin off the plane," he said as he handed the piece of polished metal to Jack.

"Thanks, Tubby." Jack took the pin and handed it to the admiral. "Here it is sir, with all my respect. From one MIG killer to another."

The admiral grasped the pin in his palm and smiled again. "Thanks, Jack."

The officers began to file out, but as CAG and Jack approached the door, the admiral stopped them.

"This is a big deal, Jack. You made us all look good. The country needed this. The President needed it to justify the coalition and everything we are doing."

"Yes, sir," said Jack.

"By the way, what is your nickname," asked the admiral. "I have been trying to recall it all afternoon. I know most of the senior officers. Strange, I can't remember yours." He frowned and tilted his head.

"Oh, sir, they just call me J.G., my initials."

"Sir."

The admiral, CAG, and Jack turned. "Yes, Tubby?"

"Sir, the skipper used to be called Phoenix. Back in the day," he said. "Prophetic don't you think?" Tubby grinned, backed to the door, and walked out.

"Now that is prophetic. I think your new nickname is Phoenix!" The admiral laughed and clapped Jack on the shoulder. "What do you think, CAG?"

"I think Phoenix it is," said CAG. "It sure fits, and I can't think of anybody in naval aviation with that nickname."

"It's done then." The admiral laughed again.

Jack and CAG walked out into the passageway. "I need to go and debrief CVIC."

"See you later, Phoenix," said CAG. He grinned, then turned and headed down the passageway. Jack headed for CVIC.

CHAPTER FIVE

Jack walked to the intelligence spaces and into CVIC. The team of de-briefers was waiting for him, the other members of his flight long gone by now. Jack filled out the forms, but his stomach was a pit of snakes. Soon they would view the tape and find it empty. He was filling out a missile-firing report when Lieutenant Commander Downey, the ship's intelligence officer, came into the room.

"We have a problem, skipper," he said.

Jack looked up and saw the confusion on the man's face. "Oh, what is it?"

"There's nothing on the tape. It didn't record."

"That's impossible," said Jack. He stood up.

"Well, sir, there is nothing on the tape."

"That means the system on the plane must be screwed up," said Jack. "Sometimes, it doesn't record." He wasn't sure how the system worked or if the tapes ever failed to record.

"Or, the RIO forgot to turn it on." Downey looked at Jack." That sometimes happens, too."

"Impossible," said Jack.

"Was it a new guy?"

"No," replied Jack. "It was Jocko. He is the best there is."

"Hmmm, Jocko." Downey nodded his head. "Yeah, you are probably right. No way he'd make a mistake like that. Not him." Downey took a breath and handed the tape to Jack. "Well, here it is. Sorry skipper, it would have made a hell of an archive to a truly historic event. By the way, congratulations, sir." He reached out his hand, and Jack shook it.

Jack turned and walked out of CVIC. His heart was pounding.

So far, in the clear!

Jack headed toward his stateroom, but it took him thirty minutes to travel the thirty yards. News of the shootdown had swept the ship, and everyone he saw in the passageways stopped and congratulated him. Jack finally made it to his door and entered the pitch-black room. He snapped on the light, walked to his rack, and sat down. He waited for the phone to ring.

He didn't have to wait long. The squadron duty officer called and informed him that CAG was with the admiral, and they wanted to speak with him. Jack headed to the blue tile area and was soon in the cabin, listening to the two officers relate their sorrow for the lost archival opportunity. It was a missed opportunity to showcase the Tomcat, the aircrew, and the navy in the most exciting MIG encounter since Duke Cunningham's and Willy Driscoll's exploits in Vietnam in 1972. Neither officer sought to place any blame on the failure to record the incident. Jack left the cabin and walked back to his stateroom. A call from the duty officer informed him that the airplane recording equipment worked flawlessly.

Jack returned to his room and stretched out on his bunk. He felt terrible for Jocko, but hell, he had had to do

81

something, and that something was to destroy that tape. He knew he still had work to do. Jocko could easily dispute the story that was now "on the street" and ruin him. But Jack was pretty sure he wouldn't do that. Jocko was above all a team player. But Jocko was also the sort of guy that Jack both loved and hated. Jack loved Jocko because he could manipulate him. He hated Jocko because Jocko knew Jack was manipulating him.

Jack lay on his rack for a few more minutes, then sat up. He grinned as his new idea came into full focus. He jumped to his feet and headed for the message center.

When Jocko landed five hours later, Jack met him in the paraloft. It was the squadron space where the pilots and RIOs kept their flight gear. Jocko and Johnny Kerns were changing when Jack entered.

"Hey, Johnny could I get a few minutes alone with Jocko?"

"Sure, skipper," replied the Lieutenant. "Jocko, I will cover CVIC and meet you at chow."

"Sure thing, thanks, Johnny." Jocko frowned at Jack. "What's up, skipper?"

"Well, I have some good news, some better news and some not so good news."

Jocko frowned again. "What's the not so good news?"

"Well, first the good news is we are being put in for the Navy Cross and Chain and Headley for the Silver Star. CAG said he is toying with the idea of putting us in for the Navy Cross for the Phoenix kills and the Silver Star for the

82

single kill. He is going to put the idea to the admiral this evening."

"Oh, wow," said Jocko. He grinned at Jack. Medals for actual combat were few and far between, and only the older aviators from Vietnam had any.

"And, the better news is I talked with the boys in the bureau. They want to send you to TOPGUN. Just like you requested. "

"You got to be kidding!" Jocko whooped and grabbed Jack in a bear hug. "I wanted to go to TOPGUN since that goofy movie came out." He grinned and started to peel off his gear.

"Been on the phone this afternoon. Everybody back there is going crazy with what the Ghostriders did today!" Jack grinned and slapped Jocko on the shoulder. "You're a war hero son!"

Jocko took off his harness and put it on a peg. He turned to Jack. "Skipper, what is the not-so-good news?"

Jack sighed and shook his head. "The tape recorder didn't work." He handed a tape to Jocko. "Here it is, but, as I said, it didn't work."

Jack watched Jocko take the tape and turn it over in his hands. Jocko slowly lifted his eyes and stared at him. He saw...suspicion?

Holy shit! He knows I switched the tapes! But that is impossible!

"The tape was clean for some reason, Jocko." Jack forced himself to look into Jocko's eyes. "Maintenance says

83

the plane works okay, but you know how the Tomcat is. Stray 'Tron's running all over the place." Jack grinned. "Hey, don't worry about it." He slapped him on the shoulder.

Jocko looked down at the tape and shook his head.

"Look, son. We got a hot vector against multiple MIGs, and nobody expected it. I sure didn't. In the heat of all of that, who knows? Maybe your regular habit patterns were broken. It's no big deal. There are multiple corroborating reports over all kinds of spook nets that confirm what we did. No question that we got all four of those guys."

Jocko looked up, and Jack met his gaze. The defiance he saw caused him to drop his eyes to the floor. He sighed and looked up.

"Look, Jocko, maybe it's for the best. I mean for me. You know the switch fuck-ups I made were pretty bad."

Jocko didn't answer, and Jack was glad for the dim light in the room. "Look, I have something to confess. You see, I told the admiral and the others that I shot the Phoenix. It just kind of came out. They put me in a tough spot, Jocko, and it just came out that way. I hope you don't mind. It just kind of came out in front of the admiral." Jack swallowed and looked at Jocko. "Hope that is okay with you."

Jocko's stare was penetrating, but Jack continued. "I need your help on this one, Jocko. Are we okay?"

Jocko looked at him for a moment then reached down and unzipped his G-suit in a quick buzz. He picked his helmet bag. "Sure, skipper. We're okay." He turned and walked out the door.

Jack watched him go, waited a couple of seconds, and then, left the paraloft. He headed down the passageway to his stateroom, smiling as he walked. Jocko would be okay. Oh, he would get ribbed about screwing up the switch for sure, but a MIG killer like Jocko won't be taking much crap. By the time Jack got to his room, he was humming to himself. Everything was going to be just fine.

Jocko left the para loft and stepped out onto the catwalk. It was dark and quiet, and he looked at the sea and smelled the salty air. There was no horizon, only a million stars overhead. He shook his head and sighed. He wasn't sure when the idea to switch tapes had come to him. He had just done it. When the plane captain had handed him the tape from the jet, and the skipper asked for it, he had switched with a spare he had in his helmet bag. During his next flight, he had thought about what he had done and was surprised that he would do such a thing.

Why?

He knew why. He had suspected that the skipper would try to hide his mistakes by changing tapes. So, he wasn't surprised when the skipper had told him the tape hadn't recorded. He was going to make it all right by "discovering" the real tape in his helmet bag. He was going to make that "discovery" as soon as he left the para loft. But when the skipper handed him the fake tape, he noticed it didn't have a blue dot on the spine. And Jocko knew in that instant that the skipper had switched tapes. The scheme to have him hot switch was so the skipper could save his

85

reputation by taking what he thought was a good tape from the jet and switch it.

Jocko sighed again and looked into the darkness. Bringing out the real tape now would cause a lot of harm and embarrassment to the Tomcat community. Jocko would do anything to prevent that. He sighed and shook his head.

Jack Grant just survived again.

Jocko stopped by the ready room and was heartily congratulated by his fellow Ghostriders, much like Jack had been hours before. But the excitement of the MIG kills was nearly seven hours old, and some of the early exuberance had died down. He decided to blow off the post-flight debrief. He had been up for eighteen hours and, besides, his pilot could handle all the questions. He walked down the passageway to his stateroom and opened the door. Tubby, Spud, and Mooch were waiting to see him.

"Welcome home, killer!" Tubby handed him a cold Budweiser. Alcohol was strictly forbidden on the ship, but that didn't stop the aviators from having an occasional "toddy." Beer was scarce since it was hard to sneak on board, took up too much space, created an empty can problem, and had to be iced somehow.

"Thanks, Tubby!" Jocko took the can and quickly locked the door behind him. He popped the top and took a long, cold drink.

"Man, that's good." Jocko belched as his roomies high-fived him.

"Now that you are a MIG killer, and a hero is it okay for a mere mortal, scum bag, douche to still room with you?" Mooch grinned and took a sip of beer.

86

"Sure," said Jocko, "as long as you make my rack every day."

"Okay, well, fuck you then." Mooch and the rest laughed, and they sat down on the bottom bunks and desk chairs. Spud squinted up at Jocko, "Well, hell, so tell us about it."

"What have you heard so far?" Jocko took another sip and sat next to Tubby.

"We heard that the skipper is now the best thing since the Red Baron. He shot two 23s with a single buffalo and then tricked the third MIG into turning into him so he could gun it. That is what I heard, but I can't believe it. Not our skipper."

"Hmm." Jocko took another sip. He thought about the tape in his helmet bag.

"What happened?" Mooch leaned forward and grabbed Jocko's knee. "How in the hell did you crawl up into his front seat and do all that?"

They all laughed and chugged their beers.

Spud threw a sock at Jocko. His eyes were wet and full with the alcohol. "I know, you guys traded places. You sat in front and did the shooting, and Jack sat in the back and fucked up the TCS switch."

Jocko laughed along with the others and took another swig. The remark hurt. He was a professional, and evidently, the word was out that he had screwed up recording the most dramatic MIG engagement in history. Killing two with one missile was unbelievable and then gunning a third was just icing on the cake.

"Hard to believe a guy like you forgot that switch," said Tubby. "But what the heck do I know, I have never been in combat like you." He grinned and slapped Jocko on the back.

"I sure thought I turned it on," said Jocko. He shook his head and took another sip.

"So, why didn't you take the buffalo shot? Why did you give it to the skipper?" Tubby looked at Jocko and frowned. "That big red button by your left knee was awful tempting, I bet."

Jocko fought the urge to tell the real story, to bring out the actual tape. Every fiber in his body wanted to see it, to have his pals see it! Every RIO wanted to shoot a missile in combat, and the Tomcat gave them that option with the Phoenix. Jocko Barnes was the first, and he bagged two MIGS with it! All he had to do was tell the story, and he would be the most celebrated back seater ever.

"Just worked out that way," he said.

Tubby looked at him with narrowed eyes. He shook his head and took another big gulp. "If you say so."

CHAPTER SIX

"CAG, the admiral wants to see you."

Frank glanced up from the message board and smiled at his ops officer.

"Thanks, Red. Any idea what he wants?"

"No sir, just got the call from the chief of staff." Frank nodded, grunted, and got to his feet.

What could he want?

His stateroom was located next to the blue tile area, so it was only a minute before Frank entered the flag office.

He smiled when he saw the admiral. They had developed a good relationship since his arrival a few weeks before deployment as the new battle group commander. Frank knew that he was a fighter pilot who grew up in the F-8 Crusader over the skies of Vietnam and that he had three hundred forty-two combat missions in that war and that he lived and breathed naval aviation. The admiral opined freely to Frank, and during their many sessions together, he offered that an aircraft carrier was the most beautiful thing on earth. The admiral had also been a CAG back in the old days and had commanded the U.S.S. Kitty Hawk, before selecting for his first star.

They were interrupted by the aide who offered coffee or water, but Frank declined.

"CAG, I am writing your detaching fitness report and need some final thoughts before I finish it. What was your ranking last time when Admiral Spence left?"

"I was number three, sir." Frank sat back in his chair and looked at his two-star boss.

"I see." The admiral nodded and repeated softly, "Number three."

"Yes, sir."

"So, how do you think that sets you up for flag selection?"

"Probably not too good."

"You're probably right. Not too good, indeed. It's pretty selective, you know. The navy picks twenty-one rear admirals from a list of 1,000 captains."

"Ugh."

"UGH, is right," echoed the admiral. "So, if you start by removing all records that do not have a number one fitness report, it gets easier for the board. Understand?"

"Yes, sir." Frank nodded and slumped in his seat.

What was this?

"I think I have told you about my concerns about naval aviation and leadership in the navy?"

"Yes, sir." Frank nodded. The admiral had confided in him over several beers in port, and he knew one thing rankled him over all others. That one thing was that the shoes ran the navy; surface warfare officers and bubbleheads…submariners. In fact, the admiral had given him a history lesson over a ton of Birra Moretti's in Naples and a ton more Goldstar's in Haifa.

"Well, those concerns are still valid. By God, the navy hasn't been run by an aviator since Tom Hayward was CNO in the early '80s. Christ, Watkins ran the show from '82 to '86, then Trost and just two months ago, Kelso took over for God's sake. It pisses me off to no end when I think about all the combat we aviators endured in Vietnam. Hell, just bringing an aircraft aboard the carrier at night was near combat, while the surface pukes were doing what, exactly? I'll tell you what they were doing. They were plowing around at ten knots, staring out the window, trying not to hit each other. They hoisted the tarps, and coiled the ropes, and sent goofy messages to each other. The sub bubbas were, well, who knew what the hell they were doing? It sure wasn't combat. Aircraft carriers were, and are, the only thing of importance anymore, and aviators should be running the company!"

"Yes, sir." CAG swallowed and looked at his boss.

"I need to ensure you have as good a shot as possible." CAG arched his eyebrows.

"Thank you, sir."

What was all of this 'about?

"Arch Smith over on Antietam is retiring. I convinced him to leave on the same day you leave. That allows me to give you a competitive fitness report ranked as number one out of two captains."

"Sir." Frank didn't quite know what that meant. "Sir?"

"It allows you to make that first cut," said the admiral. "That, and the words about your leadership on deployment, your steady hand on our Saudi ops planning, your accomplishments elsewhere during the cruise, your previous record. I took the liberty of calling your detailer over in PERS 43. You have a tremendous record, and he thinks this FITREP will get you over the top."

"Sir, I don't know what to say. I mean, I had all but given up on flag. Just didn't see how it could work."

"Well, no need to give up yet." Frank shook his head.

Wow! Wow!

"Sir, can we call your aide back? I want that cup of coffee."

The admiral laughed and motioned for Frank to join him at a small table next to his desk. He called into the adjoining room, and soon, his aide placed two cups of steaming coffee between them.

"I do have one other question for you." The admiral blew over his cup, his eyes fixed on Frank.

"Yes, sir."

"Have you ranked your skippers yet?"

"Well, uh, sir, I am just doing that now." He watched a smile stretch across the admiral's face.

"Good, I am wondering what you think of Jack Grant."

"He's a good skipper."

"And?"

"Well, I have other officers ranked in front of him."

"You do, huh?" The admiral grunted and leaned back in his chair. "How many?"

Frank had heard the admiral liked Jack, and Frank suspected it was because Jack had an unbelievable talent of getting on the right side of senior folks. The admiral's question didn't surprise him. "I have Jack around fourth or fifth. Somewhere in there, I suppose."

"Really?" The admiral grunted again. "Even after what he did in the desert? He put together the foundation of our plan, didn't he?"

"He did develop some good numbers."

"I talked with him while we made our way back to the ship, you remember that?"

"Yes, sir. Of course."

"I was impressed."

"Yes, sir." Frank swallowed and sat still in his chair.

Where in the hell is this going?

"CAG, I know you are an old Intruder guy, and I have to tell you, I do love your community. I flew a lot of missions flying cover for A-6s. God, but those guys had balls." The admiral whistled and shook his head.

Frank watched him take another sip, then put his cup down.

The admiral looked up. "You see CAG, the guy you put as number one *could* make flag. He could, but a lot of good stuff has to happen to him along the way. Just like the stuff, we are going to do for you. He has to take care of business. Do you know what I mean?"

Frank frowned and took another sip. "I'm not sure."

"CAG, Jack Grant is developing a considerable wind behind him. His shoot down of three MIGs in one engagement plus getting two in one shot and gunning the third! That is the stuff of which legends are made. That guy could go places, that is, if we take care of business for him."

Frank watched the admiral intently. He was unsure of what the man wanted.

"What I am suggesting is for you to take all of this into play when you do your rankings."

"Sir?"

The admiral leaned forward; his eyes were stern and intense. "CAG, we can get you the star, we WILL get you the star. But it will be hard to take you to the very top, to take you into play for CNO. You are a great officer, but you don't have the juice to climb the mountain to its peak. To do that, you have to have some unique piece to your background."

Frank frowned and nodded.

"I am thinking about ten years from now, CAG. I want you to think about that, too. We need an aviator with a lot of momentum to not only get into the flag ranks but also have the secret sauce to get to the top. I think we can get Jack there, but it all has to start with the number one ticket."

The admiral pushed his cup away and leaned on the table, looking right into Frank's eyes. Frank returned the gaze, then glanced down at his mug. He knew why he was here. He knew why the admiral was making a deal with Arch Smith; he understood why the admiral was giving him the number one ranking. The admiral had been preparing a package, CAG's number one ranking for Jack's. Everybody wins. Everybody, of course except the guy who had earned the top spot. Everybody but Guido. He took a deep sigh and looked back at the admiral.

"I don't know, sir."

"CAG, I know this kind of thing can bother you if you don't put it in perspective. The real question becomes not just who is the best in the air wing but who down the road is best for naval aviation and the navy. If you look at the tactical performance in the air wing, hell, just the performance during the deployment, you can come up with the guy you are now considering. Guido is the obvious choice then. But, hell, I looked at Guido's record. He has hardly been out of Oak Harbor. He is a Whidbey Island homesteader. CAG, I am asking you to sit back and look at the bigger picture. I am asking you to do what is best for naval aviation and eventually for all of the navy, not what is best for just one of your skippers in this instance in time. As you know, fitness reports are not to celebrate the past, but to give a board the ability to guide our future."

"Yes, sir."

"You have a guy, Jack Grant, who has been in actual combat. He is the only aviator on this ship besides me who can say that and one of a tiny few on active duty that can say that. Wouldn't it be nice to ensure the future of a polished, sophisticated, savvy guy who is also a real warfighter instead of just the best tactical pilot you have?"

Frank thought of the conversation he had had with Hulk earlier.

Christ, but this was ironic.

"Yes, sir. I suppose it would."

"Fantastic, CAG. Fantastic!" The admiral grinned and stood, reaching out his hand. Frank stood with him and shook it.

"I know you will do the right thing."

The admiral walked to the door and escorted Frank out into the flag spaces.

"See you tomorrow," he said, then disappeared back into his cabin.

Frank stepped out into the blue tile area and walked the few paces to his room. He entered, turned on the light, and sat slowly in his chair. Frank drew a heavy breath and reached for his letter opener. He felt the smooth, knobby end in his hands and welcomed its heft as he tried to clear his thoughts. A part of him, an enormous part of him, was elated at the idea of the admiral's support. It kept him in play. It kept him in the game. But, Jack Grant as the number one skipper? He took a deep breath and sighed.

CHAPTER SEVEN

Ike's time in the Red Sea was full of heady days as the MIG shoot down rekindled memories of past aerial glory. The Ike's aviators were all post-Vietnam era flyers who had just missed naval aviation's last war and had grown up on the stories of their heroes. But as the memories of Vietnam had dimmed, the tales of swirling air battles over Kep Airfield and daring night strikes on the Thanh Hoa Bridge were replaced with the sobering reality of potential combat with the Soviet Union. That was a scenario so unsurvivable that it was not worth thinking about, let alone dreaming of glory.

Israeli Air Force victories over Arab rivals allowed U.S. Naval Aviator's vicarious thrills during the '70s, and the IAF and TOPGUN exchanged crews for training, which in some ways injected a needed freshness. The 1986 El Dorado Canyon raid on Libya strongman Muammar Gadhafi brought back a momentary raison d'être for aircraft carriers and their crews, and follow-on aerial engagements with Tomcats shooting down MIGS kept the Red Baron blood flowing. However, all in all, the post-Vietnam period was a time of listless training and long, pointless cruises. There was not much of a reason for white-scarfed, brown-booted duelists. That is why Saddam's invasion was met with such enthusiasm in the air wing ready rooms. Iraq offered an enemy that had enough capability to be a challenge but not enough to threaten the world. The Ghostrider aerial victories on the first day of Red Sea ops intensified the energy to a fever pitch. It was one thing to plan for a training event but quite another to prepare for actual combat. Every squadron engaged in hours of training as aircrews refreshed on the workings of their ordnance and their tactics.

Planners developed rescue procedures, and aircrew drew side arms from the armory. But the days after the shoot-down stretched into a week and then into two. The adrenaline and caffeine-fueled planning sessions evolved from "standing room only" to "Hey, CVIC called. We need a body up there ASAP." The euphoria of *What If* became the despair of *What the Fuck.*

On August 23rd, USS Saratoga relieved Ike and she transited back through the Suez Canal. She left all of the war excitement and dreams of glory fading in her long, wide wake. The aircrew put the side arms back in the lockers and the charts and maps back on the shelves, and the men on Ike turned their thoughts to home. It had been almost seven months since they had departed Norfolk, and they were now very eager to return.

On the first day of the Mediterranean transit, Jack, Jocko, Headly, and Chain were awarded the Silver Star during flight deck ceremonies crossing the Mediterranean. Jack and Jocko were also awarded the Navy Cross for their downing of three MIGs in one day. Two days later, Frank and Hulk held their change of command onboard the carrier as they had selected a date on their original arrival back home. It was a morning event, and by that afternoon, Frank had packed a traveling bag and waited in flight deck control. A COD was turning up for his trip to Italy and onward to the states.

"CAG, do you have a minute?" Jocko slipped into the room. "I know the COD is about to shove off."

Frank glanced at his watch. "Sure, only have a minute though. What's up?"

"Well, sir, it's, it's..." Jocko swallowed and looked at his boots.

"Hey, son, you can talk to me. What's going on?"

Jocko glanced up, then took a deep breath. Frank saw wariness in his eyes.

"Sir, it's about the skipper."

"Go ahead." Frank frowned.

"Sir, the skipper told us, in the ready room, that the bureau is thinking about sending him to TOPGUN. To be the skipper out there."

"That is what I understand." Frank frowned again.

"Sir, the fact is the skipper isn't exactly what folks think he is."

"What do you mean?" Frank felt a sense of alarm.

"He isn't what folks think. The MIG engagements, they didn't go quite as he said."

"Oh, how so?" Frank glanced at his watch again, wishing he was already on the COD.

"Well, it just didn't happen quite like he said it did. I have something for you." Jocko reached into the leg pocket of his flight suit and withdrew a TCS tape. He handed it to Frank. "I have been holding on to this for a while. I wasn't sure what to do with it."

"What is it?" Frank turned the tape over in his hands.

"It is the real tape from our engagement."

"What do you mean the real tape? The tape didn't record."

"It recorded, sir."

"I guess I don't get it." Frank stared at Jocko.

"Sir, things happened in the cockpit, things that would embarrass the skipper. Things that are on the tape."

"I still don't get it."

"Sir, I know the skipper. I knew he would want to find a way to hide this tape because it would embarrass him. As soon as he told me of his plan to have me hot switch into the next event, I knew he was up to something."

"Still not with you, son."

"Sir, I gave him a tape that he thought was the real thing. He said he took that tape to CVIC only to find it did not work. After I returned from my second hop, the skipper gave the bad tape back to me. But you see, it was not the same tape I had given him. He switched it, probably in his room, so the story of all of his cockpit errors would not come out. The fact that I launched the Phoenix would not come out own."

"You launched the Phoenix?" Frank looked at the tape and shook his head.

"Yes, sir."

"Jesus. What a mess."

"Yes sir, but, as I said, this is the real tape, and I hope you take a look."

"Why are you giving this thing to me?" Frank was suddenly pissed. "What do you expect me to do with it? Tell the story, show the tape, make all of us look like idiots?"

"I don't know, sir. I want someone else to know, that's all."

"Why did you make the switch anyway?"

"I don't know, sir. I wanted to preserve the history of the shot. Maybe I am selfish. I wanted to have something that showed I took the Phoenix shot. I don't know."

Frank looked at the tape again and then at Jocko. "Okay, I'll take a look at it. I wish you had given this to me earlier."

"Me too, sir. I guess I didn't want to take a chance of hurting the Tomcat community. But, I thought somebody should know the truth. Somebody besides the skipper and me, I mean."

Jocko turned and walked out of flight deck control.

"CAG, time to man up." A yellow-shirted Sailor nodded to Frank. Frank looked at the crewman, put on his helmet, and boarded the COD. He took his seat, buckled in and soon felt the motion as the big airplane maneuvered toward the cat. Frank hated flying in the COD. Sitting in the back of that tube in the dark was almost more than he could endure. He had no control, virtually no way out if the young lieutenant flying the thing goofed up or if the cat misfired. He gritted his teeth as the shuttle started forward.

And then, the aircraft seemed to jump into the air, and they were off to Italy. Frank and the other passengers were leaving the Ike and heading for the USAF connector back to Dulles Air Force Base and the good old USA. He took a deep breath and leaned his head against the seat.

The hum of the big propellers and the seep of air conditioning relaxed him, and he shut his eyes. It had been a fantastic tour as CAG rand he had done an excellent job. His airwing had performed admirably the entire time he had command, especially in reaction to Saddam's thrust into Kuwait. The admiral had said great things about him and the airwing and had pinned the Legion of Merit on his uniform. And, in a meeting between the two of them, the Admiral had given him his departing fitness report. He was indeed ranked one of two with glowing recommendations for flag selection. Frank also remembered his telephone conversation with PERS 43, Captain Miles Harvey. PERS 43 was the head of aviation detailing and a powerful man. He sent all captains to their assignments and would most likely select for a star on the next board.

"Frank," I hear you got a number one ticket from Titan."

"That's right." Frank had grinned into the phone.

My, how good news does travel fast!

"Lot of talk here in the bureau about you guys, all good."

"That's good to hear."

"I am thinking about changing your orders."

Frank had frowned. He had been planning on the move to D.C. for the past six months. Betty was already practically there. Her folks lived in Georgetown, and it would take dynamite to get her to change plans now.

"You will still be in D.C., but instead of sending you over to OPNAV in some rabbit warren, I am thinking of having you relieve me as PERS 43."

Frank had swallowed and gripped the phone harder. PERS 43 was a great job. He couldn't believe his good fortune!

"You okay with that?"

"I sure am!"

Frank and Miles had chatted for an hour about the job, and at the end of the conversation, Frank had felt even better.

But the euphoria of the past subsided as Frank now contemplated all that had happened recently. The Jack Grant stuff. No matter how many times he told himself that giving Jack Grant the number one ticket was the right thing to do, he didn't believe it. He swallowed and shut his eyes as he remembered the look of entitlement in Jack's face as he read his Fitness Report with its one out of eight number. Jack should have been shocked.

"Gee, sir, I don't deserve this."

He should have been floored at his good fortune because Jack had to know, despite the MIG killing, he was not the best skipper in the bunch.

"Sir, there must be a mistake."

But Jack's eyes had reached up to him, and they had crinkled with a smile and righteousness that had turned Frank's stomach.

Frank swallowed again and tried to push the scene from his mind. But it stayed like the scent of a candle after the light is gone. It was the scent of a fix, the smell of a game. It was the scent and stench of the go-along-to-get-along chummy selfishness that Frank had managed to avoid all of his career. That chumminess wasn't part of the navy culture as far as Frank was concerned, but he knew it did exist, at the edges. He shook his head and thought of Guido.

"Sir, does a number two get you anything these days?"

"I don't know. I am sure it does."

"But it takes one to get an airwing, right?"

"Yeah." He had nodded and looked away from Guido's eyes. "Yeah, it takes a one."

Guido had sighed and abruptly stood, and Frank had stood with him. They had shaken hands, and Guido had left. But the look in his eyes, the last look in his eyes, held the haunt of betrayal.

Frank and Guido had had a bond. It had been forged during years together in the community and during long planning sessions when the only thing that could accomplish the mission was a crew in an A-6 at night. They had developed their bond during briefings to high ranking officers where Guido's expert knowledge of strike warfare and his expert delivery had won approval for critical target folders. Frank had so much as promised the number one ticket to him.

Frank swallowed to push the bile down his throat. He was glad for the darkness inside the COD. He closed his eyes and dozed until he heard the gear coming down on final approach into Capodichino, the U.S. Navy base near Naples. Moments later, he was in the lounge, waiting to board his DC-9.

CHAPTER EIGHT

While Ike steamed west, President Bush accelerated efforts to assemble a grand coalition and seek the United Nation's authorities to act. The international news media was full of pundits and talking heads and clips of meetings. In the States, the desire to know more about the gallant men who shot down the MIGS and foiled Saddam's invasion of Saudi Arabia grew. America wanted a hero, and Jack became the face of the U.S. Navy. Instead of waiting for Ike's stateside return, Admiral Turner insisted that a COD fly Jack to Bermuda where a navy jet would take him to National Airport in Washington, D.C. There was some thought and much talk about having Jocko, Chain, and Headley join, but the admiral's staff decided it would be a more clear message with only a single teller.

***

Grace Grant sat on the couch in her living room and thanked God for her calm. She thanked Him, but she also knew that He could not stop the anxiety once it decided to come back. No one, nothing, could stop it. And when it did come, she knew it would bring its companions of hopelessness and despair, and she knew she would start crying again. She glanced at the Kleenex box on the coffee table. It was a new one and full.

Grace sighed as she leaned down and kissed Harley's head. He rewarded her with a lick on the hand, and she thanked God for him, too. Her dog was her friend, her best friend. Sometimes when she thought of that, that a dog was her best friend, she wondered if it was a good thing or a bad thing. Was she blessed or just pathetic? But at this moment, when she drank in the smell of him and shut her eyes and listened to Louis Armstrong, she knew it was a good thing.

Grace played her slim fingers against the dog's soft coat and concentrated on her quietness. Quietness was a gift, and she knew it could quickly be taken. She smiled as she felt the rhythmic up and down of Harley's chest. She hoped today would be a good day. Maybe she would take a walk.

Grace was a beautiful but quiet and reserved woman, the kind of person, like unappreciated art, that can go forever and not be noticed. She was that way before the panic and more so now.

Those that explored beyond the "hello" and found her in her moments of peace would discover a wonderfully warm and generous soul with an engaging intellect. A further look would reveal deep green eyes that understood and a smile that was just hesitant enough to let you know you earned it. It was a smile that sat at the gate of lips that men used to want to kiss when she was young.

"A kiss is just a kiss; a sigh is just a sigh..."

Grace smiled as Louis's calm settled over her. She closed her eyes and remembered the early days with their kisses and sighs. She had had many suitors that wanted to kiss her. Well, unless they were naval aviators and found she was Admiral Duke Sheehan's daughter. Then they didn't want to kiss her anymore. Duke Sheehan had been the Commander of Naval Air Forces Atlantic back then and a fierce enemy of idiots with wings. Grace smiled again and thought of those early days. The days when she and Jack still loved each other.

She met Jack Grant on a Sunday afternoon at Fort Story in Virginia Beach. She was a student at Old Dominion and had never been to Fort Story, but she had heard it was a wild place with young, handsome naval aviators in abundance. The place sounded exciting, and when her classmates asked her to accompany them, she agreed. However, upon arrival, her friends vanished to the advances of familiar faces, and she found herself standing alone next to the bar. She was about to run and hide in the restroom when a young man appeared at her elbow and asked her to dance. He was very handsome, and for a second she considered declining his offer. The thought of dealing with an egocentric pilot who was stuck on himself made her weary. However, he had a hint of fragility that caused her to wonder. And she said, "Yes." They danced a couple of dances and took a walk on the beach. He was charming.

Jack called her the next day, and the following evening, he dropped by for a visit. Grace opened the door and smiled into Jack's eyes only to see them widen in alarm. She looked over her shoulder and saw her father, the admiral, glaring at them from the stairway. At least he wasn't wearing his uniform, but even in civilian clothes, he cut an intimidating figure as he walked down the steps and stiffly led them to the living room. Grace felt her hopes of dating Jack might die in that room and join the mummies of previous young lovers. However, Jack immediately engaged the Admiral in conversation about the eight A2W nuclear reactors on Enterprise and how an aviator might get into the nuclear program. That generated much interest in Admiral Sheehan because, for the first time, a suitor of Grace's was more than some shallow bag of testosterone. Grace knew her father hated that most young aviators didn't have the academic profile to get into the nuclear program, or didn't want to work hard enough to survive its rigors. His pet peeve was shallow, selfish, cocky pilots who didn't appreciate the value of their history or grasp the importance of their future. Grace thankfully endured the next two hours listening to an animated discussion on Hafnium Control Rods, calculated criticality heights, Uranium-235 and the fact Enterprise had four rudders!

By winter, Grace's mother and father had fallen for Jack. He was a very conservative young man and much of his thinking aligned with theirs. He had perfect manners, and as the Admiral told Grace, "his shoes are always shined."

Grace was thoroughly taken by his intelligence and ability to get along with her father. Jack seemed to know everything about everything. If he had a fault, it was that he was not particularly intimate or romantic. He was most awkward when they were alone, and after six months of dating, he had not so much as touched her breast. Despite all of that, she felt herself falling for him. She was not sure if she loved him or was just very impressed with him, but she agreed to marry.

"The world will always welcome lovers, as time goes by."

Grace reached for the Kleenex box. Thinking about her marriage made her begin to cry. It always did. She gently pulled her little Harley closer to her chest. She breathed him in, and the smell of him and the tingle of his tiny pink tongue made everything better.

Her first indication of Jack's selfishness came, oddly enough, during their honeymoon. Jack said he could only take a week off, so they rented a seaside bungalow on the Carolina shore. On the second day, Jack played eighteen holes of golf with the fighter wing commander and some of the guys from the squadron!

Grace was outwardly gay and joyous when they showed up in their jeeps and convertibles, but inside she was overwhelmed with the thoughtlessness of it. How could he be so, so…what? She didn't even have a word for it. When he came home that evening, drunk, she refused to talk to him. Jack's response was to pass out on the couch.

The next morning, he fixed her breakfast and tried to make up for it, but Grace sensed he was sorry because she was mad, not sorry because what he had done was so selfish and hurtful.

Grace made herself get over the golf incident. After all, they had a whole life to live together, and things settled out for a while. Of course, he followed the golf incident with a never-ending list of slights. He forgot their first wedding anniversary, for Christ's sake!

The navy stationed Jack on shore duty flying the new F-14 Tomcat and training pilots and RIOs, so there was a party at somebody's house every week. Grace liked the parties and the squadron members, but she could never get used to Jack's wandering eyes. On several occasions, she would be across the room, talking with a squadron wife and there would be old Jack, ogling some young thing. She would look at him until he eventually met her eyes. Instead of showing embarrassment, he would grin and wink. What concerned her was his lack of sexual interest in her and his evident interest in others.

Grace completed her studies at Old Dominion and took the bar exam. When she passed on the first attempt, they had a massive party for the entire squadron, and her father even attended! That caught the eye of Jack's skipper who spent much of the evening talking to her dad. Grace had done exceedingly well in school and on the exam and joined a prestigious firm in Norfolk. She was an immediate favorite with the firm's partners, and she soon became an associate. The day following her announcement of the promotion, Jack agreed to have a baby. Grace suspected he only agreed to because he was somehow jealous of her accomplishments. However, she was so happy to be having a baby!

Grace produced a child, a son they named Christopher. The little boy was a beautiful baby, but he was weak. His immune system couldn't protect him against all of the things that attacked him, and his frail body was a shaking misery of coughs and whimpers. Grace hovered tirelessly over her baby and forgot about all other things. The law firm stayed faithful to her and put her on vacation. Grace concentrated on her boy and stayed with him night and day, took him on the never-ending trips to the hospital, and nursed him with every bit of herself.

Jack got assigned to a sea-going squadron for his department head tour and was gone more than ever. When he was home, he seemed to resent Christopher's illness more than empathize with it. He became aloof and spent his nights in the guest bedroom, which was now his. Christopher struggled and would have times of relatively good health. There were periods when Grace thought that maybe everything would be okay. But a couple of weeks after his second birthday, Christopher developed a cold. It was on a Saturday afternoon, and Grace spooned him some soup and put him to bed. By that night, his fever spiked to 100, so she and Jack raced him to the navy hospital at Portsmouth. The little boy fought hard, but on Sunday morning, he died.

Grace and Jack's reactions to the death of their son could not have been more different. Grace entered a period of deep but open mourning. She not only allowed herself to think about her son; she forced herself to explore what she had lost. She embraced his death with not just tears but also with laughter as she recalled the boy's antics. She openly talked about him. She vowed never to let him be forgotten.

Jack, on the other hand, remained silent. He didn't want to talk about their son and even refused to look at the photo albums Grace occasionally laid on the coffee table.

"Why did you hang his picture?" He asked one day, pointing to the living room wall.

"Because he was our son."

"But, how can it be helpful to be constantly reminded about him? I don't get it."

"I WANT to be reminded of him?" Grace had turned to Jack with glittering eyes. "I don't ever want to forget him. And, if the price for that remembrance is a few tears, then I will gladly pay it."

And, at that instant, it became crystal clear that her husband was tragically flawed. He was not just selfish and ego-driven; he was weak. He was a man who was more of a child than the one who had died and a man who had no stomach for the realities of life. He was what fake fighter pilots wanted to be until someone--- or something---made them grow up. But, Grace was also a traditionalist and a believer in marriage. Just because she had a weak husband, didn't mean that she could not forge a healthy union from that clay. But, she also realized that if she wanted any legacy of a healthy marriage, anything with nobility and grace, then it would be her that created that history.

112

Grace wasn't sure when she fell out of love with Jack and when their arrangement became just that: an arrangement. But, she decided that if the agreement met her requirements, then she would remain in it. If it didn't, then she would leave. It was her choice; it would ALWAYS be her choice.

Grace went back to work and quickly resumed her value to the law firm. She was smart and strong-willed and a diligent researcher. She also actively participated in squadron events and was a leader of the wives' club. Jack began to show some gratitude toward her efforts until, during a party, she and Jack overheard the XO tell the CO that Grace was more valuable to the squadron than Jack. That pissed him off.

"Why are you trying to one-up me?" he asked.

"I am not trying to one-up you," Grace smiled. "I happen to believe in naval aviation, and I believe we spouses are a critical part of it. After all, we hold the family together when you are gone. Some of us hold it together while you are still here."

But as strong and brave as Grace was, she found an unrelenting enemy. It was an unseen fiend, a creeper in the shadows. And, worst of all, it attacked her for no reason. Grace met her enemy and had her first panic attack a year after Christopher's funeral. She had gone to bed and after reading a bit, had fallen asleep. In the middle of the night, Grace jerked awake with her chest squeezing so tightly she thought she had a heart attack. She gasped for breath, threw her covers back, and swung her legs to the side of the bed. She tried to stand, but her legs turned to jelly. She fell back on the bed and grabbed the post and pulled herself up.

"Jack! Jack!" she screamed. She took a step toward the door and fell to the carpet. Jack came rushing into the room, and Grace reached for him.

"Help me," she gasped. "What's wrong?"

"I'm having a heart attack."

Jack grabbed a pillow and put it under her head. He ran to the side of the bed and called 911.

Grace moaned as she gasped for breath.

What's happening to me?

A heavy weight pressed on her chest as an unexplainable fear grabbed her.

I am dying!

The vicious, raw fear gripped her. She rolled onto her side and clutched the pillow. The terror grabbed her in its jaws and shook!

Why? Why am I feeling this way? God, what's happening to me?

She cried out and rolled on her side.

Her heart would not stop pounding. She cried again. Then, the paramedics were there.

"207 over 114," she heard one say.

"Christ," said a voice. "This woman going to stroke if we don't settle her down."

Grace remembered the lights and the siren and the gurney with its cold, metal sides. The injection they gave her quickly took effect, and by the time she was in the emergency room, she was breathing normally. Her blood pressure was still high, but she was out of danger. The ER doctor ordered an EKG and blood work as well as a chest X-ray. All came back normal. Jack drove them back home as the sun was coming up, then showered and prepared for work. He seemed angry at her as if she had made it all up for some reason.

From that night on, Grace lived with the beast. The beast of panic and its return. And return it did. It never rang the bell or made a reservation. It just showed up. It crept into the house and entered Grace as a palpation, a missed beat, lightheadedness and Grace would breathe, and she would gasp, and she would grab a countertop or whatever was near to steady herself and she would pray for it to go away. And sometimes the beast did go away. Sometimes, it tricked her like that. It played with her. "Not yet," it would whisper. "Not yet."

She saw navy doctor after navy doctor, but they were unfamiliar with panic disorder. They just prescribed valium, but Grace refused to take it. She told herself she could beat this thing and continued to work.

But it always came back. If not that day, then the next. Or maybe the following or perhaps it would hide in its dark place for a month or more.

And Grace would think, "Maybe it's over!"

Maybe I'm healthy again!

She would accept invitations and plan events, and she would work late and take hard cases and go over to

Nordstrom Rack. At least to look at what they had! After all, women who are well, shop! It felt so good to be out and living and just looking!

Then, then, a missed beat. A palpitation or a wave of jelly legs and the beast would announce its attack and regardless how deep she breathed, and how hard she prayed, she found herself struggling against it again.

Jack blamed Grace for what was happening to her. When she would swoon and grab a chair for the support, he would roll his eyes.

"Christ, here we go again!"

And when the repeated trips to the ER proved inconclusive, Jack told Grace it was all in her head.

"Who knows," he said, his face angry and his eyes black. "It could be the desire of an only child to be the center of things."

Those words crushed Grace, and the once strong woman began to crumble. She took a vacation from the law office, and that made her feel even more alone and fragile. She soon stopped going to the parties, and they stopped giving them at home. She stopped going to change of commands and other functions. She gave up driving. The thought of having a panic attack behind the wheel petrified her. Jack became more and more distant and openly angry. He now had to do all of the shopping---stopping by the commissary on the way home from work, picking up dry cleaning, taking Harley to the groomer, everything. He resented it, and he told her.

Grace found that a little alcohol kept the beast at bay, so she drunk just a bit of bourbon with ice to take the edge off, and she swallowed just a bit more because she was lonely. The years went by, and Jack came back to shore duty at Oceana as a stash until he screened for command, or not. He had to fly every night, and so she had a drink or maybe two, or so, every night. Soon, her alcohol use became more and more frequent, and she openly argued with Jack. She felt his conversations were superficial, and she came to the belief that what she had thought was confidence and intelligence was just haughty arrogance.

Grace fell into a melancholy and more drinking. She ran out of things to say to Jack, and she ran out of reasons to be interested in him. It oozed away; it faded away. One less word, one less question about the day, one less smile. Before she knew it, they barely talked. Their marriage became the thing of separateness; separate bedrooms, separate dinners, separate weekends, separate lives all in the same house. Blessedly, Jack was gone from home even more frequently than before. Grace came to believe it was the forced separation of their navy life that kept them together at all.

Her blessed Harley! He showed up by accident one cold, November day. Grace was sweeping the back patio when she heard the whimper. She paused her broom and cocked her head, and there it was again. A sudden gust of wind scuffed the skeletons of dead oak leaves against the bricks, and for a moment Grace wasn't sure she heard anything after all. She took a step into the yard, and then another. There it was again, a soft cry near the boxwood hedge. She turned the broom around as she walked to the hedge and poked the handle into the green branches. She heard a little sob and pushed aside the edges of the shrub. There was the cutest little white dog she had ever seen. It shrunk back when it saw her, but she put out her hand and rubbed the soft, fluffy head. The little dog straightened and looked at her with its big brown eyes; its tail fluttered a tentative greeting against the ground.

"Hey there, hey there." Grace crouched to her knees and leaned into the opening. She patted the dog again.

"Hey there," She whispered and stroked the dog's head as she gently pulled it from its hiding place.

"How did you get here?" Grace pulled the little fluffy mass out into the open and smiled as she looked at it. The dog appeared to be okay, but it was dirty, matted, and had no collar. She looked closer and saw it was a little boy.

Grace, held the dog to her chest and got to her feet. The fur of the dog's face tickled her chin, and she felt the little animal shiver. She smiled again as the dog wiggled against her but frowned at the pungent whiff of wet fur.

"How long have you been out here, boy? Who could leave a little boy like you outside?" She frowned again at the thought of the little dog living on the street, cold and afraid. Grace pushed open the door with her foot and walked into the kitchen. Jack had his back to her, working on the daily crossword puzzle from the Virginian Pilot. Their breakfast had been solitary.

"Look what I found."

Jack turned, and Grace saw his expected frown. "Where did that come from?"

"Found him under the hedge in back. He was crying."

Grace put the dog on the kitchen counter, and as she gently examined him, the little animal wagged his tail. She looked him over then picked him up and hugged him to her. "What do you think he is?"

"I don't know," said Jack. His frown deepened. "Looks like a poodle or something. He looks cold."

Grace buried her face into the smell of wet fur and felt a pang of regret. She wanted to keep the dog, and she knew she probably couldn't. It had to belong to someone. Little Poodles don't just wander around.

"Grace, he surely belongs to someone."

"I know," she replied.

She felt Jack looking at her, and she knew he was conjuring up something negative to say. That was what he did.

"He belongs to someone, Grace. Poodles belong to people. "

She heard the sharpness catch his voice and hugged the dog more closely. The dog settled into her arms and yawned. She turned and faced Jack.

"Put an ad in the paper and go check the bulletin board at the supermarket for lost dog signs."

"We need to discuss this," said Jack. "We never agreed to a dog."

"We never agreed to your motorcycle either, Jack. Or the BMW or your $3,000 golf clubs. You are the only man in the world with twice as many pairs of shoes as his wife. There are a lot of things we never agreed on. But I...AM...KEEPING...THIS!" She stood up straight and glared at him. "I DON'T NEED YOUR APPROVAL. I AM KEEPING THIS DOG!"

Jack looked at her, and his frown turned into a shrug. He swallowed and threw up his hands. "Okay, okay, I will place the damn ad."

Grace put the dog on the floor and filled a bowl with water. She took some roasted chicken out of the refrigerator and cut it into small pieces. She wasn't sure how the dog would react to the food; he might not have eaten for days. She put the bowl down and stepped back. The little dog looked at the pan and then up at her.

He slowly walked over to the food and began to eat. He ate with intensity but not with the unrestrained greed of some dogs.

He is a little gentleman!

Grace watched him until he finished, then took him to the bathroom, stripped and stepped into the shower with him. She ran the water until it was just right, then soaped the little dog with baby shampoo and gave him a good cleaning. When they finished, she dried him off with her hairdryer.

The little dog slept in the master bedroom with her that night, curled up at her side. The next morning, she took him to the local vet who proclaimed the little pooch healthy but with no identification chip.

"What do you think he is?" asked Grace.

"Hard to say without a DNA scan, but I suspect he is a mostly miniature poodle," said the vet. "Maybe a little Cocker Spaniel thrown in? That breeding supposedly mixes the good nature of the cocker with the extreme intelligence of the poodle. See, here, his nose is not as sharp as a poodle, and his eyes are not as almond-shaped."

They started running the ad the next day, and Grace forced herself to do daily checks of the "lost dog" section at the market bulletin board. She crossed her fingers and whisper, "Please God, please God, please God," as she read the ads.

The little dog seemed to live to be touched! He was a happy little boy and rocked when he ran with his back feet appearing to skip! His ears bounced up and down, and his tail proudly plumed high in the air. He didn't bark or emit a sound and Grace thought maybe Poodles, or whatever he was, didn't bark. Then, on the third day, a car honked outside, and he cried and growled and ran to look out the window.

"He thinks this is his house now," Grace said.

Grace became more and more attached over the next days and spent every minute with the dog. She called him "hey you" because she was afraid to name him. She knew the minute she gave him a name; someone would come and take him away.

"The night of the sixth day with her dog, she rolled over in bed and touched him. She closed her eyes. "God," she said, "A week ago, I wasn't even thinking about a dog. Now, I can't live without this one. God, you have blessed me with him. Please let me keep him. If you do that, I will never drink another drop. I swear."

In the morning, two weeks later, she named the dog Harley, and she lived the next week in horror that the phone would ring and someone would take him away from her.

121

The last days of ads and bulletin board checks were the most agonizing. Grace found herself unable to do much but worry. Then, the last day of the announcement ran, and the phone did not ring.

Grace emptied her bottle down the drain, and that night, she cuddled with Harley in her bed and cried and thanked God for his blessing to her. She had never questioned Him for taking Christopher and through the grief, that at times seemed to be destroying her; she had never blamed Him. Grace e had had enough faith to believe her son's energy was meant to be in Heaven and knew she would see him there again one day. But she also felt God could grant her this little favor, this little dog. It wasn't too much to ask.

Grace also cried that night because the love of the dog bared the deep need to love something and to be loved by something. She had carried that need for such a long time! She and Jack had not been in love for as long as she could remember, maybe even before Christopher was born. But when she had those thoughts, she shook them off and just thought of how much she had loved her son for the time he was with her.

Harley gave Grace something that she needed. Harley gave her something to hug and hold and kiss and talk to and to love so profoundly that she sometimes just had to stop and pick him up and bury her face in his soft fur.

Jack initially took no interest in the dog, but the little guy was determined to bond with everyone in the family. When Jack walked into a room, Harley would run to him with his tail wagging. The look on his face said, "You are the best dad in the world!" Jack began to take Harley on errands with him---with Grace's permission. He even took him to the squadron. Sometimes he had the dog on a leash; other times, he just carried him. Grace felt the tension leave the house, and she and Jack played with Harley and even began taking walks together with him.

And then one day, it all changed.

Grace remembered that day as a bright Saturday, and Jack had carried Harley into the squadron. He wanted to check the flight schedule for the coming week. Something must have happened because that was the last day Jack had anything to do with Harley. When the little dog ran up to him to entice Jack to play or chase him, Jack turned away. When Harley tried to jump into Jack's lap, he brushed him away.

It broke Grace's heart. The dog would look at her as if to ask, "What did I do wrong mom?" Why is dad mad at me?"

She tried to engage Jack, to see what the matter was, but he just muttered, "Dumb dog," and refused to discuss it.

The tension in the house returned and oddly reminded Grace of the time right after Christopher's death. It made her feel guilty. It wasn't right somehow, but that is what she felt.

Grace and Jack returned to their *arrangement*; the brief interlude of normalcy over.

Grace now lay on the couch until Louis Armstrong was finished then walked into the kitchen to make a cup of chamomile. She ran water in the pot and placed it on the stove. Soon, it sang its song to her.

She carried her tea back to the couch and sat down. Harley bounded into her lap, and she thought about the call she had received from Jack.

"Grace, it's me. I'm in Bermuda."

Jack's voice had surprised her, and for the tiniest part of a second, she felt the excitement of the old days, the tight chested, heart fluttering early days of their marriage when she was so in love with him. But in the blink of an eye, it passed.

"Bermuda? What are you doing there?"

Grace wasn't sure where the Ike was or what they were doing.

She had received the news about the heroics of her husband and genuinely felt happy for him. He desperately needed the kind of attention he was now getting. She wished for Jack's happiness, although she held no hope that his newfound fame would somehow result in a better marriage. That opportunity was long gone.

"I'm off the ship. The navy is bringing me back early. I fly into National Airport tonight."

Grace heard genuine excitement in Jack's voice, a marked change from his other calls. They were routine, perfunctory, sterile, part of a checklist she sensed he had to get through so he could go on his liberty ashore. The calls were more business than anything since, as the skipper's wife, Grace was also a significant conduit of information. Despite her anxiety, she had managed to organize the wives to do various things: bake cookies, send posters with the children's summer photos, knit personalized quilts, and create other activities to connect the families.

"I want you to meet me there." Grace gripped the phone.

"They will send a car for you. It would be great for you to come."

"Are you sure, Jack? They will probably understand if I am not there." Grace fought to keep her voice from shaking.

"Honey, the navy thinks it's a good idea for you to be there when I fly in. As I said, they are going to have a driver pick you up in a limo."

She could hear the edge in his voice, and she knew why. The navy wanted her there, not Jack. Jack wanted what the navy wanted.

"Why, Jack? What do they want with me?"

"Honey, they want the family thing. You know, for the families."

"Well, maybe." She WAS the skipper's wife. It was the right thing to do.

"Great, honey! That's just great!" The edge had vanished. "If they send the limo, that means I can bring Harley!"

"No, Grace, I don't think so." The edge was back.

"Oh, why not?"

It's just not the place for him. Too much noise. Just not the place that's all."

"I need him, Jack."

"You do not need that dog, Grace. You can do this without him."

"You don't like him because you're ashamed to be seen with him."

"That's not true."

"It is true, and you know it." One night, after coming home drunk from the officer's club, Jack had confided that Harley embarrassed him. He wished he had a German shepherd.

"Look, are you coming or not?"

Grace listened to his hard breathing as she cradled the phone. Her hands were shaking so hard it had taken her three attempts to hang up. She leaned back on the couch and patted Harley. Then she filled her cup again and turned up the volume on her stereo.

"Sir, we need to put your seat up. We'll be landing soon." The young crewman smiled at Jack. "I hear there is a big crowd down there waiting for you."

Jack stretched and yawned and looked out the window. The pilots were on the River Visual approach to runway 19, and he could see the sun sparkle off the water below, and the snap of window glints as the plane flew by. Neat, colonial-style houses with their two-story frames and windows all in a row sat among the oak and beech and elm trees. Jack sighed and wondered if Grace would be waiting. And if she would have the darned dog with her.

He remembered that day back in the squadron. The day Harley had embarrassed him.

Jack had been in the mailroom and had overheard two squadron mates talking.

"Jesus, did you see Jack Grant?"

"Man, I can't believe he dares to carry a Poodle in here.

Do you think he knows how gay he looks?"

Jack had swallowed and held his breath. Harley was asleep in his arms.

"You know, if I flew a pussy jet, like Grant, I think I would get a fucking Shepherd, or a Pit Bull or something. You know, to make up for it."

"No shit. Grant needs a Cujo dog, for Christ's sakes!"

Jack remembered slipping out of the room unseen. But, he had heard the laughter and had hurried to his car and threw Harley in the back. He didn't look at the dog for the entire drive home, and when they pulled into the garage, he screamed: "Get out!"

***

Just as the crewman said, a crowd of hundreds of people met the plane. Of course, the top navy brass was there, and Jack met the CNO for the first time.

"Where is Grace?" The CNO looked over Jack's shoulder as they shook hands. "We wanted a family welcome."

"I'm sorry, sir," said Jack. "She is not well."

127

The CNO nodded his head, then pivoted to the crowd. "Ladies and gentlemen, Phoenix Grant!"

Jack felt himself become enveloped by the crowd, and everything became a blur of handshakes, back claps, smiles, and hugs. But he reveled in the press of the mob. He loved it! Despite the turmoil and the fact, he was meeting Senators and Admirals and Generals and the elite of Washington D.C. he never felt so assured. He belonged here!

"Sir, sir."

Jack felt a tug on his elbow, and he turned his head.

"Sir, your wife is here." A young sailor grinned and pointed to a sedan, just pulling toward the crowd. Jack gulped and watched the door open. Out stepped Grace. Of course, she was carrying Harley.

"There she is," bellowed the CNO. "Folks this is the lady that has been holding all the wives together back home." He hurried toward Grace and gave her a big hug. Harley was between them; his tail wagged joyfully.

"Come on over here, Phoenix." The CNO had Grace under his arm and walked her over to Jack.

Jack embraced Grace and smiled widely as the cameras began to pop. Little Harley squirmed free and barked as the crowd roared its approval.

The next day the front page of both the Washington Post and the Times carried a color photo of Jack and Grace with Harley between them. It was a fantastic photo, and the caption read:

America's MIG Killer. A family man and a Poodle man!

Four days later, the airwing squadrons flew off Ike and returned to their home stations.

CHAPTER NINE

Captain Miles Harvey smiled at his replacement and gestured toward his large, office chair, "Take my seat, Frank, it will be yours in a few more minutes."

Frank returned the grin, walked around the desk, and sat down. He had been "turning over" with Miles for the past four days and was just about to relieve him of his duties and see him off to his new job. Miles had selected for rear admiral and was heading to the pentagon.

Frank's new office was in the sprawling jumble of cubby holes, chipped tile, poor wiring and drafty spaces that made up the navy annex. It was an overflow space next to the pentagon that housed the navy's personnel command. As the head aviation detailer, Frank would lead a group of officers who represented all of the communities in naval aviation, and it was their task to send officers to assignments that would meet the mission of the navy, support the progress of an officer's career and, if possible, give them what they wanted.

Frank grinned at Miles again and watched his relief settle into a chair in front of the desk. "Well, Miles, I am certainly impressed with your folks here and look forward to doing this job."

"Sir, got a minute?"

Frank looked at the sound of the voice. Commander Dean Dugard, the commander placements officer, stood in the doorway. He was the last person Frank needed to see before he took the job from Miles.

"Come in, Dean," said Miles. "Pull in a chair."

Dean grabbed a metal chair from the outer room and carried it into Miles's office. He shook hands and sat.

"I got a good brief from your folks, and I think I am up to speed," said Frank. "I just wanted to see if you had any parting shots before your old boss here leaves."

"Thank you, sir. There is one thing to discuss."

"Oh, what's that?"

"Phoenix Grant?"

"Go ahead then," said Miles. "I want to talk about him, too.

Frank, I know you are aware of the plan to send Jack to TOPGUN as the skipper out there. It was beginning to bubble when you left as his CAG."

Frank felt his throat tighten. His mind flashed to the tape Jocko had given him. He had forgotten about Jack and the TOPGUN detail. When he returned home from the Ike, he had taken two week's leave and then did a six-month stint at the Joint Forces Staff College in Norfolk. "Yes, sir, I heard about that."

"You know we already sent Jocko there." Miles smiled and leaned back in his chair. "Be kind of nice to have both MIG Killers there."

"I didn't realize Jocko was going to TOPGUN." Frank felt a bit better. Maybe somehow Jocko could watch over Jack.

"I'm not so sure having Grant go to TOPGUN is a good idea." Dean interrupted the two captains.

"Is there a problem?" Miles frowned and turned in his chair to face Dean. "CNO and the Air Boss think it's a good idea. As you know, your old boss, Titan Turner, is hot on Jack. The SECNAV thinks it's a great idea. He got a great number one FITREP from Frank here. I don't get it?"

"I heard about the top-level support he has," said Dean. His chair squeaked as he squirmed.

"So, what's the problem?"

"Well, sir, the problem is Jack Grant doesn't have any bottom level support. The fighter community is mystified about how he shot down the MIGS, and most believe that somehow Jocko made it happen or it was just God's sense of humor."

Frank felt himself getting sick.

"I mean he has a reputation for being selfish," continued Dean. "His reputation is that he's a poor ball flyer, doesn't like to fly at night, can't fight the airplane, things like that."

"What do you mean, can't fight the airplane?" Miles frowned and leaned back in his chair. "He shot down three MIGS."

"Yes, sir, and as I said, that is considered, by most, to be a miracle," said Dean. "All I am saying is that he has a bad reputation in the airplane."

Miles looked at Frank. He was confused. "CAG?"

132

Frank wished he had never seen the tape. He wished Jocko had never handed him the damned thing.

"Not sure I follow you either, Dean." Frank swallowed, and his chair squeaked as he shifted.

"Sir, once the news broke that Jack was heading to TOPGUN, the Tomcat guys from Oceana and Miramar began bombarding us. I have fifty phone messages from the fighter community, begging me not to send him there."

"CAG?" Miles looked at Frank.

"Look, I don't know about the goings-on inside the fighter community." Frank looked at Miles and then at Dean. "Maybe there is some jealousy? Duke Cunningham had to put up with that as I remember. Look, all I know is that he performed for me." He felt a jolt of guilt. "He earned the number one ticket and whatever comes with it."

Miles shrugged, then turned to Dean. "The deal to send him to TOPGUN is sealed. There is no going back on it.

Besides, he doesn't have to go out there to San Diego and be the ace of the base. We want him to be visible as a spokesman. He looks like the quintessential fighter pilot. He handles scripts well, that's all TV is anyway. He can, you know, be the guest speaker at conventions, lead Fleet Week, and get on the radio and T.V. I don't care if he ever flies an airplane."

"But sir if Jack Grant is the skipper of TOPGUN he is going to HAVE to fly airplanes, and he is going to have to be good at it. He is also going to have to be a hell of a leader to hold all of those egocentric assholes together."

133

"Christ, Dean," interrupted Miles. "How hard is it to fly an F-5 or A-4 against a first tour Tomcat pilot? Half the time they probably won't even have sight of him. I'm sure he will do fine against fleet nuggets."

"Sir, we have a bunch of great pilots, great leaders, that would be perfect as the skipper of TOPGUN. Let me get their records. I can brief you on them if you want."

"I think we are beyond that." Miles leaned back in his chair. "I need you to write the orders. Get him to San Diego, get him the training he needs, and make it happen, Dean."

Dean shook his head and stood. "You're the boss."

"That's right," said Miles. "At least for another couple of minutes."

Dean exited the room, and Miles stood. Frank stood with him. "Best of luck, Frank."

Frank shook Miles's hand and watched him leave the room. He sat back down in his chair and let out a long breath.

***

Jack Grant was sitting in his office reviewing the flight schedule when Zits Bowman, the squadron duty officer, knocked on his door.

"Skipper got something for you. Message center called, and I sent the duty driver for it. It looks like it is from BUPERS."

"Thanks, Zits, give it here." Jack reached out his hand, and Zits gave him the paper. "Shut the door on your way out."

"See you, skipper," Zits turned and scurried back to the ready room.

Jack rocked back in his chair and began to read the message, and as he did, his grin grew wider and wider. It was indeed from the Bureau of Personnel, and it contained orders to "detach from command of Fighter Squadron 142 and report to the US Navy Fighter Weapons School for duty involving flying as the commanding officer".

Jack shut his eyes and laughed. TOPGUN was the most famous unit in the navy, made so by the 1986 movie--- and he was going to be the skipper! This assignment erased the disappointment he had felt since his first squadron when he was not selected to go to TOPGUN as a student. The squadron leadership had chosen Benny Johnson, and Jack had always hated him for it. Jack had researched the TOPGUN story carefully. The school offered graduate-level training for fighter aircrew over a five-week academic and flying syllabus. The school also provided training for combat air controllers and adversary pilots. The school emerged from a 1968 report by Captain Frank Ault who was charged by the Chief of Naval Operations to determine why the Navy had so many missile failures in Viet Nam and such a lousy kill ratio against MIG aircraft. Ault's report placed the blame on inadequate aircrew training, so a handful of F-8 Crusader and F-4 Phantom aviators developed a syllabus from scratch. The program was a fantastic success, as the kill ratio soared from 3.7 to 1 in 1967 to 13 to 1 by 1970. Interestingly, the USAF did not institute a program like TOPGUN, and its kill ratio worsened during that same time.

Jack had been in contact with PERS 43 about the possibility of TOPGUN but never thought it would happen. He had always considered TOPGUN to be a closed club, only for the "bros" who had been there as students. But now, he was on his way to San Diego.

Jack picked up the phone and dialed his home number. Grace would undoubtedly be there as she was more or less a hermit these days. He couldn't understand what the problem was. Grace had no reason to be anxious, no cause for panic. They had resources; he would make captain for sure, and that meant employment for another ten years minimum in the navy.

What the fuck was wrong with her, anyway? Did she want attention?

"Hello."

"Grace, it's me. I got some good news." He gripped the phone, waiting for her to respond. He could hear her breathing and the stereo in the background.

Fucking Louis Armstrong again!

"Grace." He said her name more sharply than he wanted. It came out as a bark.

"Yes."

"We got orders to San Diego, to TOPGUN." He re-gripped the receiver, unsure of how she would respond. He didn't care what she thought. He didn't want some fucking meltdown. He knew she didn't want to move from their house in Chelsea and Virginia Beach. He also knew she didn't want to move away from her parents.

"Grace." "Okay," she said.

He held the phone against his ear until it went dead.

CHAPTER TEN

Jack handed the reigns of the Ghostriders to Tagger on the first Friday in January of 1991. Friday afternoons were the preferred time for changes of command because the celebrations could stretch into the weekend. That was especially good because this was the most significant change of command event in the history of Oceana Naval Air Station. So many dignitaries attended that the mayor of Virginia Beach had to sit in the second row. Usually, the CAG was the guest speaker in such situations as he was the one that received the reporting orders from the incoming and outgoing officers. However, in this case, the guest speaker was none other than the Secretary of the Navy who began his remarks about the incredible impact the navy had on world events, to include the Middle East and the importance of the coalition against Saddam in Saudi Arabia.

Jack sat on the dais in his dress blues and listened to the Secretary. He was a bit surprised at his lack of interest in the topic but knew that was because his part was over. He had already done his part, and even if full-blown war came to Iraq, it would be over soon. Jack's interest keened, however, when SECNAV moved his remarks to praise for him and the Ghostriders. As he listened to the SECNAV, and as he eyed the crowd, he saw all were looking at him; smiling, nodding their heads in adoration. Jack grunted softly, his sword belt, worn high underneath the coat, cut into his stomach. The sword forced him to sit on his right cheek. He stole a glance down his left breast and at the "fruit salad" of color.

Beneath his gold wings, the Navy Cross was a vibrant, dark blue and it joined the red, white and blue of his Silver Star and a sea of other colors and shapes. Soon, he would add the pink and white meritorious service medal to his collection. CAG would give it to him following his remarks.

Jack and the others on the dais faced the large crowd and to the side stood the row on row splendor of the white-uniformed Ghostriders. The squadron formed in divisions with sword-bearing officers standing in front while the band assembled on the opposite side of the hangar. Perhaps the most significant fixture at the change of command was the beautifully painted Tomcat placed immediately behind the crowd. Everyone in attendance had to walk past it to their seats. Although the Navy had gone to a haze-gray paint scheme for tactical reasons, Jack instructed his maintenance officer to repaint the aircraft in shiny epoxy with the Ghostrider death's head logo in bright yellow and black. Of course, the corrosion-control shop would have to sand and re-paint the plane after the ceremony, but Jack didn't think that was inappropriate.

After all, it was his big day. He smiled as he read the name under the pilot's canopy,

CDR Jack "Phoenix" Grant Commanding Officer

He smiled again as he looked at the three, red MIG 23 silhouettes under his name.

The SECNAV finished his remarks with a salute to Jack, enrichened by the loud applause of the crowd. CAG followed with his praise of Jack and the squadron and pinned the new medal on Jack's tunic.

Jack was an expert manipulator of people one-on-one, but he was not fond of public speaking. He found himself stuttering and nervous but managed to deliver what was mostly a tribute to his squadron and their hard work. Such was naval aviation tradition as was Jack's thanks to Grace for unwavering support. He nodded to her and smiled. At least she had come this time---WITHOUT the dog. Tagger, the incoming commanding officer, gave a short speech, again praising Jack and the squadron and then it was over. Jack spent several minutes mingling with the crowd, then found Grace, talking with the chaplain. They headed to the car for the drive to the Oceana Officers' Club and the reception.

Ten days later, on the 17th of January coalition forces began Operation Desert Storm, the military operation to remove Saddam from Kuwait.

CHAPTER ELEVEN

Commander Steve "Booger" Collingwood leaned his head against the back wall of the TOPGUN classroom and watched Jocko roll through his slides. It was common practice for bro's to sit in on lectures, to provide quality control and standardization, and to inform each other. TOPGUN had the responsibility to offer cutting-edge tactics and information, and the lecture series was under continual review and scrutiny. Each lecturer endured a multi-part "murder board" before conducting an actual class. Murder boards were well named; characterized by frank and brutal questions about everything from appearance to content knowledge and delivery.

Booger smiled as he watched the younger officer. Jocko was a natural instructor. He was charismatic and intelligent and had a gift for handling the collections of type A personalities that populated TOPGUN classes. He also had a ton of credibility from his actions in the Gulf War and was a widely respected member of the fighter community. He was also a natural to give the lecture that Booger watched, "The Dog Fight Phoenix."

Jocko flipped up his last slide, **Questions**, it read.

"You know, Jocko, I have always wondered about that Phoenix shot you guys took. I know the story is Skipper Grant took it, but I don't see how, given the timing and all. If you didn't take it, why didn't you?"

Booger leaned forward to see who asked the questions. Sure enough, it was Scruffy Manus. Scruffy was a RIO from VF-51 and had a reputation for being a "code breaker;" someone who is very knowledgeable on a particular subject and tries to use that knowledge to stump the instructor.

Booger watched as Jocko smiled and nodded his head.

"The skipper took the shot because that is what he briefed we would do. He was the skipper, and it was his call."

"But you can see why I question it, right? I mean, according to this brief, you, Jocko, took a single target track lock at thirty miles to slave the TCS and got an ID. Then, the skipper makes a radio call about that ID, two MIG 23s in a welded wing, to the wingman. You return to Track While Scan so the radar can support both targets should they separate. Then, one of you fires the Phoenix. The counter goes to fifteen, and you lock the target for a follow-on Sparrow shot just in case the Phoenix misses. Then you see the fireball, and you lock the remaining MIG in the following group. All of that happens in seconds. The timing has to be perfect. And, it was the first time you and the skipper had ever flown together! Can you see why I have a tough time with this?"

Jocko smiled again and shrugged his shoulders. "I guess we were lucky."

"If you say so," said Scruffy. "But I think you took that Phoenix shot."

Jocko raised his eyebrows and shrugged his shoulders again. "Okay, guys, take ten and meet back here for the next lecture."

Booger left the classroom by the back door and went to his office. He frowned as he walked. There was a persistent skepticism within the fighter community about what happened with Jack Grant and Jocko Barnes, and Jack Grant was now the skipper of TOPGUN, the heart of the fighter community. The other thing that nagged Booger was he never saw Jack and Jocko even talking to each other. There was something between them for sure. When he first heard that Jack was coming, he called Jocko into his office to discuss the possibilities. He wanted to see if Jocko wanted to do some team thing with Jack. A team tactics brief, for instance. But Jocko showed zero interest in anything like that, and somehow ops never scheduled them to fly together. He frowned again as he entered his office and glanced at his watch. It was time for his Tailhook committee meeting. It was their last meeting before the Tailhook convention in Las Vegas, and he wanted to ensure the details were in order. This year's Hook was to be "The Mother of all Hooks" with record-breaking attendance due to the tremendous victory in Iraq. Desert Storm had lasted only forty-three days, and the United States was euphoric as the country had not had complete success in war since World War 11. Booger was primarily concerned about details since he was not going to attend Hook this year.

Booger was the XO of TOPGUN and an F-14 pilot. He was the high time Tomcat driver in the fleet with over 3,000 hours in the plane. Booger was an exceptional pilot who had come to the navy after a couple of tours in Vietnam flying helicopters. He got tired of "getting shot at by every gook with a gun" as he liked to say, so he joined the navy. He got his call sign in the training command during a flight that was supposed to be an introduction to tactical maneuvering. However, Booger out-flew the instructor to the point where, later in the ready room, the instructor proclaimed, "I couldn't get him off of me. He was like a wet booger. I flicked and flicked, and he kept gunning me."

The XO at TOPGUN wasn't a job that led to a command like a fleet squadron. The XO was usually just the senior officer after the skipper and got the job because nobody else wanted it. As the outgoing XO, Flame McCoy, explained to Booger the first day he checked in, "XO of TOPGUN is like being the pecker checker in a whore house."

Booger quickly got qualified in the F-5 and A-4 and established himself as the premier pilot and instructor. He stayed current in the Tomcat as a "guest" pilot with his old squadron, VF-21. The leadership in VF-21 also saw the benefit of having someone like Booger in their ready room, briefing, leading and de-briefing flights. Besides, TOPGUN paid for the gas, and the RIO that flew with him got some excellent training. Booger was also welcome at VF-21 because he was Booger. He was a known quantity at Miramar and recognized as one of the best fighter pilots in the navy. He was the kind of pilot that allowed TOPGUN to have and to continue the reputation that the squadron enjoyed. Many viewed Booger as an "airplane whisperer," a reference to cowboys that train horses with patience and some mysterious connection to the animal. Whisperer or not, the reason Booger was able to fly the Tomcat the way he did was because he intimately knew the aircraft and what it could do. He was a naturally curious pilot and spent countless hours exploring how the aircraft performed at different speeds, angles of attack, altitudes, and nose positions. He also exploited the Tomcat in ways few pilots could. For instance, he used his landing flaps while fighting the Tomcat because he knew the huge advantage they gave in slow-speed maneuvering. This understanding and technique came from his exploration, not from formal training.

Booger possessed the understanding of aerodynamics, and he knew the "numbers," but the difference between him and most other pilots was that he felt the art of piloting a fighter. Just like an artist that uses various oil colors to portray a particular shade and even dimension, Booger mixed subtle combinations of spoiler, rudder, and throttle with sun angle, haze level, and a critical estimation of what his opponent was doing, and about to do, to achieve victory.

"Come in, boys, come in." Booger motioned for Luke, Slim, and Jethro to join him. The three pilots tromped in and grabbed chairs in front of Booger's desk.

"Okay, so the van leaves on Wednesday, and Luke you are driving right?"

"Yes, sir." Luke was a new officer at TOPGUN, and as a newbie, he had to do crap that nobody else wanted to do.

"Good, and what are you loaded with?"

"We have the TOPGUN banner, napkins, mixer, and beer, wine, you know, the normal stuff."

"And no, ZERO, vodka or lime juice or triple sec, right?"

"That's right sir."

"XO, are you sure about this?" Slim squirmed in his seat. "Serving Kamikazes at 'Hook' is a tradition for TOPGUN. We do it every year."

"I am positive," said Booger.

"But XO," Jethro cut in. "This will be the biggest Hook ever. Christ, we beat Saddam! We have triple MIG killers with the new skipper and Jocko. We don't want to celebrate that with some piss beer, do we?"

"No beer that is cold is piss," said Booger. "Besides, Kamikazes are not a tradition. We have been serving them for a couple of years."

"But why are you so against it?" Jethro slumped in his chair and narrowed his eyes. "Is it because you screened for command a couple of days ago? Now you are some company man?"

The navy had published the squadron command list two days prior, and Booger's name was on it. He was getting an F-14 squadron.

"No, that isn't the reason," said Booger, frowning at Jethro. "Come on, man, give me a break."

"Okay, okay, sorry," said Jethro, and he slumped even more in his chair.

"Look, guys, serving a shot of liquor is one thing," said Booger. "But we don't just do that. We give a kamikaze headband to everyone that can drink ten of them."

"Yeah, it's so cool," said Slim, as he high-fived Luke.

"No, it's not cool," said Booger. "Having a bunch of drunks, mostly training command students, by the way, arcing around with those headbands, vomiting all over the

146

place, passed out in the hallways, is not cool. That is not the intent of Tailhook. The intent is to bond with all the other naval aviators past and present and vomit is not a good bonding material."

"But XO," whined Jethro.

"No, buts," said Booger. "The issue is closed. Beer, cold beer, and wine are what we are serving, and that is final. Now, get out of here I have a brief to get to."

"That's right," said Luke. "You're fighting that dude from Nellis aren't you? The air force major in the ready room."

"That's right," said Booger. "Jocko and I are taking him on." He shooed the others out of the room, picked up his kneeboard, and headed to his brief.

***

Major William "Draco" Donovan smiled as he shook hands with the navy pilot. He noted Booger Collingwood on his nametag above the gold wings.

"They call me Draco," he said. "I take it you are going to fly the F-14?"

"They call me Booger and looks like that's the plan."

"How did you get the nickname Booger? You from the south or something?" Draco smiled again.

"Something like that." Booger smiled and motioned to a tall lieutenant. "This is my sidekick and RIO, Jocko."

147

Draco shook hands with Jocko and watched Booger motion for the assembled crowd to take a seat. He fought a smirk.

Geez, why did they trot out this old commander? He must already be in his forties, and not a big fan of the gym either.

Draco turned to the six air force officers who accompanied him. "Seats, gents."

Draco glanced around the TOPGUN briefing room. It was pretty sparse, whiteboards along the walls with accompanying colored markers. There were also models of different US and Soviet aircraft attached to wooden sticks. These could be used as "wands" to hold while demonstrating maneuvers. There was also a poster that listed "rules of engagement." Draco watched Booger as he briefed them on the mechanics of flying out of Miramar and how to get to the range 120 miles away at Yuma. He had to admit that the old guy was pretty smooth; he had done this before. He copied the information Booger delivered; radio frequencies, pattern entry procedures, and so forth. Draco crisply and quickly recited the Eagle's out-of-control and spin procedures when it was his turn. Booger did the same for the Tomcat. Finally, they got to the tactical discussion.

"What can I tell you about the Tomcat?"

Draco hesitated and took a sip from his water bottle. "Not too much I don't know," he replied. "I've fought it quite a few times."

"Oh, is that so?" Booger smiled at him.

"Yeah, I probably have a dozen or so fights against the Tom," said Draco. He looked around the room, winking at the Eagle pilots around him.

"What do you figure your biggest advantage is?" Asked Booger.

Draco let the air out of his lungs," Gee," he laughed. "Where to begin." The F-15 pilots behind him chuckled and grinned at each other.

"I guess the basic thing is more powerful engines. You are flying the A model, right?"

"Correct," said Booger. "As you might know the B model has new GE engines, but I will have the original Pratt and Whitney TF- 30's today."

"Well, if your compressor stalls and you spin that thing, don't blame me." Draco laughed as did his Eagle colleagues. The Tomcat's problems with engine stalls were well known.

"Promise," said Booger.

"So, the Eagle has more power, the Eagle can put more G on the airframe, the Eagle weighs less, and in general outperforms the Tomcat throughout the flight envelope." Draco smiled again and looked at Booger. He liked to adopt the more antiseptic third-person description of "The Eagle" versus using "I." Later, during the debriefing, the third person approach made it easier for him to describe how he beat the other pilot without sounding like too much of a prick. "And, the Eagle can judge the Tomcat's speed by the position of the wings. When they are back, the Tomcat is fast. When they are out, the Tomcat is slow."

"The Eagle is a good airplane," said Booger. "I have to admit; it is an excellent airplane."

"It was built from the bottom up for fighting," interrupted Draco. "Not for intercepting."

"True," said Booger.

Draco laughed, and a sudden feeling of generosity came over him. "Hey, the Tomcat can land on an aircraft carrier. The Eagle can't do that!"

Booger smiled back at him and nodded. "So, how are you going to attack me?"

Draco was a bit startled at the question. He hesitated a second. "Well, I am going to...the Eagle is going to out-perform the Tomcat with more G available and superior power. The Eagle will eventually find itself behind the Tomcat's wing line. Since I would like to restrict the weapons to Sidewinders and guns today, I will probably be calling my first shot when around sixty to seventy degrees behind your wing, as long as the sun isn't in the way of course."

"I see," said Booger.

"And, if you get slow, I will be able to get a slashing gun shot, that is if I can't just saddle up and track you."

"Sounds like a good plan," said Booger.

Draco smiled and took a sip of water. "So, what is your plan?" Draco asked his question as a courtesy. The fact was he didn't give a shit what this old man's plan was.

"Oh, I am going to try to stay fast and not get shot." Booger laughed.

"Good luck with that," said Draco.

"How do you want to set up the engagements? Twenty thousand feet, a mile abeam at 350 or so?" Booger stood away from the podium and looked down at Draco.

"Altitude's good," said Draco. "But I would like two miles abeam and 450 for the initial set up."

"Okay, we can do that," said Booger. "And you say you want to use sidewinders and guns?"

"For today, let's use Sidewinders and guns. It keeps the beyond-visual-range stuff out of it and lets fighter pilots be fighter pilots."

"Sidewinders and guns it is," said Booger. "See you out there."

The room adjourned, and Jocko sidled up to Booger. "Geez, what a prick."

"Oh, don't get too upset. Draco can't help himself. It comes from wearing an ascot."

"No, shit. Do you think those guys know how fucked up that looks?"

"Let's hope not."

"So what is the plan?" Jocko frowned. "I don't want to get hosed by this guy. Not in front of the world on the TACTS range."

Booger laughed and clapped his RIO on the shoulder. "Me neither. So, take a seat and let's talk about this."

Booger led them to an empty briefing room and motioned for Jocko to sit.

"We know he wants the two miles abeam so he can accelerate into us and then put an eight G turn on right off the bat. He knows we are restricted to six and a half G's, so if the airspeeds are the same, physics will let him start working behind us immediately. His game plan will be to wear us down in airspeed until we can't fight him off anymore. Then, he can shoot us with either a high angle Sidewinder or slashing guns shot."

"So, like I said, what is our plan?"

Booger laughed. "You and I have flown together quite a bit. I trust you to look at our speed, fuel, and altitude and, above all, help keep sight of him. The sun will be bright and high by the time we get out there, and even as big as we both are, we can lose sight of each other for a moment. And in this kind of fight, losing sight for just a short time can be the deciding factor."

"Roger."

"What are the two things that dictate the sizes of our turning arc?"

"Airspeed and G," replied Jocko.

"Right," said Booger. "We know he has more G available and can go as fast as we can so we are going to need to confuse him.

When we turn into him on the first engagement, I am going to put the wings in the BOMB position, so they stay aft. When we pass him, we will look like we are going fast."

"Got it," grinned Jocko.

"So, when we pass with the wings back and immediately go nose-low, what does he think?"

"He is going to think we are going to scoop out below him in a huge arc," said Jocko.

"Right, and what do you think he will do?" "He will turn nose low to turn inside us."

"That's right," said Booger. "So, when we pass, I will roll, pull the throttles to idle, and put the wings to AUTO."

"I get putting the wings back to AUTO so the computer can program their movement for us but why put the throttles to idle? He is going to be awful fast."

"We have to control that first nose-low turn, or we WILL scoop out at the bottom. It has to be a bat turn."

"Got it."

"As soon as I get the nose back toward the horizon, I will hit the afterburners, and point toward where I think he is headed. If he goes nose-low our slower speed puts us inside of his turn. You will have to keep sight of him through this move."

"Right," said Jocko. "He should be high on the top of the canopy moving from right to left."

153

"That's right," said Booger. "Unless he reverses his turn and if so I can see that."

"What if he goes up?"

"The smartest thing he could do would be to go up as soon as he sees us go nose low. He could convert all of his energy to altitude and get us to lose him. He could then pick his time to pounce on us."

"So, what if he does?"

"If he goes nose high, we have no choice but to run away from him and try to separate enough to turn around and find him. In that scenario, he will most likely shoot us."

"If it is that risky, why do we go ow?"

"Because it is one way we can win, given the performance advantages he has in the scenario we are fighting. He will not expect us to be able to make that first turn. All we need is a few seconds of confusion to get the best of him. Besides, he won't go up. He doesn't want to win by swooping down on us. He wants to win by eating us up from the first turn. He wants to put the stick in his lap and pull until he hears a tone and shoots us, or pulls even more and guns us."

"You seem to know him well. Have you met?"

"No, but I know his kind."

"Okay," said Jocko. "If this works out the way we think we will be inside his turn, but he will be fast and accelerating away."

"True," said Booger. "But if I can get my nose to him and shoot something, a long-range Sidewinder maybe, it might scare him into turning into us. Besides, he will be so shocked he probably won't know what to do with all of his speed."

"Yeah, let's hope."

Booger grinned back at his RIO and winked. "Let's go and get this guy."

Thirty minutes later, Booger and Jocko were rolling out of the flight line toward Runway 24. They heard Draco call for taxi and watched his Eagle fall in behind them. The tower cleared them for a flight leader separation take off, so the two airplanes positioned on the runway side-by-side. Booger pushed the throttles up and looked at Draco who gave him a thumbs up. He selected afterburner, saw the nozzles open, and released the brakes. He let the nose fly off the ground around 160 knots, and as the Tomcat cleared the concrete, Booger raised the flaps and gear and climbed to 3,000 feet. Draco crisply and efficiently joined on his right-wing, and the two aircraft flew up and east to the Yuma TACTS range.

The Tactical Aircrew Combat Training System (TACTS) Range, is a 10,000 square mile piece of airspace located on the California/Arizona border. Instruments in the desert below the sky allowed aircraft equipped with individual telemetry pods to be viewed and recorded. Flight paths, aircraft parameters, cockpit views, weapon's envelopes, and other data can be seen real-time and dissected during post-flight de-briefs for the aircrew. The news of Booger and Jocko's fight against the hated, and grudgingly admired F-15 Eagle, filled the TACTS trailer at Miramar with a standing room only crowd.

155

Jack Grant was among the crowd awaiting the duel between the Tomcat and Eagle on the TACTS range. He had a front-row seat and watched the computer-simulated images as they took a position two miles abeam and 450 knots. Jack had often visited the trailer since taking command of TOPGUN in hopes that by watching the numbers, he could be a better pilot himself. It frustrated him because the art of aerial mastery continued to be elusive. As he watched, the TACTS operator manipulated his displays to show a God's eye view of the two planes. Airspeed, altitude, relative angles, and distances were all displayed.

Jack looked around the room to see a mix of TOPGUN instructors, local squadron aircrew, and the F-15 pilots from Nellis. Jack, of course, was rooting for the Tomcat as were all of the naval aviators in the room. There were lots of reasons to root for the Tomcat, but the primary one was the ongoing feud between the F-14 and F-15 communities over which was the best fighter. The truth was the two aircraft were designed and built for different purposes: the F-14 as a defender of the battle group and long-range interceptor and the F-15 as an air superiority fighter. In the world of dogfighting, the lighter weight F-15 was more maneuverable in the hands of the average pilot, and it had defeated a lot of Tomcat pilots.

In the F-14 cockpit, Booger checked his altitude and airspeed one more time. He glanced to his right at the F-15 and transmitted over the fight frequency. "You ready?"

"Ready," replied Draco.

"Fight's on," said Booger. He pulled turned into the Eagle and when he was nose to nose, selected BOMB on his wing sweep selector. As the two planes passed, Booger

156

pulled his throttles to idle, selected the wings to AUTO and rolled hard into the Eagle.

He continued until he was upside down, pulling across an imaginary circle toward where he knew the Eagle was heading. He pulled toward the horizon and shoved the throttles into afterburner.

"Jocko, do you have him?"

"He turned nose-low! He's at 2 o'clock," Jocko grunted over the ICS.

Booger grinned and looked where Jocko indicated. "Got him."

Booger's slower airspeed allowed him to turn inside Draco and his nose-low attitude and afterburner helped keep his speed from bleeding too much. Draco's mistake to turn nose-low put him in an arc out in front of Booger but he was at the far edge of Sidewinder missile range. Booger heard the seeker growl and pulled the trigger anyway.

"Fox two." He knew Draco would hear his shot call and hoped he would do something stupid.

Draco did just that. Instead of merely using his airspeed to stay away from Booger, he turned hard into the Tomcat, decreasing the range. Booger grinned and shot again.

"Fox two."

The men in the TACTS control room watched the first missile fly out from the Tomcat and slowly arc across the sky. It missed. Then, the second missile followed. For a second, it looked like a miss, and then the coffin symbol blinked over the Eagle. The TACTS operator keyed his mic.

"Eagle, you are dead."

"Knock it off, knock it off," said Booger. "Let's set up for another one."

The two airplanes separated, and as they climbed back to altitude, Draco keyed the mic. "Looks like you got lucky that time."

"Looks like," said Booger. He grinned when he heard the venom in Draco's voice. He knew this time Draco would be coming at him with his fangs out. Booger smiled again. He knew how to exploit that.

"Jocko, thanks, man, for keeping sight during the first turn. That maneuver only works if you keep sight!"

"I was finished reading my book back here and didn't have anything else to do."

Booger laughed into the mic and looked to his right. The two aircraft hit their altitude, and when they were two miles apart and at 450 knots, Booger keyed the mic.

"Fight's on."

As before, the two airplanes turned into each other, but this time Booger floated his turn building airspeed, and when he passed Draco right-to-right, he had 550 knots. He pulled the nose up and zoomed for the sun. During the time the two aircraft were flying back to altitude for the second engagement, Booger had maneuvered them so that when he passed Draco and went nose high, he would be able to get into the sun. Booger looked down over his right shoulder as he watched the big Eagle turn nose high toward him. He knew that even if Draco maintained sight, the Tomcat would be too close to the sun for Draco's Sidewinder to discriminate and get a solution. Booger kept climbing and smiled as he saw the Eagle's nose wander away from him. Draco had lost sight!

"Blind," said Draco. Blind is a safety call to let both pilots know that one does not have the other in sight.

"Tally," said Booger as he floated over the top.

The Tomcat aircrew in the TACTS trailer yelled when they heard this exchange. Booger's tally meant "you might not see me, but I see you."

In his Tomcat, Booger grinned again as he thought about Draco's predicament. He had two bad choices: keep his nose up and hope he could find the Tomcat, or, push it over and try to accelerate downhill like hell in hopes he could get away. Booger gently pulled the nose higher and dropped the flaps.

"185," said Jocko.

 "Roger," said Booger.

Tally," said Draco. He had regained sight!

Booger looked down to his right at Draco. He was only 600 feet away, and Booger could see the other man looking at him.

"170," said Jocko.

Booger stared at the Eagle as he assessed its airspeed.

Suddenly, the nose of Draco's big fighter shuddered, and Booger grinned as he watched him fall off to his left. Booger dropped his nose to pick up some speed.

"220," said Jocko.

Booger watched Draco bring his nose up again, and he gently increased back pressure on the stick, gliding his Tomcat over the Eagle.

"200," said Jocko. Booger selected Gun.

The two big fighters were now nosing high, each trying to gain an advantage by having the nose high enough to keep from flying out in front of the other plane but not too high to cause a stall.

"180", said Jocko.

Booger felt the stick quiver and relaxed it slightly as he nursed the rudder pedals.

The nose fell forward a few degrees, and he picked up some speed.

"200," said Jocko.

Booger milked the stick back. Slowly, slowly, the Eagle inched out in front of him.

The TACTS control operator narrowed the view, and the crowd could now see the digital airplanes next to each other.

"Christ, he is slow; how is he staying up there?" Jack asked as he looked around. Everybody was staring at the screen.

Suddenly the Eagle fell off to the left, and the Tomcat fell in behind it. The TACTS operator selected F-14 pilot view, and the navy crowd erupted when they saw the Eagle flash under the Tomcat's gunsight.

"Guns," said Booger.

The crowd groaned when no coffin appeared. The gun solution was too high of an angle and the tracking time too short.

Booger dropped his nose and unloaded for a moment to get more speed. He watched Draco pull up again and followed him. As he went over the top, he waited---waited, waited for his nose to follow through. He gingerly worked the rudders to keep the aircraft from yawing. Significant yaw at this point would most likely induce a compressor stall, and God knows what would happen then! As the nose dropped back below the horizon, he pulled hard. The nose pitched sixty degrees down in a second, and now the Eagle was right in front of him.

"Tracking," he said. Tracking is what a pilot says just before he decides to kill you.

"Tracking."

"Tracking."

Booger pulled the trigger.

"That's a kill," said the TACTS operator.

Jack grinned as the coffin superimposed over the F-15 and the crowd erupted in a roar. It was pandemonium. The F-15 pilots looked at each other in silence.

161

"Knock it off, let's go home," said Booger.

Booger made some quick notes on his kneeboard as he waited for Draco to join up and after they visually inspected each other's airplane for missing panels or leaks, they headed back to San Diego.

"Skipper, this should bring back old memories." Polack Joe Sadowski laughed as he nodded toward the digital image on the screen. It showed the cockpit view of Booger's Tomcat as he was gunning Draco, "Except, of course, your guns were real, and it was a MIG 23."

Jack grinned as the assembled crowd hooted. He looked around and nodded to acknowledge them. "Something like that, I guess." He smiled again.

Jack frowned as he looked at the screen again. "Who was driving the Eagle? Some low time guy?"

"No, sir, he is the Ops officer over at Nellis' fighter weapons school."

"Wow," said Jack.

"Wow is right," replied Polack Joe. "Booger is the best there is." He frowned and shook his head. "Except, of course, you skipper."

Jack left the TACTS trailer and drove back to the TOPGUN spaces. He was filled with pride. Pride for his Tomcat community and naval aviation. Pride for his squadron. But he also had another feeling, eating away in the dark corners of his mind.

He was jealous.

162

He knew it was crazy to have such feelings. Christ, he was the skipper! He was a MIG killer. But the matter of fact was that since he had arrived, he still didn't feel like he belonged. It was strange. He had always wanted to be admired and respected as a great fighter pilot and here, he was the commanding officer of one of the most significant assemblages of fighter pilots ever, and he didn't feel right. He could not shake the notion that he was an imposter. His mind kept taking him back to the old days when, on Friday afternoons, he would find himself alone at the corner of the bar watching legendary guys. Everybody would watch in awe as they "held court," maneuvering their hands into the position they were in when they shot somebody. Jack had envied them to the point of hatred. But, he should be past that envy now. He was Phoenix Grant! Since the day of the MIG kills and when he walked into the ready room on Ike, he had been adored and honored just like the pilots he had envied. Better even! Those guys never shot down a MIG, got the SECNAV to speak for them, or meet the CNO, not to mention the senators and all the rest. He was the skipper of TOPGUN, and he loved the way everybody treated him. But, still, it wasn't right. It wasn't right because Jack had a secret. He had felt unworthy the moment he walked into the TOPGUN spaces and met the pilots and saw all the photos of previous "bros" on the wall. There was that word again, poster. Every other TOPGUN instructor was a former student who had impressed the instructor cadre so much they petitioned PERS 43 to assign them to the school. The commanding officer, however, was not selected like that. The bureau detailed him based upon its desires, not the will of the instructors. Despite his MIG kills and newfound fame, Jack knew how good he was in the airplane, and he knew that eventually his skill level could be exposed. As he watched the TACTS tape and Booger, he felt the beginnings of regret for accepting the orders to TOPGUN.

He wished he had been assigned to the Pentagon where his credibility as a pilot would never be questioned.

Jack walked into his office and picked up the phone. He dialed the duty officer. "Have the XO drop by the office when he gets through debriefing the flight."

"Sure, skipper," replied the duty officer. "Did you hear about the XO's flight? He just gunned some Eagle driver on the TACTS range."

"That's what I want to talk with him about," said Jack.

CHAPTER TWELVE

Jack was sitting at his desk, examining an F-5 model when Booger banged on his door.

"Come in XO," he said, as he stood to extend his hand.

Booger walked in and grabbed the outstretched hand. "Skipper, I heard you want to see me."

"You heard, right." Jack gestured to a chair, "Take a seat. How did the debrief with the Eagle driver go?"

"Pretty quick," laughed Booger. "He didn't want to stick around."

Jack laughed, "I can see why." He looked at Booger. "I heard you screened for command of an F-14 squadron. That is fantastic. Congratulations!"

"Thanks, skipper." Booger smiled and shook his head. "Never thought that one day I would get my own squadron."

"Hey, it couldn't happen to a better guy. I am sorry to be losing my XO, but it is worth it to have you to lead a squadron in the fleet."

"Thanks again, skipper."

"Know which squadron yet?"

"I think it will be here on the west coast, VF-154."

"The Black Knights, great outfit! You will have a great time leading that pack." Jack smiled and leaned back in his chair. "When are you cutting out of here? Not too soon, I hope?"

"I am already current in the airplane and have all my other quals so I can get there pretty quick. I am going to leave in September, Bunny and I are taking a trip to visit her folks for a month or so, then back to work."

"You ARE going to go to Tailhook, aren't you? It'll be the biggest one yet. I was invited to sit at the head table on Saturday night!"

"Well, skipper, I would love to go, but I am going to be on leave. I promised Bunny some time to see her folks, so we will be on the road that Sunday morning, but I will be with you in spirit."

"Good enough," said Jack." Good enough." He leaned forward in his chair "So, the other reason I wanted to talk with you was about the hop today. I watched you on the TACTS range a little while ago. It was very, very impressive, the way you handled that F-15."

"Thanks, skipper."

"You know, on paper, the Eagle should beat a Tomcat. It sure looks like you didn't read that paper." Jack and Booger laughed, and Jack picked up the model. He twirled it as he looked at Booger.

"How did you do the nose swap around like that, and how could you get it to roll so fast?"

"I used the flaps."

Jack frowned. "What do you mean?"

"Skipper, we Tomcat guys are taught about the flaps for landing because of the added lift. Plus, putting the flaps down gives us the use of all four spoilers on each wing."

"Right, to give us a better roll rate in the landing configuration."

"It doesn't have to be in the landing configuration."

"But NATOPS doesn't allow the use of flaps in dogfighting."

"That's not exactly true," said Booger. "NATOPS contains a warning against firing missiles with the flaps down because you might burn a hole in them. It doesn't say anything about not using them."

"But, since we don't teach the use of flaps, doesn't that imply we shouldn't use them?"

"Not to me," said Booger.

"Hmmm," said Jack. "So do you do the same thing in the F-5 and A-4, you know, use tricks?"

"It's not a trick skipper," said Booger. "It is just using the potential of the airframe within its limits. That's all."

"Hmmm." Jack nodded and pursed his lips. He leaned back in his chair.

"Is that all you wanted skipper?"

The chair squeaked as Jack straightened up. "No." He glanced at Booger, then stood and walked around his desk, sitting on the edge. "I guess I need some help."

"Help?"

"Yes, help." Jack sighed and looked down at the floor for a moment. He didn't like having to admit any weakness.

He looked up at his XO. "Look, Booger, I want to be able to pull my weight here."

"Sir?"

"I want to contribute more. In the air."

"What do you mean?"

"I don't have the background you and the other guys have. I mean, I am not the natural dogfighter you guys are. I am just not. I wish that I was, but I am not." Jack exhaled a long stream of air and slowly shook his head. "I am just not as good at ACM as I wish. I want some help."

"Skipper, you are a MIG killer. You have done this for real, not on some training range. You don't have to wrestle around with the class to contribute."

"I appreciate that," said Jack. "Look, I know most skippers fly against the class. I want to be able to hold up my own. The skipper of TOGUN has a lot of other duties. I get that. But, like you said, I am a MIG killer. That means people expect something out of me. They expect something magic out of me, and I want to be able to give it. You know what I mean?"

"Yes, sir."

"You are the best we have, and you are a senior officer here. Hell, I couldn't have this conversation with anybody but you. I don't have the time to slowly accumulate the skills to, you know, impress the class. Could you take me out, give me some tips? That kind of thing?"

"Yes, sir. But I don't know what you mean by impress. I mean, you are the skipper. You are Phoenix Grant. You impress people by walking into the room and talking about your MIG kills."

Jack smiled and felt his face glow. The word "imposter" buzzed in his mind. "I appreciate that," said Jack. "But, TOPGUN is all about execution, not talk. Sure, I can talk about shooting down MIGs, I can talk about fighting the airplane. But I have a difficult time executing that with the class. Do you understand?"

"Sure, skipper."

"Great," said Jack. "We have flown together, and you have seen me fly, any ideas on what to concentrate on?"

"Well, skipper, if I were you I would limit myself to one plane and give it all my attention."

"Which one do you suggest? I aced the open and closed book NATOPS for the A-4 and F-5. I think I know the numbers cold."

"Sir, I heard your presentation to the class on professional excellence. It was remarkable," said Booger. "I

169

don't think there is any doubt about your ability to hold your own around here."

"Thanks, it is an easy lecture for me."

"It sure seems that way," laughed Booger.

"If you were me, what jet would you concentrate on?"

"Skipper, the F-5 is the best choice by far. It is the easiest to fly, and it patterns the MIG-21 perfectly."

"Right," said Jack. "I do like the automatic slats. It has pretty good power too for a little airplane. It is mostly a 'pull on the pole and keep sight airplane.'"

"Pretty much," said Booger. "Plus the F-5 is so small, and so fast nobody will have sight of you. Tail or head-on, it's invisible."

"But the A-4 is the ultimate dogfighter I hear. I hear you can beat any F-5 driver we have at TOPGUN."

"I have won some engagements with the A-4," said Booger. "But, skipper, as you know, the idea is not to beat the other instructors, it is to teach the students the characteristics of the MIG-17."

"I know that." Jack spat the words out and was surprised at how irritated he sounded. But he was tired of the "we are only here to serve" mantra, especially when mouthed by someone who could beat every pilot he saw. Booger was a millionaire giving to charity and scolding those who did not. Jack checked himself and forced a smile. "Look, I know the mission of TOPGUN, but you

170

have to admit there is always a personal element involved, an ego involved, right?"

"Yes, sir," said Booger. "But I try to restrict mine to being as good of an instructor as I can be, not some guy that beats the shit out of first tour lieutenants."

"Okay, got it, and I agree," lied Jack. He smiled at Booger, but he was fuming inside. He wished he had not started the conversation and hated the fact he needed Booger to help him. But, the point was he did.

"So, how do you fly the A-4? What do you do to make it so magical?"

"The A-4 takes more pilot skill to fly than any other jet I have ever flown skipper. My hands are in constant movement, stick, throttle, trim and flaps, to max perform the jet."

"So it must give you great pride to fly it so well. To fight it so well."

"Yes, I have to admit that it does. More than any other jet, except the F-14."

"Umm," Jack nodded.

Booger picked up an A-4 model and held it in his hands. "The A-4 has aerodynamic slats and can be a big problem if they don't deploy together. As you know, this jet has a roll rate of 720 degrees per second so you can get in trouble quick if they come out staggered. We have lost many A-4s to asymmetric slat extension and subsequent loss of control."

"Really," said Jack. "I didn't know that."

"Yes, sir. Most of that was back in the old days, and now the only folks in the US military that fly them are us and a couple of reserve squadrons. So, you don't hear much about the A-4 anymore."

Booger pointed to the tail of the model. "The elevator is tiny, but the horizontal stabilizer is large for the airframe, and you can move it with pitch trim. So, if you manually trim it, you can get more pitch rate."

"I remember some of that from the training command," said Jack.

"Of course," said Booger. "It's all in the books, but the application of it and the execution of it elevates it to an art form."

"Can you help me learn that art form?"

"I can sure give it a good try, skipper," said Booger. "I can have ops put some sessions together for us, that way you can have it on the calendar."

Jack thought for a second. He didn't want his private tutorials to become public knowledge. He didn't want everyone to know he needed extra help to fly. "I tell you what, Booger; I will just grab you when I see you and see if we can work it that way."

Booger shrugged his shoulders. "Okay, skipper, if that's what you want to do. But remember, I go on leave the first week in August. Then I detach to go to VF-154."

"Roger," said Jack. "Thanks for coming by to see me and, again, great work on that F-15 today."

"Thanks, skipper."

Jack sat at his desk long after Booger left the office, playing the conversation over in his head. He hated the fact he, the commanding officer, had to stoop to his XO to get tutored on how to fly a basic jet. There was no weapons' system or radar or anything exotic in the F-5 or A-4, just a stick and rudder like the old days. There was no RIO looking over his shoulder. So why was he making this such a big deal? Hell, he knew why. He was making it such a big deal because he was the CO of Fighter Pilot Central, and he was an imposter. He knew he was thinking like a kid, and that bothered him, too. He was 41 years old. He should be content letting the 25-year-old lieutenants be the aces of the base and dominate people and win all their engagements. He knew that! But dammit, the problem was he had NEVER done any of that. He had never won an engagement! Ever! And now he was in the position to maybe make up for some of that mediocrity, and he wasn't able to do it. To make it even worse, everybody treated him like he was the ace of the base. At least for now they did, and his greatest fear was that someone would look behind that green curtain and see the Wizard of Oz was no wizard at all. Christ, he was glad he had destroyed that tape.

So, now he was in the awkward situation whereby students would part the crowd in front of him and look at him with wonder, but he would sit in the de-brief like a lump of coal. Guys like Booger would stand in front of the room and lead the show. They would have the baby blue TOPGUN T-shirt in place, airplane wand in each hand and spin the magic. He would sit in silence with nothing to add. Booger and the rest of the Bro's drove the briefs and de-briefs and developed all of the learning points. He sat in silence. Oh, sure, they would say, "Phoenix, anything to add?" Or "Phoenix, does this align with what you saw out there?" The fact is that at a place like TOPGUN, you had to be more than one of the crowd. You had to be the guy that excelled in one versus one maneuvering because that, right or wrong, was the coin of the realm. He might be the skipper of TOPGUN, but he was not the leader. At least not in his mind. It bothered him so severely he sought out some past TOPGUN skippers and asked them how they "rationalized not being the King Kong fighter pilot in the command. Of course, both of them replied, "Well, I WAS the King Kong, fighter pilot."

But after some joking, both said the same things. That as the skipper, you are the coach and should not worry about competing with the players. They noted TOPGUN skippers were judged by how well the school executed its mission and the integrity of the training process. They also warned that schools like TOPGUN were always under budget scrutiny because, despite the success in Vietnam, it was difficult to prove the current value of the school. It cost a lot of money to run TOPGUN, and there were plenty of folks that wanted that money for other purposes, functional purposes. It was the skipper of TOPGUN's job to ensure that the benefits of the school were understood and that the funding remained in place.

The conversations with the former skippers always made Jack feel much better, at least until the next flight. Then he felt himself on the outside again.

CHAPTER THIRTEEN

Grace poured fresh water into Harley's bowl and tousled the little dog's head as he drank. She stood and looked out the window into the canyon. Mesquite, weeds, and scraggly shrubs choked it; typical of San Diego. The sight made her long for trees; real trees---and the color green!

She found herself smiling, and that made her happy. She had slowly gotten better over the past months. The panic was still there, but she was able to manage it, and the key to her success was her better understanding of the disease. Frustrated with the navy doctors, she had researched panic disorder on her own, and she bought several books and tape recordings on the subject. It made her feel more assured to know that others; many, many others suffered from the same thing. She wasn't alone!

Grace turned from the window to the bedroom. Time to get dressed and ready for church. It was Sunday, and she wished Jack would go with her. But, he was playing golf, as usual. The phone rang as she crossed the room.

"Grace, its mom."

"Hi, mom!" Grace smiled at the sound of her mother's voice. She missed her, and she missed dad.

"Honey, I have bad news."

The admiral, Grace's dad, was dead. He had gone to bed early that evening not feeling well, and when Grace's mother awoke to check on him, she found him lying next to her, but not breathing.

"I'm coming right away," said Grace.

Grace's mother was a strong woman, but she needed help, so Grace packed a bag and scheduled her flight. When Jack came home, she told him to follow her and to put Harley in the kennel.

Grace turned her face to the window and thought of her dad and cried throughout the flights to Norfolk. But, by the time she landed, her red eyes were dry and her sniffles wadded away in a Kleenex. Grace resolved to be strong for her mom and the family. She met her mom at the airport and hugged her and cried with her. Then she went about the business of planning a memorial and a funeral. The memorial service would be at the Oceana Chapel on Friday, and the burial would be on Saturday.

That afternoon, Jack called Booger.

"But, I can't go to Tailhook," said Booger. "I am on leave. Bunny and I are flying to Texas on Sunday morning."

"Booger, I need a representative of TOPGUN sitting at the head table to take my place. I am, you know, featured. But, shit, Grace's dad died, and we have to be on the east coast for his funeral."

"Are you kidding me? Nobody cares who sits at the head table for that thing. Everybody, there is either drunk or hungover or both."

"I don't want some lieutenant representing me. I want you to do it." Jack was getting pissed. He was receiving the very public honor he had always wanted, and if it weren't for that old bastard, the admiral, dying he would be receiving it. The guy never did him any favors

176

anyway. Marrying Grace didn't do him a bit of good. He had earned everything on his own.

On my own!

"I need someone with my stature to be there, and you are the only person who can do that."

"Skipper, I am sorry. I am. And I am sorry for your loss, but I am on leave and will be flying to Texas."

"XO, I am ordering you to be in Las Vegas, at the Tailhook banquet, for the Saturday night dinner. Do you hear me? I am ordering you." Jack gripped the phone harder. He felt his face flush.

What the fuck was Booger's problem?

The line was quiet, and Jack thought he had lost the connection.

"XO, are you there?"

"Let me get this straight," said Booger. "I am on terminal leave from TOPGUN until 0730 on Sunday morning, and you are going to order me to a fucking dinner the night before I detach. Is that what I am hearing? So that you can have a PROPER representative for something no one gives a shit about? That is fucking bullshit!"

"I expect you to be there, and I am writing the order on my letterhead. Be there, XO!" Jack slammed the phone down and gritted his teeth. Goddamnit XO!

Fucking prima donna!

He ripped open his closet door and started dressing for work. It was Monday, and that meant a fresh set of khaki's so he quickly pinned silver oak leaves on the collars, gold wings over the left pocket and his command star and name tag over the right. Shoes shined the night before sat by the chair, and he slipped them on, wiping the toes on the back of his pants. Grace was gone, so that made him happy. At least he wouldn't have to put up with her this morning, thank God. All her red eyes and sniffling.

Christ!

Jack skipped breakfast as usual and drove the fifteen minutes from Tierra Santa to Miramar, entering his office at 0700. At 0730 Slim, Luke and Jethro knocked on the door.

"What is it?" Jack had just finished writing the order for Booger to attend the banquet and was still pissed. Every time he read it, he got more pissed.

Prima fucking Donna. Mother fucking prima donna.

"Sir." The three pilots stood outside the door. Jethro was looking in.

"Come in, come on in." Jack felt his anger drain away.

"Sir, we're sorry for your loss and all, but you are still going to be at 'Hook' with us aren't you?"

"Not anymore." Jack motioned for the three to sit down, and they scooted the chairs until they were facing him. "I am flying to Norfolk on Wednesday to be with Grace's family. I'll be back Sunday night."

"Well, with the XO on leave, who's in charge?" Jethro frowned and looked at Jack.

"Well, Jethro, you are a lieutenant commander. You are in charge."

"I am?" Jethro looked at the other two, then back at Jack. He grinned widely.

"You are. However, the XO is attending the banquet Saturday night. Not sure how much more of Hook he will attend, but he will be at the banquet."

"Yes, sir," said Jethro.

"Is that all? I have a mountain of work to do before I leave."

"Sir, can we address the booze we are serving?"

"Sure, what's the problem?"

"We have always had the tradition of serving Kamikaze cocktails. It is, you know, a takeoff of the rising sun; Japan, victory in the Pacific, that kind of thing."

"Well, that doesn't make a lot of sense but, okay. What's the problem?"

"The XO told us we couldn't do it this year?"

"Why did he do that?"

"He thinks it is beneath us. That it is not the intent of Hook to do that."

"Well, that doesn't make any sense either. Fuck, is everybody fucking crazy this morning?" Jack shook his

179

head and leaned back in his chair. "Look, I don't care what we serve. Just be sure not to run out of anything. I don't want to look like a bunch of misers."

"Yes sir," said Jethro, his grin spreading across his face. "Yes, sir." The three pilots jumped up, put the chairs back in order, and left the room.

Jack sat for a while, fuming about Booger, then walked over to the ready room to see how the morning flights were going.

"What's up, Skip?" Jack stuck his head in the ready room door. Skip McCoy was the duty officer.

"Not much, Skipper. Well, I do have this one problem. Spike called in sick, and we don't have anyone for a one versus one with old Trim and Bully here." Skip motioned to two young officers standing by the desk in their flight suits.

Jack remembered the two from the class introductions. They were part of an east coast detachment from Virginia Beach. "Hey guys," he said.

The two men grinned and nodded.

"Say, skipper, are you cleared for one versus one? I can't remember where you are in the qualification matrix."

Jack felt his face grow red as the others looked at him. Their faces said;

WTF, he is Phoenix Grant. He's the skipper. He is qualified to do anything he wants!

"Sure, I can take the hop," he said.

Jack changed into his flight suit and met Trim and Bully in a briefing room. They were flying the old model F-14, and Jack felt a bit of pity for them. Their Tomcat was equipped with the Pratt and Whitney turbofans, not the new GE monsters he had had in his squadron. He just hoped they didn't compressor stall them and get into a spin. Jack led them through the brief and felt good about how smoothly it went. It was precise, thorough, offered clear understandings of game plans and learning objectives. He was in the para loft putting on his gear when Booger walked in.

"Skipper, the duty officer says you are taking out Trim on his first 1V1."

"That's right; I thought you were on leave." Jack was instantly pissed.

"Had to come back and get my new order. The one that directs me to attend Tailhook. I can use it to get a refund on my plane ticket if I don't make it back to San Diego in time to take off Sunday morning."

Jack glared at him for a moment, then bent to zip his G suit.

"Look, skipper, you know we have a training progression for this, and we haven't gotten you through it yet. I can take the hop with Trim and Bully."

"XO, I think I can handle a fucking 1V1, okay?"

Jack stood and glared at Booger. He was beginning to resent every nice thing he had ever said to him.

Booger looked at him, then sighed. "Okay, skipper." He turned and walked out of the room. Jack picked up his

181

helmet and headed for his jet; and an hour later, his F-5 and Trim's F-14 were on the TACTS range.

After checking the pods, Jack and Trim separated for some forty-mile setups to give Bully some overland radar work. Then, the F-5 and F-14 squared off at 20,000 feet, a mile and half abeam and 400 knots. Jack called "Fight's on" and both aircraft turned toward each other.

Jack pulled hard toward the F-14. His game plan was to pass left to left then execute a level, hard turn into the Tomcat. It was a straightforward move, and something a standard MIG pilot would be expected to do. Jack planned to reverse then and go high into the sun. Trim would most likely lose sight, and Jack could shoot him. Jack grinned as he pulled toward Trim, but as his nose straightened, he saw the F-14 drifting higher and higher. It confused him, and as the Tomcat passed, it pulled inverted and nosed down. Jack realized too late that by allowing the F-14 to drift high, he was giving Trim turning room to get angles on him. Jack turned left as planned, but instead of turning level, he let his nose drop to keep sight. Jack then realized that by going nose low, he was in effect flying out in front of Trim's airplane. His nose-low left turn carved a pathetic arc out in front of the Tomcat!

This is how Booger beat the Eagle! Christ, all I had to do was go nose high at the pass, and he would have lost sight of me! I could have rolled in and shot him at will!

"Fox 2."

Jack heard Trim's call over the radio and pulled as hard as he could into "the missile" hoping to cause an overshoot.

182

God but he didn't want to get shot in the first twenty seconds of the engagement!

The stick shook violently, and Jack quickly released some pressure. He felt a wave of relief when he didn't hear an "F-5 is dead" call from the operator. He accelerated twenty knots and pulled hard again.

Holy shit! The Tomcat was HUGE! It was all over him.

He pulled harder, but the stick shook again. He had to release to keep from departing the airplane.

Christ, I can't spin this fucking thing in front of the world!

"Tracking."

Christ, he is gunning me!

Jack pulled back on the stick again, but the shaking caused him to release the pressure immediately.

"Tracking."

"The F-5 is dead." The TACTS range operator's voice boomed into Jack's ears.

Fuck! Fuck!

"Knock it off," Jack said. He led the two aircraft back to the center of the range and the starting altitude.

Jack was in a daze. Everything had happened so fast, and so wrong.

Fuck, Trim had gunned him!

He slowed his breathing and tried to figure out what had happened.

I didn't expect him to drift up on me. I must have given him too much lateral displacement at the pass.

Jack directed the two planes to another side-by-side start, and this time, he planned to turn away from Trim after the pass and create a two-circle fight. That is precisely what he did, but when he came out of the two-circle turn, Trim promptly shot him in the face with a radar-guided Sparrow!

"F-5, you're dead," was his reward.

Christ, he should have known that would happen! A two-circle turn gives the F-14 the advantage of his radar.

On the third engagement, Jack decided to keep his speed down and lure Trim into a slow speed fight whereby he could use the superior maneuverability of the F-5. He passed the Tomcat at 325 knots and turned hard into it. The Tomcat turned hard too and brought his nose up, a move that Jack matched. In seconds Jack's airspeed was slipping through 140 knots.

Fuck, how is he beating me? Did Booger teach him to use flaps too?

Before he knew what had happened, Trim gunned him again!

At TOPGUN, the issue from a professional perspective is not winning or losing but teaching the student how to exploit his airplane against a replication of a MIG aircraft. That said, a TOPGUN instructor absolutely cannot allow a student to manhandle him. It's okay to be

184

shot by a student, but not continuously drilled for being stupid. Jack and Trim's debrief was an embarrassment of immense proportions as the TACTS tapes showed an F-5 that was out flown. Phoenix Grant, the hero of Saudi Arabia and killer of MIGs, had been taken to school by a kid on his first cruise.

The next day, Tuesday, the Washington Post picture of Jack, Grace, and Harley mysteriously appeared all over TOPGUN spaces with the hand-scrawled banner, "There's a new sheriff in town, and his name is Poodle man."

Jack saw the posters when he came to work and was smart enough to ignore them. He knew the culture of naval aviation and that junior officers would viciously needle anyone with a thin skin. But he fumed in his office and stayed there most of the morning, brooding. In the back of his mind, he had worried about this very thing happening: that he would get exposed for the weak pilot he was. There, in the shadows of his mind, was the ghost of concern. It had been lurking since the bureau first told him he was going to TOPGUN as the skipper. He had worried about it, but he had pushed the thoughts away.

Hey, he was Phoenix Grant!

And now, here it was. The ghost was a reality. Jack had to find some way to get the advantage and fast. If he didn't continue to fly one versus one hops with the classes, he would be labeled as a pussy, or worse. He would wear the blanket of shame, disgust, and pity. He was grateful he had the excuse of the funeral to get out of the office for the rest of the week.

***

185

On Saturday afternoon, Booger drove the six hours from San Diego to Las Vegas in record time, arriving at the Hilton at seven o'clock in the evening. His shirt was damp under the suit, and the short walk from the car to the hotel entrance sent sweat trickling down his back. He groaned with relief as he pulled the door open and felt the blast of cold air. He had always heard air conditioning and gambling were the two things that made Las Vegas possible and smiled at the truth of at least half of that story. He quickly found the elevator bank and glanced at his watch as he hit the "up" button. He had fifteen minutes to find his place at the head table.

The door opened, and he walked in and there, huddled in the floor, was a young man in shorts, and flip-flops. He was passed out, and a gooey patch of vomit covered his chest. Booger gently touched his head to see if he was breathing. The young man started at his touch and turned to face Booger then collapsed again. He was wearing a kamikaze headband.

Booger shook his head and waited for the elevator to reach the ballroom floor. When the door opened, he quickly moved across the darkened room toward the head table. He saw a knot of men surrounding Secretary Garrett and CNO Kelso and other groups standing in animated, hand waving alcoholic joy. He took his seat.

Booger stood and nodded when he was introduced as a representative of Phoenix Grant and TOPGUN, and the crowd applauded loudly. He then sat and ate the shoe leather roast beef and the tasteless mound of institutional mashed potatoes and green beans. Since he was seated at the end of the table, he did not partake of the rarified air surrounding the center. He was mostly forgotten. Just before dessert was served and before the guest speaker's

186

remarks, he slipped away and back to his car. He got back home at 3:30 a.m. His total time at the Tailhook convention had been forty-seven minutes.

***

Jack flew to Norfolk, and as the nation passed below him, he thought of the mistake he had made marrying into the Sheehan family. He had duped himself into thinking that marrying an admiral's daughter would accelerate his career. Jack had tried to impress the old bastard in the beginning, in hopes he could get a ticket to the top. Shortly after marrying Grace, when he was up for lieutenant, he had asked the old man to write him a letter of recommendation. He thought such a letter would get him selected a year early. In what turned out to be an awkward and embarrassing Thanksgiving, Grace's dad had flatly rejected the idea as "being against everything he stood for." Jack did get promoted to lieutenant commander, but he was pissed that he wasn't promoted early. He was pissed the old man had not helped him.

Jack arrived in the Sheehan home to the awkwardness of estrangement. His weak relationship with the admiral denigrated to no relationship at all, and Jack had not spoken to him or Grace's mother for years. Now, at the reception, he kept to himself and avoided the weepy eyes and hushed tones of fond remembrance. He allowed himself to the buffet and a room temperature Budweiser, but he didn't have anything to say to any of them.

Besides, he was still seething about having to miss his big moment at Tailhook. The truth was, it was Grace's threat to leave him that made him go to Norfolk. He had come home from a great golf game to find her note. He had called her with the excuse he had to take care of TOPGUN business, but she had flatly told him to get his ass on a plane.

"If you don't come to my dad's funeral I will leave you, Jack. Christ, can't you show some decency? Can't you do this for me?"

"But, I have TOPGUN to run."

"Bullshit! Put Harley in the kennel and get out here."

He had winced at the sound of the phone slamming down. But, he had picked it up and called the airlines. And, now he was here. He wished the old, panic-weak Grace was back.

He didn't care if she left; her and her dog. However, he was worried about how it would look. Family issues were frowned upon by navy leadership, and negativity was not allowed for someone on his way to being an admiral.

Admiral!

The thought of it was growing in Jack's mind. It was the MIG shoot down that opened the gate, and it was the treatment that he had received that perpetuated the notion of a star or stars on his collar. While Grace was sitting at her father's open casket, Jack went to the exchange on the base and bought a pair of silver, one-star devices. He secreted them away in his pocket to try on later. To see how they would look.

On Sunday, Jack flew back home alone as Grace decided to stay with her family. Grace insisted that Jack send Harley to Norfolk, to be with her. Jack said he would, but decided against it. Who knows, he might need Harley's leverage in the future.

Besides, it was a hassle to send him, and he didn't want to pay for it anyway. And also, fuck the Sheehans!

He stopped by the kennel to get Harley, and the joy in which the little dog greeted him pissed him off.

Why was he so fucking happy? Fucking dog.

The first thing he did after walking in the door was to put his khaki uniform together for the next day. He liked the way his ribbons looked on the light brown material with the dark blue Navy Cross, the red, white and blue Silver Star and the red and blue Bronze Star on the top row. His golden pilot's wings glowed above the ribbons, and when he put the stars on the collar, he stood back to get a good look. Jack, liked what he saw, and knew then he would do anything to make what he saw happen.

CHAPTER FOURTEEN

When Jack went to work on Monday, he was relieved to see the Poodle Man photos were all gone. He knew his performance would be the subject of most conversations for a long time to come, but he would have to shoulder the ridicule somehow. He made himself walk into the ready room and was pleasantly surprised to see that all of the talk was about how awesome and wild Hook had been. Jack listened to the banter for a while, grateful for its occupation of the JO minds. However, he tired of stories that did not include him and ambled down the passageway to his office. As he walked by a briefing room, he saw a model of an A-4 that someone had neglected to hang back on its hook. Jack walked into the room and picked it up. He rolled it in his hands for a few moments, then hurried to his office and called the duty officer.

"Have Jethro drop by my office."

"Yes, skipper."

He waited only a few moments before Jethro stuck his head through the doorway.

"Talk to me about the A-4 Jethro. I want to fly it regularly."

Jack and Jethro discussed the airplane and its place in the syllabus for over an hour, then Jack asked about the secrets to fighting it well.

"Sir, the first thing you have to do is get your slat check out of the way. If they don't program together, you

190

can't fight." Jethro held the A-4 model and pointed to the leading edge of the wings.

"Understand," said Jack. "Go on."

"I do my slat checks at 325 knots and then again at 250 knots by rolling 70-80 degrees and pulling until I feel a tiny bit of buffet. Then I pop the stick and hope that both slats extend together. Now, skipper, you mustn't have any pressure on the rudder pedals during the check."

"Why?" Jack frowned and looked at Jethro.

"Sir, if you have pressure on the rudder pedal, say the left rudder, odds are the left slat will extend before the right one and the jet will snap to the right. I mean it will snap like a whip on you."

"What do you do? How do you get out of it?"

"Well, you push forward and unload the jet. I know if you are rolling nose down toward the earth, the tendency would be to pull back but you cannot do that. You have to push forward until the slat clears and retracts, that will stop the rolling moment, and you can then smoothly pull up and recover."

"Okay, let's say the slats don't come out together, what do you do?"

"You use a little rudder trim. Let's say the left slat is coming out a little before the right. Trim the rudder a couple of degrees right and then try it again. It may take a bit to get it right in some of the jets, but you have to do it correctly. Once you trim her up, pull and have fun!"

"So, if all of that works. How do you perform this thing?"

"Well, skipper, I'm nowhere as good as the XO is at this, but he is the one that taught me so here goes. When you are flying the scooter, everybody seems to be arcing around over the top of you. They are all going fast, and you are buzzing around like a fly, waiting for one of them to get close."

Jack laughed and nodded.

"So, one of them flies by and you start heading up with him. Our A-4's are pretty close to a one-to-one thrust-to-weight ratio so we can climb with near anybody."

Jack smiled again.

"As I start chasing them uphill and the speed gets to 350 or so, I smoothly start running the horizontal trim aft as the jet begins to buffet slightly. I then pull a bit quicker to pop the slats out and begin to lower the flaps about one-third. From there I can instantaneously turn the jet and glom on to anybody up there with me. They can't get away."

"What do you do if they try to run?"

"Well, I start retracting the flaps and run the trim forward. I reduce back pressure on the stick to lower the angle of attack and increase airspeed. The slats will retract then, or if you slow down, you can bump them out again. You can follow them around gunning them all day if you want." Jethro grinned and put the model on the desk.

"Fantastic, Jethro!" Jack leaped up and clapped Jethro on the shoulder. "Fantastic."

On Wednesday night, Jack went to the Miramar Officer's Club for the weekly body exchange. Miramar was notorious for its Wednesday nights, and aviators would book rooms in the Bachelor's Officers' Quarters across the street in case they got lucky or were too drunk to find their way home. USMC aviators would come in from El Toro and Yuma, and the place would light off around 2100, or nine in the evening for the ladies.

It all started at happy hour in the WOXOF room, named for the meteorology acronym that means weather obscured and zero visibility with fog. Dancers took the stage around five, and they would soon be encouraged to take off their tops. With the breasts bouncing and booze flowing, it was a wild and beautiful time.

Someone would wind up on the stage with a girl sitting on his face, and the rodeo would begin!

Jack arrived around 2030, and revelers greeted him with the usual round of back claps and hearty hellos! He was a regular on Wednesday and a favorite of the crowd. A MIG killer and TOPGUN skipper was someone everybody wanted for their friend.

Misha showed up at 2200, and Jack nodded for her to meet him in the back bar. He had met Misha a month ago, and she was very interested in the Top Gun as she called him. They had made out in Jack's car a couple of times, and he had gotten her bra off, but they had not yet "made love" as Misha called it. In Jack's mind, he had not fucked her yet. He detested the words "made love," and in fact, he hated the phrase "I love you." He thought it was the most overused set of words in the English language. The words didn't mean anything, and people said them because they wanted the power the words gave them. A man didn't kiss a girl and reach for her tits and say, "What's your

193

sign?" He said, "I love you," so he could grab the tits some more. That is the way it worked. The first time he said "I love you" was to Debbie Bates when they were sixteen and freshmen at Grover Cleveland High School. Debbie was the only person in the freshmen class that ranked lower on the "cool person" totem pole than Jack did, and that is how he got her into his dad's car. Despite his developing good looks, he was a social zero. However, to Debbie, Jack was somebody because he had a driver's license. Since he got straight A's and that was all his dad, and mom cared about, he got the keys to their vast Nash Ambassador with fold-down seats.

Jack had found his dad's stash of Playboy and Hustler magazines, hidden behind the folders in his office. He had read some of the articles, so he knew what to do. Just after getting Debbie's bra and panties off, Jack had said "I love you" into her big eyes just before he stuck it in. He still remembered the short tryst and the delightful feeling at the end. After that, he had pulled his pants up and taken her home. He never talked to her again. Jack used the "I love you" phrase a few times in college, but usually, he didn't have to because the girls he was mounting were too drunk to hear him. He said "I love you" to Grace at the beginning of their relationship, but after a while, it took too much effort to say the words and mean them. He responded with "I love you, too," which in his mind was even triter than "I love you." However, he had to say something, so he did.

"Hey, I got an idea," said Jack. Misha was standing next to him in the darkly lit passageway behind the WOXOF room.

"What's that?" She looked up at him with her full lips, and he felt an urge in his groin.

"Let's go to my place?"

194

"I thought you didn't want to ever go there out of respect for your dead wife. I love that about you." Misha pressed against Jack and touched his face. He glanced around to ensure no one was watching. He had told Misha his wife was dead because he didn't want her to get suspicious and think he was a two-timing prick.

"I know, but something happened when I saw you walk in. I am ready to move on. It's been three years."

"But, Jack, are you sure?" Misha pressed harder against him; her face was against his chest.

Jack touched her face and tilted it towards his, "I love you," he said.

"Okay," she smiled. "Let's go."

"Just remember," said Jack. "I left the house the way it was when she died, so don't be put off by pictures or her things that you might see."

"Okay, Jack, I understand."

Twenty minutes later, Jack pulled into his driveway with Misha behind him in her car. He could hear Harley barking up a storm like he always did when he heard something outside. Harley was still barking when Jack escorted Misha inside, so he opened the back screen door and threw him out.

Jack poured two large scotches and turned on the stereo. He sat on the couch and motioned for Misha to join him, and when she did, he quickly unbuttoned her blouse. He kissed her, then took off her bra. "I love you," he said as he led her upstairs.

Jack pulled Misha down on the bed with him and quickly had her dress and panties off. She was hungry for him and practically ripped off his uniform.

That's when he heard fierce barking from the back yard.

Harley!

Shit!

Shit! Fucking coyotes!

Jack jerked on his pants and ran downstairs. He quickly crossed the living room, switched on the patio lights, and ripped open the door.

Harley was at the edge of the patio, just inside the light. The little dog leaned forward as he barked, aggressive, and wide-legged. His hair was up, and his ears were full and alert. Two coyotes were staring at him from about ten feet away.

Jack turned and ran back inside. Misha appeared at his shoulder, and they looked out the door glass. Little Harley was holding his ground against the two, larger animals.

"Jack?" Misha looked at him and frowned. Jack shook his head and opened the door. *Damned hero dog.*

He walked out and took a few steps forward. "GET OUT OF HERE," he screamed! "GET!"

Harley glanced at him and turned back to the coyotes. He growled and barked louder. He took a step forward!

Jack took another couple of steps. "GET OUT OF HERE!"

The coyotes looked at Jack, then at Harley. They turned and in an instant were over the fence and gone.

Jack turned back to the house. Misha stood in the open doorway, wearing Jack's uniform shirt.

"What's going on out there?"

Jack looked in the direction of the voice and saw Mrs. Meacham, his neighbor, peering out of her back door. It, like Jack's house, backed up to the ravine.

Jack didn't know what to do. He glanced at Mrs. Meacham.

Then he looked at Misha. "Go inside."

He turned to Mrs. Meacham and walked to her to block her view of the house. "Go inside," he called over his shoulder to Misha.

Harley gave a final bark, wagged his tail, and ran to Jack. He stood on his hind legs and looked at him as if to say, "We chased 'em away, Dad!"

Mrs. Meacham looked around Jack's shoulder, then up into his eyes.

"Who is she?"

"Just a friend," said Jack.

Mrs. Meacham frowned and shook her head. "What's she doing wearing your clothes?"

Jack looked over his shoulder at the open door, then back at Mrs. Meacham.

"She spilled something on her dress."

"Uh-hum," grunted Mrs. Meacham. "Where is Grace?"

"She is visiting her mother. She is still visiting her mother."

Mrs. Meacham looked at him and frowned again. She shook her head, turned, and walked back into her house.

Jack tried to get Misha to go back to bed with him, but she was too disturbed by what she had heard and seen. All she wanted to do was pet Harley and tell him how brave he was. She hugged him and kissed him until she finally left. Throughout it all, Jack was sure Harley was smirking at him.

The next afternoon, Jack put himself on the schedule to fly the A-4 in a two versus two fight against the class. Jack's A-4 represented the MIG 17 and Jethro's F-5 the MIG 21. They would fly against a section of two Tomcats and in one plane the crew was none other than Trim and Bully.

Instead of flying to Yuma and the TACTS range, they were scheduled to fly this hop over the Pacific in the W-291 military training area. The idea was for the two Tomcats to find the two adversaries with their radars, understand the formation of the bandits, then attack using superior weapons, radar, training, and flight discipline.

Jack hummed as he manned up his jet. He was looking forward to flying the little bird and doing some good, old ass-kicking. However, the engine started up fine, but he could not get the generator to stay online. He reset it a couple of times, but it just wouldn't hold.

"Fuck, fuck, shit, fuck!" Jack was pissed! He was going to miss a perfect opportunity to pay Trim and Bully back.

"Skipper." Jack heard the duty officer on the radio. "Go."

"Sir, the two-seater is coming back into the line. Their students' airplane went down for a hydraulic problem. Why don't you jump into it?"

Jack grinned. "Great idea. Does it have gas?"

"Yes, sir. I'll have you hot switch with the pilot and leave Jocko in the back seat. You can brief him up."

"Jocko?"

"Yes, sir. Jocko is in the back."

Jack felt an immediate feeling of unease. He had not spoken with Jocko since the paraloft incident back during the cruise. He had intentionally avoided him since coming to TOPGUN. It was just too awkward to be around him. But, what the heck, it was just a hop.

"Sure, have somebody run the book out for me to sign."

"Yes, sir!"

The plane captain ran the logbook out to him, but he just glanced at it and signed the release. As he was climbing the ladder to the cockpit, he saw the Tomcats take the runway. He saw Jethro waiting for him at the hold short. Jack jumped into the cockpit and buckled into his ejection seat.

"How are you doing back there?"

"Fine, skipper. I got a brief over the radio from the duty officer. I'm ready when you are."

"Great," said Jack. He keyed the mic, "Jethro, since we are running out of range time, go ahead and take off. Be there as soon as we can."

"Roger, see you at the north end of Papa One."

As Jack finished getting strapped in, he watched the Tomcats take off, followed by Jethro. Ten minutes later, Jack and Jocko took the active and got airborne. Jack raced toward the operating area, and Jocko checked them through the controllers. While they flew, they listened to Jethro fighting the two Tomcats.

Jack couldn't wait to get to the range. He decided to blow off the slat check. He didn't want the Tomcats to run out of gas before he got there. He caught sight of Jethro in orbit at the north end of the range and pressed to close.

"Skipper, unless you plan on staying real fast, we need to do the slat check. This bird has a history of sticking slats."

Jack gritted his teeth and looked in his mirror at Jocko.

Fucking Jocko!

"We'll stay fast. Just want to present a good target to the class," said Jack. He joined Jethro and flew tight on his wing until he heard the AIC controller call twenty miles of separation. He pulled the throttles back and dropped behind Jethro, descending to 7,000 feet. MIG pilots use trail sections just like the one Jack and Jethro had encountered over Saudi Arabia. This tactic was what they were now simulating. Jack kept sight of Jethro as the two Tomcats engaged the F-5 above him. They failed to detect Jack, and when he heard the call, "Trim is nose high to the east," he pointed his nose to the eastern Tomcat and headed uphill.

He was so glad he was on this hop!

Time to get even, Trim!

That is why they call it a wet booger!

Jack grinned as he closed within a quarter-mile of Trim who was in a nose-high arc, looping over Jethro and the other F-14.

Jack pulled up inside of him, and seeing 350 knots, started running the trim as Jethro said. He felt the stick buzz just a bit and popped it back to get the slats out. In an instant, his head whacked off the right side of the cockpit.

Jack pulled the throttles to idle and stared at his instruments.

18,000 feet, 170 knots! What the fuck?

He could scarcely see he was rolling so fast.

201

I don't get it. 170 is flying speed. Damnit. Pull it out of the dive!

"Skipper, push the stick forward! Push the stick forward!" Jocko screamed into the headset.

He heard Jocko scream from the back seat!

"Push the stick forward skipper! Push it forward!"

The airplane seemed to roll even faster. The nose was not coming up.

15,000 feet! Damnit! Thumb in the trim. Thumb in the trim! Jack thumbed the trim button in and raised the flap handle. *Fuck the flaps are up. I never put them down!*

"13,000 feet!" Screamed Jocko. "Push the stick forward skipper!"

Jack stomped on the left rudder. No help!

11,000 feet!

He pulled back hard on the stick. He had to stop the downward movement. The airplane continued to spin; it seemed to turn even faster!

10,000 feet!

"Skipper, you are passing ten grand, eject!" screamed Jethro.

He pulled even harder. Why isn't this son of a bitch pulling up? Why is it spinning? Goddamnit!

"9,000 feet, skipper, eject!"

Jack started to blackout. He saw 8,000 feet on the altimeter and pulled the ejection handle.

A violent shock of air hit Jack. He felt himself flying and tumbling---all ass over tea kettle. Then, the chute popped, and he was floating toward the sea. He looked at his risers and was relieved they were all good! He looked around for Jocko but didn't see him or his chute. Jack strained and struggled to look over his shoulder, but the canopy was hard to move.

He hit the water.

Jack bobbed to the surface and clamored into his raft. His hands shook as he dug his PRC 90 from his survival vest and called for help. He looked for Jocko but did not see him. Jocko did not answer or respond to the guard calls either. Jack crawled into his raft and waited for nearly two hours before the rescue helo from North Island Naval Air Station picked him up. He was cold and bruised but otherwise all right. However, there was no Jocko.

As he lay in the helo and flew back to the base, Jack had plenty of time to think and get his story straight. He knew he should have performed the slats check; flying combat maneuvers without doing it was a clear violation. Jocko would surely rat him out, unless he could get to him first, to get the story straight. That's all it would take. Unlike the TACTS range, the water underneath the operating area was not instrumented. He would tell the mishap board that he had performed the slats check on his way to meet up with Jethro. He did it twice, at 325 and 250, and both times they had deployed together. It wasn't his fault that during the maneuver, one of them had stuck. He figured it was his left one since he had spun right. He would tell them that he performed the recovery procedures, but they did not get him out of the spin. Jack was able to recall what he had done as his head cleared, and as the adrenalin levels lowered. He realized that he had never pushed the stick forward to unload the aircraft and get his slats to come back up.

He remembered hearing Jocko screaming at him to push the stick forward. Christ, it was just like for the MIG kills; Jocko telling him what to do. But, would Jocko back his story again? It was a lot to ask.

As he started to get off the helo, a crewman leaned to him. "You were in a two-seater, correct? Just want to make sure. We haven't seen any other chute or flare or anything."

Jack swallowed and looked at the man. "It was a two-seater. He's out there somewhere."

The navy and coast guard looked for Jocko the rest of the night. Early in the morning, they found his body. He had snapped his neck during the ejection. His automatic inflation system had kept him afloat, and his parachute had released on seawater contact.

TOPGUN was ordered to conduct a mishap investigation, and an officer senior to Jack had to be the president of the board. An old Captain with a lot of A-4 time convened the mishap board, and he wrapped it up in a week. The board was very concerned about how one crew member survived the ejection, and the other didn't and concentrated on the technical points of resolving that issue. To Jack's relief, the board did not focus on his actions as a pilot. The senior member was deferential, and Jack knew it was due to his notoriety. The board did question how Jack performed the slats check since the controller tapes showed him flying directly from the Seawolf departure point to the maneuvering area. Jack resolved the issue with his statement that he wanted to burn down fuel before he did the checks and did not do them until he was in the area and off the radar. Jack's reply was so quick and direct that the board moved to their second question: Why didn't Jack read the logbook of the mishap aircraft more closely? The plane captain had mentioned he only glanced at it. The logbook contained numerous and clear entries about a sticking left slat that had to be trimmed out for fighting. However, since Jack had discussed the airplane with Jocko while flying to the area, and had performed two slat checks before joining Jethro, that question became irrelevant. The mishap investigation found that Jack had acted correctly and that the mishap itself was due to material failure in the old aircraft. They determined the loss of the aircrew was due to an unknown ejection dynamic that would need further analysis.

Although the board cleared him, the incident shook Jack and made him think. The whole tour at TOPGUN, all eight months of it, had been difficult. He had enjoyed the prestige and the way the Navy and city leaders of San Diego County engaged him, but the embarrassment with the F-5 and now the A-4 bothered him much. There were also some rumblings about what had happened at Hook that year. Something had happened involving the abuse of women and a bunch of crap up on the third-floor hallway, near the squadron suites. A couple of admirals were investigating, and Jack didn't want to have that mess to deal with, even if he had not gone himself. Maybe it was time to leave? Besides, Grace had not spoken to him since she had returned home from Norfolk. She was pissed at him for his coldness toward her family.

"You couldn't have been a bigger jerk if you had tried!"

It had gotten so bad that he had moved out and into a room at the Bachelor Officer's Quarters at Miramar. At least, Mrs. Meacham had kept her trap shut about Harley and the coyotes and Misha, but Jack knew it would be best for him to patch things up with Grace eventually. He didn't need any crap from her surfacing and hurting his chances for admiral.

When PERS 43 detailed Jack to TOPGUN, they told him it was only for around a year, and then they had to get him "jointed." New rules for the military demanded that officers serve in joint billets (all service) to select for flag. Jack picked up the phone and dialed the number for PERS 43.

"Captain Wright's office." The voice was that of an older lady, apparently a secretary in the PERS 43 office.

"Captain Wright? Frank Wright?" Jack smiled into the phone. He didn't know that his old boss was now the head aviation detailer.

"Yes sir, that is him," replied the voice, cheerier now since the caller was an acquaintance of her boss.

"This is Jack Grant, the skipper at TOPGUN. Would you tell him I need to talk about my next assignment?"

"Surely. We will call you back if that is okay."

"That would be fantastic," said Jack, and he hung up.

Frank Wright took the message from Delores, his secretary, and frowned as soon as he saw the name. His mind shot back to Jocko Barnes. Jocko and the tape. So now, Jocko was dead.

Frank looked at the note again, mumbled his thanks to Delores, and went to his office. He closed the door and sat in his chair, rubbing the letter in his fingers.

Jack Grant. Christ!

He remembered watching the tape a couple of nights after arriving home from the cruise. His wife had gone to bed, and he was alone in the living room watching the flickering images of the Tomcat HUD and listening to the buffoonery that was Jack Grant. Frank took a deep breath and closed his eyes. The tape had reinforced in his mind an understanding of the depth of his ownership of Jack Grant. By giving Jack the number one ticket, based mostly, if not entirely, on unearned glory, Frank had unleashed Jack onto the navy.

As soon as he had arrived at PERS 43, Frank had checked up on Jack and, of course, confirmed his worst fears. The TOPGUN bros had seen through his celebrity and had carefully scheduled him for an extensive qualification process. The Hook stuff was starting to bubble, and TOPGUN had had a suite right in the middle of that mess. Also, what about his spinning an A-4 and Jocko dying in the ejection? Frank shook his head again and picked up the phone. He called in his team and quickly found a billet opening on the joint staff. Satisfied the timing would work, he called Jack.

"Sir, I didn't know you took over 43."

Frank gripped the phone and forced a smile into the plastic. "Yep, I did a short stint at AIRLANT; then they sent me here."

"That's great news, sir, congratulations!"

"Thanks, Phoenix. I appreciate it. So, Delores tells me you are looking for a change."

"Sir, I think it might be time to get moving. I know the plan was to keep me here for a year, but it has been eight months, and I think I should get the joint qualification."

"Phoenix, we are absolutely on the same page, and I was about to call you!"

"Great minds think the same!"

Frank shook his head. "Yes, they do." He gripped the phone, "My guys have been tracking you, and my placement officer has a great billet for you on the joint staff."

"Really? That would be great," said Jack. "That would be just great."

"Looks like we will assign you to the J-5, the Middle East- Africa Division. Your connection to the Middle East should be a positive."

"Absolutely," said Jack.

"How's Grace?" Frank heard the delay and wasn't surprised. Jack's relationship with Grace was no secret.

"Uhh, she's doing okay. I will tell her you asked."

"Please do," said Frank. "Look. My guys will give you a call later today."

"Roger, thanks, CAG."

Jack hung up the phone and leaned his head back in his chair. He started to call the home number. Grace and Harley were in still in the rental in Tierra Santa. The house where Harley nearly met his end. Jack needed to tell her that they were moving back to the east coast. She could live in their house in Virginia Beach while he did his stint in the Pentagon. He knew he had to patch things up.

One month later, Jack had his change of command ceremony and handed the reigns of TOPGUN over to his successor. The ceremony was well attended, and many civic and naval leaders were in attendance. The navy packed up their belongings, and Grace and Harley went to Virginia Beach. Jack had his clothes and uniforms sent to Washington, D.C., where he rented an apartment. It was perfect! As far as the navy knew, he was happily married. He was on his way to the Middle East/Africa Division of the J-5 Directorate on the Joint Staff in the Pentagon, and he didn't have Grace getting in his way.

CHAPTER FIFTEEN

The office of the chairman of the Joint Chiefs of Staff encompasses the army, navy, air force and marines and divided into eight directorates as well as other specialized staff departments. The J5 Directorate is responsible for strategy and policy, and it is further subdivided into geographical regions. Jack reported to the Middle East/Africa section. His two countries of responsibility were Iraq and Iran. Jack was excited when he heard about the assignment and immediately began to imagine how it would further embellish his career. He could see himself briefing the chairman, General Powell, on the fine points of Iraqi policy. After all, Phoenix Grant was a direct contributor to the victory of Desert Storm. Maybe he would brief the President!

Jack had never been to the Pentagon, and therefore, had no idea how it could take the dreams and imaginations of glory-bound men like him and reduce them to a harsh reality--- that his job was to finish the tasker in front of him, get it passed through the chain, then reach into the inbox and get the next one. That reality came on the first morning that he reported. He had arisen early and dressed in a sharp khaki uniform with wings and ribbons aglow, and his brown, leather flight jacket zipped neatly. An air force tech sergeant escorted him in the building and deposited in front of the desk of Colonel John S. Stoops, U.S. Army. Stoops first words were, "You are out of uniform. Navy wears either whites or blues in the Pentagon. Didn't your people tell you that?"

Jack replied that they had not to which Stoops said he was not surprised. Stoops then proceeded to tell Jack that the navy wasn't much interested in joint work or strategy and policy and that the only reason they sent people to the joint staff was because it was the law. He further opined that the US Army was the service that held the team together and that if he were a hard worker, Stoops would teach him a thing or two. Jack said he appreciated that and Stoops then explained that he was a former tank driver that was now a Foreign Area Officer or FAO.

"FAO is how the army controls the world," Stoops had confided, amid great guffawing.

Jack remembered his first lesson from Stoops, delivered in front of the colonel's desk.

"You absolutely must use the orange colored Form 136 on all materials. Form 136 provides the subject, to whom the document is intended, all signatories along the way, and a tracking number, so we know where it is and when it is to be actioned."

Jack sat, taking notes.

"Then you attach a buff-colored From 5 on top of Form 136. Form 5 is the internal tracking document within the J5 directorate. You will see that I am your first signature, followed by Colonel Toombs, followed by Rear Admiral Butts, followed by Major General Booth, and finally signed off by Lieutenant General Mays."

Jack nodded and took more notes. He was amazed at how structured and detailed the movement of information was in the joint staff.

"Questions so far?"

"No, sir just seems like a lot of signatures."

"That's how we do it here," said Stoops. He took his glasses off and gave Jack a weary, you-are-so-stupid-look. "You see in the navy you may handle communications casually, but here we do not. Here we use rules. Here the only three people that release any message from the joint staff are the director, the vice-chairman, and General Powell himself. That is how we control our message."

"Yes, sir. Just seems like a hard way to do it." Jack shrugged. "If you had better control over your message, maybe you wouldn't have all that tailhook crap to deal with." Stoops leaned back and smiled. His eyes danced with the mischief of a man who had just scored an excellent point.

Jack took a breath and sighed. The tailhook thing was growing by the day. The papers were full of the story, the investigation, the fact DOD was doing an investigation because the navy had messed up theirs so severely. Or, DOD didn't like the navy's result.

"Also, if the document you are forwarding is something that our directorate leader, General Mays, either initiated or has an intense interest in, you must also attack the blue Form 4 to the Form 5 and Form 136."

"Yes, sir."

"Questions?"

"Yes, sir, how do I know what General Mays has an intense interest in?"

Stoops frowned. "I will decide. Don't you worry."

"So, sir, you will tell me to put the Form 4 on Form 5 and 136?"

"Exactly! One more thing," said Stoops. "And this is important. When you staple the forms together, place the staple on the left side, approximately a half-inch from the left margin and a half-inch from the top, use a ruler if you need to, and staple at a forty-five-degree angle. Do not put the staple horizontally to the floor." Stoops held a piece of paper and his stapler to demonstrate to Jack.

"See, forty-five degrees, not horizontal."

Jack exited the office and from that day began the process of getting Colonel Stoops to like him. It was the way he had always approached a new assignment. One reason he had never felt comfortable at TOPGUN was that he was never sure who that person was.

Jack was surprised at how much he appreciated the rules of the Joint Staff. While the use of all the forms seemed tedious to many, he saw the value in each of them. His workday began with a 0630 arrival at his desk where he would turn on his computer and pound out responses to the myriad of questions that came to him about Iraq and Iran. Most were about Iraq, and they ranged from queries of how many pounds of chickpeas the Kurds in northern Iraq consumed every day to writing letters for the chairman in response to citizen questions. One tasker was a napkin with the words, "Saddam, Desert Storm, why is he still there?" written on it. It had come from some man in Kansas, and Jack had to write a *thank you for your interest in national defense* answer. Of course, since it was a letter from the chairman, it required a Form 4 and 5 and 136 routing package plus a trip to the editors.

Jack shared the office with a fellow naval aviator, Commander Bull Morris. Bull was an F-18 Hornet pilot who had been on the staff for over two years. He was a former squadron commander, selected for captain, and steeped in cynicism. He was also pissed because he couldn't get frocked to his new rank. The navy had a tradition of allowing selectees to pin on the new position before the Senate approved the list. However, the joint staff had no such custom, so Bull still wore the silver oak leaves of a commander. Bull was a funny but seriously disgruntled man. He was so irreverent that Jack often found him a distraction and his sense of humor as downright dangerous. At least it was hazardous from a career perspective. For instance, Bull dreamed up a purple Form 3. His Form 3 was to be used to see if the chairman, General Powell, had an intense interest in anything the J5 was interested in. The staffer must place the purple Form 3 in front of the blue Form 4 which was in front of the buff Form 5 which was in front of the orange Form 136. Bull had created Forms 6 through 135 to provide a communication path for every possible circumstance. The weird thing was that his idea, complete with a tab for every proposed form, was staffed to the director of the joint staff before his EA called Stoops and asked him why the J5 was so fucking crazy. Stoops then called Bull in for an ass-kicking, but that turned into a shit fight whereby Bull insisted that Stoops and all FAOs were assholes and that is why they weren't in their original jobs anymore. Stoops screamed at him, threatened a court-martial, and kicked him out of the office. Jack disliked Bull because his shenanigans caused Stoops to hate the navy even more than he already did, and that included Jack. He also disliked Bull because he had bigger balls than Jack.

Jack worried about how to get on Stoops' good side, despite Bull, as he walked to the metro station beneath the Pentagon and boarded the Blue Line train to Foggy Bottom. He exited, and as he walked the ten minutes to C Street and the State Department, he thought of Stoops's parting comment as he left the office.

"You know the best thing about Friday?"

"No, sir, what?"

"Only two more working days until Monday."
Stoops had laughed like a hyena, and Jack had laughed
hugely in support. The problem was it was not a joke. The
culture in the Pentagon was, "you can't make it hard
enough." The execution statement of that culture was "If
you come in at 0630, I can come in at 0600. If you stay to
1900, I can stay until 1930." Work was the only thing that
mattered, and since it was the Pentagon, anything you did
was more important than everything anyone outside of the
Pentagon did. So, you could always stay busy.

Jack arrived at the front gate, walked through the
metal detectors, and signed the log. He was escorted up to
Ms. Cates' office and walked into the familiar room.

Department of State was organized similar to the
joint staff, and it had its divisions and departments with its
subject matter experts. Every Friday, Jack met with Ms.
Cates, Bill Smith, and Sally Fry. Ms. Cates was an SES, or
member of the Senior Executive Service, somewhat
analogous to military general and flag officers. Bill and
Sally were tasker slaves like Jack.

"Team, I have good news today." Ms. Cates beamed
as she looked at the small team. "You are going to northern
Iraq!"

"What?" Jack grinned at Sally and Bill.

"You heard me right. You are going to go in two
weeks. You go in through Turkey so we will need to get
your passports stamped."

"What's the mission?" Jack had always thought covert ops--- like the CIA did---were cool.

"Undersecretary Wolfowitz has laid out some ideas, and we need to coordinate with the folks at European Command on the way in, but it will focus on analyzing what level of humanitarian support the Kurds are getting."

"How far in are we going?" Sally frowned and cocked her head. It was a perfect staffer-head-cock meant to indicate extreme interest and intellect.

"Take a look here." Ms. Cates stood and stepped over to the map on her wall. Jack took the opportunity to look at her ass when she stood. Jack thought she was hot, and her state department air of snobbish superiority made her even more so. He fantasized, bending her over her desk someday and made an effort to gain her approval and trust at every opportunity.

"The plan is to fly from Dulles into Istanbul, then on to Batman here in southeastern Turkey. You will then be driven to the border and across the Habur River near Zakho right here. As you know, there is a coalition group, the Military Coordination Command, headed by a US Army colonel, who will organize the trip from there. How far we go depends upon the security situation. That said, Mister Wolfowitz has a passion for the Kurds. I think he might be frustrated with how we left them after the war."

"How so?" Bill sat forward.

"I can answer that," said Jack, thinking of Ms. Cates' desk. "As you know, during the cease-fire following the war the Kurds and others rebelled against Saddam, anticipating we would help. We didn't, and thousands were killed and displaced. There is a feeling of guilt in some

216

corners of the Pentagon for that, and I think that is what Ms. Cates refers to."

"Exactly," said Ms. Cates. She beamed at him. "Thank you, Jack."

"Is it dangerous?" Sally asked through a head cock to the other side. Jack admired Sally and also had a huge desire to screw her even more than Ms. Cates. The thought of being with her for a long trip, even a dangerous one, excited him.

"That depends upon how far in you go."

"How far do you think we will go, given approval?"

"Well, we have re-fueling programs here in Dahuk," said Ms. Cates, pointing to the city in northern Iraq. "And then further to the south and east, we have feeding programs in Arbil. We also have a French prosthetics program over here on the Iraq and Iran border near As Sulaymaniyah at Penjwen."

"Wow, that is a long way inside the country," said Bill. He frowned as he looked at the points on Ms. Cates' map.

"It is," replied Ms. Cates, "but this map doesn't show the relief. This is very mountainous terrain, and Saddam's troops can't get up there. The Kurds and the fact there is a No-Fly Zone in the north keep him away."

Jack and the others discussed the trip for the rest of the hour, and when he left and boarded the train for his ride back to the Pentagon, he felt that maybe he would do something meaningful in the job after all! Maybe there was an opportunity to shine on the trip to Iraq besides just bedding Sally. Jack grinned as he watched the scenery fly past.

Maybe I can brief the chairman when I get back!

Jack returned to his office and turned the computer back on. He sighed with relief to see no new taskers in his box. He had met a girl in Old Town the previous Saturday and was supposed to meet her for happy hour at Fort Meyers at 1800. He could tell she was dying to screw him.

"Any good word from the mountain?" Bull swiveled in his chair to face Jack. His grin was cynical as usual.

Jack didn't want to tell Bull about the Iraq trip yet. He didn't want to hear how much bullshit it was. He wanted to believe it was something important.

"No, the usual stuff."

"You know if you put your feet at a forty-five-degree angle when stapling, your brain will automatically send your hands the correct message. It works."

Jack frowned and turned to face Bull. "Fuck you, Bull. Some of the stuff we do matters."

"No, shit?" Bull chuckled and leaned back in his chair. "Hard to believe some version of this won World War 11."

Jack stood to leave when Bull stopped him.

"Some dude from the navy staff dropped by looking for you."

Jack frowned, "Oh, yeah. What did he want?"

Bull stood, walked across the room, and handed Jack a yellow memo paper. "He wants you to call him at this number. It's about Tailhook. I think he's a lawyer."

Jack frowned again as he looked at the slip of paper. He heard guys were getting calls to come and tell their story. "Thanks," he said as he walked out.

***

"Have a seat, commander."

Jack took a chair and faced the woman across the table. Her name was Ms. Duggan, and she had presented credentials identifying her as from the office of the Joint Staff Inspector General. Beside her sat a navy lieutenant commander, the lawyer whose number he had received from Bull.

"You are Jack Raymond Grant?"

"Yes, ma'am." Jack squirmed in his chair.

"You were the commander of TOPGUN from January 1991 to October 1991?"

"Yes, ma'am."

"Why so short of a tour?"

Jack felt a quiver of fear. Ms. Duggan was the kind of woman Jack feared more than anything. He could tell she was not impressed with him. Worse, she was probably smarter than him.

He gulped and looked at Ms. Duggan's dark eyes. They were fixed, like a shark's. They offered no clue of what she knew or wanted. Jack shivered. He most certainly did not want to screw Ms. Dugan.

"Time to move on," mumbled Jack. "Time to get joint qualified."

"I see."

Jack swallowed. Ms. Duggan's eyes never moved from his.

Why is she so fricking intense?

"So, you didn't leave early to get you away from command, your command, a command that had participated in Tailhook '91?"

"No." Jack took a breath to steady himself. "No, it was just time to move on."

Ms. Duggan stared. "And I read here you say you were not at Tailhook in 1991."

"That's right."

"That's interesting. You were a star of the show weren't you?"

"I was asked to sit at the head table. Because, because of the MIGs I shot down."

"Of course, the MIGs." Ms. Duggan's face broke into a smile but her dark, ever-piercing eyes ensured Jack that nothing was remotely funny.

"The MIGs," she repeated. "That's why you are a hero, isn't it? That's why you had to be there, with your friends and admirers, isn't it?" She frowned and cocked her head. "Can you prove you were not there?"

"I already made statements about this," said Jack. "I went to my wife's father's funeral, Vice Admiral Sheehan."

"I can read your statement, but how do I know you went to the funeral? Do you have receipts? Old airplane stubs?"

"I didn't keep that kind of thing," said Jack. "We stayed in Grace's family house. I don't have any receipts for anything."

"So, you can't prove you were not at Tailhook?"

"I can get about a hundred witnesses that saw me at the funeral." Jack took a deep breath. He knew he sounded too defiant. But this was all bullshit. He had been told the whole thing was a witch hunt, and that the previous navy investigation had been thrown out. They were looking for scalps!

Ms. Duggan lowered her head and studied the papers in front of her. Jack heard her take another deep breath. She looked up.

"What about the suite? What about the TOPGUN suite?"

"What about it?"

"Who was in charge of it? Who was the responsible officer for what happened in the suite?"

221

Jack hesitated. The previous navy investigator had not asked him that question. Since he had not gone to Hook and since the TOPGUN suite was not part of any sexual allegations, the heat had all gone elsewhere. "I don't remember. One of the guys."

"One of the guys?" Ms. Duggan sat back in her seat and stared at Jack. Her face was hard and red. "One of the guys? That is the kind of crap I get from all of you. Nobody seemed to have a senior officer involved in anything. Just some of the guys. Well, BULLSHIT! She slapped the table.

Jack jumped back. He had not expected this. He looked at the lieutenant commander who appeared as shocked as he was.

"I want someone senior. I want the name of someone in your command senior enough to answer for over thirty-six reports of drunken, puking, headband-wearing idiots. I want to know whose idea it was to pour kamikazes like they were water and get young men so drunk they walked around the hotel lobby with their balls hanging out. I want a name! If I don't get the name of someone who was there, then the only other name I have is yours. You were the commanding officer. Ultimately, YOU were responsible for what went on whether or not you were there."

Jack gulped and looked at the lieutenant commander again. He looked at Ms. Duggan and then back at Jack. "I suggest you provide Ms. Duggan with some responsible person, the person who coordinated the suite activities and approved them. Someone like your XO maybe. Was he there?"

Ms. Duggan sat up straight, and her face brightened. "Exactly! Who was the XO at the time, and what was his role in this?"

"Well, he was the coordinator of the suite," said Jack, grateful to get the heat off of himself.

"Would he have approved what alcohol you were serving, and how you served it?"

"Yes," said Jack. "Absolutely." He felt immense relief. For a second, he had thought his career was over.

"And who was the XO?"

"Commander Steve Collingswood."

"And did he go to Tailhook?"

"Yes, he did," said Jack. "Yes, he did."

CHAPTER SIXTEEN

Jack, Sally, and Bill flew from Dulles to Istanbul, landing there mid-morning. They were escorted through Turkish security and onto a Turkish C-130 for the flight to Batman. Colonel Fred Thompson from the EUCOM J3's office met them there. He was a FAO like Stoops but had a genuine and convincing air of optimism about him that Jack found strangely irritating. He was like a cheery smile on a cloudy day; bullshit and out of place.

Jack and the others followed Fred across the tarmac to a Quonset hut for briefing before the ride to Zakho.

The hut was small and dark, but there was a pot of coffee brewing and some comfortable couches. Once seated with cups in their hands, Jack and the team turned to Fred.

"There are approximately 30 million Kurds spread across Turkey, Syria, Iraq, and Iran, the largest group of people without a country in the world. This presents problems since Kurds have a distinct identity and a strong belief that the land beneath their feet is theirs---wherever those feet happen to be."

Fred fished into his pocket, found a small cigar, and lit it. He blew out a mouthful of smoke and continued.

"You will like the Kurds. They are handsome people, straightforward, loyal, charismatic, and hardworking. In some ways, they are the perfect victim. They will try to convince you into recognizing Kurdistan as a separate country, but you must be very careful about that. It flies in the face of all the Turks believe and is not in agreement with the UN Security Council understandings either." Fred paused and took another puff on his cigar.

"The Kurds are tribal and oriented around their family unit. These families align into groupings with fierce loyalties. Best to stay out of the middle of that kind of stuff."

"What about terrorism?" Sally put her cup in her lap. "What about the PKK?"

"Good question," said Fred. "The PKK is not a family-centered group based upon generations of loyalty like the others, but a separatist group. It is recognized as a terrorist group by the Turks and by the United States. They have mounted many attacks over the years against the Turkish government, and that opposition continues today. They have been pretty active lately and their leader, Ocalan, has been fanning the separatist talk. The Turks are pretty nervous. All of southeast Turkey is a combat zone. You will leave Batman in SUVs, but you will wind up in armored personnel carriers toward the last part of the ride with Turkish air cover."

The briefing continued for another hour; then the team mounted their Toyota SUVs for the ride. The trip went as the colonel forecast, and by late afternoon the group, ensconced now in an armored personnel carrier, rumbled across the Habur River Bridge into Iraq. Meeting them were Army Colonel Oscar Sturgis, and members of the coalition force representing France, Great Britain, Australia, and Turkey. The team shook hands all around while nearly a dozen Peshmerga fighters stood in the background. Jack observed them closely. Their dark eyes were in constant motion as they surveyed their visitors, and they had an alert but relaxed air about them. They were not quite arrogant but not at all threatened or cowed. When

Jack made eye contact with them, they maintained it but showed no anger or challenge. They were all armed with a combination of assault rifles, grenade launchers, shotguns, and pistols. While most wore baggy pants, loose shirts, and vests or light coats and a turban-like hat, a few wore blue jeans, sweatshirts, and tennis shoes. All were chain-smoking American cigarettes. Soon, the team jumped into SUVs for the short ride to the MCC compound; a collection of concrete structures surrounded by cinder block walls. Sandbag covered guard posts with two to three Peshmerga at alert dotted the enclosure.

"Are the Iraqis up here? What are you defending against?" Bill asked the question as the team assembled outside the SUVs.

"Whatever comes our way," said Colonel Sturgis. "You see Saddam might not be here, but his money and his influence are everywhere." He led them into the planning room where they joined members of the coalition team. Colonel Sturgis stood at the head of the table and smiled again.

"During your time here, you will likely be approached by locals who want to know the status of American favor. They will want to be reassured that America has not forgotten them and that Saddam isn't coming back, and so forth. They may try to curry your favor or seek some advantage. "

"What do you mean?" asked Jack.

"Everything is tribal here. People identify first with their clan, and so they act in that belief. It gets murky because they also will include friends in that mix. So, they will do things to support that group that takes precedence over the larger society. For instance, take the fuel and food

226

situation. You will hear about shortages, and it is a fact that there are chronic shortages of food and cooking and heating oil across the region. However, much of the shortage has to do with the redistribution of the goods that do make it here."

"What do you mean?" asked Bill.

"You guys know that UNSCR 665 imposed sanctions on Iraq. The idea was to put pressure on the populace that would result in a popular uprising, the overthrow of Saddam, and Jeffersonian democracy throughout the region."

"That is pretty cynical," said Sally.

Colonel Sturgis glanced at her and smiled. He looked at the map for a moment then turned back to the group. "Tonight, you will meet Mr. Henri Lever. He is a Belgian and is the representative for the United Nations High Commission on Refugees in Iraq. He is part of the architecture put in place by well-fed, overpaid, and ignorant diplomats that do their dark work in the UN headquarters in New York. Over forkfuls of fillet and foie gras, they develop with great flourish some of the most un-executable and ridiculous ideas you can imagine."

"Oh, come on," said Bill. "That's a bit much, isn't it, Colonel?"

"Take yourselves," said Sturgis. "You advise decision making about things and people you do not know or understand. You gather in your group and spend countless hours agonizing over some demarche that supposedly will influence Saddam. But, it cannot be worded too directly because then you will have to do something!" The colonel stood, and Jack could see his ide, animated eyes. "You deliberate over words. You can't say, 'we will demonstrate resolve. That means we might have to do something physically. So you change the words to, 'we will reserve actions,' but the word action is too direct. So you say, 'we will consider responses,' and on and on."

Jack and the team fell silent, and Jack recalled the time they spent four hours trying to create a single paragraph in response to Saddam's withholding of inspector visa's. He had begun calling a demarche a "demarche mellow" because of its lack of impact. A term that Ms. Cates quickly forbade him to use in her presence.

"Look, I know you mean well. We all do." The colonel looked around the room and smiled. "The problem is that so much of the United Nations' stuff, the sanction stuff, never, ever works. All it does is deprive the population of resources while the corrupt government in place finds a new way to take what is left. So the fuel and food that does get up here is intercepted and siphoned off by Iraqi bureaucrats, Kurdish bureaucrats, and others. And, other folks like Henri take their share too."

"How can that happen?" Bill frowned and stared at the colonel.

"Henri may work for the UN, but he is also an opportunist. This gig in northern Iraq is just another opportunity. He once told me he gets paid around $600,000 from the UN as a salary plus he has a staff of twenty plus every expense is paid for as well. But my contacts here tell me he makes millions off of the trade with Iran and Turkey. You see, he uses the limitations imposed by the very organization he works for to provide him business to overcome those limitations."

228

"Wow," said Jack. "Does he get access to the stuff that Operation Provide Comfort provides?"

"Probably," said Sturgis. "Eventually, he probably does. It comes in by truck or helicopter, and we give it to the Kurdish leaders. I imagine Henri is in the mix somewhere."

"Why doesn't the MCC distribute it fairly?" Sally was mad.

"I don't have the resources here to be the distributor of goods. I provide the security for the stuff when it comes."

"I thought UN Security Council 687 and 688 provides security. By setting up the No-Fly-Zone and preventing Saddam from coming up here."

"Nothing the UN does provides actual security," said Sturgis. "That's what I have been talking about. All the resolutions and demarches in the world won't provide a lick of security. In the end, it takes guns and physical power to provide security. Anything less is just bullshit for diplomats."

Jack and the others fell silent again, and the room took on an awkward chill. The colonel took a seat at the table and cleared his throat.

"Let's talk a bit about that security. As you have seen, we have a mix of coalition forces and a strong contingent of Peshmerga fighters. For those of you who are not familiar, the Peshmerga are Kurdish soldiers." The colonel looked around the room at the team. "Their name, Peshmerga, means 'those who die first, or those who sacrifice their lives.' They have been defending Kurdistan

229

for centuries and have a deep hatred for Saddam and the Iraqi army. I think you know what happened in Halabja where Saddam gassed 5,000 Kurdish women and children to death. Well, that was a sliver of the 100,000 Kurds Saddam ordered killed during his Anfal operation so the Pesh will have no problem engaging any Iraqi they see."

"Why does Saddam hate the Kurds so much," asked Jack?

"They reject the central government in Baghdad for one," said Sturgis. "They have a long history of independent thinking, and they align culturally more closely with Iran than Iraq."

"Really?" Jack was feeling good about the trip. He was learning things that could be useful for him later with Ms. Cates.

"Many believe they are descendants of the ancient Medes. They refer to the Medes in their Kurdish anthem. And, they sided with Iran during the Iran, Iraq War. That was unforgivable from Saddam's perspective. So, Anfal was an attempt to purge them. As I said, the Kurds will have no problem engaging any Iraqi. They are superb fighters, although they can become somewhat undisciplined when the shooting starts."

"What do you mean?" asked Sally.

"I mean if one bullet will stop a man, they will put one hundred into him."

The colonel looked up as a young officer entered the room. "Henri is here."

"Roger," said Sturgis. "Show him to the dining room." He looked at Jack, Sally, and Bill. "You are about to meet an insufferable prick who represents much of what is wrong with the international effort here. He is a tick upon these people and a leech upon the American taxpayer. However, as criminally disgusting as he is, and no doubt you will find him that way, he does provide a service that we need. The UN agreements are fragile and come under constant scrutiny and criticism. Many see situations like Iraq as opportunities to pad their accounts and so holding the structure together is critical. Henri does that. For the wrong reasons, perhaps, but he does. So, come meet Henri and let's have some supper."

The group followed Colonel Sturgis through a long, dark hallway until it opened into a large room lit by flickering electric lights and a fireplace. Electricity was sporadic in northern Iraq, and the MCC had diesel generators to catch the load when it failed. They were fortunate as most of the 4 million Kurds had no generator and if they did, no diesel to run it.

Sturgis introduced the team to Henri Lever, and Jack found him just as imagined: arrogant, profuse, irritating, and his opening dialogue with the colonel said it all.

"Greetings Henri, now that you have met the team, could I interest you in a cocktail?"

"Certainly, scotch please."

"Good, I just got a few bottles of Cutty Sark on the last helo."

"Cutty Sark!" Henri glared across the table at Sturgis. "What do you mean?"

231

Sturgis appeared perplexed. He looked at Henri and shrugged his shoulders. "What?"

"I expected Chivas, the Royal Salute 21. That's what I serve my preferred guests."

"That stuff is $170 a bottle, Henri. A bit rich for US taxpayer blood."

"Then, Johnny Walker Blue Label."

"That's $150 a bottle, Henri. Look, we are on the government dime here. I have Cutty Sark, Jack Daniels or Budweiser. Your choice."

"Why are you Americans so cheap?"

"Look, your salary, your staff, expenses, your fucking Land Rover are all paid for by American taxpayers."

"My compensation is from the UN," sniffed Henri.

"Exactly my point," said Sturgis. "And we know who pays that bill don't we?"

"Alright, well, then, Jack Daniels." Henri exhaled a deep sigh of resignation.

"Very good," said Sturgis. "How about the rest of you?"

"Coke," said Sally.

"Make it two," said Bill.

Jack wanted a whiskey, a double. It had been a long day. But, for some reason, he couldn't make himself join Henri. "I'll have a bottle of water."

The group sat at a round table and was served in large, steaming bowls by Kurdish staff members. The MCC employed them to better connect to the community. The menu was simple and consisted of rice, vegetables, and roasted goat. A bowl of apples, oranges, and bananas was dessert. Of course, Henri complained.

"Why is there no beef?"

"There is no beef, Henri," said Sturgis as he looked upon his guest. "Because there are no cows." He gestured toward the table. "But as you can see there are goats so please enjoy."

"I like raisins and dates in my rice." He looked at Sturgis and then up to the bowl carrier.

"Raisins and dates are on the next helo," said Sturgis. He winked at Jack. "I will be sure to save some for your next visit."

Henri sniffed with irritation, picked up his knife and fork, and began a stream of consciousness about why he was so wonderful.

"The 4 million Kurds here revere me, and they know I am the reason they receive the food and fuel and medicines they need," he said amid smacking lips of rice and goat. "They know it is NOT Provide Comfort," he wagged his finger at Sturgis. "Oh, they will bow and scrape in front of you, but THEY know, they know, who their savior is."

"Perhaps," said Sturgis. "But I don't want to be anybody's savior. I want to keep Saddam from killing them or starving them to death."

"Well, then, we are a team." Henri smiled and held his glass up for a toast.

"Agreed," said Sturgis. He smiled and held his glass forward as Jack, Sally, and Bill did the same.

The meal lasted for an hour, and, blessedly, Henri had to leave. Sturgis did manage to find a bottle of Jack Daniels to give him as a parting gift, and that seemed to salve his pique. After Henri departed, Sturgis motioned for the team to sit.

"I want to introduce you to the two men who will be escorting you. They are both senior Peshmerga fighters, and they are familiar with the programs we have going on in northern Iraq."

"Why didn't they come to dinner?" Asked Sally.

"Because they don't like Henri," replied Sturgis. He stood and walked to the door. After a few moments, he reappeared followed by two men.

"This is Akam," said Sturgis. He gestured to a dark, bearded man wearing the traditional Peshmerga outfit of baggy pants, loose shirt, short coat, and head covering. He had an assault rifle slung over his shoulder. The man bowed slightly and touched his heart.

"And this is Cobar." Sturgis gestured to the other man who was a virtual opposite of Akam. He was clean-shaven and had dark brown hair and gray eyes. Cobar wore tennis shoes, blue jeans, a Rolling Stones T-shirt, and a sleeveless parka. On his head, he wore a red, Saint Louis Cardinals baseball cap. He, too, had a rifle slung over his back. Cobar also bowed while touching his heart, and the team rose and shook hands with the men.

The group quickly took seats and Sturgis laid a map of Iraq on the table. "We are here, at Zakho," he said, pointing to the northernmost part of Iraq. You will travel south through Dahuk and Mosul tomorrow morning."

Jack watched Sturgis trace a line to a point on the map and shot a glance at the two Peshmerga. Akam's eyes, dark and expressionless, were glued to the map. Cobar's eyes danced, and he had a slight smile. He must have felt Jack's gaze because he looked up, winked, and then looked back at the map.

"At Mosul, you will see a fuel depot. Not much really, but I wanted you to at least see it," said Sturgis. He frowned and looked around the table. "I don't want you to spend too much time there. Take a look and keep on going, okay?"

"Why is that?" Jack frowned.

"You run out of the mountains as we go south, so it is easier for Saddam's men to filter in. Plus, there are a lot of people around the fuel, and some of them are up to no good. Safer in Arbil here." He pointed to the map. You can stay with friends."

Jack nodded and looked at Cobar, who grinned back. He glanced at Akam, but the silent man's dark eyes remained on the map.

"Should we have guns?" Sally looked at Sturgis.

Sturgis laughed and leaned back in his chair. "Sure, I can loan you all a nine millimeter. Do you know how to use it?"

"We had to refresh with them before flying over Iraq," said Jack. "We shot at floating garbage bags off of the fantail."

"I have never shot one," said Sally.

"Me neither," said Bill.

Probably too late to start now," said Sturgis. "These guys can do the shooting." He motioned to Cobar and Akam. "Jack, I can loan you one for the trip."

"Thanks," said Jack. He liked the idea of being armed. He also liked the idea of being able to tell people he had been on the ground in Iraq, armed to the teeth, on a dangerous mission.

"You mentioned flying over Iraq," said Sturgis. He looked at Jack and smiled. "Were you in Desert Storm?"

"No, I was in Desert Shield."

"Oh, you missed the show then." Sturgis frowned. He looked disappointed.

"No, he didn't," said Sally. She put her hand on Jack's and smiled at Sturgis. "Jack is the guy that shot down three MIGs at the very start of the war."

Jack looked at Sally and smiled.

"You're THAT guy!" Exclaimed Sturgis. He leaped up and extended his hand.

Jack stood and smiled as they shook.

"Cobar, Akam, this is the navy pilot that shot down the three MIGs. Remember, we were talking about it the other day."

Akam leaped to his feet and snapped to attention. He looked at Jack and once again bowed and touched his heart. Cobar did the same but then grabbed Jack's hand in a vigorous shake. "It is a great day to meet you," he said. "You kill Saddam's murder pilots."

"As you can see, the Kurds are not too fond of Iraqi pilots." Sturgis laughed and looked at Jack. "What's it like to shoot down an enemy plane? To win in aerial combat?"

"It is a feeling of accomplishment," said Jack. He smiled back at the adoring faces. "It's you or him, so if you win, you avoid death. If you lose, it is almost certain." He loved the horrified look in their eyes. "The key is not to lose." His laugh allowed everyone to segue away from the seriousness of his comments, and Colonel Sturgis motioned to their seats. They all sat back down and focused on the map.

"Road is very rough, here to here." Cobar's finger moved along the thick curvy line that represented the road from Arbil to Al Sulaymaniyah. "Here is maybe a problem." He pointed to a lake between Arbil and Al Sulaymaniyah."

"Why?" asked Jack.

"The area near the Dokan Dam is sometimes a rendezvous point for nefarious characters," said Sturgis. "It is possible to have trouble there. Akam and Cobar are familiar, though; it should be okay."

Jack looked at Cobar and grinned. He was beginning to feel a bond with the Kurdish fighter. "How do you two feel about it?"

"We have fought many times together." Cobar looked at Akam. "He is fast and smart and not afraid of death. I trust my life with him."

The solemnity of Cobar's statement stilled the room, and everyone looked at Akam. Akam looked up from the map, nodded towards Cobar and shrugged.

"He is better with the shotgun."

Everyone laughed, and even Akam allowed a slip of a smile.

They continued to pour over the map for another hour and then decided to turn in. Tomorrow would be a long day. Jack and Bill bunked together, Sally had her room down the hall and Cobar, and Akam just disappeared. Jack waited until he heard Bill snore, then crept out of his room. He quietly entered Sally's room and tiptoed across the floor.

She was asleep, laying on her side, and Jack stripped off his shorts and slipped under the sheets. She moaned as he caressed her warm shoulder, and he moved his hands down her side. Sally was naked, and as he touched her, she rolled toward him. He planted a kiss on her lips, and she pushed back. Then, seeing who it was allowed him to kiss her again. His fingers explored her awhile in the dark; then he went to work.

Just before dawn, Jack arose from the warm bed and put on his shorts. He opened the latch and crept toward his room. As he opened the door, something made him turn, and he noticed the outline of a figure at the end of the hallway. He squinted in the poor light, the gray through the window just coloring the room. He made out the outline of a cap on the figure's head. It was Cobar. Jack opened his mouth to speak but then shut it. If he spoke, he would signify he knew that someone was there, that the light had been enough. He would acknowledge that he was coming from another room. But if he remained silent and just entered his room, then, in a way, nothing had happened. Jack opened the door and went in. He lay on his bunk, and the next thing he knew Bill was shaking him.

"Come on, man; time's a-wasting. Breakfast in five minutes."

Jack groaned as he stretched and shut his eyes against the burn of sleeplessness. He shook his brain awake and then tasted Sally on his lips. He smiled through a yawn as he stretched again and remembered the night before. It was a night of manly accomplishment, and so the ache was good. He ached from being up all night with, and that was worth any tiredness he would have that day. The fact that it was State Department pussy made him laugh out loud. Jack smiled and whispered to himself, "This is a fighter pilot's morning."

CHAPTER SEVENTEEN

Jack arose, washed as well as he could in the sink and combed his hair. He liked not having to shave. He and Bill had been advised to grow beards to fit in with the locals. Ironically, it was Cobar who was the only clean-shaven man in the traveling group, and that was because he couldn't grow a beard.

The team was gathered around the table when Jack walked in, and he carefully kept his eyes off Sally. Now that he had had her, she was no longer interesting. Coffee, chai, eggs, yogurt, bread, cheese and fruit were on a serving counter along with a couple of boxes of American cereal. Jack poured himself a cup of coffee, grabbed a banana, and sat down. He felt Sally's eyes on him.

Breakfast was a festive affair as Cobar excitedly told them of his night standing guard and how he kept awake by listening to Talabani Peshmerga make love to their goats. Cobar and Akam were Barzani affiliated, and although the two parties united against Saddam, they had real divisions. Jack laughed as Cobar told his story and noticed that Akam remained silent, sipping his chai. Jack felt good that these two men were going to escort them. Two Cobar's would have been uncomfortably frivolous; two Akam's, uncomfortable severe.

Just before they stood to leave, Sturgis gave them vehicle assignments. Although all could fit in a single SUV, redundancy was the watchword in northern Iraq. Sally, Bill, Akam and one Peshmerga guard were in one vehicle while Jack, Cobar and two Peshmerga were in the second. The trip was to consist of four days and three nights on the road with stops at Arbil and Al Sulaymaniyah on the way out with a second stop at Arbil on the trip back. The route was to take Highway 2 from Zakho through Dahuk and Mosul to Arbil on day one. The team would travel overland from Arbil to Dokan then take Highway 18 to Al Sulaymaniyah on day two. The return trip was a mirror with a stop at Arbil on day three then back to Zakho on day four. Just before the left, Sturgis gave Jack a Beretta nine millimeter pistol and three ammo clips.

The two SUVs took off around eight in the morning, and the trip to Mosul was out of the mountains and straightforward with a solid, paved road and Kurd-manned random checkpoints. When the team got to Mosul, they stopped for lunch. The two SUVs pulled up to a peeling, whitewashed building with tables on the sidewalk. A screen-less open window framed hunks of meat hanging from black, metal hooks with men working an open pit behind it. Customers sat at the tables, fanning away the large, green flies that preferred them over the meat.

The team took seats at a dusty table while the Peshmerga took guard positions. Jack thought it a bit suspicious to have that kind of protection, but nobody seemed to notice or care.

"What's on the menu?" Sally grinned at Cobar, and Jack felt a pang of jealousy.

"Goat," said Cobar with a smile as he winked at her.

Sally shaded her eyes as she looked at the window. "Do you think the meat is good?"

"Yes, of course. Is goat," said Cobar. "Is good."

"Well, okay." She turned back to Cobar and smiled again. "Looks like it is goat all around," said Jack. "I do suggest we get it well done though." He frowned at Sally and Bill. "Are you sure you want to be drinking that?"

Sally and Bill had finished the water on the table and were working on a second. It had been a hot and dry trip as they had forgotten to pack bottled water.

"What wrong?" Cobar frowned and looked at Jack. "Yeah, what's wrong?" asked Bill.

"Don't think we should drink open water," said Jack. "We aren't from around here."

Cobar said something in Kurdish to a waiter, and moments later, he brought a tray with cold, bottled water as well as a heap of goat meat, onions, and bread.

Everyone dived in, and an hour later, the group was driving by a large depot filled with fuel trucks.

"The trucks come from the south and also from Iran," said Cobar.

"Iran?" Jack was confused.

"Yes. The oil is brought here to refine for use. Iran is a great partner with the Kurds."

"But what about the UN sanctions?"

Cobar just laughed, and the caravan continued through the depot.

After viewing the depot, the caravan continued to Arbil. The terrain reminded Jack of the Sierra Nevada in

California. Vast swaths of evergreens and knots of hardwoods gave way to the stark landscape of a high desert plateau. It was a rugged place where gurgling streams of white water raced by the cars only to turn blue as they tumbled into deep pools. The road ran by villages of stone and wood and concrete; houses and outbuildings surrounded by fields of grazing sheep and goats. If the forests reminded Jack of the Sierra Nevada, the villages told him of trips to Mexico. They told of hard people living a hard life.

The SUVs traveled a couple more hours until they reached a small town. Cobar, driving the lead car, pulled into a gas station and they filled both vehicles. Jack remained in the front seat and watched a Kurdish man approach Cobar. They greeted each other and engaged in a conversation; several times pointed to the car. Finally, Cobar embraced the man, then returned to the SUV. Akam paid for both, and they jumped in and started down the road.

"Who was that?" asked Jack.

"A friend," said Cobar.

Jack shrugged and settled into his seat. They drove on, and he nodded off a few times, jumping awake when the car hit a pothole or bump. He was soon able to re-energize his batteries and enjoy the rest of the trip.

The rural landscape of sheep, goats and small villages gradually gave way to a more dense set of houses and stores and streets of cars and people. Finally, they were in Arbil. Cobar insisted that they view the citadel in the center of the town, so they left the highway and entered the city. Jack was surprised to find that over one and a half million people lived there. He just assumed that all of

243

northern Iraq was sparsely populated, mountainous and barren. This trip was undoubtedly proving him wrong. As they drove into the center of town, they could see the citadel rising from the ground, burnished gold by the setting sun.

Cobar explained that the stone walls went up 100 feet at an angle of 45 degrees and the top was the oldest continuously inhabited place on earth. Jack smiled at the pride he saw in Cobar's eyes and voice, and the excitement of his narrative. Jack was surprised at Cobar's pride.

They drove the circular artery around the citadel then headed south-west toward the home of Cobar and Akam's friend.

"We go to a friend's home," said Cobar.

Jack looked across the seat at him and nodded.

"His name is Adan," said Cobar. "We have known him since we were small boys." Cobar looked in the rearview mirror at Akam, then out the front windscreen. "He is the best friend of my life. His wife is Kagul, and they have a young granddaughter, Navciwan. "

Jack frowned at the tension in the car. Something was wrong. "Why the serious face?" he asked.

Cobar stared out the window. He turned and looked at Jack and took a deep breath. "There had been a terrible thing in their house." He looked at the road again.

They rode in silence for a few miles, and Cobar looked at Jack. "Adan and Kagul had a son, Kolan. Kolan and Akam and I were best friends. Kolan had a wife. They were both killed by Saddam."

"Jesus," said Jack.

"You look like Kolan," said Cobar.

"I do?"

"Yes." Akam turned from the window. His dark eyes found Jack's, and he nodded his head. "You could be a twin brother." He turned back to the window. "When I met you the first night at MCC, I was shocked by you. Akam, too. We did not show but shock. That night I sent word to Adan. I did not want them to shock. There is already sorrow in the house." Cobar sighed and gripped the wheel.

"Maybe we should not stay there."

"I do not think we have much choice," said Cobar. "You remember the man at the filling station? My friend?"

"Yes."

"He is sister's husband. He asked if you were the one."

"What do you mean?" Jack frowned and turned to see Cobar's face.

"The one with the MIGs. Saddam has a one million dinar bounty on your head."

"What?"

"Word travels fast here. We have nothing else to do but gossip."

"A bounty?"

"Yes, it is common practice for Saddam. No one knows even if he pays or not."

"I don't believe it. Me? A bounty?"

"Yes. So, we must be careful. Stay at my friend's house. Go quickly to Sulaymaniyah to see minefields, then back."

Jack sat back in his seat, trying to absorb what he had heard. He felt a strange pride about being important enough to have a bounty on his head. An image of Steve McQueen and his sawed-off rifle side arm flashed in his mind. But the pride was quickly replaced with concern. He was in a hostile area, out of his environment, wholly dependent upon men he did not know. He wasn't sure what a dinar was worth, but a million of them had to be significant enough. He frowned and touched the Beretta in his jacket pocket.

The caravan proceeded through the city and soon was traveling down dusty side streets and for the first time, Jack noticed Cobar continually checking the rearview mirror. Akam seemed more alert, too, and neither man talked. The silent, heavily armed Peshmergas with them were also alert, their heads incessantly swiveling.

Jack was relieved when they finally pulled off of the street and through a narrow alley into a courtyard. They all got out and stretched, and Jack could tell by Sally and Bill's banter that they knew nothing of a bounty. He decided not to say anything about it. They couldn't do anything but worry anyway.

They grabbed their gear and followed Cobar and Akam into a large, dark room where they were introduced to Adan. He stared at Jack with wide, confused eyes, and his hand trembled as he placed his hand to his heart and bowed in the custom. Sally and Bill were busy messing with their luggage and didn't appear to notice. When it was their turn to be introduced, they just smiled and nodded.

Adan led them into an inner room, seated them around a circular table, and served small glasses of chai.

"We must be alert," said Cobar.

Adan nodded and sipped his chai. He looked up at Cobar and Akam, then at Jack. "Yes. Many enemies."

Jack was aware it was customary for Kurds to first talk of family and exchange best wishes before talking about any business. Doing otherwise was rude. He was surprised at Cobar's opening. He saw Sally frown and open her mouth to speak. Then her eyes looked up and brightened, "Well, hello there."

They all looked, and there stood a young girl.

"Navi, go." Adan motioned with his hand. He looked angry. Jack looked at the girl, and she was staring into his eyes. "Kagul!" Adan yelled for his wife.

Jack kept looking at the girl. Her dark eyes were filling with tears as Kagul rushed into the room. "Navi," she said.

"Go!" Adan motioned again.

"Navi." Kagul took the girl's hand, but she jerked it free and ran to Jack. She hugged him and put her face into his chest.

"*Bav*," she sobbed.

247

Jack looked at Adan and frowned.

"Navi." Kagul gently took the girl by the shoulders and pulled her back.

"*Bav. Bav.*" Kagul pulled the girl to her and held her. Then took her by the hand and led her out of the room.

What was that all about?" Bill frowned and looked at the others. "Yeah, what's the deal? What's going on?" Sally stared at Jack, confusion in her narrowed eyes.

"*Bav* means father in Kurdish," said Cobar. "Jack looks like her father."

"He looked as you do." Adan nodded to Jack and took a sip of chai. His hand trembled as he placed the cup in its saucer. He looked at Jack, his eyes old and wet, "he looked as you do."

Jack swallowed and felt the stillness in the room. He looked back at the older man.

Adan took another small sip and sighed. "The girl has not been well. These are the first words from her in over a year." He placed the saucer and cup on the table, stood and put his hand on his heart. "It is a miracle you here. Perhaps Navi can be freed. It is a miracle."

Everyone stood as Adan left the room.

Cobar looked at Jack. "Adan and Kagul lost their son and daughter-in-law to Saddam murderers. They were Navi's parents. But maybe it is good you are here." He smiled and nodded. "Maybe it is a miracle as Adan says."

"Son looks same," said Akam, gesturing toward Jack. "Miracle or not, we should have stayed somewhere else," said Sally.

Cobar looked at Akam and Jack; then, he shifted his gaze to Sally and Bill. "Saddam has a bounty on Jack. One million Dinars. We had to stay here."

"What?" Sally and Bill spoke in unison.

"Looks like the MIG thing is causing a problem," said Jack. "You have to be shitting me!" Sally frowned and shook her head.

"Afraid not," said Jack.

"How dangerous is it?" Bill looked at Cobar.

"It is pretty dangerous. I did not find out until we were almost here. Too late to turn back before."

"We can't go back without looking at the French prosthetics lab," said Bill. "Ms. Cates made me promise to take extensive notes and prepare a report. It was the real reason she wanted us to go in the first place."

"How dangerous is it for just one car to go?" Bill walked to the map. "Maybe a borrowed car?" He looked at Cobar and then at Akam. "The three of us could go to Sulaymaniyah with an escort in a borrowed car and take a look at the stuff Ms. Cates is interested in. Jack and Sally can head back."

Jack frowned but remained silent.

Cobar and Akam started talking in a wild, hands waving riff. It was in Kurdish, so Jack, Sally, and Bill had no idea what they were saying. After minutes of argument interspersed with head nodding, they stopped. Cobar looked at them and smiled.

"The trip from here can be off the highway until Dokan at the dam. It will be reasonably safe for one car. Akam and I will escort Bill, and the other Peshmerga will take Jack and Sally back tomorrow morning."

"Great," said Bill.

"I think that is a super idea," said Sally.

Jack shrugged. "Okay." He was surprised at his disappointment. It's not that he wanted to do the mission; he could care less about the Kurds. But the ordeal with the little girl had spooked him. It was if she made a connection to the place with him. He had an uncomfortable feeling of owing something. It was weird. The fact he looked like her dad, and she began to talk all of a sudden. It was a bit of a miracle like Adan had said. But, he didn't give a shit about what happened here. What he did want though was the ability to tell the story later about how he smiled in the face of danger and traipsed around Iraq with armed Peshmerga guards, armed to the teeth, with a bounty on his head. He had already begun to write portions of his next fitness report in his head.

Bill, Sally, and Cobar discussed the idea for a few more moments while Akam and Jack watched. Adan appeared in the door, and for some reason, they all stood. He was beaming!

"She talks!" Adan walked to Jack and clasped his hand. "She seems to now understand her bav is dead. But he is still with her. It is a miracle."

"Wonderful!" Cobar grinned and grabbed Adan's shoulders, and Akam vigorously shook his hand. Sally and Bill clapped and smiled.

Fuck, it was a miracle.

Adan led them into the dining area, and they sat down to a table of goat meat, bread, onions, and fruit. Kagul and Navi joined them, and Navi held her grandmother's hand as Adan passed the plates. Navi looked at Jack and smiled. She seemed to be at peace.

They talked and laughed as they ate. The goat was tender and the bread fresh and the onions crisp. They were nearing the end of the meal when Sally pushed back her chair. "I am not feeling so well."

Jack looked at her and was startled at the paleness of her face. "You know, I am not doing very well either," said Bill. He wiped his forehead with a napkin and closed his eyes.

The others in the room looked at them and then at each other. "The water," said Jack.

"What is this?" Adan frowned and looked at Cobar and Akam. "They both had water for lunch. Not from the bottle. From the stream."

"Oh," said Adan. The stream can make strangers sick."

"It's too soon, isn't it?" Jack looked at Cobar and then at Sally and Bill.

"I think it takes a couple of days to get sick from bad water."

"Well, whatever it is or whatever it is from, I feel terrible," said Sally. "I need to go lie down."

"Me too," said Bill.

Kagul stood. "Come, let me show you to your rooms." She led them out of the dining hall.

The next morning, Sally and Bill were too sick to come to breakfast, and Bill was undoubtedly too ill to go on the trip to Sulaymaniyah. Jack, Cobar, Akam, and Adan discussed the danger of the situation while they ate breakfast. Adan assured them all was safe in his house until Sally and Bill could travel, so they planned to stay in Arbil. They were sipping chai when Bill walked in. His face was a pasty white, his eyes were red, and his hair was a mass of tangles. He looked awful, but he was dressed.

"Let's go," he said.

The men at the breakfast table stared at him a moment, then Jack stood and helped Bill to a seat. "You're not going anywhere."

"But, I have to," said Bill. "I promised Ms. Cates I would look at that project. It is in danger of getting un-funded unless we can make specific recommendations."

"You too sick," said Akam. He set his jaw, and for him, the matter was closed.

"You are too sick," said Cobar. "It is impossible for you to go. It is a challenging trip, even if you feel good."

"I HAVE to GO!" Bill slapped the table. Spit dribbled from his lip, and sweat beads popped over his eyebrows.

"Look, I will go." Jack startled himself with his words. He wasn't sure why he had said them.

"What?" Cobar frowned in confusion.

"I can go in Bill's place. Let's have Sally and Bill stay until they can travel. Who knows, maybe they can leave later today?" He looked at Cobar and Akam. "The three of us can go."

"But you are the one they are looking for." Cobar shook his head. "Not a good idea."

"Put me in clothes like Akam is wearing and I will be okay. They don't know what I look like, especially if we are in a different car. They are looking for an American in a big SUV." Jack was surprised at how quickly his plan rolled out.

"Akam?" Cobar looked at his friend. Akam pursed his lips and frowned as he thought through the idea. He shrugged his shoulders.

"Let's go."

One hour later, Jack was standing in front of a mirror dressed in baggy pants, a loose shirt and short vest with a Kurdish head cover. He hadn't shaved since leaving the states, and with his dark hair and eyes, he looked like a local. Jack stuffed his Beretta in his waist and walked into the living room. Cobar grinned when he saw him.

"You look like Kurd, and I look like American."

Jack chuckled when he looked at the jeans, T-shirt, tennis shoes and ever-present baseball cap. "I think you are right."

Akam grunted approval and walked out to start Adan's car. It was an old Mercedes-Benz.

"We will be back day after tomorrow," said Cobar.

Adan and Kagul touched their hearts and bowed, and Navi ran to Jack and grabbed his hand. She kissed it and then ran out of the room.

Jack smiled as he watched her go. He hadn't done anything but be there. But, that was enough to help the little girl out and as small as it was, it was the first thing he had ever done for anyone in a long, long time. He thought of Grace for a second but then shook her from his head. Time to hit the road.

The plan was for Jack to drive since only locals would dare to drive in that backcountry. Cobar sat in front with him, and Akam took the back seat. The back roads to Dokan were mountainous and narrow, and the ride was jarring and uncomfortable. It was too hard to talk, so the three men jostled in silence for hours until they finally joined highway 18. Just west of the dam they entered an uphill stretch that was a winding road with switchbacks and curves, allowing them to see what was ahead. As they negotiated a narrow, left-hand turn, they saw the roadblock ahead. Jack pulled the car over.

"It could be some locals trying to get a tax," said Cobar. "If so, they won't mess with us."

Jack nodded his head and gripped the wheel. "Any chance it is PKK?"

"Not down here," said Cobar. "They are after Turkish military targets. Nothing here for them."

"What if it is somebody looking for me?"

"Could be," said Akam.

"Okay, let's turn around," said Cobar. Jack started to make a U-turn when a truck with four armed men pulled up behind them.

"Stay," said Akam, and he opened the back door and jumped out. Jack looked at his rearview mirror and watched him approach the truck. The four men pointed their rifles at Akam, and the driver pointed toward the Mercedes and shouted. Jack could feel his heart pounding, and he fought to keep calm. He glanced at himself in the mirror. He looked just like they did. Nothing to worry about.

The conversation continued for five more minutes before Akam suddenly turned and walked back to the Mercedes. He had no sooner shut the door when the truck pulled up so close it tapped the back bumper.

"Drive to the checkpoint."

Jack put the car in gear and pulled out on the highway. The truck was right behind him.

"They believe the American is in the car," said Akam. "They believe it is you." He looked at Cobar.

Cobar nodded and took a deep breath.

"What do we do?" Jack gripped the wheel to keep his hands from shaking. He had never been so scared.

"Turn me over to them at the checkpoint," said Cobar. "You and Akam keep going."

"No," said Akam. "They would discover you in moments; then they would kill you and chase us down."

"Then what?" Jack was frightened and gripped the wheel harder. The checkpoint appeared around the corner. It was three hundred feet away, and three guards manned it.

"We drive to the checkpoint," said Cobar. "Jack, get as close to it as you can. I will take my pistols in my jacket. Akam, when you get out of the car, point your rifle at me and hold the shotgun in your other hand. We have to make them think I am the American. Order me to get out, and I will put my hands in the air. We will walk toward the truck. When I yell, throw me the shotgun. I will aim for the checkpoint guards, and you aim for the men in the truck. Jack, when you hear the shooting, sit still. Be ready to go as soon as we jump back into the car."

Jack's head was spinning! He couldn't believe what was happening!

A gunfight in Iraq? Jesus!

"Okay," was all he could find to say. He looked at Cobar again. "Okay."

"Don't leave us," said Akam.

"I won't," said Jack. He swallowed and gripped the wheel harder.

"Don't be afraid," said Cobar. "One miracle already happened because of you. Maybe we will get another. "

Jack was so terrified he could hardly breathe. He was afraid to look at the guards. He was too scared to even look in the mirror.

For Christ's sake, what was he going to do? For Christ's sake!

The guard put his hand up as Jack slowly drove toward him. As he got closer, the guard screamed at him and unshouldered his rifle.

"Get out!" shouted Akam. Akam jumped out of the back and motioned to Cobar with his assault rifle. "Get out."

Cobar opened the front door and got out. He put his hands in the air. The truck stopped behind the Mercedes, and the men in the back began to leap off the end.

"Now," screamed Cobar. Akam threw him the shotgun and Cobar shot the closest gate guard. He went down, and Cobar pumped the gun and shot the second guard. Akam opened up on the truck and put a clip into the knot of men boiling off of the back. Two went down immediately. He pulled out his pistol and shot the third man and the driver. Cobar pumped again and shot the third guard, clearing the roadblock.

Jack stomped the accelerator and rolled over the dead guard. He looked in the rearview mirror and saw Cobar glaring at him in confusion. He saw Akam put two shots into the truck driver.

Everybody else was on the ground.

Jack stopped the car twenty yards from the roadblock. He looked in the rearview mirror and saw Cobar and Akam glaring at him, puzzled looks on their faces. They shrugged and jogged toward him. They were only steps away from the car when another truck rolled into view. It had many men in the back.

Cobar and Akam turned, saw the truck and reached for the door. Jack stomped the accelerator.

"Stop," yelled Cobar. He looked at Jack in confusion. "Stop!" Jack watched the rearview mirror as he drove forward. He saw Akam stuff a fresh clip into his rifle and turn back toward the oncoming truck. Smoke and shell casings spewed as he opened up. Men fell off the back of the truck, and Jack could hear screams over the sound of the roaring Mercedes. He saw Cobar pump three shells from his shotgun into the men. Jack kept his eyes on the road as he negotiated a curve then looked down on the scene during the traverse. He saw Akam take a bullet in the chest and blood spurted out of his back. He fell to his knees, firing a wild arc of bullets as he went down. Cobar ran to his side, knelt, then stood and fired a blast at the truck. He reached down for his friend, grabbed him around the waist and staggered to his feet, pumping his gun with one good arm. Cobar pumped and shot again. He backed up as he fired. For a second Jack thought about turning around and getting them, but then he saw a half a dozen men open up with their rifles. Cobar and Akam were caught in an obscene, horrifying dance as the energy from all the automatic weapons hit them. Jack looked at the road, pushed the accelerator to the floor, and raced up the hill. He drove and drove, nervously looking out the back but also afraid there would be another roadblock around every corner. Finally, when he felt safe, Jack stopped the Mercedes and got out. He walked around to the front of the car and shot through the driver's front window. The glass shattered into a milky run of fissures and breaks, and he shot again. He shot the Beretta into the air until it was empty and threw away the two extra clips Sturgis had given him. He stepped back into the car and drove into the outskirts of Arbil.

It was two in the morning when Jack parked the car a couple of blocks from Adan's house. He didn't want a Mercedes with bullet holes in the windshield out for display. He hurried up the street and knocked on the door. After several minutes Jack saw the lights inside come on, and Adan answered. He was bed frazzled, wearing a night robe and frowned when he looked over Jack's shoulder.

"Where are Cobar and Akam?" He opened the door wider to let Jack in.

Jack hurried in and turned to Adan. "Are Sally and Bill still here?"

"No, they left last night. But where are Cobar and Akam?"

"They are dead," said Jack. "We were ambushed at the Dokan Dam."

"What?" Adan's eyes flew open in shock. "Here," he gestured toward the dining area, "come in."

Jack followed him, and the room brightened as Adan flipped on the lights.

"Sit, I will make chai. But tell me what happened."

Jack had had plenty of time to rehearse the story on the way back to Arbil, so he sat down and began. His story was the truth about what happened up until the time he ran over the guard's body and left his two friends.

"Akam fired at the truck and Cobar shot the guards at the roadblock. One of them shot at me through the windshield, and I got out and shot him."

"With your nine millimeter?"

"Yes, with the gun I got from Sturgis at the MCC. Cobar shot the other guards at the roadblock and Akam finished off the ones in the truck. We were getting in the car to escape when a second truck came up. They were too close to run so Akan, and Cobar both jumped out and screamed at me to go."

Adan leaned back and shook his head.

"I didn't want to," said Jack. He put his hands up to his face. He needed to pause for effect. Jack slowly pulled his hands down and looked at Adan again. "Please believe me. I didn't want to leave them."

"It is understandable," said Adan. "Here we look out for our guests, Jack, whatever that requires."

Jack felt the relief drain from him. Adan believed him! "Please, Jack, go on."

Jack paused with a long breath. "I took off as they directed. But I could see them in the rearview mirror. Cobar and Akan were firing with everything they had."

Adan alternately frowned and nodded with the story.

"The men on the second truck fell and screamed and for a second," Jack stopped and looked at the floor again. He sighed and looked back at Adan. "For a second it looked like we could win. I stopped the car and backed up to Cobar and Akam and hopped out with my gun."

Jack stopped to gauge Adan's reaction. His eyes were wide with interest and belief.

"I emptied a clip into the men at the truck and slid in another. Cobar and Akam were firing their rifles non-stop. All I could hear was the rattle of the automatic and the boom, boom of the shotgun. I thought we were going to make it."

Jack forced his voice to break again. He swallowed and shook his head. "But the men in the truck kept coming, Cobar yelled at me to get out. He said, 'Don't let them capture you, Jack! Don't let them capture you'. I jumped back into the car, turned and emptied my last clip into the men at the truck, and took off." He put his face in his hands.

"It must have been terrible," said Adan. His voice was soft. "You must have been very frightened. In a strange country, vulnerable."

"Yes." Jack raised his head and looked at Adan's understanding eyes. "Yes, I was terrified. But I am humiliated. I lived." His voice broke again, and he looked to the side. He swallowed and looked back at Adan. "I lived, but they died."

Adan stood and walked to Jack. He put his hand on his shoulder. "You did all you could. I will send men to recover their bodies. I will also tell your story; the story of the three heroes. It is a miracle that you survived. But now, we must get you out of here."

A Peshmerga guard drove Jack back to the MCC, arriving there around noon the next day. Jack told his story to Colonel Sturgis, who wrote a detailed report of the incident. When he finished, Jack was the hero at the Dokan Dam. He was the one that fought desperately against tremendous odds but got away. He was the one saved by his Peshmerga friends. Jack was a mixture of Admiral

261

Nimitz, John Wayne, and Indiana Jones, and he smiled when he read the report. He took a copy of it to make sure it would be in his next fitness report. He also took the Beretta, a gift from Sturgis to a fellow warrior.

Jack returned to his desk in the Pentagon, and, indeed, the Sturgis report was not only the centerpiece of Jack's next fitness report but also the centerpiece of some close hold meetings in the Pentagon. Since the administration, and therefore the chairman, didn't want US involvement deep into Iraq known, the report did not circulate out of a small group. However, Jack was invited to meet with General Shalikashvili, who had just replaced General Powell as the chairman. He also met the CNO and was a guest speaker at the navy's all flag officer convention that year. These were indeed heady days for Jack Grant, a man who was uniquely charmed and destined for great things. He went back to working taskers and completed the minimum 24-month tour in the Pentagon. Following that, he was detailed to War College at Fort McNair in Washington, DC, specifically the Industrial College of the Armed Forces course of study. Jack selected for Captain and was detailed back to San Diego as the deputy commander of Carrier Air Wing Fourteen.

Grace was working on a legal brief for her boss when Jack strode in. Harley barked and ran to him, tail wagging and writhing to be picked up. Jack inexplicably reached down and patted his head. Grace raised her eyebrows at his momentary affection but remained seated.

"Got orders to an air wing." He smiled.

"Yes, you told me," said Grace. "In San Diego."

"Yes, CAG Fourteen." He smiled again. "You coming with me?"

Grace looked at him a moment, then shook her head. "Work is going well here. I am feeling better. I think it best to stay."

Jack shrugged and grinned. "It's probably best. I will be gone most of the time anyway."

"Yes," she said. "It's probably best."

The job of deputy commander of an air wing is the best deal in the military. All you do is fly. Jack had no real responsibilities except to get current in the airplanes the air wing flew. He was senior to everyone, but the CAG and the CAG was too busy to bother with Jack. Jack spent much of the next year getting requalified in the new F-14D Tomcat and initial qualification in the F-18 Hornet, EA-6B Prowler, A-6 Intruder, S-3 Viking, E-2 Hawkeye, and SH-60 Seahawk. He attended schools and endured his re-qualification in swimming and the infamous upside-down-inverted-while- blindfolded-helo-dunker. At the ship, he only flew the F-18 at night since it was so much easier than the Tomcat.

Jack also was a guest speaker at all kinds of events as the navy milked his MIG killer and Hero of Dokan Dam status. Jack's celebrity caused a bit of a rift between the CAG and him, but Jack wasn't concerned. The CAG wouldn't dare write any bad paper on him; after all, he was doing what big navy wanted. After fifteen months as DCAG, Jack and the CAG had a change of command and the new commander of Naval Air Forces Pacific, Vice Admiral Stan "Titan" Turner, was the guest speaker. His glowing words about Jack left no doubt that Phoenix Grant was going places.

In May 1996, Carrier Air Wing Fourteen and CAG Jack Grant deployed to the western Pacific on the USS Carl Vinson.

CHAPTER EIGHTEEN

The Vinson departed Alameda and journeyed down the California coast where she joined the other ships in the battle group and flew on the air wing. Once the squadrons were aboard, and the pilots' night current again, she headed west. The group stopped for three days in Hawaii, a visit on the outbound leg that is bittersweet. A seasoned sailor knows that to endure a six or seven month deployment, he must make the mental "switch" to the "I-am-gone-now-mode." The thought of being away from home can be overwhelming, almost inconceivable. Until this psychological adjustment occurs, the first days and even weeks of deployment are times of long, sad faces. Leaders know to keep their charges very, very busy during this initial sea period. Operations and training exercises filled the days and nights. Once the Sailor mentally adjusts to being gone, he is a much happier person. Hawaii interrupts that transition.

Jack had an excellent time in Hawaii, of course. The local leaders catered to him, as usual, and the Honolulu Star-Advisor carried a half-page article about the "Warrior CAG." Even Medal of Honor winner, Senator Daniel Inouye, visited the carrier and met with Jack in a Flag cabin reception. After three days, the Vinson and her group pulled out of Pearl Harbor and at 1000 commenced flight operations. Jack flew an F-18 Hornet that first night and landed on the pinky recovery. He ate a quick dinner in Wardroom One, then watched the night recoveries from CATTC. The CAG was the absolute king of CATTC, and he had a chair in the center of the gallery with his name on it. Nobody else ever used it. He watched until he got bored, then went to his office. He was sitting there when his DCAG, Captain John "Otter" Wilde, knocked and came in.

"What's up?" Jack smiled at Otter. His DCAG was a likable guy, excellent pilot, and leader and did much of the heavy lifting for the staff. He was the guy that had to carry all bad news to the worst possible recipients.

"Cag, I just landed on event seven."

"Have a seat." Jack motioned to the chair in front of his desk.

Otter sat down and leaned forward. Jack could see he was agitated. "I just landed on event seven, and Kathy Hodges answered my ball call. She controlled my pass."

Jack frowned and picked up his letter opener. "So?"

"So, CAG, she is a COD pilot. She only flies during the day." Jack frowned again.

"So what is the problem? She is an LSO, isn't she?"

They were interrupted by a knock on the door and LCDR Herb Coin; the CAG OPS officer stuck his head through the opening.

Otter looked at Jack. "CAG, I asked Herb and Rowdy to come down." He motioned to Herb who sidled in followed by LT Rowdy Gates, the senior CAG LSO. The two men stood next to Otter. Jack leaned back in his chair and twirled his letter opener.

"CAG, I know you weren't an LSO, but I was, so I am pretty current on this stuff." Otter motioned to Rowdy who handed him a thick book encased in blue plastic. "This is the LSO NATOPS, and I want to read you a passage."

"Okay," said Jack. "Go ahead." He still wasn't sure what the issue was.

"Here in 2.4.2, it says, 'The LSO shall remain proficient in the landing environment.' CAG, that line does a couple of things. It authorizes our staff LSOs to fly squadron airplanes and to receive flight pay, but it also requires them to be proficient. To me, that means to be current. So, if you are going to wave pilots aboard at night, you need to be current at night. The COD only flies in the daytime, as you know. So, Kathy Hodges has no business waving people at night because she does not fly at night."

"But, isn't she under training?"

"Yes, sir. She is an LSO under training who has been to LSO School, and her commanding officer provided the recommendation letter. But she should not be waving at night."

"Why not? Don't LSOs under training wave at night? Under our CAG LSO supervision, of course."

"Sure, but the other LSOs under training are all pilots that fly at night."

"Well, what did she do?" asked Jack. "Just walk up to the platform and take over?"

"No, sir, she approached Rowdy this morning," said Otter. He nodded at Rowdy.

267

"Well, sir, Kathy approached me in the wardroom and said she wanted to wave at night. Perry Mason was with her."

"Our JAG?"

"Yes, sir. She said it was a requirement for her career progression. I told her I wasn't sure she should wave at night, but she said Tailhook changed all of that."

"What?" Jack frowned and looked at Otter. "What about Tailhook?"

"She just said that things are different for women in the navy these days. Thanks to Tailhook."

"Sir, that is a bunch of bullshit," spat Otter. "This has nothing to do with gender. Male COD pilots don't fly at night either. Or wave airplanes at night."

"Get the JAG down here," said Jack. He didn't like the sound of this. "And how does this lead to her being on the platform tonight?"

"Well, sir, I guess that is my fault," said Rowdy. "The Tailhook thing spooked me, so I told her to come on out."

"I can't believe this," said Otter. He glared at Rowdy, then looked at Jack. "The key to the LSO-to-pilot relationship is trust. CAG, you know how it is. When you are coming aboard some shitty night, and the deck is moving, and you have already boltered once or twice, everything in your body screams for you to pull power and land. You do not want to go around again. And CAG, it is the voice of the LSO, that says, 'deck's down, hold what you got' that keeps you from sucking power and planting

268

the jet. But that voice has got to be believed. And it is believed because of the trust the pilot has in that LSO. Trust because he knows the LSO is a pro and confidence because he knows the LSO is a pilot too. A pilot that flies in that shitty weather himself."

Jack winced as he twirled his opener. He always thought LSOs were a bit stuck on themselves. Gods of the platform and all. He had never had a particularly good relationship with them. He was about to speak, but a knock on the door stopped him.

"Come in."

The CAG legal officer, LT Cyrus Mason, walked in. Everyone called him Perry after the TV character.

"So, what's the story with Kathy? I understand she approached you?" Jack nodded toward Perry.

"Yes, sir, she did." Perry swallowed and looked around the room.

"What did she want?"

"She just said she wanted a legal opinion on something then took me to see Rowdy."

"Did she threaten any action?" Jack sat up, now intrigued.

"Not directly. Kathy said she thought becoming an LSO would help her career and that the artificialities of the past that kept women down were over because of Tailhook."

"What artificialities?" Otter leaned forward. His face was red.

"You know, sir." Perry looked at the floor, then at the DCAG. "Things that the navy put in the way of women."

"What about other COD LSOs that are men. Do they wave at night?" asked Jack. He was now concerned. He didn't need any more Tailhook shit in his life.

"Of course not," said Otter. "As I said before, airplanes that fly in the day, like the COD, have LSOs that wave in the day. They go through a qualification process for that, but they are never fully qualified LSOs because they don't fly at night."

"But doesn't that hurt their career?"

"Their career as what? COD pilots do not have a career like the rest of us. They are never going to command a ship or an air wing or a shore station for that matter."

"Is that fair?" Jack could see Otter was getting pissed, but he didn't like the idea of any perceived unfairness to women. It might cause him trouble.

"What has fair got to do with it?" asked Otter. "What is right is to have qualified pilots, trusted pilots, wave our people aboard this carrier. That is the only important thing."

"Perry, what is your thinking on this?" Jack looked at the JAG. He wanted to give someone else an opportunity and to let the DCAG cool off.

"Well, sir." Perry took a breath and scuffed the deck with his shoe. He did not look at DCAG. "I think she might have a point of some kind. It depends upon the language in the LSO manual, I guess."

"The language is pretty clear," spat Otter. "It says SHALL…not should, or maybe, or kind of. It says the LSO SHALL remain proficient in the landing environment."

"I tell you what," said Jack. "Perry, you get with Rowdy and come up with some facts on all of this. Ask the bureau for help. Ask the AIRPAC JAG what he thinks. In the meantime, let's let Kathy wave at night like she wants. Under heavy observation, Rowdy. Who knows, maybe she will get tired of the cold and the wind up there and give up on her own."

Jack avoided looking at Otter, who stood and motioned to the door. "You guys clear on out now."

Jack watched them file out, except for Otter.

"CAG the air wing will despise this. Everybody has had enough of the Tailhook crap. Every single guy here has had someone they know drawn and quartered by that fucking mess, and a lot of innocent guys have lost their careers. Having a person who is not qualified to wave at night just because she is a woman will be seen for what it is. A capitulation to political correctness."

Jack looked at Otter, then leaned back and looked at the ceiling. He was mentally pacing through his risk matrix. Loss of the "love" of the air wing was not trivial, but he knew he could overcome that. After all, he WAS Phoenix Grant for God's sake. What would be much more difficult would be if Kathy got hold of some newspaper or congressperson or whatever and made a significant case out of this. That is not a risk he wanted to take.

He glared back at Otter. "Then DCAG I suggest you get in front of this and explain to whoever needs it that it is about the career progression of a junior officer who is in a non-typical career path for naval aviators. A young officer that wants a little help."

"Oh bullshit, CAG. It's me you are talking to now, not some PR puke. Do you forget about the risks involved here? The risk to the ship, you, more importantly, to the air wing? What if she gets behind some guy throwing a bad pass at the boat?"

"That's what we have the CAG LSOs for." Jack lowered his voice. He didn't want people out in the passageway to hear their business.

"It's hard for the CAG LSO to fix something inside the wave off window CAG. And as we know, Rowdy isn't that strong, to begin with."

"DCAG, I don't want to argue with you about this. I have made up my mind. If we turn up something from AIRPAC or the bureau, we will turn it off. I promise."

Otter looked at Jack and slowly took a breath. He shook his head, turned, and walked out of the room.

CHAPTER NINETEEN

Often, West Pac battlegroups conduct port calls in Singapore, Hong Kong, and other exotic places but the Vinson Battlegroup schedule forced it to continue west after Hawaii. The battlegroup transited the Malacca Straits, exiting at the northern mouth, then headed west once more. The Vinson's first mission for the deployment was a bilateral training exercise with the Indian Air Force and their new MIG-29's. The Indians had purchased over fifty of the 4th generation fighters as a hedge to F-16s that Pakistan had acquired from the US. The training exercise was so delicate that a contingent from the American consulate in Mumbai flew to the carrier, landing via COD.

Jack, DCAG, and the skippers from the F-14, F-18 and E-2 squadrons met the visitors in the flag mess for lunch where Admiral Summersly and his Chief of Staff welcomed them. The consulate group leader was the embassy air attaché in New Delhi, a USAF Colonel who was also a former F-16 pilot. His name was Hank Corning, and Jack found him to be an insufferable prick. Jack felt that Hank fashioned himself as the reincarnation of Lawrence of Arabia, only in India, and his every word and action was condescending and elitist. He also reminded Jack of the pilot Booger fought back in TOPGUN, BEFORE the beat down. Jack would have excused himself and left the details to DCAG, and the skippers had it not been for Jennifer Fletcher. Jennifer was a USAF Major and the public affairs officer in the consulate, and she was the leader of the consulate group of staffers and note-takers that formed the group. Jack thought she was the hottest thing he had seen since leaving San Diego, and he forced himself not to stare at her during lunch. He wanted to bang

273

her in the worst way. He could tell by her glances and the way she smiled at him that she was doable.

"Now that we know a bit about how you view the region, maybe we can get into some specifics about the exercise." Jack took a sip of coffee and rattled the cup back into the saucer. "We read the backgrounder message traffic, but what do you want to get out of it? What's not in the message traffic?" He watched Hank nod his head in the broad, powerful way superegos do to show appreciation for the little mind of a lesser being.

"I am glad you bring that up CAG." Hank blessed the room with a smile and leaned back in his chair.

"Sir, sorry for interrupting, I still need to do the piece on the CAG. For the article, the embassy promised to the New Delhi Times." Jennifer smiled and looked at Hank. "Could I get some time with Captain Grant?" She smiled again as she looked around the table. "The Times was established just last year by Dr. Govind Narain Srivastava, and the paper wants items that will be out of the norm for Indian readers. We suggested an article on Captain Grant, and they were thrilled."

Jack felt his face flush. "We can go to my cabin if you wish. Your staff is also welcome."

"Leave them here," interrupted Hank. "We need to capture the details."

Jack could have kissed the prick for that but instead stood and beckoned to Jennifer. "Follow me." He looked at Otter and smiled, "DCAG be sure to get the essence of what they want."

"Yes, sir," said Otter.

274

Jack walked to the flag mess door, turned to ensure Jennifer was following, then continued down the passageway to his room. He entered, turned on the lights, and deftly locked the door behind his guest. He turned and embraced her, kissing her deeply. She responded just like he knew she would, and he reached up to her breasts. She moaned as he massaged her and he unbuttoned her shirt and took it off. He reached down to her belt, loosened it and slid her trousers off. Soon she was naked, and he had her kneel in front of him as he unzipped his flight suit and dropped it to the floor.

Back in the meeting room, Otter listened to Hank drone about the importance of India to the cosmos, then interrupted. "So, tell us the requirement."

"Yes," said the COS. "The admiral is very interested in ensuring we support the embassy and the consulate. We understand the delicate balance here between India and Pakistan."

"We are grateful for that," said Hank. "You see the Indians purchased over fifty MIG-29s during the past couple of years to offset the F-16s we sold to Pakistan. This training is the first opportunity the US has to temper some of the concern India has for our Pakistan relationship."

Otter shrugged and took a sip of coffee. He could give a shit about Pakistan or India. All he wanted was to get the details and go to his flight brief.

"So, what kind of presentations do they want? What do you want to achieve by all of this?" Otter looked at his watch.

"Yes," added the COS. "The message traffic alluded to positive scenarios and outcomes. What does that mean?"

"The Indians want to know if their MIGs are capable of beating the Paki F-16s. Hard to figure that out of course without them fighting each other. Lord knows we do not want that to happen. So, the Indians approached us about an idea whereby they face airframes that are equivalent to the F-16 flown by western pilots. That led to this initiative."

"I see," said the COS. The admiral will be very interested in that. It didn't come out in the message traffic."

"No, of course not," said Hank. "We couldn't say that in any public forum. So, the idea would be to conduct static events that allow the Indian pilots to flex their new hardware and tactics. You have a lot of former instructors in your squadrons, don't you?"

"Yes, we do," replied Otter.

"So, we ask that you set up the events in a classic two versus two format, you know, around fifty miles separation to start. That will give them some time to work their radars before engaging. And if you could use mixed F-14 and F-18 sections, it would be perfect. That will let the Indian pilots see both airframes."

Otter nodded and sipped his coffee.

"Of course, the weakness in this plan is that the Tomcat and Hornet are not equivalent to the F-16. But we can't do anything about that."

"I guess I don't get you," said Otter.

Hank laughed. "Look, guys, these are MIG-29s. They will probably be more than most of your guys can handle doing your best. I don't think you need to hold anything back."

Otter frowned and leaned back in his chair.

"I mean, I've beaten the hell out of F-16s with my Eagle, and I've fought the Tomcat and the Hornet," said Hank. "I think the MIG-29 can match you any way you want it."

"Okay," said Otter. "I think we got this." He started to stand.

"But what if it doesn't go that way?" asked the COS. "The message traffic mentioned positive scenarios and outcomes. What if the MIG-29 pilots have difficulty?"

"Well, I don't think that is a possibility," said Hank. He chuckled and shrugged. "But if it happens by some freak set of events I would hope you modify your presentation." He turned to Otter. "Let's you and I conduct the face-to-face brief for the events. We can always modify with message traffic or telephone. We have your contact information."

"Fine." Otter stood, and he and Frank left for a squadron briefing room.

An hour after Jack took Jennifer to his room, they dressed, and he handed her some news clippings he kept in his desk drawer. He had several copies of various articles about the hero of Desert Shield and the Dokan Dam.

"Take these," he grinned. "Write your article with them."

Jennifer took the clippings and turned to go when they heard a knock at the door. Jack frowned but quietly unlocked and opened it.

"CAG, I was hoping to see you." It was Kathy, the COD pilot. "Kathy, just the person I was hoping to see." Jack opened the door wider. "This is Major Fletcher from the consulate. Maybe you can give her some perspective about life out here as a female pilot."

"Really? That would be great!" Kathy smiled.

"Jennifer, this is Kathy Hodges, one of our COD pilots. She might have flown you aboard."

"She did," beamed Jennifer. "Hey Kathy, got a minute to talk?"

Jack watched the two women walk down the passageway. He was humming as he shut the door and headed to his shower.

Down the passageway, Otter held a brief meeting with the Tomcat and Hornet skippers. "Take the tanks and rails off the Tomcats on the roof. Take the laser pod and the centerline tank off the Hornets. Put the A team on the flight schedule. I want guys out there that know what to do with the jet. I will have Air Ops add airborne tankers to the schedule. I want you to kick the fucking shit out of those guys."

The next day, the COD with the embassy team left on the first launch and Vinson steamed north to a position off the Indian coast near the MIG-29 base of Jamnagar. It was the home of 28 Squadron, the first Indians to receive the Fulcrums. As the ship moved toward the exercise area, the Hornet and Tomcat aircrews studied the Fulcrum and honed their tactics.

Otter led the first event from a Hornet's cockpit, and his wingman was "Marshall" Dillon, a Tomcat pilot with the capability to play the big fighter like a banjo. They used superior tactics and simulated launches of Phoenix, AAMRAM, and Sparrow missiles before merging with the MIGS. Then when in visual range, ravaged them with Sidewinders and guns. All of the training sorties that day went the same as the CAG Seven fighters butchered the Fulcrums in engagement after engagement. The only shot the MIGs called all day was a long-range Hail Mary that, upon analysis, most likely killed his wingman. The CAG staff compiled a roll of gun camera film, TCS footage and recordings that they entitled, The Jamnagar Turkey Shoot.

That night, Jack was doing paperwork when Otter walked in. "CAG, got some film of today's flights if you want to look." Jack hesitated. He was busy and would prefer Otter handle the MIG-29 business. It was just some low-level tactical stuff, and he didn't want to mess with it. But then he smiled. Otter had been cold to him since the situation with Kathy, the COD pilot, and he wanted to smooth things out.

"Things go well today?"

"Things went exceptionally well today." Otter smiled as the phone rang.

"Hang on a second, DCAG. Take a seat."

Jack wanted to play the tape with Otter there, to appease him. No reason to have his right-hand man pissed at him. He picked up the phone.

279

"CAG, its Major Jennifer Fletcher, from the consulate."

"Hey Jenny, what's going on?"

"Look, Hank called, and he was distraught with all of you out there."

Jack frowned. "What's the problem?"

"The commander from 28 Squadron came to visit Hank tonight. He was outraged at what had happened today. He told Hank he was mortified by the embarrassment his young pilots had suffered during what they thought were to be western training flights. Instead, they had faced graduate-level scenarios from seasoned Americans who didn't want to provide training; they just wanted to stroke their egos."

"I haven't received a debrief of the day yet, but if your MIG drivers expected us to just fly out in front of them, I guess they were surprised."

Otter smiled and gave him a thumbs up.

"CAG, we had an agreement for training. We had an agreement for positive outcomes. You are putting us in a very precarious spot."

"Well, maybe your idea of training and our idea of training is different. In the navy, we train like we fight. And we fight to win."

"That may be so," said Jenny. "But I also train like I fight. I came out to the ship for one reason: to fight for my career. And if you don't have your guys fly out in front of mine tomorrow, I am going to tell the ambassador how you let me suck your dick in your stateroom."

Jack almost dropped the phone. He glanced at Otter to see if he had heard. Otter still had a tell-them-to-go-fuck-themselves grin on his face.

"What, what?"

"You heard me, CAG. I promised the ambassador that he would be very pleased with this training event. I promised him that his pilots would be very uplifted. My career depends on this. So, I will tell the ambassador that after you forced me to suck your dick, you put that thing of yours in my ass. After your Tailhook business, I don't think he will have any trouble believing me. Do you?"

Jack swallowed and gripped the phone tighter. "DO YOU?"

"No, no, I guess not."

"So, unless you want the whole world to know all of this, change your routine, or I will talk. Get it?"

Jack felt sick. He looked at Otter's big grin. "Get it?"

Jack heard the phone click. He looked up at Otter. "We have to change things for tomorrow."

"What do you mean?"

"I mean we have to give the MIG drivers a break, let them win a couple."

"Why? Why would we ever do that?"

Jack struggled for an explanation and shrugged.

"CAG, why would we ever do that?" Otter looked bewildered.

"I think it is the right thing to do. You know, for diplomatic reasons."

"Diplomatic reasons? If those fucking idiots are stupid enough to buy MIGs, then they can fucking die in them for all I care. Fuck them!"

"Look, Otter, it's complicated." Jack felt his face get red.

"There is nothing complicated about it. The job is for men to fly training sorties against men. That means to bring all you got and then debrief what you brought. It doesn't mean wimp around and get shot for goodwill."

Jack was pissed! Fucking Otter and his small fucking mind! "Don't fucking argue about it DCAG. Call the fighter squadrons and tell them I said so. Limit to four G's, no afterburner. Period!"

Otter looked like he had been shot. He glared at Jack for a long time, then shook his head and walked to the door.

"Look, Otter."

Otter opened the door then turned to Jack and shook his head. "Jesus, CAG, what happened to you?"

CHAPTER TWENTY

"CAG, you have a minute?"

Jack looked up and saw Admiral Summersly standing in the doorway. He leaped to attention. "Yes, sir."

The admiral walked in, followed by the COS. "Can we talk in private?"

"Yes, sir." The admiral and the COS took seats in front of Jack's desk.

"What can I do for you, sir?"

"Jack, first of all, I want to tell you how sorry I am about your wife. I never met her but hope your trip can bring some closure. Some relief to you."

"Thank you, sir." Jack swallowed and drew a deep breath.

Grace had been placed in a hospice by her mother. Jack had received a Red Cross message the day before with an urgent suggestion to come to her bedside. He hadn't seen her in over two years.

"We anchor in about ten minutes; I have the barge ready to take you to fleet landing. I understand you have your tickets?"

"Yes, sir. I leave Bombay, I mean, Mumbai this afternoon."

The men chuckled nervously at Jack's mistake. The Indians had changed Bombay's name the previous November. It was easy to forget.

"Good, good. And to be clear, you will rejoin us when we pull into Jebel Ali."

"Yes, sir."

"Good. Good. Jack, I am concerned about the timing here. We just got message traffic on a plan called Desert Reveille. It involves attacking Iran from inside the gulf with one or more carriers. To this point, it has been only a powerpoint brief given to successive battle groups when they enter the gulf. We are the third group to get it. We will get the brief from the battle group we are relieving; we update it, then we brief Fifth Fleet. Heretofore, it has been more of a drill than anything else. However, a BIG difference for us is a requirement to work with an air force component that is establishing in Qatar right now. They are setting up a composite air wing with a colonel leading it. He will be your counterpart."

"I understand sir, but why now and why Qatar?"

"Some Black Ops chatter indicates the Iranians will do something at the Atlanta Olympics. Qatar allows the Air Force to use targets in the south while we would look at ones to the north."

"Yes, sir," said Jack.

The admiral frowned and looked at his hands. He took a deep breath and raised his head. "Look, CAG, I hate to bring this up now but the follies last night disturbed me."

"Yes, sir." Jack swallowed and took a quick breath.

284

"I know I am a surface warfare officer, but I have seen quite a few Foc'scle follies and last night was unbelievable."

"Sir, I think they were just blowing off some steam." Jack leaned back in his chair and tried to calm himself.

The follies were a fucking disaster!

"I don't think so, Jack. The follies I have been to feature the normal JO hi-jinx, I get that. But last night. Last night they were pointed at you and not in fun. Your squadron JOs were cruel, Jack. It doesn't make sense to me why they would act that way."

"Sir, I think…"

"CAG." The COS interrupted. "What was the deal with the chocolate on the kid's nose? Christ, I hope that was chocolate?"

"Sir, it was just a JO wearing my name tag, making fun. That's all."

"I don't know." The COS shook his head. "He showed up every few minutes and said, "Anybody seen the admiral?""

"Every time he did it, the house came down." Admiral Summersly shifted in his chair. "That humor directly implicates me."

"Yes, sir," said Jack.

"Jack, evidently, the air wing thinks you are brown-nosing me. Why would they think that?"

"Well, sir, the JO crowd always thinks that."

"I don't think so," said the admiral. He looked at the COS. "The whole follies had that as the theme," said the COS. "I mean, the guy with the Indian accent pretending to have anal sex with the Hornet pilot. That was disgusting. And the whole time he is saying, 'Take this for the CAG.' I mean, wow! That was terrible."

Jack swallowed and looked down at his desk. He picked up a pen and took a breath.

It had been terrible.

"What was that all about?" Asked the admiral.

"It was because CAG instructed the air wing to let the Indian MIG-29 pilots beat them," said the COS.

"What?" The admiral frowned and looked at the COS and then at Jack. "I saw the tape your staff made after the first day. Our guys got the best of them, but it seemed pretty straight forward. Besides, the Indians just got those jets. It will take time to exploit their capabilities. I think our training will inspire them to learn quickly. Did you see the tape?"

"Yes, sir." Jack lied. He never did look at the tape Otter showed him.

"Then, I don't get it," said the admiral. "Why change what you were doing?"

Jack looked at his hands to avoid the gaze. He thought of Jenny's warning. "I just thought it might be better to ease up on them." He looked at the admiral. "To give them a more valuable experience."

"Well, air-to-air training is your business. But I sure wouldn't have changed what you were doing." The admiral shrugged.

"Yeah, CAG," smirked the COS. "we got message traffic from the consulate, and there was no issue with the first day of training. Nobody said they wished you would fly out in front of them."

"And what was the deal with the 'Roger balls, I have your balls in my hand.' What was that all about...with the female voice?" The admiral frowned at Jack.

Jack took a deep breath and swallowed again. "Sir, the CAG LSO came to me asking to let the female COD pilot wave the air wing at night."

"Okay, so?"

"I thought it would be good for her career."

"Okay, that still doesn't explain follies."

Jack shrugged, but the COS cleared his throat. "Admiral, she only flies in the daytime. As you know, the COD doesn't fly at night."

"Okay."

"LSO NATOPS says that an LSO must be familiar with the landing environment. That means the LSOs must fly aboard the ship at night if they are to wave at night."

The COS paused and looked at Jack. "So the air wing took exception to CAG letting a woman pilot that only flies in the day wave them at night. They see it as a politically correct move that you, the admiral, wanted."

"Me?" The admiral sat up and frowned. "Me? How does that happen? What do I have to do with it?"

"Sir," Jack started to speak.

"COS, would you leave us alone?" The admiral glared at Jack.

"Yes, sir." COS pushed his chair back, stood, and left.

Jack watched the door close, then turned to the admiral.

"CAG I know there is a tradition in naval aviation to encourage your junior officers to be, shall we say, colorful."

"Yes, sir."

"But, they are still officers, CAG. And officers need to show some bit of dignity. Don't you think?"

"Yes, sir." Jack took a breath to calm himself.

"You appear to have lost control of your air wing, and worse, they have lost control of themselves. That, CAG, is NOT the kind of leadership that I reward."

Admiral Summersly stood and walked to the door. He opened it, then turned back toward Jack.

"We'll also need to talk about Desert Reveille when you get back."

"Sir, I will put a planning team on it now."

"Good. Make sure the DCAG leads the team. I need the best plan we can develop."

"Yes, sir." Jack watched the admiral open the door and leave. He walked to the door and locked it then went back to his desk and slumped into his chair. He leaned back and rested his neck against its high back. The King's Throne was what his skipper's called the chair. He didn't much feel like a king now. The air wing, his air wing, had lost respect for him. And he was Jack Grant!

That night Jack was sitting in his office when he heard a soft cry from his bedroom. He ignored it. He was on an aircraft carrier; there was nothing in his bedroom. But he heard the call again, and then again. Jack walked to the door, and as he put his hand on the knob, the weeping grew louder. Fear seized him, and he wanted to run but pushed open the door. A figure was on his bed, and he didn't want to see who or what it was. He didn't want to walk any closer, but something made him. He walked to the figure and pulled back the sheet. Grace sat up in the bed. She had a hideous grin, but she had no eyes. Jack tried to run. His feet wouldn't move. Grace came closer; he couldn't move! Grace's face started to distort. Then, it was Christopher's head on her body. His baby mouth opened, and his teeth fell out one by one. They made a ping when they hit the floor.

Ping…ping…ping!

The Christopher baby mouth said, "Bav, Bav." But, it was the voice of the Kurdish girl, Navi. Jack tried to run, but he couldn't move. Christopher moved closer and closer. Jack could smell the cough syrup on his breath. It was for babies; Grace had gotten it. He came closer and closer, and Jack began to scream.

289

Jack jerked up in bed. His heart was racing, and he switched on the light. It took him thirty minutes to calm down.

It was just the nightmare again.

CHAPTER TWENTY-ONE

Jack opened the door to the house in Virginia Beach, and a joyous Harley met him. Despite his advancing years, the little dog was still full of energy and playfulness. He stood on his hind legs like a miniature polar bear and whined to be picked up. Jack ignored him and walked across the living room, but the dog insisted on friendship. He stood on his legs again and whined. Jack sighed, reached down, and patted the dog. Then, he surprised himself and swooped the little creature into his arms. He felt a tightness in his chest as he nuzzled the dog.

Why did I do that?

He was surprised the dog still liked him. If dogs held grudges, Harley didn't appear to hold one toward Jack; despite the fact, Jack had spurned him over and over. He put Harley down and went into the kitchen. It was empty, so he walked out the back and found Grace's housekeeper, Maria, smoking a cigarette on the patio.

"I'm going to the hospice," he said. He waited for Maria to speak, but she just put her cigarette out.

"I'll be back this afternoon." Then, for some reason, "Look after Harley." He frowned as he said it.

Why do that? She looks after him anyway? He shook his head and headed to his rental car.

Jack pushed open the door of the Coastal Peace Hospice and walked to the receptionist's desk. He made himself appear cheerful, despite the situation and despite the fact, he had not slept much since leaving the Vinson.

The meeting with admiral Summersly and the air wing's treatment of him had continually played in his mind.

He introduced himself to the receptionist, Dottie, according to her name tag, and showed her his identification. She showed him the elevator, and moments later, he exited on the third floor. A young man who introduced himself as Joe led the way through the tangle of rooms and hallways. Jack felt uneasy. It was a clean place, mocked by the occasional, bright vase of flowers. As if a plastic daffodil could hide the final battlegrounds of the dying.

"Grace is in here." He opened a door, and they entered a small room. It was sparse with no windows and painted in pale green.

Darker green linoleum covered the floor, and a nightstand and chair were the only pieces of furniture besides the bed. It was a single, placed against the wall, and Jack saw a figure curled on the edge. It was Grace, and above her on the wall was a portrait of Jesus, His head uplifted, and His hands stretched forward.

"Where is all the stuff?"

"Stuff?" Joe frowned.

"You know, the monitors and other medical equipment."

"There is nothing to monitor," said Joe.

"But she, she looks..." Jack was shocked at what he saw laying on the bed. Grace was a bag of bones. She was on her side, facing the room, and he could see the sharp outline of her shoulder blades against the blue cotton nightgown. Her right arm was above the sheet and her wrist and fingers poked out like Halloween props. Her once-proud gob of beautiful hair was a mat of greasy strings, sweat-plastered to her head. Her face set in a frown, brows knitted, mouth partially open. Jack could hear whimpering.

"Uhh, uhh, uhh, uhh…"

"Jesus." Jack slumped into the chair.

"You haven't seen her for a while?"

"No," mumbled Jack. "Not in a couple of years."

"She has been here for two weeks. Her mother brought her in."

"Her mother?"

"Yes, a strange situation. Grace's mother brought her in, carrying her dog. The three of them stayed together for most of the day, then the mother and the little dog left. Grace went downhill almost immediately."

Jack looked at Joe. In the weak light, he was unsure if his expression held pity, sorrow, or scorn.

"I was gone." Jack looked back at Grace. He felt the urge to explain. "I'm in the navy."

"Yes, we know. You haven't had any recent contact with your wife, have you?"

"No." Jack followed Joe's eyes to his wife. "Not for a long while."

"She has ovarian cancer. She is very sick. She only has days left."

"How can you tell?"

"Because I do this for a living," said Joe.

Jack was again confused by Joe's tone. He couldn't quite tell the intent.

"What happens now?"

"She will continue to fail. She hasn't moved for two days, hasn't eaten. Her body is resisting, but it is shutting down."

"Does it hurt?" The whimpering seemed like anguish.

"She is on morphine for pain relief. The whimpering and panting you hear is her fight. It is her fight to stay alive as long as she can."

"I thought people came to hospice because they want to die?"

"No, they come to hospice TO die. Whether a person wants to or not, the body will try to stay alive as long as it can."

"Jesus." Jack took in a quiet breath. He felt himself swallow as he looked at Grace. "Will she be like this until the end?"

"Pretty much, yes. Grace will move occasionally. She will moan. She won't open her eyes anymore now. She will frown and cry. And, she will reach out, grasping the air."

"Reach out?"

"Yes, we call it plucking. Grace will reach out with her fingers and pluck the air. We aren't sure what it means, but it happens during the final days."

"Does she know we are here? That I am here?"

"She knows that we are here," said Joe. He leaned over Grace. "Miss Grace, Miss Grace."

Grace continued to whimper but moved her right arm with a slight twitch.

"Miss Grace, your husband is here."

Jack swallowed, and despite his best efforts, his eyes welled.

He felt his chest tighten as a tremendous feeling of guilt swept him.

Grace groaned and moved her arm. She raised her fingers and then dropped them to the bed.

"It's all right, Miss Grace." Joe picked a sponge from a bowl of water on the nightstand. He squeezed it, then gently wiped Grace's forehead. He dipped the sponge again and rubbed her neck, then turned to Jack. "You can do that for her if you want to. I'll come back a little later."

Jack took the sponge and dipped it into the water. It was cool.

He squeezed it and started to wipe Grace's forehead. But, he stopped. He dropped the sponge into the water and sat down. He didn't want to look at Grace, so he looked at the floor. Tears welled in his eyes, and he couldn't stop them. The tears pissed him off. They frustrated him. He hadn't given Grace a second's thought for so long. So what was the deal with the tears?

He swallowed and picked up the sponge again. He began to wipe her forehead.

Grace's breathing was deep and ragged, and she would stop for long moments. The first time she stopped breathing, Jack thought she was dead. He felt another, different, touch of guilt because it relieved him. It didn't make him happy, but it eased him. He could settle the thing and be on his way. He wiped her forehead for a while longer. She seemed to fall asleep. Just as he started to leave and find Joe, she took a loud, ragged, deep gulp of air. It almost lifted her off the bed. Jack had never seen anything like this, and it was fascinating and horrifying at the same time. He continued to watch his wife as the cycle of breathing and not breathing played, as the slit between life and death closed and opened again. But, after a while, he just felt disappointment when she started to breathe again. And he felt guilty, but, by now, it was familiar.

"Uhh, uhh, uhh, uhh." The whimpering was never-ending.

Jack sat in the chair and felt his head nod. He must have dozed because when he jerked awake, it was late morning. He looked at Grace, then stood and walked to the edge of the bed. He reached down and touched her forehead, and he didn't know why. He couldn't do anything for her. He wasn't even sure if he wanted to. Her forehead was hot and clammy.

"Grace. Grace, I'm here." She didn't make any move to indicate she heard him.

He swallowed again as fresh tears filled his eyes.

Jesus, why the tears? Christ!

She looked so fragile and helpless, lying like an old rag doll.

Like an old rag doll all alone.

Ovarian cancer? Why wasn't he told?

But Jack, why didn't you ask?

He knew why no one told him. No one told him because he didn't give a shit about Grace. He didn't deserve to know.

Jack wiped his eyes, but they filled again.

She had nothing. One nightgown. Maybe a toothbrush.

Nothing! Here she was dying alone, and he was the only one with her, and he was nothing but a prick who hadn't loved her enough---if he ever did love her.

Jack was shocked at his feelings. He didn't care about her!

WHY AM I CRYING?

He couldn't control himself. He couldn't stop the crying. It didn't make any fucking sense.

He slumped back into his chair and squeezed his eyes shut.

Why did he feel so guilty? A lot of marriages fail? I didn't give her cancer.

Hell, I don't even have to be here.

He sat in the chair and struggled with his thoughts. Thoughts he could not control, and he listened to Grace moan and whimper. Occasionally, she would stop, and he would look up, wondering if that was it.

Had she died?

Was he hoping she had died?

But then the whimpering would start again.

That afternoon, Grace started plucking. Jack was dozing in the chair when he heard the covers rustle and saw her lying more on her back. Her right arm was reaching into the air, and her fingers were plucking at something. She was whimpering, her eyes shut hard and her face set in a deep frown.

Jack stood and walked to the bed. "Grace. Grace."

She made no indication that she heard him but kept plucking and whimpering.

Then, her hand dropped, and she rolled onto her side again.

Jack wiped new tears away and looked for a tissue. Joe would be by any minute. He glanced at the nightstand and saw a small, cloth-covered box sitting in the back corner. He took it and sat back in the chair. He turned the box in his hands and put his nose to it. The box held a faint smell of Chanel. Chanel had been a favorite of Grace's.

Jack opened the box. Grace's wedding ring and the fake Rolex he had bought for her when they were first married lay on top.

"It's real," he had said to her glowing eyes. It wasn't the first time he had lied to her, but it was the time he always remembered because of her eyes. Eyes that had been wide with happiness and she had squealed with delight. "I saved up all my cruise money to get it," he had lied. The truth was he had paid thirty dollars. As far as he knew, she always thought it was real. And here it was after all this time.

A folded letter was under the ring, and Jack lifted it out of the box. Under the letter was Harley's collar and Jack cursed aloud as his eyes welled.

Jack angrily swiped the tears from his eyes and face.

Goddamnit!

He opened the letter. It was from Mrs. Meacham, their old neighbor from San Diego.

Grace, I am sure your husband told you about your brave little Harley and how two coyotes almost attacked him. I heard the barking, you know I can't sleep and looked out the window just in time to see Harley chase them away. He is such a good dog; protecting your house and all. I am sure Jack DID NOT tell you about the hussy that was in your home. I saw her at the door, wearing one of Jack's shirts. I want you to know that too. If I can ever be of help, you have my number and address.

Maude

Jack folded the letter and put it in his pocket. No reason for anybody to find and read that. He closed the box and swallowed hard.

So Grace knew about Misha.

She had never confronted him. In the short conversations, they had had since he had moved out she had never mentioned anything about that night.

Joe came in later that afternoon and brought Jack a sandwich and some juice. He also turned Grace over on her other side and wiped her face with the sponge. He hummed softly to himself as he worked. Jack sat back and watched him, strangely uncomfortable with it all. Here a total stranger was so attentive and caring for a woman he didn't know while he, her husband, hadn't even tried to contact her for two years. He wondered how Joe could do such things, day after day, year after year, caring for others who would never know him, never even acknowledge him.

What makes a guy like Joe tick?

I mean, maybe guys like him get off on this kind of thing?

Jack frowned as he watched and shook his head. Joe was not representative of how things were or how people were. Jack was sure of that. Joe was an outlier. People like Joe were important in places like this, but that was about it.

Then why do I feel so guilty?

He sat for a while after Joe left then went to the lobby to see if Dottie was there. He could probably convince her to go back to his hotel room with him. Jack knew she wanted to have sex with him. But, as he walked across the lobby to her receptionist stand, he realized that he had no interest in sex. That confused him, so he just asked if she had any aspirin.

Harley met Jack at the door and was as excited about seeing him as before. A thing that Jack could hardly fathom. But, he picked the little dog up once again and rubbed his ears and patted his back. The short tail whacked back and forth. Maria appeared, then left, and Jack heard her car drive off. He found Harley's food bowl and filled it from the bag then sat down to the Carl's Junior Double Whopper with cheese and bacon he had bought on the way home. Harley alerted on the burger o Jack gave him the bacon. He didn't know why because he loved bacon more than the burger.

After dinner, Jack sat on the couch, and Harley jumped to his side. They watched television together until Jack could no longer stay awake. He went to bed, and Harley plopped down beside him. Jack pushed him away so he could have room to sleep, and turned out the light. Some hours later, he awoke to feel the little beast snuggled up next to him. Jack started to push him away again, but, hesitated. He reached over and stroked the dog's furry head and petted it. Jack took a deep breath and smiled. It all seemed to be the way it should, and Jack wondered why he had been so distant to the little dog in the past. And why so distant and troubled with Grace? He couldn't remember what the trouble had been. He spent the night in a fitful, sleepless struggle and returned to the hospice at 0800. Joe was attending to Grace when he arrived.

Jack took the chair and watched as Joe gave Grace a sponge batch. Her body sagged as he moved her, the muscle tone long gone. Her skin was like paper against her bones, and her breasts sagged down her chest. Despite the tremendous invasion of privacy, Joe took immense care to cover her as he worked, treating her with the utmost respect and dignity. The entire time he talked to her in soft and reassuring tones, telling her what he was doing.

"Miss Grace I'm going to turn you on your side, okay?"

"Miss Grace, I'm going to have to remove your nighty now."

"Miss Grace, this is going to be a little cool on your back."

"Miss Grace I'm putting on some cream okay? It will make you rest more comfortably."

That afternoon, Grace's whimpering grew louder, and she began to pluck continuously. Jack left the room and found Joe talking to another staff member in the hall. They went back to Grace's room together.

"Is she trying to tell us something or get something? Does she need water or anything?"

"No. Many patients do that during the final stages. I think she is reaching for something only she can see."

"Reaching for what?"

"Only she knows," said Joe. He walked to the bed and put his hand on Grace's forehead, stroking it gently. "Maybe a child or maybe her mother. Did she have a pet? Who knows, maybe Jesus?" He looked up at Jack, then back at Grace. "Maybe all of that."

"Should I bring her dog?"

Joe didn't answer, so Jack walked to the bed and stood beside him. He looked at his wife for a long time. Then he whispered, "What do you think she is reaching for?"

He felt Joe's eyes turn to him.

"I think she is reaching for you."

Jack swallowed hard to hold back the tears. He stared down at the bed and heard Joe walk out of the room.

"Why would you be reaching for me?" Jack whispered to his dying wife. "I never did anything but hurt you." He dropped to his knees and put his head on the bed. The tears came, and he sobbed into the sheets. Everything was wrong. Everything was wrong. All of his life he had schemed and manipulated and lied and made things up and tore things down and he had never walked in a straight line anywhere. But somehow everything he did worked out. Didn't that mean something?

I am the luckiest man I know. And I don't understand why.

Jack returned to the chair and must have dozed. He raised his head and saw that Grace had stopped plucking. She lay quiet and on her back. Her mouth was open, and she was breathing in deep gasps. He could see her pulse in the veins of her throat, and her lungs softly rattled.

He reached down and touched her forehead; he couldn't keep the tears from falling on her. His nose was running, and he sniffled the wetness away as well as he could.

"Grace, I am so sorry. I am so sorry."

Since he had walked into the room the first day, he had hoped she would not open her eyes. He had hoped she would not hold him in her gaze. He knew they must hold hate, contempt, maybe even pity. Pity, a thought he had never had. Why pity the great Jack Grant? He did not want to see those eyes now. Maybe that is why in his nightmares she didn't have any. But now he prayed she would open them. He wanted her to look at him one last time. Maybe something would happen, perhaps he could say something to keep her from hating him from Heaven. He wanted to see her move her hand, moan, and do anything to let him know she heard him. He leaned forward to her; to will her to open her eyes and forgive him. He looked over her bed, desperately hoping and waiting to see a sign, anything. He had a terrible feeling that if she died without forgiving him, everything he had ever done would go unforgiven. She and Christopher would not see him in Heaven. He took the sponge and gently wiped her forehead. He tried to sort out the confusion in his mind. But her eyes did not open. There was no forgiveness. There was only the faint movement of the bedclothes as she breathed.

Jack returned to his chair, slumped into it and closed his eyes.

"Jack, Jack, wake up." He opened his eyes, and there was

Grace, sitting on the side of the bed. But she looked different. She looked just like she did when they first met. She was beautiful!

"Look, Jack, look at who is here."

Jack smiled as Grace reached behind her, and he watched Grace laugh as she brought out something in the sheet. He smiled as he looked back up at Grace, but her face had grown contorted. Jack felt fear rise in his throat. He tried not to look at what was in the bundle. But he couldn't take his eyes away. He couldn't shut his eyes.

"Here you go, darling," said Grace. But her lips didn't move. The sound just came out. "Here are your boys Jack" She ripped off the cloth, and there was Harley. It was Harley, but it had the head of Christopher. The head turned toward Jack and smiled.

"Bav," it said. Jack felt himself scream as he jerked awake.

"Jack, Jack, wake up. Wake up, you are dreaming."

Jack opened his eyes, confused, and still scared. He looked up and saw Joe.

"Jack, wake up. Man! You must have had a nightmare."

Jack looked into Joe's eyes and felt the terror leave him. He took a shaky breath and sat up in the chair. He took a couple of deep breaths and started to stand. He looked at Grace.

"Just stay in your chair a moment." Joe dropped to a knee and put a hand on Jack's shoulder.

"She's gone," he said.

Jack looked into the kind eyes. It took a moment for him to understand.

"What?" He stood and walked to the bed. Grace looked even tinier and frailer than she had before. But there was a sense of peace in her body. Her eyes were softly closed, the frown was gone now, and her mouth was smooth and relaxed. Jack looked around, but Joe had disappeared, and for a second he was afraid. Afraid that the nightmare would come back. But that fear vanished as he stood over her. He looked at her and frowned. He was so confused he could hardly think. The tears were gone, and he wondered what had caused them. He felt a peculiar emptiness; not sadness necessarily, or if it was, it was sadness for him, and not her. He wanted her to forgive him while she was still alive but frowned as he thought of that. Why was that so important anyway? He felt a nag, an odd wariness; that something that should have happened inside him didn't. He felt a fear that something that he was supposed to have learned wasn't understood at all. But worst of all, he felt an uneasiness that he had never experienced before. It was a fear that maybe all of his life, he had been entirely wrong about everything. He stared at Grace for a while longer, then leaned over, kissed her forehead, and left.

Jack stopped by the house and, once again, his new, best friend, Harley met him. He was surprised how much he had grown to like the little guy and how much he was going to miss him.

Jack made the final arrangements for Grace's memorial service; much of it had already been done by the officers' wives club. It was a low-keyed affair at the base chapel. He had her body cremated and the ashes placed in a vase that he left on the fireplace mantel because he didn't know what else to do with them.

Since he was going to be returning from cruise in a couple of months, Jack instructed Maria to maintain the house and look after Harley. She had already agreed with Grace, so it was no surprise. What intrigued Jack most was the fact she never said a word to him. But, as he opened the door to head to the airport, he turned to her.

"Is there anything you want to say to me?" She looked at him and took a breath.

"You are a pig." She turned and walked out of the room. Harley followed her.

CHAPTER TWENTY-TWO

"CAG, have a minute?"

Jack looked up from his desk and nodded to Otter. He hadn't talked to his DCAG since his return to the ship.

"Come in Otter." Jack allowed himself a quick frown as Otter walked in and took a seat. He knew the COD pilot and MIG-29 issues were still between them.

"Sir, you know that while you were gone, we did some planning on Desert Reveille."

"Yes, I am just looking at the folder now. What do you think?"

"Sir, it isn't executable."

Jack sighed. He suddenly felt weary. He didn't need any of Otter's fucking practicality now. Jack leaned back in his chair and fought for patience. "Otter, this is a plan that was first created at least a year and a half ago, maybe more. It is our job to take the plan, make the small changes to it that our particular air wing composition requires and brief it up the chain. So, what do you mean not executable?"

"I mean the folder has a plan for a night, precision attack against multiple targets in a congested area that is heavily defended."

"We do that all the time. We did that in Desert Storm."

"Sir, in Desert Storm we had a wide, wide set of potential targets that Saddam had to defend. He had to defend his entire country and don't forget, we used stealth and Tomahawks and jamming, and other stand-off weapons. What we have here is an attack on a postage stamp."

Jack frowned and looked at the papers in his hand. Otter was a King Kong Hornet pilot who was a renowned expert at striking targets. Jack highly respected his opinion when it came to *all things bomb*. "Okay, Otter, back up and give it to me from the top."

"Well, sir, the target folder requires we permanently destroy the capability of the patrol boats to sortie from both Bushehr on the north coast and Bandar Abbas down south. Bushehr has a mix of twenty-four Bog hammer, and Mod Kaman patrol boats and Bandar Abbas has twenty-two. The target areas are small and congested and to ensure we sink the boats we need to put a thousand pounder on each one with a delayed fuse to detonate beneath the keel to break it."

"Right, so what is the problem?"

"Sir, given the briefed altitudes for delivery, the bombs will fall for thirty-five seconds, and they have to be supported by the laser designator the entire time of fall. The pilots will have to be in a turn over the target area that entire time to ensure the pod remains uncovered and lasing the target."

"Show me the slide of the target area."

Otter opened his folder and flipped to the slide with Bandar Abbas and Bushehr. The patrol boats appeared as small, white spots on the satellite images.

Jack stared at the images, then turned his head toward Otter. "Go ahead."

"Well, sir, if we are going to hit the targets at night, we will have to somehow de-conflict over this small area, or we will hit each other. That means we either do it by time or distance."

"How do the plans that were handed to us by the other battle groups address this?"

"That's just it. The other groups didn't address it. Nobody took this seriously."

"What do you mean? How do you not take a target folder seriously?"

"Because nobody thought we would ever do this."

Jack frowned and grunted. "Go ahead."

"CAG, to execute this the way the folder has it planned now, we would have to put a string of twenty aircraft over each target area separated by time to avoid hitting each other in the dark.

Nobody would have their lights on. Even if it were only thirty seconds apart, the strike group would be in a left-hand turn over the target area for twelve minutes from the first plane to last. They have Soviet SAMs out the ass as well as Improved Hawks that we gave them. Sir, we would get slaughtered!"

"Why don't we take out the SAMS before we strike?"

"Not enough assets on one carrier. And, if we use Tomahawk or air launched cruise missiles the Iranians will most likely sortie the boats out to sea. It has to be a single punch at the target set."

"Hmm," said Jack. He sat back in his chair. "Is there any other way to do the mission without bombs? What about mines?"

"Mining the harbors won't work because the bottom's too deep and too soft. We can't guarantee a high enough kill rate when they transit."

"Rockeye and cluster bombs?"

"We looked into the numbers, CAG and they will booger those boats up a lot, but they won't necessarily sink them."

"So, where does that leave us?"

"Sir, it leaves us with 1,000-pound laser-guided bombs. The same ordnance the other groups chose."

"So, you do think there is a way that we could do this thing? Hit these targets?"

"Yes, sir. But it would have to be a daylight strike so we could concentrate the strikers and we would have to drop gravity bombs so we would release the weapons and get the hell out of there. That is the only way to do it."

"Geez," moaned Jack. "That takes us back to the Vietnam days. You know how we got criticized for using dumb bombs during Desert Storm. We looked like stooges. The US Air Force was lighting up everybody's TV with videos of precision strikes, and all we had was file tape of

Tomahawk launches from ships. Nobody would approve something like that."

"Then we should throw this folder away," said Otter. "The plan, as it now exists, the one we received, cannot be executed. Period." He sat back, his face pinched in anger.

"Tell me again the reason why we have to disable the boats permanently? You said mines were no good? A couple of aircraft with cluster bombs could do a lot of damage."

"Sir, the bottom of both ports is very poor for mining. We can't get even a 50 percent likelihood of sinking them with mines, and if we drop Rockeyes on them, it will just blow off the tops of the boats. They won't sink them."

"Maybe, but if you blow the tops up, they can't operate them."

"Sir, if we start something with Iran, they will shut down the Straits of Hormuz and the carrier will be stuck inside the gulf indefinitely. Eventually, they will get the boats fixed and come out and kick our ass."

Jack winced, and his eyes automatically went to the map on his desk. The Straits of Hormuz was a narrow chokepoint and the only passage from the Gulf out to the Indian Ocean. It was dotted with islands and Iran had missile launchers on many of them.

"Well, that explains the hard-kill requirement. And I can see why nobody took this requirement seriously."

"Yes, sir. I think the previous battle groups thought of it as a planning drill. You know, something you have to do just because you are here."

Jack slumped in his chair. "And, of course, something that has to be briefed to Fifth Fleet."

"Yes, sir."

"What does the air force say? You talk to their colonel yet?"

"Yes, sir. I talked to him on a covered circuit the other day. He laughed when I said we had to uses dumb bombs in a day strike."

Jack sighed. He had to brief Admiral Summersly on the plan that afternoon as the first step before briefing Fifth Fleet.

"Otter, how did the other battle groups get by with this if the flaws were so obvious?"

"Oh, that's easy CAG." Otter offered a rare smile. "The guys that know how stupid it is are too junior for the brief. The guys that are senior enough for the brief are too stupid to know."

Jack pursed his lips and nodded. He wasn't sure which category Otter had him in but didn't want to ask.

"Anything else, sir?"

"No, thanks, Otter. When is the brief to the admiral?"

"You must not have heard about the change?"

"Change?"

"Yes, sir. You are to helo into Fifth Fleet headquarters this afternoon and brief the three-star."

"Vice Admiral Renfro?"

"Yes, sir. The same."

"Oh, my God! You have got to be shitting me!" Jack winced and took a sharp breath. Vice Admiral Renfro was a notoriously aggressive surface warfare officer who either loved you or hated you.

"What about the brief to Admiral Summersly?"

"According to his air ops officer, he thinks this is a done deal. It has been planned by two battle groups in front of him that are run by aviator flags and not a shoe like him. I think he sees this as a social visit and an opportunity to impress the three-star more than anything. After all, nobody believes we are going to attack Iran."

"Okay, Otter, thanks. I will see you at the helo."

"Yes, sir." Otter turned and left the room.

Jack sat for a few moments, considering a trip to see the admiral and explain the situation. But, since the plan would never be executed anyway and because he was already in trouble with the admiral, he decided not to. That afternoon Jack and Otter jumped on the helo for the flight into Bahrain, and Fifth Fleet headquarters.

"CAG, I take it this is the same plan that the previous battle group had?" Vice Admiral Renfro looked away from the briefing slide and focused on Jack.

"Well, sir, we did scrub it thoroughly, but the group in front of us developed a pretty good plan to base from." Jack smiled and nodded his head. "Of course we do have the F-14D, and the Nimitz group only had F-14As."

"What does the F-14D got to do with this? They don't drop bombs."

Jack gulped. He had thrown in the F-14D bit to show they had a little more to offer. He didn't see the question coming.

"Well, sir, well, they have the Joint Tactical Information Display System."

"Got it. But what does JTIDS on a Tomcat have to do with bombing patrol boats?" Renfro turned his chair and fully faced Jack. "I guess I don't get it?"

Jack felt his face grow red. He was in deep shit if he couldn't find a way out of this. He felt Summersly's eyes on him too!

"Sir," as you know, JTIDS allows the Tomcat to link with the E-2 and the Air Force AWACS if available and will give the battle group commander better situational awareness. That's all I meant." Jack gulped again, hoping that he had escaped.

Renfro continued to stare at Jack.

"Sir, it gives the decision-makers more clarity, and we wove that into the plan."

"Hmmm." Renfro narrowed his eyes and nodded his head. "Hmmm. Okay, I guess that makes sense." He smiled for the first time since they had sat down for the brief.

"Good Job, admiral." Renfro smiled at Summersly, and Jack knew he was in the clear.

"Clear the room except for the table." Renfro looked at his deputy who immediately shooed out all of the supporting staff. Once the room cleared, Renfro leaned back in his chair.

"Gentlemen I hope you scrubbed your plan well because there is a growing chance that we will use it."

Jack took a deep breath.

Holy shit!

Vice Admiral Renfro continued. "We have black program intercepts that indicate the Iranians are going to do something during the Olympics."

Jack glanced around the room. Everyone was staring at the three-star. He couldn't believe what he had just heard. The room was silent except for the hum of the projector fan.

"Sir, how can that be? Isn't Iran sending athletes to Atlanta? I think I saw something like that on message traffic." Summersly leaned forward.

"Yes they are, but that doesn't matter to them. Besides, the Iranians might do it in a way that does not point back to them. The inputs we get are consistent. I was briefed into the SAP analysis, and there is no doubt of the possibility. "

"But, admiral, the idea of attacking Iran from inside the gulf seems to be risky. How would we ever get back out? The Strait of Hormuz is one hell of a chokepoint!" Summersly looked at Renfro and frowned.

"Maybe so, but waiting for them to attack us is a hell of a lot riskier. I suppose you have all heard of the USS Stark?"

"Yes, sir," said Summersly.

Renfro looked around the room. "For those of you that don't remember, Stark was attacked in 1987 by an Iraqi Mirage and hit with two Exocet missiles. The ship saw the airplane from hundreds of miles away, the ship twice radioed the airplane and asked it to identify itself, but took no action. The missiles hit her, and thirty-seven U.S. Navy Sailors died with twenty-one more wounded. The skipper was courts-martialed, and the Tactical Action Officer resigned over the matter. Do you have any idea what would happen if we let those boats out? If they swarm a carrier and hit it multiple times?" Renfro took a deep breath as he looked around the room.

Everyone looked at the floor.

"Look, gents, there may be a very fine line here between attacking and defending. All I know is if we get put on alert, and there is any indication at all I am not going to have another USS Stark on my hands. Do you all understand?"

"Yes, sir," said Jack. He heard the others also respond. "Tell me about your plan? I don't need the background just show me the attack phase."

"CAG." Admiral Summersly looked at Jack.

"Go to slide eleven," said Jack.

"Sir, you can see the disposition of the boats here in Bushehr and Bandar Abbas. You can see they are tightly bunched, and if they are all in port, which they often are, there are twenty-four here at Bushehr, which will be our targets and twenty-two at Bandar Abbas."

"Got it," said Renfro.

"The strikers will launch at night and proceed to populate a command and control orbit stack here for the North group and here for the South group." Jack pointed to two places on the map. They are one hundred miles from the coast, and the aircraft are stacked 1000 feet apart in altitude. The lead aircraft is 24,000 feet, which is also the delivery altitude. Once the code word is sent, each airplane will push from the stack based upon his time and altitude. We fill from the bottom of the stack first. All aircraft will have lights off, with no radio chatter for the duration of the attack." Otter kicked Jack's leg under the table.

"Good," said Renfro. "Continue."

"Sir, each striker, will carry a 1,000-pound laser-guided bomb and once in the target area will identify his target, designate it and release his weapon. The strikers will pass the target area at thirty second intervals." Jack felt Otter kick his leg again.

"How long will they be over the target area? I see the dispositions of the SAMs." Redd frowned slightly and swiveled to look at Jack.

"Sir, the thirty-five second time of flight is something we cannot factor away. The Iranians defend the area with Improved Hawks, SA2s, and SA6s. If we go in any lower, the guns will get us. However, we plan to desensitize the plan with opsersizes."

318

"Opsersizes?" Renfro frowned again and looked quizzically at Jack. He then looked at Summersly, who in turn scowled at Jack. Jack had wracked his brain on the helo ride over for some way to counter the time-over-target problem. If there was one thing Jack Grant could do, it was the ability to bullshit. He had come up with the opsersize idea just before the helo had touched down.

"Yes, sir." We have already planned the routes from the orbit points to the target areas with the correct package size and disposition. With your permission, we will now fly daily and nightly packages with enough regularity to desensitize the defenses. After we do this for a while with no adverse effect, the Iranians will drop their guard. In the event we get the word to carry out the attack, we turn the exercise into an operation and strike them."

Renfro stared at Jack, and Jack held his breath. If Renfro bought it, he was a hero. If not, well, who knows.

Renfro turned in his chair and looked at the briefing screen.

The target area slide was still showing. "Hmmm," he cleared his throat.

"Sir, I think our plan, a modified version of the Nimitz plan whereby we desensitize Iran with opsersizes, will work," said Summersly.

Renfro looked at him for a moment and then back at the screen.

Summersly shot a look of pure terror at Jack.

Renfro continued to look at the screen, and Jack felt his fear grow. Everything could blow up right now!

Renfro turned to the room, then to Summersly and smiled. "Admiral, I think you might have something here. Not optimum, of course, but your opsersize idea just might work. Good job, great job!"

Jack felt the pressure blow out like a party balloon.

Summersly looked at him and smiled broadly.

"One question, Admiral Summersly." Renfro leaned back in his chair. "What about all this staff help we are supposed to get for this exercise? Have you gotten any of the Maritime Component Commander staffers yet? "

"The COD is supposed to bring the first batch in this afternoon."

"Good," said Renfro. "You know the navy has been trying to get into leading the joint air game for some time now. We need something to counter having the air force lead every air action we have. This MCC group is our attempt to counter that. It will be interesting to see how they can link with CENTCOM, and us for that matter."

"We're ready for them," said Summersly. "We will have to berth them all over the place. They are using parts of CVIC and wardroom one for planning spaces. Kind of a mess."

"I imagine it is," said Renfro. "But shouldn't last too long. This Desert Reveille op will be over as soon as the Olympics finish. Besides, this allows us to prove we can man a joint planning element on an aircraft carrier."

"Sure hope all of this is just an exercise in communications," said Summersly. "I would hate to have to go after Iran from inside the pond."

"Hopefully, we will never find out," said Renfro. He stood, and all participants in the room scrambled to their feet.

"However, remember the Stark," Renfro frowned. "Not on my watch, By God." He strode out of the room.

Otter did not look at Jack or talk to him during the flight back.

When the helo landed, he walked away before Jack could corner him. It didn't bother Jack that much. He wanted a good relationship with his DCAG, but, if not, what the fuck? The important thing was that the admiral seemed to like him again. He started walking off the deck when he felt a hand grab his shoulder. He turned to face Admiral Summersly.

"You did a superb job back there, Jack." The admiral smiled and gripped his shoulder. "I don't know where you came up with the opsersize idea, but it was brilliant."

"Sir, it is a variation of mirror-image strikes we always plan." Jack felt the bullshit roll off his tongue.

"Well, however you did it, it was brilliant." He winked and headed toward the hatch to his spaces.

Jack grinned and then broke out into a broad smile. His magic had not changed. The Phoenix was still the master of the universe!

Jack entered his room and had no sooner taken off his flight gear when he heard a knock at his door.

He opened it. There stood Otter. "Come in. Have a seat."

Otter walked in but remained standing as Jack sat down.

"Sir, that plan is a fucking disaster waiting to happen, and you know it. You had the chance to put a stake in that goofy shit, but you didn't."

"Easy, Otter," said Jack. "Watch your tone with me."

"You are a coward," spat Otter. "Every decision you make is designed to make you look good regardless of what it does to the rest of us."

"Stand down, mister!" Jack took a deep breath.

"The fucking Indian MIGS, the un-qualified female LSO, your no over-night liberty policies and now this. Everyone in the air wing has lost confidence in you."

"I am the CAG! Nobody has the right to lose confidence in me except the admiral."

"I cannot believe you," said Otter. He slowly shook his head. "It's not about YOU. It's about the wing!"

"You just ended your career, Otter." Jack stared into his DCAG's eyes. "No CAG has ever fired his DCAG before, but I am going to make an exception. I hope you have the damned professionalism to keep that fact to yourself until after the exercise is over. Then you will be out of here on the next COD."

"Fine, I would rather haul shit for FEDEX than serve with you." Otter spun around and walked out.

Jack stared at the door, breathing hard. He slumped into his chair and put his head in his hands. He knew what Otter said was true. He knew the strike plan couldn't work. He knew it but went along with it because hell, it would never happen anyway and he didn't want to deal with changing it.

What fucking difference did it make?

Was he a wimp, or was he just pragmatic? What fucking difference did it make?

But there was one thing Otter was sure right about, and that was how the air wing felt about him. He could feel that now. He could sense it and see it now that his eyes were open. Christ, he was the expert on being an outcast. Until the MIG kills, he had ALWAYS been an outcast. He knew what it felt like to be disliked.

Do they think I'm a coward?

He knew they did. He knew they did.

Jack kept his head on his hands and closed his eyes.

He was standing in the living room of the house in San Diego. He saw Harley, wagging his tail with his big brown eyes looking up. But Harley was a little boy, knocking on the door. His big brown little dog eyes were little boy eyes, and they were full with fear! Harley looked over his shoulder and back at Jack. He kept knocking and knocking. Jack could see his lips move.

"Let me in! Let me in!"

Jack tried to move his legs. He had to get to the door and let him in. He knew what would happen if he didn't.

The coyotes!

There was a shadow over the boy, and Jack could hear panting. It was the coyotes!

"Let me in. Dad, let me in!"

Jack tried harder. His legs wouldn't move. His feet wouldn't budge. He tried, and they wouldn't budge.

"Let me in dad!"

The shadow grew darker. "DAD! DAD!"

Jack jerked awake and grabbed the arms of his chair.

Christ! God Almighty!

He sat still as his breathing returned to normal. He took a couple of big breaths and slowly let them out.

It was only a dream. It was just THE dream. He had been having some version of it since he heard about Grace in the hospice. Her face flashed in his mind now. How fragile and sad and sorry she looked in that bed. Already dead but just waiting to die. Christ, he had been such an ass to her.

Why am I so fucking tired?

Jack leaned back in the chair. He hadn't gotten a good night's sleep in days. He fought the urge to go into his bedroom and turn the light out. He sat in the chair for a long time and wondered if he dared see the flight surgeon. Maybe get something to help him sleep. He sure as hell wasn't going to tell him why he couldn't sleep. But he could use something. Something like the air force guys used to fly those long hops to Iraq in their F-117s. He started to reach for the phone when the door opened, and his admin chief poked his head through the opening.

"Got some mail off the COD, sir, and a message from BUPERS."

"Thanks, Chief." Jack took the mail, and they chatted for a moment. The chief offered condolences about Mrs. Grant, then left. Jack looked at the stack of mail and saw a note from his ops officer.

Sir, you got a call from Pers 43 about your old XO, Booger Collingwood. He wants you to call him back ASAP. Capt. Roby DSN 882-3974.

Jack picked up the phone and began to dial. He still had trouble believing he could call the States from his desk.

"Phoenix, this is Curt Roby, thanks for calling me back." "Sure, Curt, what's up?"

"Sir, Booger Collingwood has his retirement letter in, and I am wondering if you might help."

"His letter? What do you mean? He is the skipper of VF-154, isn't he?"

"Afraid not," said Curt. "Booger got caught up in the Hook scandal, and just before his change of command; they sidelined him."

"What? Hook was over two years ago."

"It took a while for DoD to get the whole mess from the navy. Figured we were covering up, I suppose. Then they had to redo a bunch of stuff. It has been one ugly mess for sure. Bottom line is Booger is taking a fall for the TOPGUN suite. They say he attended Hook and he was in charge of setting up the suite. That's right, isn't it?"

"Yeah, he was the XO. The XO oversees that kind of thing."

"They say he either came up with the idea of the Kamikaze shots or at least supported the idea and that he supported strippers in the suite."

"You have to be shitting me!"

"No, sir. That is what the report says. Booger didn't fight it. He just put in his letter yesterday. I am calling to see if you would be willing to make a call to the DOD IG. My JO detailers here tell me the word on the street is that he was against the idea of hard liquor in the suite and only attended the banquet at the last minute. He did that because you had to go to a funeral for your wife's father."

Jack gripped the phone and took a deep breath. "What do you think the DoD IG wants to hear from me?"

"Well, if you said that Booger was not in favor of the Kamikaze thing and that he was in attendance only for a few hours at the banquet I think they would let him go. They would forget the whole thing. At least that is what their guy is telling me."

"I wonder whose head they would be looking for then?" "Don't know sir, don't know how you guys planned the suite for Hook. I know that if Booger is free and clear, we need to say so and get him to pull his letter. He is a great American, and we need him in command."

"I'm not sure how I can help."

"Make the call Phoenix; just make the call. I'll give you the number."

Jack felt tight in his chest. If he got Booger off the Hook, he would just be putting himself on it.

"I don't think I can help." His voice sounded weak.

"You can't help, or you won't help?" Jack could hear the irritation in Curt's voice.

"Either way, I am not making the call."

"But, Phoenix, you can save this guy. I mean, look what he is doing for you. He hasn't said a word in protest. If he hadn't gone to Hook for you, it would be YOU in the hot seat. It would be YOU held liable for the Kamikaze thing and the strippers."

"Sorry I can't help you."

"You have GOT to help him. You are the only one who can!" Jack hung up the phone, rocked back, and stared at the wall.

His eyes found the TOPGUN plaque he had displayed there. Every visitor commented on it. TOPGUN had such a tremendous reputation.

A wave of depression hit him. The same wave that crashed over him daily now. Sometimes it held him for hours. He thought about seeing the flight surgeon again. But he knew he couldn't do that.

Jack leaned back in his chair and closed his eyes. He dozed for a second until he heard a knock at his door.

"Come in." He leaned forward and sat up straight as the door swung open.

"Hey, CAG!"

Jack opened his mouth in shock. His old CAG, Captain Frank Wright, stood in the door. He leaped up, walked around his desk, and stretched out his hand.

"Sir what are you doing here?"

"I'm leading the MCC staff. Just got off of the COD."

"Wow! That is fantastic. I lost track of you after you went to the pentagon. I heard you selected for one star, though!"

"Yeah, even a blind squirrel can find a nut," laughed Frank. "I picked it up on the last board."

"How did you get here?"

"I have some time until my senate confirmation comes through. The bureau sent me here to do this while I wait."

"Sit down, have a seat, and let's chat."

"Love to," said Frank. "But I have a staff meeting with my folks. I'll take a rain check on the chat."

"Yes, sir." Jack shook hands with Frank again, and his old boss walked out of the room. As the door swung shut, Jack smiled.

Maybe having his old CAG back would change things. It was also a good thing he selected for flag. It was a good thing to have Frank going places. He could take Jack with him.

CHAPTER TWENTY-THREE

"CAG, Frank Wright here. Can I get the rain check on that chat now? It's about the Desert Reveille plan."

"Sure, come on over." Jack frowned as he hung up the phone. DCAG had briefed Desert Reveille to the aircrew, and the strike package was flying mirror images of the attack each night. It had been a week since Frank had come onboard and Jack wondered what he wanted.

Moments later, he heard Frank's knock and invited him in.

"Sir, take a seat, what's up?"

"Thanks, Jack." Frank sat in the chair facing Jack's desk. "Since coming on board, we have concentrated on establishing communications and procedures to operate with Fifth Fleet, other battle group assets, associated in-theater commands and Central Command. I just got to the target plan this morning, and I wonder how you got it approved."

"What do you mean?"

"I mean it isn't doable. Is it?"

"Well, sure I think it's doable." Jack swallowed. His old CAG still intimidated him.

"I ran into Otter in the passageway. Hope you don't mind, but I wanted to make sure I hadn't missed something before taking your time up. I asked him how he was going to string all those planes across the target area without getting shot to shit."

"What did he say?" Jack swallowed again.

"Strangest thing. I thought he would blurt out some rationale. Something I had overlooked. But he just said, 'talk to CAG.'"

"Look, sir, I know there is an issue with stringing the strikers over the target, but I think our opsersizes have softened the Iranian resolve and I think we give their SAMs too much credit. I still think the thing is executable. Besides, we aren't going to attack Iran."

"How can you be so sure?"

"Because nobody in their right mind would order such a thing."

"They might if they thought a good plan was ready to be executed."

"It is a good plan." Jack swallowed and looked at Frank.

"Mind walking me through the numbers? I can't figure how the hell you string that many airplanes over the target for that long, all on predictable flight paths with twenty SAMs firing at them? How?"

"It's only twelve minutes over the target up north and eleven down south. We can do the strike."

"Jack, the rule is thirty to sixty seconds over a point target area like this. You know that."

"I still think we can do the strike."

Frank looked at Jack for several seconds. "No, I think you know it can't you can't do it, but you got the folder, and you didn't want to challenge it publically. I think bit by bit you just got stuck with this and now that things are heating up, you don't know how to get out of it. I think that is what is going on here."

Jack didn't know what to say. He took a deep breath and looked at Frank.

"Jack, how can you sit on a war plan that you briefed and blessed and say it is executable when you know it can't and shouldn't be flown? And if you don't know it isn't executable, then you are in the wrong job."

"You put me here!" Jack felt his face growing red.

"And it was a mistake!"

"What do you mean?"

"I ranked you as number one based on the MIG action. And on the recommendation of Admiral Turner. It wasn't my idea, but I went along with it."

Jack was stunned. He blinked at his old boss. He didn't know what to say.

"Look, Jack, that's all in the past now. Get the admiral and let's talk about the plan. I will go with you. We can say that analysis of the opsersizes indicate they didn't pan out as you thought. You need to re-plan. There isn't any harm in that."

"I'll look like an idiot. I can't do that." Jack rubbed his face and sighed. "Look, CAG, sir, just let this go. We are NEVER going to attack Iran anyway. Never."

Frank looked at Jack, then shook his head and reached into a satchel. Jack had noticed it when he came into the room and assumed it had briefs and reports. Frank took out a tape and held it up.

"I want to play you something. That VCR work?" Frank pointed to the box over the television.

"Yes, it works."

Frank walked to the unit, turned it on, and shoved the tape in. It whirred for a moment then the image of a Tomcat HUD popped up. Frank turned up the volume.

Dragon, Dakota, say status.

"That is Jocko's voice," said Frank.

Dakota, Dragon, two groups of suspected horses vectoring south towards you. Ten-mile trail. The lead group now bullseye zero one zero for fifty-five. Hail Mary. Hail Mary.

Dragon, Dakota copies horses, and Hail Mary. Master Arm on skipper, select Phoenix.

Roger.

"That's you," said Frank.

Horses and Hail Mary.

"That's your wingman. You remember this?"

333

"The tape?" Jack felt his stomach turn. "The tape from the MIG engagement? How?"

"Let me forward it," said Frank. He hit the forward button. "Here."

Skipper, I am going to slave the TCS to the radar and see if we can get an ID on these guys.

Good idea.

Got him.

Confirm horse.

There are two of them, welded wing. Confirm, TWO horses in the lead group. In range for the Phoenix, skipper.

Shoot now, and they will never see the missile coming. Take the shot, skipper!

Take the shot!

Fox three.

"Whose voice is that?" Frank paused the tape.

Jack shook his head.

"Who said Fox Three? Who shot the Phoenix?" Frank stared at him a second then hit the play button.

What happened?

"That sounds like you asking 'what happened,'" said Frank.

I had to get it off the plane, skipper. It will be doing Mach five by now and will hit them from directly above. They won't see it coming.

Sure. Sure.

Frank paused the tape again. Jocko shot the Phoenix, not you."

Jack stared at the frozen tape; he felt himself shiver as he took in a deep breath.

He looked up at Frank and swallowed. "That's right."

"Let me fast forward it a bit," said Frank. He toggled the button, and the tape whirred. Then they heard Jocko.

Got the second guy locked. Skipper, come hard left and put him on the nose.

Crossing under and visual.

Mile and a half away, he's turning into us. Shoot him, skipper!

Fox one.

Select Sparrow!

"You're in min range; the radar broke the lock. Select Sidewinder.

SHOOT.

I can't get a tone. I can't get a tone!

335

You still have Sparrow, select Sidewinder!

I can't get a tone! I can't get a tone!

You're in guns! You're in guns.

Frank and Jack heard the sounds of heavy breathing and grunting followed by the distinctive buzz of the Tomcat's Gatling gun.

Splash one horse!

"Sounds like you had some severe switchology problems," said Frank. He turned off the tape.

"Yeah," said Jack. He slumped against the wall and closed his eyes. "Yes, I did."

"I guess I can see why you didn't want THAT version going around."

"How did you get this tape?"

"When you asked Jocko for the tape, to take it to the post-flight debrief, he figured you were up to something. So, he gave you a blank one he had in his helmet bag."

Jack frowned as he remembered the sequence. It seemed so long ago.

"Jack, what did you do with the tape he gave you?"

"I exchanged it for a blank one in my room. I gave the blank to CVIC and destroyed the tape Jocko gave to me."

"And you knew the tape was blank and that Jocko would take the hit for screwing up the recording?"

"Yes." Jack shook his head and walked to the couch. He slumped down against the arm.

Frank sat on the edge of Jack's desk. "I was going to rank you somewhere in the middle. Somewhere behind Guido and the others. The fact was, I didn't think you were ready for higher command."

"Look..."

"Let me finish," said Frank. "The admiral called me in after the shootdown and convinced me that you were the man to get the number one ticket. He also lined me up to get selected for flag in the process."

"Sir, I..."

"Let me finish, Jack."

Jack sighed and shook his head. He felt drained.

"Chains of events happen because people do not do what they are supposed to do, what they pledged to do. I set Phoenix Grant in motion by giving you that number one ticket in exchange for a favor from the admiral. That led to TOPGUN and Jocko's death."

Jack stood. "I didn't kill Jocko. He died in an accident. It was a fucked-up plane!"

"Maybe," said Frank. "Maybe, but at any rate, I put you there."

Jack couldn't look at Frank. He sat back into the couch. "My actions also put you in a position to ruin Booger. You could have helped him."

337

Jack looked up at Frank. "How do you know about that?"

"The captain detailer in PERS 43 is a good friend of mine, Jack. I know all about the TOPGUN suite, about Booger getting blamed for what you set in motion. I also talked to a lot of TOPGUN junior officers. They told me what went on there. All of it."

Jack slumped even deeper against the couch.

At least Frank didn't know about Harley, how Jack's shenanigans almost got him killed. And Frank didn't know what a shitty husband Jack was. Jack looked at the floor. He thought he was going to throw up. He felt his chest tighten as a blackness of guilt descended upon him.

"And now, because of me, you are in a position to do great harm to this country." Frank stood and stared at Jack. "The other battle groups didn't take this seriously because it wasn't tied to the Olympics in Atlanta. They knew nothing would happen on their watch, so it was all bullshit to them. The first guy who did the folder probably figured to throw in some buzz words, night precision, laser-guided, and so forth. Just something to brief and get off his plate."

Frank leaned back and looked at the ceiling. "But, you know, from a professional perspective, from the perspective of protecting the art of aerial combat, that guy, and every CAG after him should have stopped this thing. They should have raised the bullshit flag over it."

"That would have been hard to do," mumbled Jack.

"Not for the first CAG. But it did get harder and harder as it became more or less accepted."

"But, given nobody believed we would ever attack Iran, what would have been accomplished?"

"Well, for one thing, a realization that we need new weapons," said Frank. "New weapons that give us greater stand-off precision."

"What do I do?" Jack could hardly speak. The only energy left in him was guilt. A thought of Grace flashed through his mind, but he frowned and shrugged it off.

"You need to call the admiral and get this thing stopped," said Frank. "The Olympics started a week ago. If anything at all screwy happens, who knows what will result."

"I need to think about this," said Jack. His mind was a swirl of confusion.

"Don't think about it for too long. If you don't, call it off, I will. And I will give the admiral this tape too. For Christ's sake, Jack, stop the dominoes from falling. You have done one selfish thing after another since the miracle of that shoot down of yours. I have been selfish, too, to be honest. But I am through being selfish. For God's sake, call the plan off."

Frank stood and walked to the door. Jack shut his eyes and leaned his head against the wall. He heard the door open and close, and he felt a shot of relief for being alone. But, he wasn't alone. Guilt was in the room with him. Guilt he had managed to hide so well for so long. He sat on the couch for over an hour after Frank left, thinking of Grace, thinking of Christopher. He thought of Harley and Jocko. Finally, he went to see the Chaplain.

Jack knew Chaplain Roy Devore while attending services on Ike. He began to attend as soon as he arrived on board because the admiral attended them. Jack had no particular faith or belief and never went to church ashore. However, he heard the admiral was a devout man and would certainly look favorably upon another Lamb of God. Jack also went on liberty with Roy because Roy went on liberty with the admiral. Roy was a Catholic and enjoyed good wine, good cigars, and good food. Jack researched the Bible enough to have conversations on most topics that Roy and the admiral bridged.

As Jack maneuvered through the passageways and down the ladders to the Chaplain's office, he agonized over what to do. What to say? How could Roy help him? Would talking to a Chaplain do him any good, or was it just what people told other people to do when they had no answers themselves? The real problem was that Jack's relationship with Roy was not based on actual companionship or trust or even friendship, but upon Jack's manipulation of those things. Roy might not know it, but Jack liked being with Roy for what he got out of Roy, not anything that he was willing to give. He still had no idea what to say when he opened the door to the religious ministries office.

"CAG, to what do I owe this honor?" Roy beamed as he stood and extended his hand.

Jack smiled as he shook the hand.

"Come in. Have a seat." Roby gestured to a battered chair. "Want some coffee?"

"No, but thank you," said Jack as he sat down. He glanced around the tiny, cluttered office and sighed.

"Sorry, again about Grace. I did not have the honor of meeting her, but I wish that I had."

Jack looked at Roy and blinked at the man's genuineness. He felt the now-familiar shot of guilt run through his frame.

"Thank you," said Jack. He swallowed against the knot in his chest.

"We missed you at services while you were gone."

Jack swallowed again. The warmth of the Chaplain mocked him.

They sat for some moments, and Jack sensed Roy's patience in the silence. He looked down at his hands, clutched in his lap and was relieved by the unanticipated calm. The two men, sitting in this small room inside this massive warship wasn't awkward at all, and that surprised him. He could feel Roy looking at him, but it wasn't a bad feeling. He could hear Roy breathing. Slow and even and comforting.

"I...," Jack trailed off as he forced himself to look into Roy's eyes, and he swallowed as he found them warm and kind.

"I'm in trouble, Roy."

"Oh, in what way?" Roy frowned and leaned toward him.

"I." Jack put his head down and rubbed his eyes and face with his hands. He felt sick. "I am not a good man, chaplain." He raised his head and looked at Roy. "I am not the man you think I am." He sighed and leaned back in his seat. "I am not a good man."

"What kind of man are you, Jack?"

Jack put his head down and shook it from side to side. "I am selfish, Chaplain. I am selfish. Everything I do, everything I have ever done for as long as I remember has always been about me."

"Oh, come now, Jack. You seem to be a fine fellow. A fine officer and leader." Roy gently slapped Jack's knee.

"I abandoned my wife." Jack swallowed and looked into Roy's eyes. "I think you Catholics have a thing about that, don't you? About marriage forever?" He put his head down again. "Jesus, I just walked away from her, from Grace, when she needed me the most. I let her suffer the loss of our son alone. I let her suffer her sickness alone. I just let her suffer. You know?" His voice was thick and broken, and his eyes burned. For some reason, he couldn't stop talking. "She suffered from panic, and I didn't give her a second's thought. All she ever wanted was someone, was for me, to give a shit and I didn't. I didn't! What if I do get into Heaven, God knows that won't happen. But, what if I do and she won't talk to me there?"

"Jack, it is Heaven. She will talk to you."

"But I was so bad. I was so bad."

"Jack, we often magnify things when loved ones die. I am sure you weren't as bad as that. She stayed married to you, didn't she?"

Jack slumped his head and looked at his boots. The laces were uneven. "I didn't shoot the MIGs with the

342

Phoenix." He looked at Roy and then let his gaze move past him to the crucifix on the wall. "My RIO did that. But I took the credit, and he let me." Jack glanced into Roy's eyes. There was no disapproval or alarm. Not even a frown. "I gooned the switches and would have never shot the other MIG if it weren't for my RIO and I took the credit for that too, and he let me."

"Sounds like he is a good man."

"He WAS a great man!"

"Was?"

"Yes, was. Jocko was a great man. You see I spun an aircraft into the water and killed him. I blamed it on the airplane."

"Jack, come on now. Accidents happen in your business. Surely you can see that?"

"Roy, I set up my XO to have his career ruined. I could have saved him, but I didn't." Jack felt a tear slide down his cheek. He quickly wiped it with the back of his hand, but another followed. He shamefully wiped it too but couldn't stop the rest. He sobbed and put his head in his hands. He felt Roy's comforting hand touch his back as he shuddered and collected himself.

"Chaplain, I left two friends to be killed in Iraq." Jack looked up at Roy and for the first time, saw alarm in the Chaplain's eyes.

"I could have stayed, and they could have fled with me, but I left them. And my friends got killed, protecting me!" He did not want to look at Roy anymore and let his eyes drop to the floor. He breathed through his mouth, and slowly, his chest stopped heaving. He shook his head and sighed and wiped his eyes.

"I am the wickedest fucking man I know." He looked at Roy and swallowed.

"Jack, sometimes it takes a time of wickedness to bring out the good." Roy patted him on the knee again. "The apostle Paul was a wicked man before seeing the light on the road to Damascus. History is full of men who experienced evil but then experienced good."

"But Roy, it never stops with me. There is no road to Damascus for me." Jack looked at the Chaplain and again saw the crucifix over his shoulder. "I approved a strike plan that I knew was wrong. That I knew couldn't work, and I can't make myself admit it."

"What do you mean?"

"The plan we call Desert Reveille. The plan to dissuade Iran from attacking the Olympics, or punish them if they do, is wrong. It won't work, but I approved it anyway."

"Then go and change it, Jack. You can do it. Go and change it."

"Oh, Roy, you don't understand." Jack straightened in his chair. "The plan has been approved by the President. It is in motion."

"Well, surely if it is that bad, someone along the way would have stopped it. Lots of people from you to the President."

"That's not the way it works, Roy. The people up the chain approve a concept; they leave it to us to do the details. They TRUST us to create a workable plan."

"Jack, I think you are in a bad way now. I think you are punishing yourself and that is a healthy thing to a point. I am sure the plan is okay."

"Roy, the problem is nobody has looked at it. Everybody thinks that someone else has looked at it."

"Have you talked to the admiral about this? You know he is the most reasonable man."

"I haven't talked to him yet. But the Olympics started already. Changing the plan, at this point, would make him look like a total idiot. It would make all of us look like idiots." Jack looked at Roy and then rubbed his eyes with his hands. They were damp, and he knew they were red.

"What do I do, chaplain?" He swallowed and looked at the priest. "What do I do?"

Roy looked into his eyes and then leaned forward and took his hands. Jack could feel the warmth in them. "What would make you feel right, Jack?"

Jack let out a breath and stared at the crucifix. He slowly shook his head. "I don't know. I don't know, maybe if I could do something truly heroic, something that would make up for all of this."

"Then, go find the mission and do it," smiled Roy.

"That truly would take a miracle." He shook his head again and looked back into Roy's eyes. "And, I need a way to stop the strike. To stop this insane plan."

"Then find a way to stop it, Jack. You can do that."

Jack took in a deep breath. "And that would take another miracle, Roy." He looked at his hands. "What do I do, Roy?"

"Do the next right thing, Jack. Forget the past. Forget all the rest for now. Forget the things you have done that you aren't proud of. Jack, when you walk out the door, just do the next right thing that you can do."

"And then what?" jacked looked at Roy and sighed. "And then what happens?"

"Who knows, Jack? Maybe your miracles will happen."

"Successive miracles?" A slight smile crossed Jack's lips.

"What do you think the chances of for that?"

"I don't know, Jack. But it all starts with the next right thing."

CHAPTER TWENTY-FOUR

Jack sat in the Stingers' ready room and listened to his ops officer deliver the Desert Reveille brief over Vinson's closed-circuit television. The CCTV provided briefs to each ready room located throughout the ship.

Jack's mind was a swirl of confusion. Part of him wanted to hold on to the path he was on. After all, it had always worked out. But, part of him wanted to come clean and tell the admiral about the flawed plan. After he left the chaplain's office, he decided that he needed to fly. Maybe the next right thing was to fly a great hop! Perhaps that is what he needed to do to get everything in perspective. He still didn't like flying at night, but the Desert Reveille plan was a night-focused event, so he had no choice if he wanted to lead it. Mode 1 to touchdown in the Hornet also helped! And, he wanted to lead because, just like in Desert Shield, if there was going to be any glory, it would be fleeting.

Jack felt better as he listened to the brief. He felt better in the ready room's respectful environment in which he was the king. Yes, maybe the next right thing was to fly a great hop.

"Gents, we launch at 2100, so it will be good and dark. When you get airborne, tank if you are scheduled, but monitor the attack frequency. Remember that point Ramage is both the orbit and push point, so turn your lights off at least ten miles before arrival. Stay on your altitude until time to push and do not descend before Ramage. Once you get to Ramage at your push time, descend to 24,000. That is the attack altitude. Proceed inbound to the target area at 500 knots, find your aim point, and release your ordnance.

No talking on the attack frequency unless there is an abort. Abort is the only radio call on the attack frequency. Got it?"

Jack listened quietly and took some notes. The other Stingers on the launch were also taking notes.

"The code word for the attack is Skillet Handle. Copy that? If you hear Skillet Handle, get in position to execute the plan. We will pass the push time with the code word, so skillet handle two-three means the first plane's push is at time twenty-three after the hour. CAG is first so he will go to 24,000 thousand to push. The rest of you are stacked above him by 1,000-foot intervals and will push thirty seconds after he does. So, the airplane at 25,000 feet will push from Ramage at time two-three plus thirty seconds after the hour. The guy at 26,000 will push at time two four and so on. Did everybody get that? Any questions call me here in CVIC at 4721."

Jack watched the rest of the brief and then went to his stateroom. He kept his flight gear there, and at 2015 he was on the deck pre-flighting his Hornet. His airplane had a laser pod on the left-wing and a 1,000 pound LGB on the right. He also had an AAMRAM missile and two Sidewinders as well as a fully loaded gun.

Jack took his time inspecting 307 for the correct pressures, no leaks, good tires, good bomb, and missile mounts. 307 was his favorite plane in the wing because it had the best navigation system and the best Mode 1 capability. It took him exactly where he had to go and landed him once he got back to the ship.

She was a good bird, except for a reoccurring gripe about the radios. Once in a while, the volume would vary from the selected level. It didn't happen on every hop, and maintenance couldn't duplicate it on deck.

Jack read the gripe but didn't think anything about it. After all, it was good old 307! He climbed up the ladder and hopped in. The plane captain helped him strap in, and twenty minutes before launch the yellow-shirted director gave him the turn-up signal.

As soon as he was airborne, Jack raised his gear and de-selected afterburner. The night's plan was zip lip, so he made none of the standard radio calls. He climbed away from the Vinson, then returned overhead, found the tanker and took on 2,000 pounds of gas. He then proceeded to Ramage at 24,000 feet.

While Jack was flying to Ramage, a nail and shrapnel-filled pipe bomb, placed in Atlanta's Centennial Olympic Park, detonated, killing a visitor, Alice Hawthorn, and injuring over 100 others.

News of the explosion shot around the world and at Fifth Fleet headquarters Vice Admiral Renfro received a SPECAT FLASH message alerting him to the event. He directed his aide to get RADM Summersly on the red phone, and when he heard the two star's encrypted, metallic voice, he ordered the code word for Desert Reveille, "Standby for Skillet Handle. Standby for Skillet Handle."

Summersly turned to his aide and ordered, "Stand by for Skillet Handle." He hung up the phone and raced to the Combat Information Center. His aide called the senior watch officer in CIC and repeated, "Skillet Handle, Skillet Handle."

The senior watch officer transmitted on the attack frequency "Skillet Handle, Skillet Handle.

Jack heard the call. It was very faint, but the words exploded in his head. He could not believe it was happening. They were going to execute Desert Reveille!

He immediately completed the checklist for arming his weapons.

The waypoints on his navigation computer pointed to his target, a patrol boat in Bandar Abbas. He listened intently to hear the push time.

Back on Vinson, confusion reigned. Was Skillet Handle a go?

The Senior Watch Officer certainly thought so, as did his watch team.

Summersly burst into CIC and saw the aircraft heading to Ramage. That was the standard route of flight for the opsersizes, so he thought nothing of it. The atmosphere in CIC was loud and chaotic. He saw his chief of staff and talked into his ear to overcome the noise and confusion. "Anything come in over the purple net?"

"Sir, all we know is something detonated at the Olympics in Atlanta. As you can see, all the jets are heading to Ramage."

"Good," said Summersly.

"Yes, sir," said the COS. "I never thought we would do this?"

Summersly nodded and looked at the screen. Then he frowned, panic creeping into him. He grabbed the COS by the front of his jacket. "What do you mean...DO THIS?"

"Sir?" The COS leaned back, confused.

"What did you mean when you said, 'do this'?"

"Well, sir, you know. Skillet Handle. Desert Reveille."

"What!" Summersly grabbed the COS by the shoulders. "I directed to STANDBY for Skillet handle. Have you received new orders?"

"Sir all we have is from the senior watch officer. He said you directed Skillet Handle."

Summersly ran to the senior watch officer's station and swiveled him around in his chair. "What did my aide pass to you?"

"Sir, he passed Skillet Handle."

"Christ, I said to standby for Skillet Handle."

The admiral looked over his shoulder and saw his aide. He rushed to him. "What did you pass? What orders did you pass?"

The aide, visibly shaken and stuttering, said, "Sk, sk, Skillet Handle sir. Skillet Handle."

"Sir," the COS broke in. "We have not issued a push time; we can abort the attack. We can just direct the strikers to belay the last order and standby. I will pass the word."

"Good, good," said the admiral. "Confirm all jets have the word."

The senior watch officer keyed his mic on the attack frequency. "This is War Bonnet, repeat War Bonnet, belay the last order. Stand by for Skillet Handle. I repeat, stand by for Skillet Handle. All aircraft acknowledge on this frequency. Time four seven."

In 307 Jack turned the volume of his radio up. He could barely hear.

"Repeat, time four seven," said the senior watch officer. Jack heard the time hack and glanced at his wristwatch. Christ, it was four seven now!

He looked at his NAV; he was right at point Ramage anyway! Jack took a deep breath, pointed toward his target, and pushed the throttles up. He turned the radio to the strike frequency and accelerated. As the Hornet moved toward the coast, Jack Grant smiled at the calm inside of him.

He was going to do the next right thing.

The admiral stood next to the watch officer and listened as the strikers all reported n. It took eight anxiety-ridden minutes, but they all reported in except for CAG.

"Do we have radar on him? Where is he? Who is controlling the stack?"

The senior watch officer glanced around the room. "Chief, who is controlling Ramage?"

"Sir, it is Hopkins."

"Where is Hopkins?"

Sir, he is at the end." The chief ran to a Sailor operating a radar console in the corner of the room. The Admiral and the senior watch officer followed him.

"Hopkins, where is CAG? What is CAG's side number?" The admiral grabbed the senior watch officer.

"Sir, he is in..." he looked down a list on his clipboard. "He is in 307."

"Hopkins, where is 307?"

"Sir, he is on his way to the target." He grinned broadly, "He is looking right on, sir."

"Christ, get him on the radio, try all the freqs!" screamed the admiral.

"307, War Bonnet." Hopkins paused, then keyed the mic again.

"307, War Bonnet."

"307...307, War Bonnet, over."

Admiral Summersly grabbed the mic from Hopkins. "307, this is the admiral. Come in." He took a deep breath. His hand shook as he keyed the mic again. "307, come in."

Jack could easily see the coast, and he could see the blur of his target in the cockpit FLIR image. He flew a bit closer and dropped his nose to accelerate. As he did, his radar detection RAW gear indicated he was being scanned from the right front quadrant of his aircraft. The warble in his headset confirmed the strobes on his screen.

"Captain, captain, the airplane is not turning around! It is coming!"

Air Defense Captain Adlan Ravli jerked awake. He had been dozing, as was his habit at the end of his shift.

The night shift had become annoying as the Americans routinely flew profiles towards the coast, only to turn around. Captain Ravli had become convinced they did it to provoke him. He had told his men to stand down from their quick alert status and had told the second colonel, his deputy, to leave for the night and be with his new child.

"How far?" He jumped from his chair and quickly crossed the room.

"Sir, the plane is here. At Bandar Abbas." The radar operator pointed to the blip.

"Target the aircraft with the I Hawk. Prepare to fire on my command."

The image of the patrol boat sharpened on Jack's FLIR, and he re-checked his cockpit switches. The warble in his headset quickened in frequency, and Jack knew the Iranians targeted him.

A missile battery radar had locked him up!

He rechecked his switches, the target was designated, the laser was on, just a bit closer and he would drop his 1,000 pounder.

"Prepare to fire." Captain Ravli barked the command. The airplane was close now. It was so close.

"Fire!"

"Missile away," replied his operator.

"Fire again!"

"Missile away."

Jack heard the warble in his headset change again and knew a missile was tracking him. He smiled. He was at peace.

Everything was going to be all right. Jack sharpened the image on his FLIR. The aim dot was right on the superstructure. Jack hit the pickle button on his stick and felt the lurch of the weapon leave his airplane. He lowered his left wing to keep the laser aimed at the target.

Do the next right thing, Jack. Forget the past. Forget all the rest for now. Forget the things you have done that you aren't proud of. Jack, when you walk out the door, just do the next right thing that you can do.

"And then what happens?" Jack whispered into his mask.

Who knows Jack? Maybe a miracle will happen. Perhaps a miracle will happen, and everything will be as it should.

Jack concentrated on the target. He felt good. He felt good because he was doing the next right thing. In his right periphery, he saw a streak of light. Jack saw the hot glow of something streak past his left side.

It was the Iranian Missile! It startled him, and he shut his eyes, expecting an explosion. He swallowed…but…nothing! He opened his eyes and saw a red point of the exhaust falling toward the sea.

It had failed to detonate!

He glanced at his FLIR and saw it whiten. The blast from his bomb had hit the patrol boat and saturated the FLIR filters.

Direct hit!

Jack jammed the throttles into afterburner, swung the Hornet toward the coast. He dumped the nose just as an explosion shuddered his airplane.

A second missile!

Jack's Hornet rocked violently, and both engine fire lights came on. He instinctively pulled the throttles to idle. Both lights went out, so he jammed them back into afterburner.

The explosion shook Jack out of his reverie. He had done the next right thing; the Desert Reveille plan was finished. And, somehow, he had survived.

He looked at his instruments, relieved there was no further indication of fire or damage. His stick felt steady in his hand. He dived toward the deck to get out of radar range of the missile sites.

"Sir, the second missile hit him!"

"Are you sure?"

"Yes, sir. I observed the point of intercept. The missile and the aircraft are no longer on the radar!"

"Fantastic! Allah be praised!" Captain Ravli smiled and clapped the operator on the back. As he turned, the rest of the men in the darkened room cheered and clapped. They had shot down an American!

Jack leveled off at two hundred feet, then slowly lowered his altitude to fifty feet as he streaked across the sea toward the ship.

CHAPTER TWENTY-FIVE

"Does anybody here know what just happened?" Admiral Summersly turned to the men in his cabin; Otter, the COS, and Frank.

"Otter?"

"Sir, we know that the orders to stand by for Skillet Handle did transmit. Every other pilot on that flight heard it and acknowledged it. We know that CAG was in a position to hear the transmission. He was on a high altitude ingress so he should have heard."

"He was in 307," said Otter. "I flew it earlier today, and it has an intermittent radio gripe. It goes off frequency occasionally. It's insidious so the pilot may not know until he realizes nobody is talking to him."

"Could that problem cause the radio to lose volume? On its own?" Summersly nervously wiped his face.

"Possibly." Otter nodded his head. "I had a good debrief from the electricians and reviewed all of the gripes on 307. There were times when it tuned lower than the setting."

"So, it is possible that he could have had the radio on the right frequency, at the right volume but didn't hear the recall order?"

"Yes, sir, it is possible."

"How close did he get?" The admiral looked at the COS. "How close did he get to the target?"

"Unsure, sir. His radar return was right in the target area though."

"Where is he now?"

"Don't know that either, sir. Nothing on radar. Looks like two I Hawks intercepted him. At least one hit."

"Did he try to evade the missiles? Shoot decoys or flares?"

"The tape doesn't show any evasive maneuvering before impact. Impossible to tell at this point if CAG deployed any countermeasures."

"If he was supporting his bomb, he would not be doing anything evasive," said Frank.

"For God's sake, why not?" asked COS.

"So he could keep his laser on the target," replied Frank.

"If he was hit, any chance of rescue?" Summersly looked at Otter.

"Sir, we have helos in the area," said Otter. "They can't do much until daylight."

"Are we hearing anything on the Iranian frequencies?"

"Yes, sir, stuff coming in from NSA. Nothing but jubilation over the shootdown. No mention of looking for a downed pilot," said COS.

"So, what do we think?" Summersly looked around the room.

"Sir, I would like to say something." Otter cleared his throat.

"Go ahead. Please."

"I told CAG he was a coward. I told him that because we both knew the plan was not executable."

"What?" Summersly leaned forward. He looked at Otter, then at the COS.

"Couldn't be done like planned. Too much time over the target, too many SAMs, too small of a target area. Couldn't be done."

"Then why didn't he tell me?" Summersly glared at Otter, then at the COS. "Why didn't anybody tell me? Why didn't YOU tell me?"

"Sir, believe me, I wanted to. But CAG forbade me to do it.

"I told Jack the same," interrupted Frank.

Summersly looked at him in shock.

"I told him to come clean about it and tell you. I was sure he was going to do it. After his flight tonight."

"Jesus." Summersly rocked back in his chair and stared at the ceiling. "Jesus. So, he continued to the target area, not knowing the attack had been called off? "

"Who knows," said Frank. "Jack might have heard the recall and pressed on anyway, or he might not have because of the radio. With Jack, you never quite know what the motivator is."

Summersly looked at him and shook his head. "It still just doesn't sound right."

"Admiral, admiral!"

The men looked toward the door. A lieutenant stood in the opening. "Sir, we have contact with Captain Grant."

"Contact?" Summersly stood and looked at the messenger. "Yes, sir, he is inbound to the ship. And his code report indicates he hit his target!"

"What! He bombed Iran? Jesus Christ! COS, draft the flash message that indicates pilot reports delivering ordnance on planned target/patrol boat at Bandar Abbas. More to follow."

"Yes, sir," the COS dashed out of the room. "Otter, go and meet him. Frank, you go too. Get him up here ASAP. And all of you," the admiral pointed to the men in the room. "I want all of you back here to discuss this. After CAG arrives, we need to get to the facts very, very quickly. We need to understand what happened and then pass that up the line."

After Jack contacted the ship, he was vectored for an immediate approach and flew a smooth pass right into the three-wire. It surprised him since he was so excited from the attack. He parked his Hornet, shut the engines down, and climbed down the ladder. A mob of men stood near the back of the plane, and Jack joined them. Flashlights showed a score of jagged tears and holes in the rudder and tail section.

"It is a miracle this thing flew," said the squadron maintenance chief.

Jack smiled at the word miracle and began to look his airplane over when Otter and Frank appeared at his side.

"Lot of folks want to talk with you," Frank yelled over the sound of the wind and plane engines.

"Yeah, I imagine," grunted Jack. He allowed Otter and Frank to lead him off the flight deck. Once on the 03 level, Frank turned to Jack. "I need to talk to you for a few minutes alone. Before we see the admiral, let's go to your stateroom, you can take off your flight gear there."

Jack shrugged his shoulders, "Sure."

"Otter, tell the admiral we are on our way."

"Will do," said Otter. "But don't take long. He is worked up."

Frank and Jack walked the short distance to his stateroom, and once inside, Jack began to take off his gear.

"I noticed your bomb is gone." Frank leaned against the wall, a frown on his face.

"I dropped it on my target."

"So, the US has attacked Iran, then?" Frank took a chair and shook his head.

"Well, wasn't that what Skillet Handle meant to do?"

"Yes, I guess it was," sighed Frank.

362

"What happened? What started all of this?" Jack slumped into the chair behind his desk.

"Something blew at the Olympics in Atlanta, and the Fifth Fleet passed to standby for Skillet Handle. That came to us, and the Admiral told his aide to tell the senior watch officer to stand by for Skillet Handle. Of course, the aide left out the *stand by* part when he told the senior watch officer. It all went to shit after that. You and all the other strikers headed for the command and control point. Didn't you hear the recall?" Frank leaned forward. "Everybody else did. We know about 307's radio."

Frank waited for an answer, but Jack was fiddling with his gear. "CAG."

Frank frowned and touched Jack on the shoulder. "CAG, did you hear the recall?"

Jack looked up at Frank. He smiled and leaned back in his chair. "Sure."

"What?" Frank looked shocked. "What? You heard it? You heard it? Then why in hell did you proceed?"

Jack sighed and grabbed the arms of his chair. He looked at Frank for a long time. He shook his head and rubbed his face with his hands. "Something happened to me out there."

"What do you mean?"

"I don't know. Something."

"What the fuck do you mean, something? What happened?"

"I DON'T KNOW!" Jack's hands shook as he gripped the chair. "I DON'T KNOW!" He felt his face grow red. He swallowed and shook his head again.

Christ!

Jack leaned back, took a deep breath, and looked at Frank. "I don't know. He shrugged his shoulders. "I guess I continued because I wanted to stop the insanity of the plan. I wanted to prove that a night attack on a target area that small was impossible to execute. I figured I would get hit, but losing me and one airplane would be worth it." Jack paused and took a deep breath. A wry smile crossed his lips. "I didn't expect to actually get to the target, let alone hit it, then survive."

"You mean you were on some suicide mission?"

"I don't know, sir. I …something like that."

"Jack, listen to what you are saying," said Frank. "You say you intended to execute a suicide mission to save the navy from a bad plan. That is quite remarkable. I mean, all you had to do was to tell the admiral. Remember I am the guy that tried to get you to go to him? All you had to do was do what I said. He could have contacted Fifth Fleet. The plan would have been scrubbed." Frank frowned at Jack and leaned back in his chair. "I find it incredible that instead of having a conversation, you head for the target."

Jack met his gaze but said nothing.

"Do you realize how crazy it sounds? How unstable you sound?"

"Maybe I am unstable," spat Jack.

"Look, Jack, there is more in play now than any of us know. We don't have any idea what the Iranians did in Atlanta if anything. We don't have any idea what the folks in CENTCOM or the Pentagon are planning. We do know, now, that an American fighter bombed Iranian soil. God knows what that is going to do. There is already lots of confusion from the message traffic we are reading. But I do know one thing." Frank Leaned forward. "If we do have to take further action against Iran, or explain the action we have taken, a story about a suicidal CAG going after a target will not fucking help. If you come out with your, 'I was going to kill myself to cleanse my soul' story, you will destroy our credibility. It will make us all--- by that I mean all of the military---look very questionable. Questionable, in a time when we can't have any concerns about what we are prepared to do. For Christ's sake, the President would end up apologizing for you."

Jack frowned but remained silent.

Frank looked at him and shook his head. "What is going on with you?"

Jack winced, leaned forward and plucked a pencil from his desk. He rolled it in his fingers.

"Come on, Jack, it's a fair question."

Jack sighed and looked at Frank. He nodded, "Yes, I suppose, it is." He eyed the pencil as he rolled it. "As you know, I have had a lot on my mind lately; I have been thinking about a lot of things. I guess it caught up with me."

"You mean the stuff we talked about before?"

"Yes."

365

"Christ, I didn't realize you were at the point of killing yourself over it."

Jack sighed again. He scratched the side of his head and ran his hand down over his neck. "I guess it was seeing Grace that got me going." Jack looked at the pencil and pursed his lips. He felt tight in his chest, and for a second thought he might cry. He swallowed and looked at Frank. "I mean, I feel like I am having some kind of break down."

Frank frowned but remained silent.

"I have been a cheater all my life." Jack swallowed and looked at the wall. Away from Frank. "I cheated and manipulated in high school, college, flight school. But, the funny thing is that everything worked out. You know? Everything, and if I wasn't cheating and manipulating, sheer good luck just filled in. I mean, you know my story." He looked Frank who nodded back.

"I selected for command because the other department heads got fired. If that hadn't happened, I would never have been a Tomcat skipper." Jack paused, unsure how much he wanted to say. He looked at Frank.

"Go ahead, Jack. It's alright."

"You saw the tape. The thing about killing the MIGS, the glory that got my career going. That's all a lie, as you know. I mean, it was my back seater, Jocko, who talked me through the whole engagement. He is the one that shot the Phoenix that made me so famous. Without him, I would have never done any of it.

And, to repay him, I threw away the tape that contained his heroics. And he was okay with it." Jack's hands trembled as he stared at the pencil. As if there were

366

answers somewhere in the wood and graphite core. He looked at Frank, and seeing no disappointment, continued. "It was also luck that you gave me the number one ticket. You told me you didn't want to, and I understand why. It was a ticket I knew I didn't deserve. But it happened. I fucked over my XO at TOPGUN, told the NCIS investigators a bunch of crap that ruined his career and got me out of the TAILHOOK scandal. Even worse, I screwed up and spun an A-4 and killed Jocko in the process. All because of my ego. Frank, I abandoned my friends in Iraq. The story about me having a gunfight is all bullshit. I ran and left them to die. And my lie made me even a bigger hero. For Christ sakes, I selected for CAG early! And then there was all the mess about The COD pilot and the MIG-29s. I screwed that up because I didn't dare to do the right thing. I even got a blowjob in my stateroom. From the Air Force Major." Jack swallowed and looked at the ceiling. "Christ, do you believe me? Do you believe a guy like me exists?"

Frank frowned but said nothing.

"So, when I saw Grace, all this stuff came rolling up to me." Jack swallowed and turned to the wall. He took a deep breath and swung back to Frank. "I almost killed her little dog, for God's sake! He stood off two coyotes while I was trying to bang a chick I picked up at the officers' club. I am just a fricking, worthless piece of crap, Frank."

Jack took a breath and looked at his hands. He rolled the pencil in his fingers. He didn't want to look at Frank and was grateful for the moments of silence that followed. Finally, Frank cleared his voice.

"So, what did you want to happen, Jack? Why did you proceed to attack?"

"I want to be who everybody thinks I am." Jack felt a tear run down his cheek and quickly wiped it off. "I just want to be the man everybody thinks Jack Grant is."

"Well, you have another chance at that, Jack. Because it is now time for you to ACT like the man people think you are. So, the suicide or cleansing moment or whatever the fuck that was all about can't be part of this. You aren't on the Oprah Winfrey show; you are in the US Navy." Frank leaned forward again. "I think 307's radios failed sometime after the mistaken code was sent. You headed to the target, never realizing the strike had been called off. You were the leader, the first man down the line. You had no idea or way of knowing what was happening behind you. As far as you knew, the orders were to hit those boats and take them all out. So, you pressed to the target because that is what professional naval aviators do."

"But, that isn't true," said Jack. "I did hear the recall. I did press on despite that."

"So, NOW you give a shit about the truth? You haven't cared much about that before."

Jack winced at Frank's stinging words. He looked at the floor.

"Now is the time to be Jack Grant," said Frank. "Now is the time to capitalize on another one of your miracles. Now is the time, once again, for you to lift glory from a pile of shit you have created. We need a hero, Jack, not some flawed figure who wants to come clean. Nobody cares about clean at this point."

"So, in other words, I win again?"

"Yes, Jack, you win again."

368

Jack leaned his head back and sighed. His mind whirled in doubt. He was so sure about what to do when he was heading toward the target. He was so sure his survival was a sign; it was time to come clean on all of the crap he had done. He was so sure it was time to end the charade and somehow start all over.

"We have to go see the admiral," said Frank. He stood and looked at Jack. "And you have to be Jack Grant."

Jack sighed and stood. He nodded at Frank. "Let's go."

They walked out of Jack's stateroom and the few feet down the passageway to the flag spaces. Frank led the way into the Flag cabin. The admiral stood when they walked in. He extended his hand to Jack.

"Good to have you back, CAG."

"Thank you, sir."

"Seats, gents." Summersly took a seat at the head of his table.

The aide offered seats next to the COS and Otter.

"Well, let's get to it. We have messages to send ASAP." The admiral leaned forward. "Can you tell us what happened?"

"Yes, sir." Jack took a breath and swallowed. "I heard the code for the attack and immediately headed for the launch and martial point. I was the lead, and the given push time gave me a tight window to get in position. But, I made it and commenced to my target on time."

"Did you hear the recall?" Summersly's gaze was intense. Jack looked at the admiral and saw the concern in his eyes. He knew the man's career was on the line. He glanced around the room. Hell, all of them had some part to play in this. Jack looked back at Summersly. Frank nodded slowly and winked.

"No, sir," he lied.

"Damn!" Summersly frowned. "We heard about the radio problem with your airplane."

"Yes, sir," said COS and Otter in unison.

Jack felt the tension leave the room. Everybody was off the hook. It was an airplane malfunction! Or, at least they thought they were off the hook.

"But Jack, why in the hell did you take an aircraft with a known communications problem?" The admiral frowned. "Especially as the strike leader."

"Sir, it was an inconsistent gripe. It didn't happen every flight. Besides, 307 has the tightest navigation system in the airwing. As flight lead, I had to make sure I got us to the exact target run-in line."

"Yes, I suppose so," sighed the admiral. "I suppose so." He looked at Jack, then at the others. "You reported that you hit your target."

"Yes, sir, if you look at 307's cockpit recorder, you will see I hit my target." Jack looked at Frank. Frank smiled.

"About the plan. I hear others cautioned you that it wouldn't work." Summersly looked at Jack, then at Otter and Frank. He rocked back in his chair and cocked his head. "How is it that the Iranians hit you? The very first airplane on what could have been a twelve airplane stream. How do you explain that?"

"Sir, we have the tape." The aide interrupted and scurried through the door. He had a VHS tape in his hand. He inserted it into the player, and the men looked at the screen. The image of the Bog Hammer appeared accompanied by the sound of Jack's breathing. As the picture sharpened, the audio warbles of radar track and then missile guidance blared. The bomb appeared as a dark streak; then the FLIR brightened until white out. The tape went black.

"Well, it appears you hit your target," said Summersly. "But, to my previous point. How do you explain the fact the Iranians hit you?"

Jack had had time to think during the tape. "Sir, it's not on the tape of course, but as I was approaching the target area, the coast was black. I saw pinpoints of light, but for the most part, black." Jack fixed the admiral with his most sincere stare. If there was one thing Jack Grant could do, it was to bullshit. It was time to make shit up. "Then, suddenly, lights came on. I think the Iranians must have monitored us and heard the recall. They heard the communications that followed and that alerted them. That explains their ability to target me. If we hadn't chattered up the radio with the recall stuff, a stream raid would have worked just fine. Skillet Handle would have worked."

Summersly frowned and started to speak. He took a deep breath and slowly nodded his head. He smiled and looked at the COS. "Can we corroborate any of this? Develop the kind of linkage CAG suggests?"

"I am sure we can," smiled the COS. "I mean, there is no real way to prove it didn't happen that way."

"Good," said the admiral. "Draft up a message that details the incident. Ensure we say aircraft tape indicates direct hit on target boat. Be sure the 307 issue is clearly explained and CAG's reasoning for taking the airplane. Emphasize the CAG's story about the lights coming on."

"But, sir won't that raise questions about why he pressed to the target? After he knew the Iranians might be alerted?" The COS frowned and paused in his note-taking.

"NO," said Frank. "Jack is a professional aviator. He got the word to attack, and he did. That is all anyone needs to take out of this."

"Great," said the admiral. "COS, tell the captain to get the ship as far away from Iran as he safely can, the other side of the gulf. Put that in the message too. Then show it to me in fifteen minutes. No longer."

"Yes, sir," said the COS. He jumped up and ran out of the room.

"CAG, get with the DESRON commander and work with my staff to get the other ship's skippers over here. We need a plan on how to defend the battle group if the Iranians counter-attack.

Frank, your folks in the maritime control center are in this, and we need your input for sure."

Jack, Otter, and Frank stood and walked out the door and down the passageway to Jack's office.

"Get some sleep," said Frank. "Otter and I will take a whack at this thing and give you an input and status brief in the morning."

"Thanks," said Jack.

"Boss." Otter looked at Jack. It was dark in the passageway, but Jack could see his eyes. "Good job out there, sir."

Jack was stunned. It had been a long time since Otter had said anything positive to him.

"It was a good plan," said Jack. He turned and walked to his room. He shut the door behind them and walked through his office into his bedroom. He sat on the edge of the bed and flopped back on the covers. Christ, but it seemed like forever ago when he had turned the radio off and headed for the target, positive he would not return.

He had been so calm!

It had been the next right thing, as the chaplain had said.

But now, now what? He didn't know what to think. Things had all changed back. He was, once again, the old Jack Grant. He closed his eyes and fell into a troubled sleep. Grace was in his dreams. Grace and Harley. And just before he awoke, it was Grace and Harley and Jocko.

Jack jerked awake and blinked against the fog in his head. What was the dream about? He remembered Grace and Harley, and then Jocko. But there was no story to it. He arose, showered, and walked into his office. Otter sat in the chair across from his desk, thumbing through an old copy of Navy Times. He glanced up when Jack opened his door.

"Morning boss."

"Morning Otter." Jack sat behind his desk and gave his deputy a wary eye. Last night, in the passageway, he had seen a different attitude from Otter. All the COD pilot, MIG-29 stuff was water under the bridge? Did Otter now have some admiration for him?

After all, Jack had attacked Iran, alone, and had hit his target and returned. The stuff of legend.

Otter obviously had not slept all night. His dark eyes were bloodshot and weary. He gulped from a large coffee cup, still wearing his flight suit from the night before.

"Pandemonium across the ship as you can imagine," said Otter. He took another gulp. "Washington is in an uproar and everybody wants to know how the attack on Iran is related to the bombing in Atlanta."

"I imagine so," said Jack.

"We got a good air plan for defending the carrier in case the Iranians want to send out their air force," said Otter. The E-2 and Tomcat boys did an excellent job with it, and the AEGIS ops officer supports the plan. Defending in the air is easy. It is the boat thing that was always the problem."

"Yes," nodded Jack. "Defending against a swarm of patrol boats is the reason the Desert Reveille plan was designed in the first place. And now I have given them the reason to swarm. I can see why everybody is in an uproar."

"Don't be too hard on yourself. You didn't give the code word to attack, and you didn't hear the recall."

Jack looked at Otter to see if there was anything behind his words. Had Frank spilled the beans? Did he know or suspect anything?

Otter nodded, "Yep, you did the right thing, boss," and took another gulp.

Jack's phone rang, and he picked it up.

"CAG, COS here, got some good news if you can believe it. Can you come down and see the admiral?"

"Sure, be right there." He hung up the phone and smiled at Otter. "Time to see the big guy."

Jack and Otter walked the short distance to the blue-tiled area and entered the admiral's cabin. Summersly, Frank Wright, and the COS were seated at the table.

"Sit down, gents," said the admiral. He waited for Jack and Otter to sit, then smiled. "Our boys in the Pentagon say there is chatter that indicates the Iranians believe we mined the approaches to the patrol boat bases in Bandar Abbas and Bushehr."

"Really!" Jack sat back in his chair.

"That's what they say," said the admiral. "The chatter also indicates Iran thinks the single plane attack last night was an attempt to draw them out so they would hit those mines."

"What?" Jack, Frank d Otter all spoke in unison.

"We do know the Iranians approached the Swiss this morning and asked them to intervene. The blast in Atlanta has caused much international concern, and the

375

Iranians are afraid we are about to do something. Some folks at State believe this brings an opportunity to dialogue with Iran."

"So, the attack was a good thing?" Otter asked with a smile. "Strangely enough, maybe it was," said the admiral. "What was a tremendous mistake, now seems to have been the right thing to do. Amazing how things work out sometimes."

Jack smiled with the others, but he felt oddly uncomfortable. He glanced briefly at Frank, who was looking right at him. "Just play along" was in his eyes.

"Well, let's get to work." The admiral stood, and the others followed suit.

Jack walked out of the flag spaces and headed back to his room. He opened the door and started to walk in.

"Jack."

He turned to see Frank coming down the passageway. "Could I have a minute?"

"Sure, come in." The two men entered the room, and Jack gestured toward the couch. "Have a seat."

Frank sat down and smiled at Jack. "Good job in there."

"So, is everybody off the hook? Is the admiral going to be okay?"

Frank smiled and leaned back, "I don't think so. We bombed a sovereign nation without authority. Regardless of the good things that might have come out of this, we fucked up. There wasn't supposed to be a strike, but there was. Somebody will pay for that."

"Who?"

"Well, we both know it should be you."

Jack nodded and looked at Frank. "I suppose you are right about that."

"But, it won't be you," said Frank. "Hell, it CAN'T be you. Not now."

"Then, who?"

"Summersly."

"The admiral? Why?" Jack frowned and leaned forward from the couch.

"Think about it, Jack. He is in charge. He issued an order that was misunderstood and then acted upon. He is the fall guy on this."

"But, it wasn't his fault. He is a surface warfare officer. It was my fault."

"Jack, to be blunt, there are a lot of carcasses strewn in your path. The two-star is just the latest."

"Well, at least the weakness of the plan is exposed. At least I did that. That is what I wanted to do in the first place."

"You are right about that, I don't think anybody is going to execute that plan anymore," said Frank. "But, we both know there was a much better way of doing that than what you did."

"Maybe," said Jack." Maybe you're right."

"About your suicide mission. Do you plan on flying right away?" Frank frowned and leaned forward. "I am worried about you."

"I'm okay," said Jack. "Everything is back the way it was anyway."

Frank frowned again and started to speak. He looked at Jack, then stood. "Get some more rest CAG." He walked out of the room.

For the next week, the Vinson battlegroup huddled in a defensive position in the gulf, as far west as it could get. The news reports about the Olympic bombing revealed one dead and 111 injured with another dying later of a heart attack. A security guard named Richard Jewell was the main suspect, although his motive was unknown. The Iranian connection to the bombing wholly dissolved. Ironically, the incident gave the U.S. and Iran a reason to resume talks via the Swiss.

Frank Wright was correct in his assumption of falling heads. RADM Summersly was relieved of command. Ten days after the event, the COD brought his replacement, RADM John Franklin, USN. However, Frank did not accurately assess the damage. He was removed from the one-star list due to his mismanagement of the Joint Maritime Component Commander mission.

Vice Admiral Turner, Commander Naval Air Forces Pacific, petitioned the SECNAV's office to urge Rear Admiral Franklin to submit Jack for a Distinguished Flying Cross. Franklin agreed.

The Carl Vinson and her battle group relocated to the north end of the Persian Gulf to support Operation Southern Watch, a UN-sanctioned program to prevent Saddam from using aircraft against his people in the southern marshes. While there, Vinson and Pentagon planners developed Operation Desert Strike to punish Saddam for his attempts to shoot down U.S. airplanes and his actions against the Kurds in the north. Initially, the plan used CAG 14 for the attack, but that plan was altered to use USAF and USN cruise missiles. Jack and Otter fought aggressively to use CAG 14 aircraft, but they were overruled. Twenty-seven cruise missiles were fired at Iraqi targets.

Operation Desert Strike was a letdown for the Vinson and her airwing. Their only action was escorting USAF B-52s and some post-strike sorties, protecting against an enemy that never showed.

Finally, they left the gulf. The USS Carl Vinson and CAG 14 journeyed across the pacific toward home. During a flight deck ceremony, Jack was awarded the Distinguished Flying Cross, the Bronze Star, and an Air Medal. Given his previous decorations, Jack Grant was the most decorated naval aviator on active duty. As the carrier neared the coast, all CAG 14 squadrons prepared to fly off to their home stations. On the day before the fly-off, Jack went to find Chaplain Roy. He had not talked with him since their conversation in the chapel and before he had attacked and bombed the patrol boat.

Jack dropped by the ship's library and chapel in the hopes of finding Roy, and, luckily, he was there.

"Got time to chat?"

"Sure," said Roy. He stood and gestured toward a couch. "I was wondering when you would drop by."

"What made you think I would drop by?"

"Our last conversation ended in me, suggesting you do the next right thing. I wondered if you did that. With your actions?"

Jack sat down and looked at the chaplain.

"So, did you? Did you do the next right thing?"

"It seems to have turned out okay."

"That's not what I asked you?"

Jack looked down at his hands. He felt Roy's eyes on him. It was not an uncomfortable feeling. After all, that is what he had come for, and he knew the eyes were kind. He looked up.

"I heard the recall. I knew it was called off. I went anyway." Roy nodded his head but remained silent.

His understanding was infuriating!

"I wanted to do something that would end the plan!"

"You could have just gone to higher authority and done that."

"Yes," said Jack. "But I also wanted to do something that would absolve me."

"Absolve you?"

"Yes, of all the rotten things I have done."

"You could have come to me for that. Confession is a lot easier," chuckled Roy.

"I think you know what I mean," said Jack.

"I know what you mean, Jack."

"But, instead of dying a cleansing death and exposing the bad plan, I live. I am now more powerful than the man I wanted to kill off."

Jack looked at the chaplain and shook his head. "The story is that I was unwitting about the recall but heroically proceeded anyway. And, somehow, initiated a dormant conversation with the Iranians. It is now a classic, Jack Grant success story. But, the admiral and Frank Wright are cashiered because of me."

Jack looked up at the ceiling and sighed. "Christ, I destroy people left and right." He sighed again and let his eyes drop to the floor. He could feel Roy's eyes on him and knew he didn't have to talk. But he wanted to talk! He looked into Roy's eyes. "I do know this. I thought I was doing the next right thing when I turned down that radio and headed to the target. I just knew it! But it wasn't. Roy, I don't know what the next right thing is or if I can even realize it."

"Jack, our life is a string in front of us. There are never-ending opportunities to do the next right thing. They appear, disappear, and reappear — a little like Mary's Cheshire cat. But there are opportunities all along the string. That is why it is called the next right thing."

"But, I don't know what that is."

"Well, it isn't a suicide bombing mission. I can tell you that," said Roy.

"Yes, I suppose you are right."

"How did it go with Grace? I haven't talked to you since you got back."

Jack sat back. The chaplain's change of subject surprised him. He looked down at the floor. He was glad the chaplain asked him the question. He wanted to talk about Grace.

"Do you realize, I never tried to find out what was wrong with her?"

"What do you mean?"

"I mean, the panic attacks. The anxiety. I never tried to get to the bottom of what was wrong with her."

"You took her to a lot of doctors from what you have told me."

"Yes, but we never got a solution. Nobody wants to deal with emotional problems, especially if you don't want to choke down all their pills."

"She didn't die of panic disorder, Jack. She died of cancer."

"She died a long time before she got cancer, Roy. And I didn't do anything about it."

Roy didn't answer. He just had kind eyes.

Jack talked to those eyes for an hour. He told them about his experience in the hospice. He spoke to them about his uncontrollable tears and about some guy named Joe. A guy he didn't understand but wished that he did. He told them about the way Grace had died.

"She was reaching for something, Roy, and Joe thought it was for me. But that isn't possible. What have I ever done to have her want to reach for me?"

"Then give her something to reach for, Jack."

"But that is a selfish way to think. Isn't it?" Jack shook his head and took a breath. "Did you know that I prayed for her to open her eyes so she would forgive ME? Do you see how pathetic I am? She is in a hospice, and I am praying for her to forgive ME. It is always…hell; it has ALWAYS been about me."

Jack looked at Roy. He wished the man would not be kind. He wished he would curse him. Jack looked at the floor and shook his head.

"Jack, you have the power to make *it* about someone else." Chaplain Roy's voice was soft. "We all have that power. We all can put someone other than ourselves in the center. It's just hard to do sometimes."

Jack looked at Roy, then let his eyes drop to the floor.

"Find a way to do that, Jack. You play the lead role in your story. Find a way to make that leading man the man you want him to be."

"I don't know how to do that," said Jack. "I never have before."

"You've never had these doubts before either, have you? You've never had these questions about yourself, have you?"

"Well, no."

"Then maybe it is time for you to change yourself, Jack. Maybe now is the time."

Jack looked at Roy for a long moment. He rose to leave. "See you next week?"

Roy smiled and stood. "I will be on the dais with you and Otter at your change of command."

"Say a good prayer for me, then," said Jack.

"I will," replied Roy. "Then, what?"

"I am going to take some leave. I also need to get Harley and take him to my niece's in New Mexico. She wants the dog, and it's the last thing I can do for Grace. She wanted the dog to live out his days with someone that loved him.

"Will you fly or drive?"

"I fly to Virginia to pick up Harley. Grace's friends are watching him. Then we will drive. I need some time to think about all of this."

"Good," said Roy. "Family or friends along the way?"

"No, I am planning to stop in a little place in Missouri," said Jack.

"Oh, where?"

"A little place called Theodosia Village. In the Ozark lake country. My dad took us there once when I was eleven. I always planned to go back and visit."

"Sounds like the right thing to do, Jack. And, who knows, maybe you will find some answers there."

Jack nodded and took a deep breath. "Thanks, Chaplain." He turned and walked out of the room.

The following week whizzed by as Jack and his staff prepared for the change of command. There were a million details to deal with; even the CNO's office called!

A navy change of command is a time-honored event that allows the Sailors and officers of a unit to see the physical turnover of authority. A dais often used and those on it include the officer relinquishing command, the officer gaining command, the reporting senior officer, a guest speaker and, of course, the chaplain. Roy, Otter, Jack, Rear Admiral Franklin, and, finally, the guest speaker, Vice Admiral Stan "Titan" Turner, proceeded onto the dais in reverse seniority. They individually trooped through a double row of side-boys while receiving salutes and the welcome of the yeoman's pipe. The band added the traditional "ruffles and flourishes" for the two flag officers' entrances. For Air Wing Fourteen, this event went as planned, and once all were on stage, Chaplain Roy delivered the address. It was an uplifting and grateful message, and he ended it with a special request for Jack.

"And, Father, a special blessing on Captain Grant as he proceeds down his road. Support him as he seeks his questions and grace him as he uncovers his answers."

Jack felt his face glow and was grateful for his bowed head. "Amen."

385

"Thank you, Chaplain." Jack turned to Roy and smiled. "Thank you for your words and your stewardship of this command. Thank you for your friendship with me." He shot a salute to his friend and then turned back to the crowd. A large assemblage of guests was in front of the dais, seated in folding chairs. A contingent of Sailors stood in formation.

"At my first change of command, I had the Secretary of the Navy as my guest speaker. It was a pretty big deal." Jack smiled as the crowd laughed. "At my last change of command, I had the Commander of Naval Air Forces, Pacific, Vice Admiral Turner, as my guest speaker. Jack gestured toward the three-star to his left. That was a pretty big deal too." The crowd laughed some more.

Jack paused and looked across the sea of smiling faces in front of him. It was a beautiful, crisp day in San Diego, and the ceremony USS Vinson was a magnificent venue.

"I am also blessed to have him here today. And there is a reason for that." Jack looked down at his speech and took a breath. He looked up and above the eyes of the crowd, to the waters of San Diego Bay.

He took another breath to settle himself.

"For my previous changes of command, I wanted the prestige of senior and powerful guest speakers. And, because of the events surrounding me, I could have that. I have, indeed been fortunate. The CNO's office informed us that he was available for this event if I wanted." Jack paused again and looked in the faces of the crowd. They were all smiling, glad to be a part of this special moment for a special man. But, I declined the CNO's gracious offer," said Jack. "You see, I wanted Vice Admiral Turner to be here since he was the first flag officer to advocate for me. He convinced my CAG to give me the number one ticket. A ranking I did not deserve." Jack looked at Vice Admiral Turner and smiled at his confused frown. "He has supported me since the days when I was a skipper. I owe much of my success, my command of this air wing, and my reputation to him." Jack smiled again, saluted, and turned back to the crowd.

"But, I do not merit his advocacy or his support." Jack paused, and the crowd quickly quieted. There was a low buzz in the audience, and he scanned the faces. Their eyes narrowed, and their smiles sagged in confusion. They wanted him to say something funny---to explain---so they could smile again.

"Admiral Turner thought he saw in me, a future, naval aviation leader. I dare to say, he saw in me as a person that one day could take the torch from him, and carry it to the pentagon." Jack paused again, then continued. "But, I misled the admiral. I misled all of you." There was a collective gasp from the crowd.

What did he say?

Mouths gaped open and frowns found their places. People looked at each other, then around to others. Had they heard him correctly? Was this some kind of stunt?

Jack turned to Vice Admiral Turner and slowly shook his head. "Sorry about the surprise, boss, but this is the best way to do this." He shifted his gaze to Chaplain Roy. Jack nodded to him. "This is the next right thing to do chaplain."

Jack turned to the crowd. He stared at his speech and then, carefully folded it and put it in his breast pocket.

He looked down for a moment, then swallowed and met the confused gaze of his guests.

"I am not the man you think I am," he said. "I am not the man, not the officer that the navy thinks I am." Jack swallowed again and felt his eyes grow wet. "In fact, I am a fraud." He took a deep breath...No turning back now.

"I have lived a completely self-centered life." Jack forced himself to scan the crowd slowly. If this self-immolation was to be worth-while, he had to look into the fire. He had to see their eyes when they turned from a friend and advocate to disgusted disbeliever.

"I have conducted myself with only my self-interests in mind. I neglected the needs of my wife. I left her to more or less fend for herself. I don't know if you knew her. Grace was her name. She suffered from anxiety and the loss of our son, and I just walked away from her. She died a little while ago. She died in a hospice because I didn't take care of her."

The crowd gasped again — more confusion.

"I selected for fighters out of the training command because I manipulated the instructors and because I got access to the computers and changed my scores. I screened for squadron command due to a total fluke of luck. I did not shoot the Phoenix missile in Iraq. My RIO shot it because I was too timid and if it were not for his direct coaching, I would not have shot the other MIG either."

Jack cast a look at Otter. His face was set in a deep scowl. Changes of command were supposed to be unique and special, not gut-wrenching. Jack turned and scanned the crowd again. He now saw anger amid the confusion.

388

"I was not a hero in Iraq and did not survive a shoot-out with Saddam's men. I ran out on two, brave men who were battling for me. I left them to die."

Jack paused as his voice broke. He didn't want to look at the crowd anymore. He didn't want to see their looks. He gripped the sides of the podium and felt the tears drop from his cheeks.

It was so quiet he heard himself swallow.

He held onto the podium for a few moments, then straightened and turned toward Vice Admiral Turner. "Sir, I know I am now an embarrassment to you, and for that, I have no excuse. But, I can fix this. I can fix it now. Sir, I resign my position as Commander, Carrier Air Wing Fourteen and, furthermore, I resign as a Captain in the United States Navy. My signature is on the documents, here at the podium."

Jack saluted. Vice Admiral Turner, unsure what to do, looked at Rear-Admiral Franklin. Both men stood in confusion. Jack turned and walked off the dais.

That afternoon, Jack visited Rear Admiral Franklin's office. His aide gave Jack an endorsed letter of resignation and forwarded it to Commander Naval Air Forces Pacific, VADM Stan "Titan" Turner. VADM Turner's Chief of Staff met Jack in the foyer of the headquarters building on NAS North Island. He informed Jack that the Admiral did not wish to see him but endorsed and forwarded his resignation request.

CHAPTER TWENTY-SIX

Theodosia Village is a hamlet of 230 people, located where Highway 160 crosses the Little North Fork arm of Bull Shoals Lake in Ozark County, Missouri. An actress that nobody ever heard of, named Tava Smiley, hails from the village, but, other than that, it is off most peoples' maps. History has it that the town started around a post office in 1886 with the first postmaster named Kirby. The creation of the dam in 1951 did much for regional flood control. It also created an opportunity for a marina to support all the fishing and pleasure boats that took to the lake. It was at this marina that Cooks' café took a prominent position to serve the visiting fisherman, hunters, and skiers as well as the locals. It was in the café parking lot that village constable Cletis Bower lounged in his truck with hopes of catching sight of Doctor Ruthie Jenkins.

Some say the Bowers were runners-up to the Kirby family when the original postmaster was appointed. They also say that is why the Bowers have been irritable and cranky ever since. Whatever the reason, the family did have an ill-tempered side and that, of course, made them well-suited for being preachers and, or, lawmen. Preachers have to be cranky since they spend most of their time looking for the bad in people and lawmen have to be cranky since they spend most of their time finding the bad in people.

Cletis was scouting the café because he knew Ruthie was in there having lunch. He started to move his truck to a better spying spot when he saw the van with out-of-state plates drive up. As was his heritage, he began to look for something wrong.

Jack and Harley had had a great ride together across the country and had bonded into an inseparable duo. Harley was a living bandage to Jack's wounds, and his "love" lifted him. He realized that to be loved when you don't deserve it is a precious gift, even if it is from a dog. Jack thought a lot about his transformation and prayed that it was real. His cleansing had begun with his self-doubts at TOPGUN and the death of Jocko. His unbelievable cowardice in Iraq had plagued him much but the fact he was able to bring some closure to the little girl, Navi, gave him hope that perhaps he was intended for some good. The stuff on the Vinson with the Indians and the COD pilot, his behavior with the Air Force Major, all mixed in and caused him to doubt himself more. Listening to himself on the tape was, perhaps, the piece that caused him to snap. The "suicide mission" to Iran was God's way of laughing at him for trying to find the easy way out.

The career-ending change-of-command speech was the cathartic moment for Jack. It was his way of proclaiming to himself that Jack Grant wasn't going to be Jack Grant anymore. He was going to be someone much, much better. And on the nights on the road when he stroked his dog's fur and watched somebody else's local news, he felt that maybe he could be saved. Saved from himself, of course, and liberated from the expectations he had set in others. He knew that he could never pay for what he had done. Lives and careers had been lost because of Jack Grant, and he suspected someday a bill for that would have to be paid. And on those nights in those motels, he thought hard on what Joe had told him, and what Chaplain Roy had said. Jack hoped that he could in some way, be a man that Grace could have reached for. Jack thought these things with some tears and remorse but mostly with determination. Harley made the connection to Grace for him and the link to being a better person for that matter. He knew that dogs make you a better person, so he considered it divine providence that he had Harley as a traveling companion. Maybe the spirit of fifteen thousand years of dog and man could make him whole again! It was childish to think, but in the flickering light of motel televisions with a ball of fur at his side, it didn't seem too unrealistic.

Jack and Harley took backroads and country lanes across Virginia and Kentucky and then began their journey into the beauty and wildness of Missouri. Hoping for a lunch of fried catfish, Jack pulled their van into the parking lot of Cook's Café in Theodosia Village. Jack remembered it from his boyhood trip and couldn't wait for more. He jumped out with Harley following him.

"Wait there, mister."

Jack picked Harley up and turned to see a man in a wrinkled, khaki uniform, stepping out of a pick-up. The man had a badge over his left breast pocket and wore a pistol on his side.

"Yes, sir."

"Dogs need to be leashed here in Theodosia Village."

"Sure, I am putting it on him now."

"Dogs need to be leashed *at all times* in Theodosia Village."

"Yes, sir."

"We take animal control very seriously. Don't want no dogs running around free."

392

"Look, officer, we just pulled up and got out of the van. He wasn't wearing a leash in the van. I am holding him as you can see."

"You weren't holding him a second ago. I seen him on the ground without no leash."

"Okay, officer, I have him now. I will leash him and never let him off it until I leave town. ll that satisfy you?"

"When you leaving town?"

"Not sure, after lunch."

"Let me see your license and registration."

Jack looked at him in disbelief, then shook his head. "Yes, sir, let me leash the dog." He opened the van door, grabbed Harley's leash, and clipped it onto his collar. He put Harley down and handed his driver's license and the van registration to the officer. The officer took the documents, but Jack noticed he kept looking over Jack's shoulder toward the café. Jack followed his eyes and saw a woman in the window. She was sitting at a table, her profile to the parking lot. Jack looked back at the officer.

"You have a California driver's license." "Yes, sir."

"What are you doing here?"

"Passing through."

"From where?"

"Virginia."

"California, Virginia, what gives?"

"I was in the navy. I moved a lot."

"I see," said the officer. He looked over Jack's shoulder again, then studied the documents for a few more moments.

"Keep control of your animal," he said. He handed the license and registration back to Jack, looked in the café window once more, then turned and walked to his truck.

Jack frowned as he watched the officer walk away, then turned and smiled at Harley.

"Let's go, boy."

The two of them walked to the café, Jack tied Harley to the front rail and walked inside.

"Howdy!" A blonde woman with the pitcher of what looked like iced tea smiled at Jack.

"Howdy to you!"

"Looking for some lunch?"

"Sure am, but do you have a place, maybe outside, where I can eat with my dog?"

"You didn't leave him in the car, did you?"

Jack turned at the interruption. He smiled into the flinty, gray eyes of a striking brunette. Her pretty face was set in a frown.

"No, ma'am, he is tied up on the front porch. I would never leave him in a car."

"Oh," smiled the brunette. Her eyes softened, and she leaned from her booth and extended her hand. "I'm sorry for being so rude, but I have seen a lifetime worth of dogs that died in their owner's cars."

Jack took her hand, warm and firm, and smiled again. "No problem at all, ma'am. What puts you in contact with so many dogs?"

"I'm a veterinarian," the woman said. "Ruthie Jenkins."

"I'm Jack Grant. It's a pleasure to meet you."

"One animal lover to another." Ruthie smiled and returned to her seat.

Jack turned to the waitress. "Miss, do you have a patio out back?"

"We sure do," she smiled. "Go get your pooch."

Jack nodded and pushed out the front door. He walked to the rail, untied Harley's leash, and led him to the door. He glanced over his shoulder at the parking lot and saw the officer staring at him. Jack waved, but the man just glared.

"Come on, boy."

Jack pulled open the front door of the café. As he crossed the room, he stopped at Ruthie's table. "Care to join us?"

Ruthie looked at Jack, and then her eyes fell to Harley. "Sure, if he is with us."

"He is always with me," said Jack.

Ruthie looked up at him and grinned. She looked past Jack towards the parking lot, "I can't leave yet anyway."

"Oh, how's that?"

"The constable has a thing for me. Follows me everywhere."

"The guy with the badge? Harley and I met him."

"What did you do, spit out some gum?"

"Much worse," laughed Jack. "Harley jumped out of the van without wearing his leash."

"A true criminal," said Ruthie. "But, be careful around Cletis. He has an inflated sense of worth and power in this small village."

"I don't plan to mess with him anymore," said Jack. "May I help you with your plate?"

"No, I can manage." Ruthie picked up her glass of ice tea and plate and followed Jack to the outdoor patio.

They sat under a large, oak tree, and Jack ordered the fried catfish sandwich and a child's burger for Harley. Ruthie munched on her lunch.

"Lived here all your life?" Jack smiled at Ruthie and looked around the patio and at the lake. "Beautiful place."

"No, we used to visit when I was a kid. I'm from Saint Louis. I grew up there, graduated from college, graduated from vet school, and started working in the city. But, I got tired of the never-ending requirement to wring more money out of the customers. You know, people will do almost anything for their pets, and so, vets can take advantage of that. Anyway, I decided to move to somewhere small."

"Well, you accomplished that?" Jack laughed, and Ruthie laughed with him.

Cletis started his truck to reposition himself. He had seen the California Virginia guy stop and talk to Ruthie. And he saw her get up and follow him.

Fucking jerk. That prick was with Ruthie.

Cletis shook his head. Ruthie had a spell on him. He couldn't get her out of his mind.

She wasn't just beautiful; she was powerful. She mattered! She had an office in Gainesville, the best vet shop in Southern Missouri. Heck, she couldn't walk into a basketball game or across the floor of the auction barn without being mobbed by people who wanted to talk to her. Cletis figured that as a member of the leading family in Ozark County, Ruthie Jenkins belonged to him.

Cletis drove his truck around to the side of Cook's so he could see the patio. Sure enough, there was Ruthie. She was talking to the guy from California or Virginia, or wherever he was from.

For the next two hours, Jack found himself thoroughly enjoying Ruthie's company. She told him about herself, and he told her he used to fly planes in the navy and that he was now retired. Harley liked her, too, and hopped into her lap. Ruthie welcomed the little dog, petting him and rubbing his ears. Harley's half-closed eyes said he was in heaven!

Ruthie had a way about her that, no matter how he fought it, reminded Jack of Grace. He smiled and carried on his part of the conversation, but he had a battle fighting the memory.

It was selfish. Ruthie had the right to be Ruthie, not Grace. And, Grace had the right to be the only Grace.

But as he fought the thoughts, he knew that Ruthie, the Ruthie in front of him, was who he needed to talk to right then. For once, Jack didn't find himself looking at a woman as just a potential bed mate. For once, he was listening to someone to hear what THEY wanted to say. Jack was shocked when his watch showed so much time had passed.

"Well, I guess we have to go." "You sure?" Ruthie frowned.

"Yes, it's a long way to New Mexico."

"You can leave him, you know." Ruthie ran her fingers through Harley's curly hair and stroked his ears.

"I got used to his company," said Jack. "I'd miss him on the rest of the trip."

"I'm sure you would," she said. "But, if you change your mind, you know where to find me."

"Thanks," smiled Jack.

"I feel odd saying this." Ruthie frowned and took a quick sip of tea. "But I wish I would have met you in an earlier life."

Jack looked at her. He frowned, then quickly smiled. "I'm afraid if you had met me any earlier, you wouldn't like me at all."

"How so?"

"Let's just say I am a better man now."

Ruthie nodded. "Well, travel safely."

Jack stood and reached to shake her hand, and Ruthie let Harley jump to the floor. He touched Ruthie's hand, then quickly hugged her. He shut his eyes and smelled her hair.

Jack slowly pulled back and looked into Ruthie's eyes. "I'm glad I met you now." He grabbed Harley's leash and walked him out the door. It was hot outside, so he unhooked Harley's collar and opened the van door.

"Get in, boy."

"Stop right there, mister."

Jack turned, and there stood the officer. He was hands akimbo, looking like he owned the world. He wore his trooper hat low and silver sunglasses perched on his nose. He looked so much like the arch-typical, southern sheriff, Jack almost laughed.

"Yes, sir."

"I told you not to have your dog off the leash in Theodosia Village."

"For Christ's sakes, I am letting him in the car."

"He's off the leash. That's the law. You're going to have to surrender your animal."

"Cletis, for God's sake, what are you doing?"

Jack heard the café door slam and turned around. Ruthie frowned as she walked toward the two men. She shaded her eyes with her hand. "He let the dog loose so it could jump in the van."

"Doctor, I don't tell you how to do your business," spat Cletis. "Don't tell me how to do mine."

"He isn't causing any trouble, Cletis."

Cletis ripped off his sun-glasses. His eyes were balls of hate. "He didn't need to let the dog loose to get it in the van. It's just laziness. Laziness with animals is what gets folks hurt!"

Jack was shocked at how angry he was. "Sir, we can just leave and let you go about your business."

"This IS my business!" shouted Cletis.

"Okay, okay," said Ruthie. "Now, Cletis, we can work this out. Maybe Jack can pay a fine?"

"Jack? Jack? My, aren't we all friends." Cletis glared at Ruthie then turned to Jack. "There is no fine for stray dogs in Theodosia. Doc, you know that. Not anymore?"

"What are you talking about?" Jack frowned and looked at Ruthie.

"Last year, a woman in Douglas County died from *Capnocytophaga.*" Ruthie took a deep breath. "Only case I have ever seen or heard of in Missouri."

"What the heck is that?" Jack frowned again. He was worried. The goofy, southern sheriff thing was no longer funny.

"It is a bacteria found in around seventy percent of dogs, and very, very rarely it can be toxic to humans," said Ruthie. "Only ten cases were reported to the CDC in the whole country last year. And, most of them were not life-threatening."

"What does that have to do with Harley?"

"Nothing," said Ruthie. "Absolutely, nothing."

"It was a stray dog that licked that woman," said Cletis.

"Nobody ever proved that," said Ruthie.

"Like I said, it was a stray dog that licked her and killed her," said Cletis. "So the Theodosia Village council passed a law to put down all stray dogs." Cletis glared at Ruthie and Jack.

"You have got to be kidding me?" Jack shook his head.

"When did you pass that law?" asked Ruthie. "That's preposterous!"

"We did it a couple of months ago." Cletis smiled and rocked on his heels. "It's the law now." Cletis glared at Jack. "Mister, you need to get that dog out of the van, now." He pushed his sunglasses back onto his face. "NOW!"

"And you intend to put my dog down?" Jack gritted his teeth.

"That's the law, mister."

"I can't let you do that?"

Cletis took a step back. His hand touched his holster.

"I am not about to let you kill my dog because of some bullshit, local ordinance."

"Cletis, just let the man go," said Ruthie.

"Get the dog from the van," said Cletis. He reached for his revolver and pulled it out of its holster. He pointed it at Jack.

Jack was stunned.

What the fuck is happening?

"GET THE DOG, OR I WILL SHOOT HIM IN THE VAN!" screamed Cletis.

"Okay, okay," said Jack. He backed up to the van and opened the door. Harley wagged his tail. He was ready to get on the road!

Jack looked at Cletis. He leaned past Harley and reached into the glove box. He grabbed his Beretta; the gift from Colonel Sturgis.

Jack stepped away from the van and leveled the gun at Cletis. "Put your weapon down," he said.

Cletis took a step back. Jack saw his jaw drop. His sunglasses didn't hide the surprise.

Jack gripped the gun harder. "DROP IT!"

Cletis stood still. Jack saw his pistol twitch. "PUT IT DOWN!" screamed Jack.

Cletis opened his hand, and the revolver clunked to the ground.

"I'm not going to let you, or anybody, kill my dog," said Jack. He breathed hard. "Ruthie, are you willing to help me?"

"Just don't shoot, Jack," she said. I'll help you."

"Get your car and take Harley out of town, or whatever it takes to get him out of the jurisdiction of this idiot."

"I'll take him to my office in Gainesville."

"Good. I'll give you 30 minutes, then I'll let Cletis go," said Jack. He looked at Cletis. "Unless I have to shoot him."

"You realize what you are doing?" Ruthie opened the van door. She turned back to Jack.

Jack chuckled. "Believe me; this is the best thing I've done in a long, long time."

"Okay, I'll get Harley safe," she said. "Then, I'll find the county sheriff and put an end to this."

"I appreciate that, Ruthie. And, if anything happens, take care of Harley, will you?"

"Nothing is going to happen, Jack. But don't worry about Harley. I'll look after him."

Ruthie grabbed Harley from the van. As she walked by Jack, she whispered, "Whatever you do, don't trust him. He has been a little frog in a tiny pond all of his life. He is dangerous, Jack."

"Thanks, Ruthie." Jack watched her take Harley to her car. He kept the gun on Cletis but watched until they were out of sight.

"You realize the shit you're in?" Cletis spit then shook his head and scowled.

"I realize it."

"Just for some dumb dog? You draw down on a lawman for some old dog. And, it ain't like that dog can hunt or anything. He's just a lap-dog. He's good for nothing."

"He's MY dog, Cletis. And he's my friend."

"Dogs ain't friends! And don't think just because this is a little town, you're pulling a gun on a lawman isn't a big shit."

"It's not just about the dog."

"What, then?"

"This is about you and Ruthie, and you know it. You're mad at her because she won't have anything to do with you, so you want to kill my dog."

Cletis lurched forward. "BULLSHIT! This is about the law! This is about keeping this town safe from them lickers."

"Don't make me shoot you," said Jack. "I'm beginning to want to." He gripped his gun and leveled it on Cletis's head. "You're wanting to kill my dog is just wrong. And I'm not going to let you do it."

"IT'S THE LAW!"

"Not for my dog, it isn't."

Cletis shook his head again and squatted on his haunches. A small crowd had gathered, and Jack could hear their conversation, buzzing in the background.

"Why don't you rush him?" Cletis yelled over his shoulder. "Hey, Goddamnit, he won't shoot you! Rush him!"

The crowd watched and whispered.

"You bunch of fucking pussies!" Cletis scrunched up his face and clenched his hands. "I won't forget this!"

The crowd was unimpressed. It was a good day in the Village. The weather was warm and dry.

Jack checked his watch and thirty minutes later, lowered his gun and turned it toward Cletis, handle first. Cletis eyed him for a moment, then stepped forward and snatched the weapon. Cletis picked up his revolver and stepped back.

"I surrender, sir," said Jack. He held his hands in the air. He thought he heard Harley bark and almost turned around.

"You fucking bastard," said Cletis. He pointed his revolver at Jack.

BOOM!

Jack was on his back.

His ears rung. Or, was it the sound of his heartbeat?

He was on the ground. He wanted to get up, but he couldn't move his arms.

He struggled and gasped.

Got to get up.

He struggled some more. Then, some more. He kicked and kicked at the Missouri dirt in the driveway.

Then, his lungs filled with calm. It was going to be okay. He tried to raise his arms again, but they wouldn't budge. But that was okay.

He tasted copper, and he knew it was the taste of his blood. He had heard about that. Jack swallowed against it. He coughed and rolled onto his back. He felt his eyes flutter. He was looking outside through the living room fan.

He liked the blinking of his eyes. It made the clouds dance. It calmed him.

He reached up and saw his hands in front of him. He watched his fingers pluck and try to grab at her light.

"Hey, Grace," he whispered.

Made in the USA
Las Vegas, NV
07 July 2021